Worlds Broken

Worlds Broken

K. J. Winghart

To order additional copies of this book, contact:
Xlibris
844-714-8691
www.Xlibris.com
Orders@Xlibris.com
835026

To Eugene Schneider
Because he would've been the first in line to buy this novel
meant for teenagers just because his granddaughter wrote it
Love and miss you every day, Grandpa

1

ONE OF MY favorite things about water is the way the sunlight seems to be entranced in an entirely choreographed dance with everything that's under the surface. The kelp to my left, swaying side to side, allows slight rays of light green to shine through onto a sea anemone. Two fish no larger than the palm of my hand chase each other in and through the poisonous plant.

As I swim farther toward the coral reefs, I notice a shadow looming above me. As I turn and look up, I smile and reach to glide my hand along Luna's underbelly to welcome my old, manta ray friend. Luna swims around me playfully before taking her usual spot at my left side.

A pool of small fish frantically swims in the opposite direction as they see her swimming closer. I spot a small crustacean taking advantage of some algae buildup on a rock and quickly grab it for Luna's snack. I used to have a hard time keeping up with her, but now we swim as equals. She doesn't even mind the spear I carry with me anymore for these hunting trips.

It was Dad who taught me to swim. I was younger than most,

only reaching six months the first time he took me out into the water. Dad always said that I was a natural. Made for the ocean. But then again, everyone here is. He just always had a way of making me feel like I was special. Different, but in a good way.

Mom always tells me that the second I was in the water, it was near impossible to get me out. By the time I had reached three years, I was swimming circles around the five-year boys. Well, with the exception of one very annoying, very egotistical boy.

By my thirteenth year, I was one of the best hunters in Maurea. Not because I'm particularly good at any of the actual capturing of the fish, but simply because I could spend twice as long underwater. Most hunters last around twelve minutes while I was staying under for closer to twenty. The extra eight minutes does a great deal when all the other hunters leave the water, and the fish think it's fine to come out and swim freely again. Not that we necessarily need the compliancy.

Everything about us makes living underwater easier. Our long, golden-white hair shines when the sun pierces through the ocean's surface and attracts fish right into our vicinity to strike. Our toes are webbed to make us swift and efficient underwater. Not so different from a sea otter's, actually.

My dad used to tell stories about people from a long time ago. Apparently, people's toes were separated. Seems strange. Frankly, gross, if you ask me. What good are separated toes? You can walk on land just fine with them webbed.

"They simply didn't need them, Adira," he would tell me. It's hard for me to understand, I suppose. I've never seen anyone outside Maurea. I've never met anyone that wasn't of the Dorian. And I'm okay with that. I love my home and my people. All of a sudden, I feel a slight tug on my foot. Vince. He gives me a thumbs-up and heads for the surface, and I follow.

"You swam by at least three different pools of mature fish back there. Were you planning on hunting at all today, or did you and Luna just want to swim in circles all day?" my closest friend asks with a grin. I splash him in response.

There was never really a time when Vince and I weren't friends. With both our fathers being a part of the Legions, when their friendship grew, ours did as well. Dad died around the same time as his mom, too. That kind of loss brings people together.

Our families rarely did anything apart. He also happens to be one of the most sought-after male mates in all Maurea. Vince has a softness about him that makes others feel safe. His hair is never out of the low tie he keeps drifting just below his shoulders. Where most people's eyes are a stark blue, his are a softer shade that one might say is almost gray. He's abnormally tall but doesn't demand a strong presence like most men do. I find myself in a constant state of peace whenever he's around. Ever since I can remember, I've wanted for us to go beyond friendship, but he's never seemed to hold the same sentiment. My time is quicky running out that I'll have to even have a chance with him.

"You remember we have that meeting with my dad today, right?" Vince breaks me out of my thoughts as he maneuvers to float on his back on the surface. I slowly float to my back as we chat.

"I thought today was just a mannerisms lesson. I know my mom isn't a member of the Legions, but I'm sure she can handle those," I respond.

"He was saying there's a change in plans." Fine by me. The mannerism sessions are one of the most boring parts of being an Heir. According to Simon, it *is* one of the most important, though. We have to come across to the entirety of the Dorian as not only the ones that they can put their trust in, but also the ones to be respected and listened to. My family is from one they call the *Originals*. I never really learned much about what that insinuates. You'd think we could learn more about *that* rather than learning how to speak like we've all got a kelp stalk up our ass. But my father's father's father and down and down the line was a part of starting what we call the Legions. As the eldest of his kin, it's my job to take over his spot. Even if I have only reached twenty-two years.

"Hey! If you two are going to wade around and chat all day, I'll be sure to consider it in your rations of the week," squeals Walter.

How this guy ended up being in charge of the hunting on the island is beyond me.

"Our bad, Walter," Vince yells back, straightening out in the water. "Adira was just talking a break from being the one who brings in the most fish each week. It's taxing work, I'm sure you understand." Walter scowls before plunging back underwater. We burst into laughter.

"Well, aren't you my hero," I mock.

"Always have been, always will be," he responds with a wink that makes my stomach flutter. He dives back underwater, spear in position. I follow. Vince has a more direct hunting style. He goes into the center of pools and uses his strength and agility to get as many fish as he can in the short period of time that he has before they all scatter too far out of reach. My hunting takes a little more patience, but as Vince pointed out, I usually get the most results. I simply wait. I usually find somewhere where it is easy for me to be as still as possible, and I wait for hungry fish to come to me by attraction of my hair. After about seven minutes, the first fish comes to investigate. I position the angle of my hand on the spear to best strike. This part is all about speed. The less struggle, the better. To avoid as much pain as possible, I aim directly through the gills each time. Right between them is the main artery. It takes seconds for them to bleed out. Sometimes, I get lucky, and the blood attracts some larger prey. Sharks come to investigate from time to time but will often abandon the hunt once they see the more powerful predator. Us. I don't relish killing sharks. I think they're beautiful, intelligent creatures. They aren't my favorite taste either. But the ones that are stupid enough to try to take us on are quickly taken care of. There aren't many things in the ocean that we are prey to. After being under for around ten minutes, most of the hunters have started breaking for the surface to make their way back to shore. Perfect. It takes no more than three more minutes for me to fill my spear with seven more fish. There's too much blood wafting around me at this point that I have to move to a new spot to wait out more prey. After about eight more minutes, my spear is full with twelve fish.

My chest starts to tighten as my body begins to beg for oxygen. Luna finds her way to me as I begin my ascent to the surface. She knows when to make herself scarce when I'm hunting. Right before I break the surface, I hear my mother calling out to me from our family's hut.

"Adira! Time for lessons!"

If I ignore her, maybe she will think I couldn't—

"I know you can hear me. Get yourself out of the water and dried off. The rest of the heirs will be here any minute."

I break the surface of the water more on instinct to inhale oxygen after being without it for so long rather than compliance with my mother's wishes. I run to where it is just Walter and Vince left waiting on the shore to drop off my day's catch.

"Always a pleasure, Walter," I say with a smirk. He only grunts in response before hauling the day's load on his back and heading toward the hut where others will be waiting to count and divvy amongst all the Dorian.

"I'll see you shortly. Give Lana a kiss for me, won't you," Vince says with a smirk.

"Give her one yourself once you get there, you flirt," I chide back at him. He laughs in response and runs toward his family's home to change for the lessons.

I run toward our family's hut, still dripping. Our family's home is like everyone else's in Maurea. It was made a *long* time ago, but there's always additions and repairs to be done. It's not surprising being that it's made of a combination of a mud from the ocean floor and sand that, when dry, seems to be as hard as a rock. That is, until it rains. Luckily, it's a rare occurrence when the rain will damage a house enough that anything is completely washed away. But the days following thunderstorms are usually filled with work from everyone on the island diving for the mud and touching up anything that might have washed away. My mom is frantically sweeping sand from the floors even as I track more of it from the living space all the way back to my room. I stop by the twin boys' bedroom to hand them two shells I found for them to add to their collection.

"Now, boys, Luna picked these out special for you. I made sure that they are very similar, all right?"

"Thanks, Addi!" Liam and Avery scream in unison. Every time I give them new ones, it's as if they've never seen a seashell in their lives. And even if I come in with two identical shells, there is always a quarrel over who should get which one. I leave my six-year brothers to their bickering to quickly change into one of my favorite and most comfortable blouses made from seaweed and different seagrasses. Not the most fashionable, but far more comfortable than anything made from kelp.

"Adira! I need you to run to Walter and get our fish for the next week!" my mom shouts to me from outside my room.

"Mmk," I yell back. I head out of my room and give each of the twins a kiss on the head as I exit our home and set out to see my *favorite* person in the whole world. Walter acts like I'm one of his least favorite people, but I am his best fisherman, so he can't complain. Not much at least. I pass by most of the huts that house families on my way to the fish keep and see that most families are in the middle of making supper for the evening. The smell of burnt seaweed is wafting from Geode's hut when I'm five homes down. I look up to check the sun's position to determine if I have time for a quick pitstop. Eh, it'll be short, but I can't resist. Old man Geode really is one of my favorite people.

"Geode!" I shout when I start coming up on his hut.

"I know that's not my favorite fisherman coming to say hi to me! She hasn't been around in ages!" He chides with a smirk that brings out the wrinkles around his eyes.

"I see you've managed to burn part of your supper again," I kid. He scoffs at me with a look of disbelief on his face.

"I don't know how you kids are eating it these days, but if it doesn't crumble into oblivion in your mouth and taste like flames, I'll have nothing to do with it!" I can't help but laugh. "Did you stop by to sneak me a couple more of those little fish I love so much?" he asks in an exaggerated whisper.

"I unfortunately come to you empty-handed. I just smelt your supper from five places down and thought I'd offer my assistance if you needed it."

"Bah." He waves his hand at me. "I'm old, girl, not an imbecile. Now tell me, tell me." He sits down in a chair and motions for me to sit. "Have you talked to"—he looks around and leans in closer to me to whisper—"*you-know-who?*" This man absolutely loves gossip. Luckily, he'd never tell a soul a thing that is said to him. He calls himself the keeper of secrets and told me they're so priceless that he'd never sell them out to anyone. Geode might know some secret about every single Dorian on Maurea.

"No, I haven't yet. Opportunity hasn't come up," I respond. He balks at me.

"Girl, if you don't suck it up and *make* an opportunity, I'll come over and burn all of your seaweed before you can say *barnacle*." I laugh at his delicate way with words.

"Always sticking your nose in other people's business," I chide.

"Then quit shoving it under my nostrils, girl, and I'll leave you alone." I look up to see that I'm on my way to being late if I don't get moving. Geode notes my gaze.

"Get on out of here, Adira. Tell that mother of yours I say hello. And don't show up empty-handed next time. It's rude to get such amazing advice from someone with no payment," he says with a wink. I laugh again.

"I didn't ask for the advice, you know," I say.

"But you'll always get it, sweetheart. On your way now," he shoos me away. I give him a wave as I run the rest of the way to the fish keep. Walter is still counting when I show up.

"Walter! Just the man I was looking for." He looks up at me and groans with a roll of his eyes before turning back around.

"What do you want, Adira?" he asks with a gruff.

"I'm great, thanks for asking. Mom just sent me to get our share for the week," I say with an overexaggerated smile that makes his frown lines go impossibly deeper. "And possibly two fresh catches that haven't been salted yet?"

"You know that they aren't going out till tomorrow. You know the

rules. And why don't you go out and get to fresh ones on your own?"
He points at me with his disfigured hand. I always wondered if part
of the reason he's so angry all the time is because he never was able
to have a mate. That must get lonely.

"Look, the heirs are coming over tonight, and Mom doesn't want
to be a bad hostess. Can you let it pass this one time?" I ask, softening
my tone. He gruffs again and doesn't respond.

"I'll go out extra early tomorrow to make up for it." He pauses
again and finally turns around and, with a gravelly groan, points
his head in the direction of where a few rations have already been
counted out. I run over and grab them along with two large tuna and
swing the bag over my shoulder.

"You're the best, Walter. I owe you!" I shout as I walk out.

"Yeah, yeah," he responds. I run the rest of the way home and
come in tracking more sand. My mom scoffs as I head to the back of
the hut to store the week's rations in our salt room. I come out with
two large fish that my mom will cook up for everyone that comes
tonight. Right when I get the fire started, I hear a knock at the door.
Just as I walk out, I see my mom inviting in our first visitor, Lane.
The first of the heirs to arrive.

Lane waltzes in with his hips guiding him as usual and makes a
show of thanking my mom for her hospitality. How in character of
him. Lane has a way of charming every single woman that he ever
graces with his perfect teeth and long curly hair. He always keeps it
down—letting it drift to his collarbones. He refuses to ever put it up.
Lane is the top of every girl's choice of mate in Maurea. Even more
sought-after than Vince is. His perfect genes scream at you from a
mile away, and he knows it.

"Miss Lana, I cannot begin to thank you enough for having us all
here today. Your home is *almost* as charming as the hostess herself."

Come on, Mom, I know you're not feeding into this bullsh—

"And, Adira, can I just say you look—" He looks me up and down,
pausing too long for comfort at the V in my blouse. ". . . exquisite."

His ability to trigger my gag reflex never fails.

I pull up on my blouse, hoping he will take it as the thousandth clear sign of my disinterest in his gazes. I know exactly how attractive Lane is but have always been thoroughly repulsed by him.

"Lane, welcome." It's all I can manage to say to the walking, talking block of testosterone that won't get out of my personal space.

I notice the sun starting to set, so I take advantage of the opportunity to escape from his debauched gaze to light all the lanterns. My mother looks thoroughly mortified at my lack of manners as I scurry off. Sometimes I wonder if me and Vince are the only ones in all of Maurea who can see how much of an ass Lane really is.

I take my time lighting the lanterns so that by the time the hut has adopted the soft glow, everyone else has arrived. There are five of us total.

Leia is coming into her twentieth year. She's a very simple and quiet girl, but kind. She's actually a very talented musician. You will rarely see her in the water, but you can always hear her beautiful voice whenever you walk by her family's hut. Eliot, already in his twenty-fifth year, takes a great pride in being an heir. Born a leader, when the day comes where we must choose who is the top Legion of Maurea, I have no doubts he will follow in his mother's, Pandora's, footsteps. Although Lane might try to take it from him solely for the title. And then there's Vince.

As uncomfortable and tedious as these sessions are, I'm grateful to have him here with me. If nothing else, he's a calming presence.

"You're going to give your mother quite the headache if you keep dragging half of the ocean in here with you." He moves a strand of soaked hair. I blush at the small touch. He's put his hair back into his usual low tie and is wearing one of his nicer shirts.

"Let me guess. Another meeting with an ogling potential suitor after this?" I reply while sloppily putting my mop of wet hair into a knot on top of my head.

"Maybe. By the way, who are some that you've been meeting with?" Before I am able to respond, Simon, Vince's dad and my father's oldest friend, walks into our hut.

"Simon, what a surprise. Welcome to our home," my mom says. "Though I believe tonight is just one of the mannerism sessions." I guess I wasn't the only one who had no idea that there was a change in plans tonight. Not that I don't enjoy Simon's company. He's always been like a second father to me. Lane is aware of this and averts his gaze from me to feign an interest in a conversation between Leia and Eliot.

"There's been a change in lesson plans. I, along with the rest of the Legions, have decided that you five have had enough training on what to say and how to act in a manner that represents the Legions. It's time you all learned why it is that the Legions exist and just how important your role as one of them is."

To hear Simon speak is to be mesmerized. He conveys it so whenever he talks, it comes from a deep place of importance and wisdom. It doesn't matter who you are or what you're doing. When he speaks, his demeanor demands not just hearing, but listening and digesting everything he says. There are few people I respect more than him.

"But before that, I need to stress the importance of what is coming up for each of you. As you know, you cannot take over the position as Legions until each of you has chosen a mate."

I was dreading this conversation. Some are able to get away without ever choosing a mate. Those that seem to have genetic flaws are prohibited from ever choosing one. But if you are one who has what is considered "pure genes" or are a member of the Legions, you have to have a mate. Most members of the Legion happen to have both. With Vince never really showing interest, I had hoped that my having green eyes where everyone else has blue would make them reconsider my obligation to choose a mate being that it is *technically* a genetic flaw. However, my ability to stay underwater longer than most is a trait that is considered to be too important not to pass on. The window for mate selection is coming to an end, and I haven't even started looking at suitors. The only person I'd ever want to be with is Vince, but he's had so many suitors inquiring about him that it's basically impossible at this point. Not that he'd be interested in the first place. I had hoped that Vince might one day return the affection that I've felt toward him. I never brought it up directly, so I guess that's on me. But once women started lining up behind the door to be potential suitors for him, I've lost a lot of my nerve. I'd planned to talk to him eventually and just finally get everything out in the open before the ceremony, but the time just hasn't presented itself yet. And the last thing I want is to hurt him or ruin the relationship that we have. I only hope that if he ends up choosing someone else that they will deserve him. Not that anyone could.

"The ceremony will be taking place in four weeks' time. I expect all of you have been taking this matter seriously as this isn't just about the person you will be spending your lives with, but it is also the person whose genes will be shared with your kin. The Legions have faith that you will make your decision carefully and wisely."

Well, that's great.

"Now, for a heavier subject." Yeah, like the conversation about the person you're stuck with for the rest of your life is light chitchat.

"Over the next few weeks, I am going to tell you of things that you will no doubt question. But what I have to teach you isn't just from the Legions, it's from the Originals. This information may not come into purpose in your time as the Legions, but it will happen someday. And if that day is during your lead, you need to be prepared." He pauses to look each of us in the eye and then politely asks my mother to step out of the room.

"Make no mistake, the information you will receive is that of utmost secrecy. No one outside of the Legions and Heirs must ever know of what we will discuss. Not even your mates. Do you all understand?"

No one speaks, but we all nod in unison. I've never held much interest in being a part of the Legions. It was just something that I simply had to do. A duty. But to think that I am about to be a holder of a history that is sacred *and* secret is enough to spark my interests in the Legions more than it ever has.

"All you have ever known has been Maurea and the Dorian," Simon continues.

"Your world has always been the ocean. Nothing else has ever existed outside of that. Your lives have revolved around the sea and what it can provide. But there are worlds beyond Maurea, and there are people that are not Dorian. We are one of five worlds that is a part of the planet called Earth."

Nothing he is saying is making sense. I look around at my fellow heirs to see I'm not alone in my confusion. I look to Vince for some reassurance, but he looks just as taken aback as the rest of us. When our eyes meet, I furrow my brows, asking him if he knew about any of this. He shakes his head in response.

"There is a history that goes much further back than that of the Dorian people. It's nothing like that of Maurea's history. Instead of peace, there's been war. Instead of fruitfulness, famine. Instead of growth, destruction. Instead of harmony, terrorism. And this is just the surface of the true history of mankind and its many faults and difficulties.

"Where you only know of the ocean, there are parts of the world that are covered in plants that come out of the ground rather than from the sea. Some so large that they reach to over forty feet tall. There are vast scapes of land that are nothing but sand. There is rain that comes in a soft, frozen state and covers miles upon miles for months at a time. And there are creatures that live in each and every one of these lands. They have adapted, just as the Dorian have.

"Our purpose started out as an experiment to see if people were capable of true adaptation to harsh environments. No one ever thought it would go this far, but here we are, approximately one thousand thirty-seven years after the fact, and the Dorian have not only survived, but adapted and thrived." He ignores our stunned stares and continues on. Deciding to get all of the impossible information out in the open at once.

"We are currently in an ecosphere. The Dorian exist only inside of here. There are three other ecospheres that exist along with us. Maurea is the oceanic ecosphere. Tragdome is the forest ecosphere. Sentri is the jungle ecosphere. And Avil, the desert. All created for the same purpose as Maurea. Inside of each ecosphere are people that look similar to you or me, but vastly different at the same time. Still people, but with stark differences in physical and mental characteristics. We have never had contact with the other ecospheres since the Originals, so there is no way to tell just how different they are or if they have even survived the experiment started long ago. But outside of each and every world, the rest of the Earth lies beyond."

I hear everything that Simon is saying but feel as though he's speaking a different language. There is only Maurea. There is only the Dorian. I have so many questions but feel unable to even speak one word. One thousand thirty-seven years? And what is a desert? Or a jungle or forest? It feels as though my whole life I've believed a fallacy. If it's been so long, how are we supposed to know how the other ecospheres have adapted? Or if they even exist? Do they know *we* exist? I thought it was just us. It has to be just us. As though Simon can hear the questions of my thoughts, he concludes,

"We are not alone."

2

I THINK SIMON KNOWS that we all need our own time to process everything that he laid on us tonight. He leaves shortly after, promising to answer any and all questions we have over the next few weeks. Leia is the first to leave. She worries her bottom lip as she goes to thank my mom for her hospitality and quickly leaves the room with tears welling up in her eyes. Vince shoots a glance toward her before giving me a quick side hug and a look that tells me we'll talk about this all later and heads after her, I'm assuming to comfort her. Eliot clears his throat, thanks my mom with all the quiet authority he holds, and heads out of the hut. When it's just me and Lane left, I inwardly roll my eyes.

"Adira!" my mother chastises. Okay, so not so inwardly, I guess. Lane just gives a quiet chuckle and offers me his elbow.

"Take a walk with me," he says with a nod toward outside. I take a deep breath. I *really* don't have the patience to deal with him right now.

"Lane, we just got some really intense information, and I would really like to—"

"Adira," he cuts me off. "Take a walk with me." I grind my teeth together so hard it feels like my jaw is going to crack. I look down at his elbow that he still has out, offered to me. I drag my gaze back to his before ignoring it and leading the way outside. I walk quickly, but he matches my stride without any effort.

"So, do you wanna talk about it?" Lane breaks the silence.

"Not with you," I snap back. He snorts as if it was just a quip from a child. It just goes to further infuriate me.

"And why not, may I ask," he responds in his light, carefree tone. Gosh, he really is irritating. I turn around and stop us in our tracks.

"Because, Lane. You're a pompous ass who is honestly the last person in all of Maurea, no, scratch that. In all of this Verth that I'd like to talk about this monumental, life-changing information with." For one moment, it looks like there's a semblance of hurt in his eyes, but he recovers as quickly as it's there.

"Earth."

"What?" I ask.

"You called it *Verth*. It's *Earth*." I see red. I honestly think that I might hit him. I imagine how good it would feel for my fist to connect to his stupid, perfect face and to mess up his stupid, perfect hair.

"Are you going to hit me?" he asks incredulously. Some of the anger subsides due to the surprise that he guessed exactly what I was thinking.

"It's not a terrible idea," I mutter as I continue walking. Swimming is a lot harder with a messed-up hand. Best not.

"Don't worry, I won't take it personally," he says with a grin.

"No, please, feel free to take it personally," I retort. He lets out a soft laugh before we fall into silence. We walk on the beach until the stars take over the sky before he finally breaks the silence.

"You're angry." I bristle at his comment. Sure, I'm confused and shocked and a little staggered from what we just heard, but angry? I subtly look toward Lane trying to figure out his angle. We've never really had a lot of conversations in the past. He's always been in a world of his own with his own big head at the center of it. You never really see him without some girl or one of his other pompous friends at his side. Why he cares enough to even talk to me about this is beyond me. What I really want is to talk to Vince through all of this, but he went off to comfort someone else. A pang of jealously hits me. He just went to comfort her because she was crying. Vince is a good guy like that. But it feels like my head is going to explode with all these thoughts and questions. At least I know that whatever I say to him, he can't spread it around since we're the only ones who're allowed to know the information in the first place. It's that knowledge that loosens my tongue.

"I don't know if it's anger," I finally reply. For a moment, he looks surprised that I even answered.

"Hm," he sighs in response.

"What do you mean 'Hm'?" He smiles as if I just made a joke.

"Fine, if you aren't angry, then what're you feeling?" he asks.

"Um. Confused? Mostly just confused, I guess. Shocked."

"You're lying," he answers. I flinch back.

"Excuse me?"

"I said you're lying. Tell me what you're really feeling," he demands.

"Why do you care, Lane?" I snap. He gives me a contemplative look and has a slight tick in his jaw.

"Didn't say I did," he responds. I scoff and turn around to go back toward my home. I don't need this right now.

"Where're you going?" Lane calls after me.

"It's not like you care!" I yell back. He runs to catch up with me and grabs my hand to turn me around. He has a frustrated look on his face as he runs a hand through his hair.

"Look, just tell me what you're actually feeling right now. For once in your life, Adira, just say what you want to!" Once again, I see red.

"You don't know anything about me, Lane. Back off." I keep walking as he stays put where he stands.

"I'm angry!" he shouts. I stop my stride and take a breath before I turn around. He's staring me down and looks at me with something that I can't quite name. All of the usual swagger that he holds melts away and is replaced with anger and hurt.

"I'm angry," he repeats quieter. "I feel like I've been a damn fool my entire life. I feel small and insignificant. And I am *furious* that my father knew we'd come into this information eventually but waited for Simon to tell me. That the bastard couldn't give me this *one thing*." He yells and then turns to sit in the sand, facing the ocean. I realize he probably needed to talk this out with someone just as much as I did. I stay where I am for a few minutes before deciding to go and sit a few feet from him. He looks slightly in my direction but doesn't break the silence.

"I can't be angry," I say softly. He turns to me.

"Why not?" Tears start to well up in my eyes.

"Because if I'm angry, I have to be angry at *him*. And I'm finally at a point where I'm not constantly consumed with anger at him. I'm not ready to go back to that." Lane looks over to me for a moment before averting his gaze back to the ocean. After a while, he stands up and pushes his hair back from his face as if he's putting the mask of unruffled perfection back on.

"Good night, Adira." He walks away, leaving me at my spot in the sand. As he goes farther and farther away, I find myself looking forward to the next time he takes the mask off. I didn't realize that just getting that small bit off my chest would make me feel lighter. It's as though I've been able to pass along part of the load to someone else, even if it's just for a short time. Even if that person was *Lane*.

It still feels like my head might explode not only from everything that I've learned today, but also from what I believe is the first candid conversation I've ever had with Lane. He would be the one to wait to show that he has a human side until the day that our lives seem to go up in flames. I look out at the sea and let my tears flow freely. Here I thought the ocean was the whole world, because it's *my* whole world. As I look out, I wonder what lies beyond and if I even want to know. Will I even be content here knowing that there's more out there? I love Maurea. I love my people. There's not much to see up on land. It's just sand and whatever structures we've created throughout the last 1,037 years. But the ocean has the real views. It's a whole world that is separate from the land. One with color and life and a surfeit of possibilities. The ocean was always enough for me. I realize that the dominating emotion that I'm feeling with this isn't anger or confusion, it's fear. What if the ocean won't be enough for me anymore?

I let the stars witness my tears until it feels as though I've run dry. Eventually I stand on stiff legs and walk back home. Mom is waiting up for me as I walk in. She seems to be weaving a basket while both Avery and Liam are passed out with their heads lying in her lap. The sight brings a grin to my face.

"Do you want to talk about it?" she asks.

"So much," I respond.

"But you can't," she says with an understanding look. I nod in response as she sets her basket aside. I go over to sit by her.

"I never really got good at this," I say, grabbing the basket she's almost done with. She gives a soft chuckle.

"You'd have to be out of the water for longer than two seconds to learn, Adira." I chuckle at her soft reprimand.

"You're probably right," I say as I set it back down. She starts rubbing a hand through Avery's hair.

"I know you can't tell me the details. But just know I'm here for you, okay?" Here I thought I couldn't possibly have any tears left in me.

"I know, Mom. Thanks." She gives me an understanding smile before looking down at the boys.

"Want to give me a hand getting the boys to their room?"

"Yeah, of course." I gently untangle Liam from Mom's lap and cradle him in my arms as Mom picks up Avery. We carry the boys to their room and set them gently on their beds before blowing out the lantern and leaving their room. I head toward my room, hoping that a good night's sleep will help calm the tides of my endless thoughts.

"Adira," my mom calls.

"Yeah?" I say through a yawn.

"I am proud of you. Terrible basket weaving and all," she says with a smile. I give her a tired smile back.

"Thanks, Mom."

"And he would be proud of you too." With that, she turns to her own room, and I see the soft glow from her lantern go dark. It's all I've ever wanted, really. To make him proud. I just don't know what to do at this point. I feel like I want to dig my head into the sand and scream and pretend this day never happened. But it did, and now I have to do something about it.

I go and lie down on my bed hoping that the exhaustion of my body will overrule the alertness of my mind. Tomorrow. I'll figure it out tomorrow. At least I can go to bed feeling just a trace lighter than I did earlier. I find myself hoping that Lane feels the same way, just a little lighter.

~~~~~~

"So, you're telling me that not only are there four different worlds called ecospheres, and they not only reside in a *planet* called *Earth*, but that there are *other* planets that exist in a social system?" I ask incredulously.

"*Solar* system. And yes," Simon replies. I honestly think my mind might explode all the way to Jurpiter. Today's lesson is about different sciences that have been studied by the human race. I can't get over the fact that I live in a world inside of a world inside of a world . . .

"This information is hardly important in the grand scheme of things, so let's move on, shall we?" Simon says.

"Hold up, are there people on every one of these planets? Honestly, how many people exist!" I can't help but ask.

"Of course not. The mere idea of life existing out on other planets is absurd," Eliot chimes in.

"Uhhh, I call bullshit," Lane retorts.

"*Language*, Lane," Simon cautions.

"My apologies, Simon," Lane responds with his best smile. "I'm just saying, mathematically, it's completely logical to assume that life exists on those other planets. Just last week we didn't think there was anything outside of our pretty bubble. It's not a stretch to assume that of other worlds," he concludes with a braggart look toward Eliot. He turns to me and gives me a wink. "Adira has come to the smarter conclusion."

"I really don't need you standing up for me, Lane." I snap at him.

"Oh, but here I am, doing it anyway," he responds with his usual bluster. I roll my eyes at him, and he gives a silent chuckle at my reaction. I really shouldn't let him get under my skin so bad. I turn toward Vince to complain but am stopped short by the glare he's aiming toward Lane. Good grief, I didn't think it was that big of a deal . . . I nudge him with my knee until he looks at me.

"Chill," I whisper. He gives one last dirty look toward Lane.

"Sorry," he whispers back. He's been off ever since we got the big news a week ago. I haven't really been able to talk to him much about it. Our week has been filled with us asking endless questions. Today is the first day that Simon's taken charge and just started giving lessons rather than the constant question and answer.

"Now, the next topic we will be discussing is one that you all need to know because if one of them were to happen, it would suggest the integrity of Maurea has been compromised. Natural disasters," Simon says.

"Well, that sounds lovely," Lane mutters under his breath.

"Would you shut up?" Vince shouts at Lane. The hut goes quiet, and Lane's eyebrows shoot up at the sudden outburst. He turns to Simon and suavely states,

"My apologies, Simon, please continue." What was that about? Maybe I should talk to Vince. It's clear that something is bothering him. He's not an angry guy, so I can't begin to understand why he's come across that way in the last week. I decide that after today's lesson, I'll bring it up to him. If you can't get tough love from your best friend, then who can you get it from? Simon breaks the silence and continues with his lesson.

"There are different natural disasters that certain parts of the world are prone to depending on their climate and geography. Today we will focus on the ones that affect oceanic areas—being that Maurea is just that.

"The two major disasters for oceanic areas are called tsunamis and hurricanes. Maurea and the ecospheres may be over a millennium old, but they were built to withstand time, which means that we shouldn't get any real natural disasters here. As you know, we get the occasional storm, but nothing to the magnitude of either of these. If something similar to them were to take place, it would be safe to assume that the integrity of Maurea would be fractured. We have protocols in place for if such an event would happen, but it hasn't for over one thousand years, and I'd be surprised if it occurred during your time as Legions."

"Or maybe we'll be just that lucky," Leia murmurs. I chuckle softly. Lane leans over toward Vince.

"Uh, Vince, Leia just spoke. Are you sure there's not a temper tantrum you'd like to throw?" Lane throws in Vince's face. Vince turns bright red and seems to shrink down in his chair.

The rest of the lesson goes by in a bit of a blur. I keep getting distracted thinking about how I'm going to talk to Vince. Simon finally dismisses us, and Vince immediately bolts out of the room. I follow after him.

"Hey! Wait up!" He stops but doesn't turn toward me. I catch up to him and grab his arm to turn him around.

"Hey, you wanna tell me what all that was about?" I ask.

"Lane just annoys me, is all," he mutters.

"Um, yeah, join the club, Vince. You've never let him get to you before. Why now?" He sighs and sits in the sand and pats the ground next to him. I sit down.

"I'm kind of overwhelmed. We've got the mating ceremony in a few weeks, and now we have this news on top of it. I haven't made any sort of decision yet on who to choose, and it's just getting to me. All of it. Lane is just the most annoying thing around for me to let it out on, I guess." I can't help the small laugh that comes out of me.

"Who do you think I should choose as a mate?" My heart drops into my stomach. *Me, you should pick me.*

"Um, who do you want to pick?" I ask instead. Red climbs up his face as he stares down at the sand. Is he going to say it?

"Do you think it's better or worse when two people are friends before they're mates?" My heart is racing so fast it's going to beat out of my chest. I don't know why he doesn't just come out and ask me, but if he wants to go this backward way about it, fine.

"Better. Way better, in fact," I say in the flirtiest way I know possible. He gives me a grin before standing up and offering a hand down.

"Thanks, Adira. I think I've made up my mind." A smile breaks across my face. *Ask me, Vince. Just ask.*

"I've gotta go help Dad with some stuff. I'll see you at tomorrow's lesson, yeah?" And then he's gone. I can't help the disappointment that crashes in my chest. Why didn't he ask me? There are too many variables if we wait until the day of the ceremony and do it there. I'm not sure where Vince's head is at, but I know I don't want to push him into anything. If he wants to wait, I can handle that . . . right?

3

THE NEXT THREE weeks were spent with the heirs and Simon and were filled with lessons of the history of mankind. Our hunting responsibilities were put on hold at the Legions' request so that we could spend more time in the lessons. I knew what we were learning was important, but every cell in my body wanted to run from the hut and straight into the ocean.

Some of what we learned was beautiful. We learned of creatures that could do the strangest things. A smaller animal called a monkey is one of my personal favorites. They seem to be a more mischievous creature than the rest.

Simon also spoke of plants that were scattered all across land. One day, he drew something called a tree. Simon said that the trees had many uses, such as aiding in the construction of homes. Whereas ours are made entirely from mud dug from deep under the sand and different seagrasses with kelp, seaweed, and animal skin on the roofs to prevent water from seeping through when it rains. Simon told us that there were hundreds of different kinds of trees, and that depending on where you were on Earth, a different species of tree dominated the landscape. It's a beautiful thing to imagine.

However, much of what we learned was of horrors I wish I could forget. Children starving and begging for food from strangers, vast miles of trees being cut down for foolish purposes, leaders of nations exploiting their people, war across all corners of the planet. It seems that for every positive, beautiful thing that the Earth has, there's something evil to take it away.

Today we learned about a man so many people loved and so many more feared. He was afraid of a group of people and made it so that all of his followers grew afraid of them too. The fear grew to hate until he led them to murder millions of these poor people after torturing them in ways I didn't know mankind was capable of.

Ever since the lessons started, night after night I've had strange dreams about the day's topics. Some are delightful. Last week I had a dream I was jumping from tree to tree with a monkey at my left side the whole time. I woke up giggling when the creature was so startled that food came flying out of his nose! Other dreams make me wish I could never fall asleep again. Some of bloody war, some where my stomach physically hurts from being empty for far too long in a vast, desert land of nothing, some from hatred being spewed at me in the streets. After today's lesson, I have a strong feeling that rest is not going to come easily tonight.

I walked back home after the day's lesson in a haze. It wasn't until a strong gust of wind left a coolness against my face that I realized I've been crying.

"Adira!" I turn to see Vince running after me. I quickly wipe the tears away. Not that my crying is anything new to Vince.

"Are you all right?" he asks. Not a trace of discomfort or unease. How is he taking all of this so well? Other than the anger, he seems completely unfazed.

"If I said yes, would you believe me?"

He looks at me with his half smile and uses his thumb to wipe away a lingering tear.

"Not exactly, no," he answers with a chuckle. I can't help but laugh too.

"What would you say to a swim?" Like he even has to ask. But the sun is almost set, and it's never a good idea to stay in the water after dark.

"It's a little late for that, don't you think?"

"Now, the Adira I knew would never turn down a good swim," he mocks, starting to take off his shirt and shoes.

"Well, if you're going to be competitive about it," I retort as I throw off my blouse and sandals. I never leave home without my swimming clothes on. We both sprint toward the water. I take a full intercostal breath before I submerge myself beneath the surface. Even as I hold my breath, I feel as though I'm finally able to breathe after weeks of suffocation. If there's anything I've learned from these lessons, it's that my body is *literally* made for the water. And I am more than happy to oblige.

We swim down toward the coral reef where I find Luna making a meal out of a small fish. Once we come into sight, she abandons her feast to greet us. It feels as though it's been years since I have seen her. She swims extra close to my left as we continue on.

As we start to approach open ocean, Vince waves to get my attention and points to a humongous shadow out past the reefs. I can't remember the last time I saw a blue whale, but they're a mesmerizing sight to see. One of the most magnificent giants that ever existed. I decide to swim closer and get a better look, despite Vince's furrowed glimpse of concern.

Another creature we've learned about in Simon's lessons are called elephants. They are the largest animal that walks on land, and yet, according to Simon, this ocean giant is still larger than twenty of them.

I stop swimming when Vince grabs my leg. I turn to see that I have swum over one hundred feet from the drop-off of the reef. I know I've gone out too far. I know that it is time to turn back. I personally know just how dangerous the ocean can be at night. But despite that knowledge, I turn back around to see that the whale is staring back at me. At first, he just floats there, as if contemplating what floats less than two hundred yards from him. Curiosity must win out, and he slowly starts to swim in our direction. Vince immediately makes a break for the surface to do his fastest swimming toward shore. Just as I am about to join him on the surface, the whale lets out a large moan as if he's asking us not to go. I turn to see that he continues his swim toward me. I am stuck between panic and curiosity. Every part of my mind is screaming for me to swim away as fast as I can—even if there's no possibility of outswimming the giant. But my mind doesn't work with my body, and I go frozen, unable to move. The giant moves closer and closer, and I notice his mouth is not open in their usual form they take on to do filter feeding. He's not on the hunt for food. He doesn't see me as a meal. He comes toward me with a look that almost resembles curiosity. The whale slows until he slowly floats up to meet my eyes. My heart is pounding so hard that I can hear it in my ears.

Fear turns into fascination and humility as the creature's eye becomes parallel with mine. His eye is larger than my entire face. My dad used to always tell me that you could read a person's every motive if you cared enough to look them in the eye. And for a moment, as I look into the eye of this magnificent creature, I see him. I see grace. I see kindness. I see a gentle spirit.

I reach out my hand to touch the largest animal on Earth. And I find myself swelling with a love and a pride for Maurea that I didn't know I could have before. Because despite there being so many more worlds in a much larger planet called Earth, my world has the Earth's largest and most gentle giant. And he trusts me enough to allow me to momentarily be a part of his vast world. I feel extraordinarily humble as I wade there in the ocean with him. I have no control over what is happening at this moment, and yet I've never felt so free. A burning starts to grow in my chest as my lungs beg for oxygen. I put my forehead to the snout of my new friend, hoping that he can know and understand my gratitude. I turn my back to the whale as I start my swim toward the reef. Once I reach the drop-off, I look back to see him swimming off into the vast ocean. He doesn't leave before letting out a low groan of farewell. I wave to Luna before I break the surface. Vince runs up to me frantically.

"Are you hurt? What happened? I wanted to swim down to help you, but I didn't want to aggravate it in any way." His trembling hands on my arms make my shoulders shake.

"Vince, calm down. You know most whales aren't like that. I wish you could have been there . . . I've never experienced anything like that in my life. I—" He still hasn't stopped shaking. I've never seen him so jolted. I take both of his hands in mine.

"Hey, I'm sorry I freaked you out. I shouldn't have gone out so far. Relax." His shaking eventually starts to subside, and he looks from down at his feet to meet my eyes. He wraps me in a hug so tight I can't breathe.

"You can't be so reckless, Adira. If something were to happen to you, wha-what would I tell your mother? Or brothers? What would *I* do?" I feel terrible for scaring him so much. I wish I could tell him I was sorry for what I did, but I'm not.

"Do you want to sit for a while?" I ask. I can't tell if the wetness on his face is from the ocean or tears.

"Yeah, sure. Ha. Sitting isn't a bad idea."

He sits next to me on the dry sand as we look across the ocean to see the last strands of light escaping under the horizon. *This* he freaks out about but doesn't think twice on learning that the world is so much bigger than we knew our whole lives. After I hear that his breathing has slowed down, I break the silence.

"How are you handling all of this so well?" I ask.

"What do you mean?"

"You know what I mean," I retort. He gives me a contemplative look but stays silent. Minutes pass in silence.

"I suppose I always assumed." I give him a quizzical look.

"Not that I assumed all of the details that we've been learning about," he continues, "but I always assumed that there were others out there. Even if it wasn't necessarily a conscious thought that I had. When we learned that we aren't alone, there was a part of me that went 'Ah, I knew it,'" he says with a smile.

"You always were a smart-ass, weren't you?" I nudge him, and we share a laugh. There's another long stretch of silence as we watch the last drop of sunlight disappear.

"It doesn't have to be a bad thing, Adira."

"You're right. Nothing terrible about war or famine. Hey, I'm hanging out with Hitler later if you want to tag along."

"That's not what I mean." He laughs.

"It's just a scary thought, Vince. I know Simon says that the whole reason these different ecospheres exist is to see how far humanity can go, but I can't help wondering if they were running from something. I mean, look at the history of humanity. If I was dealing with famine, war, and poverty, I might want to run into a giant bubble as well," I say. I can practically see the complex thoughts forming in his mind through the furrow of his brow.

"Yes, there are terrible things that have happened throughout the world. But there are also a lot of good. You have to remember that it was people from out there who created our home.

"The way we speak, our mannerisms, our language, the way we behave together as a community, the way we hunt, and everything that we are came from people who don't look like you or me. The Originals were just ordinary humans trying to make humans extraordinary."

I know he's right. Damn, I hate it when he's right. As the first stars start to pop out in the night, a cold wind blows over the waves, which sends chills down my spine.

"We should be getting back home. We've got another full day tomorrow," I say as I stand up and brush the sand off the lower half of my body.

"I'll walk you home."

"Actually, I think I need some time alone with my thoughts. The twins will undoubtedly demand an unruly amount of attention tonight," I say with a small chuckle. "Thanks, though."

"Don't go off making friends with an elephant on your way. Straight home," he teases.

We go our separate ways; I find my thoughts drifting back to the whale. Vince's words still linger in the back of my mind. He's right, there are beautiful things about the other worlds we don't have here. But tonight, I forgot about the monkeys and the elephants and the wars and the terrible things that make the rest of the world feel so dark. Tonight, I dreamt about the whale and the sea.

4

THE CEREMONY INVOLVED with choosing your mate is a two-day process. The first day is when most of the exciting things happen. It starts in the morning where the current Legions name off each person who is in the pool of that year. For most, they get to decide what year they choose their partner. However, you cannot be a part of the ceremony until you have reached twenty years and must participate before you reach thirty years. With Leia reaching twenty, this year is one that is especially exciting for Maurea being that it is the year the Heirs will be paired. Tomorrow is the day that marks the start of the ceremony. Tomorrow I will learn who I am to spend the rest of my life with and fulfill my duty to pass along the Dorian genes. No pressure.

It's interesting to think of this whole process with my newly acquired knowledge. We've always known that gene selection was something important. We knew that if you had an unwanted anomaly in your makeup, then you wouldn't be allowed to have a mate. Even with those who were told this was going to be their fate, there's never been uproar or unrest about the ancient law. We knew that this decision was never just about us. We just never knew why. Why no one cared enough to ask, including myself, is enigmatic. To think about how this sacred practice is the reason my toes are webbed, my hair is golden, and I can stay underwater for so long, I can't help but wonder if the other ecospheres have made it as far as the Dorian. What do they look like? Do they even look like people anymore? Do they wonder the same thing about us?

My thoughts drift to Vince. I wonder why he hasn't made arrangements between him and one of the many suitors that has been lining up to be paired with him. Why he hasn't just made plans to be with me if that was what he was hinting at before. If two people wish to have each other, they make it known in the beginning of the ceremony. Those who haven't made such arrangements are put into a separate pool where they will either be chosen by someone or the Legions will make a pair. For those of us in that pool, we are all given numbers so we know which order we will have the opportunity to claim a mate. If we are claimed, we are unable to oppose. It's considered the highest praise to be chosen. Male or female can be the one to make the choice. Part of me wishes that I would have taken time to get to know possible suitors before getting to this point in the process. But I also know that I would inevitably find flaws in each of them that I deemed too annoying to deal with for the rest of my life. All except one . . . I've decided that if Vince doesn't ask, I will leave the decision for my mate up to the Legions. They know what's best for the entirety of Maurea, they'll know who I can best serve alongside. I haven't bothered getting to know many of the possible suitors, so I shouldn't be at risk for being selected specifically by anyone. To think I only have two more nights where I'll be lying in this comfortable, old bed in my small room of my family's home feels bittersweet. I've been dreading tomorrow for so long that it feels almost like a relief that it's finally here and about to be over with.

The sun has set for hours now. I wonder if I am the last person on Maurea that is still awake. Likely not. There are nineteen other people whose lives are also changing tomorrow. The sound of scampering footsteps makes its way toward my room. Not the only one awake even here.

"Addi?" Liam coos from the doorway. A smile tugs at my lips.

"Liam, what are you still doing up?" He fiddles in the doorway, playing with a loose piece of seaweed around the entry to my room.

"Are you gonna leave us tomorrow to go live with different boys?" he asks quietly.

"No. I still have tonight and tomorrow here with you, Avery, and Mom. And I'll come by all the time to visit. And of course, drop off more shells." This pulls a smile out of him.

"I think Avery is just really going to miss you, so I wanted to make sure you were going to come back all the time. I think he even said that he wouldn't even fight over the shells anymore or somethin'." He looks down at his feet.

"Come here." I gesture toward myself. He climbs up the bed and onto my lap. I start rubbing small, soothing circles on his back.

"Does Avery know that he has nothing to do with me leaving?"

"Um, I'm not sure."

"Well, do you think you could pass along a message to him for me?" He nods enthusiastically.

"If I could stay here forever and ever, I would. There's a duty for each and every member of the Dorian people that is way bigger than you or me or Avery. It's very important that we do everything for our people that we can. Just like Dad did."

There's a sadness and pain in his eyes. He already lost someone so important, and now he feels like he's being abandoned all over again. I wish I would have paid closer attention to the boys during the hard times. I was so consumed with my own grief I had forgotten that they're old enough to feel that too.

"Liam, no matter how long I'm gone, I will always come back." His bottom lip starts to tremble as he rests his head on my chest. I rest my chin on top of his head.

"This isn't a bad thing. After all, in a couple days, you'll have a big brother." He shoots his head up.

"Do you think he'll play with me and Avery!" The sudden change in demeanor makes me laugh.

"Absolutely. Who wouldn't want to hang out with you guys?"

"Well, thanks for letting me know that stuff. I think Avery was starting to get really sad about it." He lays his head back on my chest.

"I'm not going anywhere," I whisper. There's a long beat of silence. I begin to think that he may have fallen asleep.

"Addi, can you sing Lady Blue?"

"Do you promise to go straight to sleep afterward?"

"Yes!" he shouts much too loudly.

"Okay, okay, shhhh." I start to sing the old and familiar lullaby. By the second line, Liam's eyes are closed. By the fifth, I hear a light snoring. I pick him up and carry him back to the room he shares with Avery. All the while singing.

Upon an old ocean Blue
I saw a wave of beauty
She roared and thundered to and fro
As if a sacred duty
Oh, beauty Blue, why do you moan
From where'd you come or where to go
I wave farewell to Lady Blue
But forever see her in the morning dew

5

THE MORNING COMES far too soon as my mother comes rushing into the room to make me presentable for the ceremony.

"It's a big day, Adira. Big big day!" I do my best to rub the sleep from my eyes.

"Yeah, Mom, I know." She hasn't stood still for a second. She starts rummaging around my room trying to find something, making it look like the twins ran through here on a rampage.

"Mom, can I help you find something?"

"I had a dress put in here a week ago, and it's gone missing, Adira. How do you lose things so easily?" As she is running around the room, I notice a beautiful dress that I hadn't even realized was there until just now. Made entirely of different seagrasses, it looks as though every shade of green is present on this dress.

"Mom." She turns to me, and I point. She sighs of relief and drops the three blouses of mine she has in her hand onto the ground.

"Oh, thank goodness. Go ahead and slip it on." I start taking off my nightclothes as she goes and grabs the beautiful dress.

"I've never seen this before. Did you make it?"

"Actually, it was my mother who made it for my ceremony years ago." I slip on the dress, and it hangs perfectly on me. The bottom of the dress goes all the way down to my toes with a slit on the left side that runs up to my upper thigh. The straps are less than an inch and fall over my shoulders to reveal my bare back. The front hangs loosely around my breasts.

"You are a vision, Adira. The greens of the dress make your eyes look greener than anything I've ever seen." Water starts to well up in my mom's eyes.

"Well, hopefully some young suitor likes something a little different." I don't know why I feel embarrassed or the need to cry myself.

"I wore this the day I said your father's name." I stop short as I am admiring the dress.

"*You* claimed Dad?"

"Oh what, did you think I was going to let someone else snatch him?" she says with a smirk as she starts to put small braids throughout my long hair.

"I guess I always thought you two had arranged your match ahead of the ceremony," I imply.

"I'm not entirely sure your father even knew who I was before I said his name that day. But I was the third one who got the chance to claim someone, and the two in front of me were men. Your father, of course, was every girl's choice. But nevertheless, I was the first one who got to him," she says with a smirk.

I always thought of my mom as too shy a person to stand up for what she really wants. I can envision her in her prime wearing this gorgeous dress, being the envy of every other girl in the pool.

"What was it like . . . the first night?"

There's a long stretch of silence. I turn to see that she has tears running down her face. Grief and longing so evident in her expression.

"Adira . . ." She stops braiding and takes my hand to sit with me on my bed.

"Your dad and I didn't fall in love right away. I know that's how everyone wants it to be, but that's not the way it always goes. Within about a year, however, I was smitten with him and he with me. The feelings don't always come overnight. If you get someone you may not have had in mind, the world isn't ending. And in the end, your mate is for a purpose greater than yourself or romance."

I can't decide if her words are more comforting or discouraging. I always thought she and Dad were in love from even *before* the beginning. That they had chosen each other ahead of time. It's what everyone wants to think about their parents, I suppose.

"Um, it may hurt a bit at first. But eventually, the pain will stop, and you will see that there is something, uh, very special and enjoyable about the act that is the . . . threshold of carrying on your genes." My face starts to cringe.

"Okay, Mom, I get how that part works." We both burst into laughter. It feels nice. As though a long tension has finally been broken. Although I can imagine that breaking tension with laughter during the ceremony is something that would be frowned upon.

"Well, I am going to go and make sure that your brothers are decent and ready to go. I'll leave you to your thoughts."

As she leaves, I exit our hut to look out at the vast ocean. I hadn't been able to go back since the encounter with the whale. I had hoped to get a quick swim in this morning to let out some nerves or even to just have some time with Luna. But my conversation with Liam ended up going late. I turn back when I hear my brothers calling after me. My mother has changed into a beautiful blue dress, and my brothers are in their best ceremonial clothes. Avery runs up and jumps at me quickly, being met with a chastisement from my mother about not messing up my hair or dress. I sneak a wink to Liam as he walks with me. I look back on the place that has been my home for the last twenty-two years, thinking about how this is the last day that I will be able to call this hut my home. I turn away from the hut to walk hand in hand with Avery, Liam, and our mother toward the most important ceremony of my life.

~~~~~~

The ceremony is held outside where the longest stretch of sand is uninterrupted by homes. The whole beach is decorated with shells laid down in intricate designs. All of Maurea comes to this ceremony every year. I've known every one of the Dorian my entire life, but for some reason, seeing them all this year at once, it feels like the population of Maurea has tripled. There are two areas marked off by pillars of fire that represent where the pairs go once they've been announced, and another where we will wait our turns until we either claim a mate or someone claims us. I'm the last of the heirs to arrive at the ceremony. I lock eyes with Vince as I walk toward the small group with Simon at the center. Vince breaks eye contact to take in the beautiful dress. I find myself blushing at the wordless compliment. Vince and Eliot are wearing the same ceremonial garb that most men will wear to ceremonies such as this. Lane is wearing the same thing but with decorative shells wherever he can manage to place them. Leia is in a beautiful, long white dress that hangs loosely over her body. I can't pull off white the way she can. Which is fine, because the process of dying seagrass white is time-consuming and smells terrible until you air it out for at least two weeks. It was worth it for her, though. She really is a beautiful girl, and the dress is stunning. I wonder who she is going to be paired with today. My thoughts were that perhaps she and Eliot would make a good pair. Both quieter in their demeanor, but with a kind and genuine heart. Lane is most likely going to be paired with India. She is no doubt the most beautiful of everyone in the pool this year. She knows this *almost* as much as Lane does. This is the first year that she had reached enough years to be able to take part in the ceremony. When she heard Lane would be a part of it, she put her name in. No doubt that those two have arranged their match already.

"Today is one of the most important days of each of your lives," Simon says. "I know each of you will make the current Legions proud. Remember, you have a duty that is higher than anyone else in the pools today. Choose wisely. We wish you all the happiness in the world."

The sound of the ceremonial conch shell signals the ceremony is about to begin. Before I am able to walk and join the others, Simon stops me.

"Adira, can I have a moment?" I was hoping to talk to Vince to make sure that we had some sort of plan, but the look on Simon's face makes me pause.

"Of course." Vince looks back at us and then continues on forward with the others.

"I know this isn't a day you have been looking forward to. It wasn't one that your father really was either. But he did it, same as you, because it was a duty." I look down at my feet. Shame reddening my cheeks. I thought I had hidden my distaste for being paired better than that. Simon takes my chin to move my gaze back up to meet his.

"Your dad would be so proud to see you here today. And as I'm sure Lana told you, they ended up very happy in the end. You will, too. I believe that fully." Maybe Vince has talked to him about how he will choose me. I can feel tears welling up in my eyes. Today would be so much easier if Dad were here today. Simon wipes the tear away and pulls me into a hug.

"Tomorrow, when it is time for the ceremonial binding, if you would like, I will be there at your side." It's customary that the father of the female mate accompanies her to the binding. Apparently, it's part of an ancient practice from the Originals. I had been dreading the obvious absence of my father during the ceremony. The fact that Simon would stand in his place makes tears fill my eyes.

"It would be an honor, Simon. I can't thank you enough."

"The distinct pleasure to stand in his place is all mine, dear. Now hurry on and catch up with the others. Now is not a day to be running late," he says with a smirk. I compose myself with a deep breath and hurry on to catch up with the others.

Those who have made arrangements ahead of time break off and stand to one side of the ceremonial hall. The rest of us stand on the other. Surprisingly enough, none of the heirs have made preconceived arrangements. Not unless you count me and Vince's weird conversation. Between both of the groups stands the current Legions: Eliot's mother, Pandora; Lane's father, Paul; Leia's father,

Harold; and Simon. Whenever the four Legions come together, there is always a space between Harold and Simon that is left open in solidarity for my father. Pandora steps forward to begin the ceremony.

"On behalf of the Legions, I would like to welcome you all to this monumental occasion in these young Dorians' lives. When the Originals settled on Maurea, they started a tradition and a vital step in the progression and biological advancement of our people." She turns to face the six people who have already made arrangements.

"You all have made a preconceived choice to plan who your partner will be to carry on the blood of our people. Your dedication to the mission of the Originals is seen, appreciated, and respected to the highest degree." She then turns to us who have not made any previous plans.

"You all must be feeling quite anxious," she says with a slight chuckle and smile. It is met with nervous giggles down the line.

"But we as the Legions applaud your faith in not only us, but in your fellow young Dorian that stand beside you. Take comfort in knowing that we, too, know how difficult this decision is, and do not take it lightly. For those of you that are chosen, it is of the highest compliments you can receive. For those that choose to have us select your mate, thank you for your faith in our decisions. Please come forth and draw a number for your order."

We each walk forward one at a time to pick a number from the Legions for when we will have our opportunity to either pick a mate or have the Legions choose for us. I step up after Leia to claim my number. There's fourteen of us. I receive the number 6. Good enough, I suppose. Right in the middle. I wonder what number Vince received. As I look at the seven males that are in my pool, I know I at least won't get chosen before Vince can claim me. I can only hope that no female goes before me and chooses him. I'm so nervous now that we're here. This was stupid, we should have come together as a pair. In my heart, I know that with Vince, it would be easy as *breathing*. Number 6. I try to catch his gaze. Please, don't let it be too late.

"For the three pairs that stand before us, I congratulate you on your decisions. The Legions offer their full blessings to each of you," Pandora concludes to the other six. She then turns to us.

"Number one, please step forward."

A woman, Jasmine, who has reached twenty-five years, steps up first. She claims a twenty-seven-year male who seems pleased with her choice. They walk together toward the Legions to receive their blessing. Two males, one after the other, are called next to make a selection. No one has chosen me yet. Only three more people to go. My palms start to sweat, and I feel as though everyone inside of the ceremonial hall can hear my heartbeat as it thumps inside my ears. Pandora calls out for number 4. Vince walks forward. YES! Here's the moment I've dreamt of my entire life. Here's where we go beyond friendship and find what we're really capable of as a pair.

"Vince, what is your selection?"

There's a long pause. Longest yet. I try to take the silence as a good sign. He locks eyes with me, and I shoot him the biggest smile I can manage. He returns the smile before turning to the Legions and stating in front of all of Maurea.

"Leia."

A smile starts to spread across her face as she walks to his side to stand before the Legions and receive their blessing for the match.

I can't breathe. There's a pain in my chest as I feel the blood drain from my face, and I do everything I can to hold back tears. Am I this stupid? It really was just me all along. How can I feel so betrayed when he was never mine in the first place? I feel so naive. Foolish. Did he know? Will he laugh about it in bed tomorrow night with her? I am stuck in a moment of shock when I all of a sudden hear my name called. Is it my turn to pick now? What happened to number 5? I look up to see that it isn't my turn to stand before the Legions and state who I choose. I have been claimed by number 5. I swallow hard as I walk forward to stand next to my mate before the Legions. Pandora states for all of Maurea to hear,

"Lane and Adira, we give you our blessing."

6

THE REST OF the ceremony goes by in a blur. I can't shake the shock of what just happened. India hasn't stopped glaring at me as if I wanted this. She ended up being paired with a male who was in his last year of eligibility for the ceremony. How ironic. At least I'm not the only one leaving the ceremony feeling disappointed. Lane hasn't moved his hand from around my waist since we were paired. I see my family walking toward us, so I break from his grasp to go and hug my brothers. The twins run up to me, and I sink my face into their white curls. My mom puts a hand on my shoulder before she goes to greet Lane.

"Lane, welcome to the family," she says warmly.

"Lana, thank you for raising such an exquisite daughter. It's an honor to be a part of your beautiful family." He really does try to sell it for everything that it's worth. He turns toward me and gives me a look that makes bile rise up in my throat.

"I promise to take excellent care of her." My mom turns away from him right before he wets his lips and bites the corner of his bottom lip as he looks at me up and down, as if some prized trophy. My mom comes and wraps me in an embrace and whispers in my ear.

"Remember, give it time." She puts me at arm's length, and I give her a nod. It's all I can manage until I'm alone to process this without the eyes of others. His parents, Paul and Camille, walk up to greet us. Camille wraps me in a hug far tighter than comfortable or necessary.

"Oh, Adira, you are a vision. We are so pleased with Lane's decision to pick you."

Paul gives me a handshake and nod of acknowledgment before he turns to his son.

"Congratulations, son. I had thought we talked about you choosing India, but I suppose that is a conversation we can save for *later.*"

Um . . . I'm right here?

"Yes, I have to admit I was slightly hesitant due to the deformity and all. But our family's genes have always come through in the end, so I have no doubts our grandchildren will take from their handsome daddy. So, no worries, dear. Nevertheless, welcome to the family!" Camille says.

Deformity? I guess I see where Lane gets his charm from.

"I don't know, I think the green eyes are rather charming," Simon says as he walks up to greet us. Vince and Leia trail behind him. Vince won't look me in the eyes. All the better. I don't have anything to say to him at this point. Simon walks up to Lane and shakes his hand to congratulate him on the match. Leia comes up to me and gives me a hug to whisper in my ear.

"Did you know? Did you know he would pick me?" she says giddily. All I want in this moment is to hate her. To make it her fault. But in my heart, I know that it isn't. The only person at fault is me for having any feelings other than friendship toward Vince. I set myself up for this.

"I hadn't the slightest clue," I say forcing a smile.

"Congratulations on your match, Adira. Your kin will no doubt be some of the most gifted and beautiful on Maurea."

All I'll be good for it seems.

"Thank you, Leia. Congratulations to you as well." She smiles, and we exchange a kiss on each cheek before she goes off to meet her parents. Vince begins to walk toward me to embrace. I put my hand out to shake his hand. He looks down at my hand and, with a disappointed glance, takes it in his own.

"Congratulations on your match, Vince. I hope you'll be very happy." Hearing myself out loud, I know my tone sounds harsh and insincere. But in reality, it is what I want at the end of all this. For him to be happy and be with a woman who does that for him. I just thought that woman would be me. *I would have made you happy, Vince. I'm sorry you thought it couldn't be me.*

"Adira, I—"

"You don't have to explain yourself. You owe me nothing. Leia is beautiful. You two will make kin to be envied over. I wish you nothing but the best." Just as Vince is about to say something, Lane walks up to interrupt.

"Vince! I have to say, you picked quite a gem. Congratulations on your catch. I must say, I thought you would steal my own with all that time you two spend together but—" He puts his hand back around my waist and pulls me into him.

"We all know who this catch belongs to." I can feel the bile rising in my throat again.

"I don't *belong* to anyone," I say, elbowing his side hard enough he lets out a small wince. "Now if you would both excuse me, I'd like to go home with my family." I break from his grasp and turn to walk away when Lane grabs my hand.

"I will see you tomorrow, my dear." He bows and gives me a wink as he kisses my hand. I pull my hand away and shoot one last glance at Vince before I run up to Avery and Liam.

"All right, you two, who's ready to go home?"

"We are!" the twins exclaim. I remember how boring I found these ceremonies when I was their age. They've probably been begging my mother to go home since the moment they knew who their new brother would be. The very thought makes me sick. I make a promise to myself to not let Lane's temperament influence my brothers. I give myself a second to mourn any notion that I had that I would be coming home tomorrow with a man my brothers could look up to as any sort of fatherly figure. My mom kisses Camille on each cheek before joining us to depart.

The walk back to our hut was silent other than the sound of the crashing ocean to our right. Every once in a while, one of the twins would try and make joke or mimic the sounds of different sea creatures. When we get back to our home, I strip off the dress as soon as I'm alone. I look at it as it lays on my bed and think about how much promise I was feeling the first time I saw it this morning. Now, I can't soon enough get it out of my sight. I slip on my kelp blouse and trousers before heading out into the living space to see my brothers having all of the seashells I have ever brought back for them in a pile on the floor. They try blowing into each and every one of them to try and recreate the conch call from this morning. Avery starts blowing so hard he starts to turn bright red. I can't help but giggle at my silly brothers. My mother has changed out of her dress and is in her own comfortable clothes. She nods her head slightly toward the door.

"Come with me, let's go take a walk."

I follow her outside, and we start our trek along the beach. Both of us are quiet for quite some time. My mom is the first to break the silence.

"I know Lane wasn't your first choice," she says.

"He was my last choice, Mom. After never choosing a mate at all," I spit out.

"Adira, Lane's family has some of the strongest and most adaptable traits out of all the Dorian people. You may not love him now—you may not ever learn to love him. But what's most important is the fact that he will be an excellent mate for you to carry on Dorian blood."

"Yeah, Mom, I'm very aware of my obligation to screw. But, Mom, what if it didn't matter as much? What if life was about something more important than all of this?"

"Adira, what could be more important than your people?"

I have nothing to say to that. Because there is nothing more important. I wish I could tell her everything. I wish I could tell her that it used to be about something more. I wish I could tell her about weddings and fairy tales and all the things that used to go into choosing a partner and how none of it had to do with passing down genes. I wish I could tell her that I love Vince. But I know I can't. I thought I would leave today feeling like I gained another family. Instead, I stand there on the sand feeling more alone than I ever have. I look out toward the ocean and find my thoughts once again drifting to the whale.

"I think I'm going to go for a swim," I say while undressing down to my swimming clothes.

"All right, be safe. And don't stay too long. The boys will want to spend some extra time with you tonight."

She starts to walk back toward the hut as I run toward the water. I breathe deep before I submerge myself into the waves. As if Luna was waiting for me, she drifts up to my side as we swim toward the reef. A small pod of dolphins swims to greet us. Friendly and playful creatures, dolphins are. But we don't see them super often. I look up to watch them race toward the surface to jump and spin into the air. The water is cooler than the last time I was in. It wakes me up from the daze I was in from the ceremony. I swim quickly to the drop-off to see if by some off chance, my gigantic friend still resides in these open waters. It seems as though he has moved onto bigger and better spaces. I envy him. I long for bigger and better places. But yet, here I am, world growing smaller and smaller leading to tomorrow. I turn back toward the reef to enjoy the rest that the ocean has to offer. A sea turtle that looks to have reached about eighty years or so swims peacefully across the blue. I swim back toward the dolphins. One of them is in a particularly playful mood and uses her nose to nudge me around, all the while chirping and whistling. I stroke her back before taking hold of her fin as she leads me around in the water much faster than I could ever hope to swim. Luna has a hard time keeping up, so she swims back down to the coral reef to make a feast of some crustaceans. The water seems to be getting colder, causing me to start to shiver. The shivering causes me to run out of breath faster than usual. I let go of the dolphin's fin and head to the surface. I crawl back onto the sand to see Vince there, holding my clothes.

"What do you want, Vince?" I grab my clothes from him and start to get dressed.

"Adira, can we just talk?"

"Vince, what do you want me to say? There's nothing *to* say here."

"Why are you mad? I had no idea Lane was going to try and claim you. He never told me anything. It's not like me and Lane are close, Adira."

"Leave it alone, Vince." I turn to walk away. Vince follows me close behind.

"No, I'm not going to leave it alone. You haven't looked me in the eye since the ceremony, and I just need to know what's going on! What happened, Adira? Did he hurt you?"

"No, of course not. Now leave. It. Alone." He grabs my arm and holds me in place.

"Vince, let me go."

"No, not until you tell me what the hell is going on! Why is it my fault you got Lane as a mate?"

"Because *you* didn't claim me first!" The second it comes out, I want to take it back. He stares at me in shock and lets go of my arm. Tears well up in my eyes, and I feel my face burn with embarrassment. Neither of us knows what to say now. After a while, Vince breaks the silence.

"You never told me," he murmurs softly.

"Oh really? I thought that when you were asking about choosing someone who was a friend, you were talking about *me*, Vince. I told you to go for it. And look at that, you did. I was just stupid enough to think it was me. Besides, would it have even made a difference if I just said it directly to you?" I ask.

"Of course, it would, Adira. Are you kidding me?"

"Then why didn't you? You picked Leia. If you felt something in even the slightest way, why on earth wouldn't you just say *my* name?" Tears start rolling down my cheeks. I can see Vince's eyes starting to fill with tears as well.

"Adira . . . I don't . . . Leia just made more sense. There weren't any complications with her. You're too important. What if we couldn't adjust? You never told me, Adira. I can't read your mind or know what you were thinking. I thought you'd end up with Eliot since you talk of him so highly. She expressed some interest a while back, and we started talking more, and I think she is someone that I can learn to love and that she can learn to love me." He starts to walk toward me, putting out his arms as if he is going to try his best to comfort me. I step back.

"I wouldn't have had to learn, Vince." He stops in his tracks.

"Adira . . . I—"

"You don't have to say anything. It doesn't make a difference anymore."

With tears still streaming down my face, I turn to walk away from him when he grabs my hand and spins me toward him. Before I am able to react, his arms are around my waist and his lips are crashing against mine. My lips instinctively start to move with his as I melt into him. I reach my hand up into his hair as he moves his hands underneath my shirt and up my back. This feels so right. As if the last twenty-two years has been leading to this. But I know the longer we go, the more it will hurt once we inevitably stop. I push back from him, finding myself out of breath. We both just stand there for a second in shock as to what just happened. He looks me in the eyes as he takes my hand and puts his forehead against mine.

"I'm so sorry," he whispers. I push away from him to walk away. "So am I."

~~~~~~

As we walk in separate directions toward our homes, I touch my lips to try and soak in the heaviness of what just transpired. I try to stay in that positive and joyful mindset that I have finally had my moment with Vince, but as I stride closer to my home, each step brings me closer to reality. Tonight is my last night here. Tomorrow, I am officially paired with Lane for the rest of my life. The reality is that tomorrow, the forbidden kiss will have made it even harder to move on. How am I supposed to just be his friend now? Every time I see him, I know I'll be haunted by the moment we shared. I'll think of his hands on my back and wonder where they may have gone if we hadn't stopped. Part of me wishes I could forget everything that just happened. That I could forget about Vince and do my best to create a happy life with Lane. But I know it's too late for that.

I walk into our home as my brothers come running past me out the door. My mother calls out to them, "Stay close! Come back in before it gets too dark!"

She busies herself cleaning up the boys' mess of shells still on the floor.

"Why don't you leave those for the boys to pick up?"

"It would be more work for me to get them to pick them up than it would be for me to just do it myself. I'm a bit too tired after the long day to put up any sort of fight," she says with a chuckle.

"Hah, they are a bit of work sometimes, aren't they?" I respond. I help her finish the collection of all the shells and carry them into the boys' room. I go and sit on Avery's bed as my mom sits on Liam's.

"I'm going to miss this place."

"You're not leaving forever, Adira. I know you'll come by all the time."

"Of course, I will. I just know it won't be the same." I distract myself with one of the shells that I gifted to the boys. I find its smooth texture oddly soothing. I wonder what creature used to call this tiny shell home. Was it as scary for them leaving this shell to find a different one as they grew? I suppose that's all this really is. It's me growing out of my home and having to move to a different one. I wonder which home we will be assigned to. Maybe one of the newer ones? As I place the shell back with the others, I notice that all of the shells are trembling on the surface in which they sit. I look around the room and see all the lanterns have also started shaking.

"Mom, what's going on?" I can see my own panic mirrored in her eyes. She shoots off the bed and runs into the main part of our hut. I follow her close behind as I watch everything we own tremble around us. The walls start to crumble, and the roof of our home starts to shed around us. We know we need to get out of the house, but the shaking ground makes my legs feel weak and unstable. I feel as though I don't have full control over my body. I start to panic until I feel my mom's hand take my own. I move as fast as I can with my arm around her to the outside of our hut. We come out to see other families all around us escaping their collapsing homes. Everyone is running around trying to make sure that their loved ones are safe and accounted for. I look around to try and find Liam and Avery in all of the madness, but I can't spot them anywhere. Finally, the trembling stops.

"Mom, where are Liam and Avery?" She looks past me in horror, unable to speak.

"*Mom!* Focus! Where are Liam and Avery!"

With a trembling finger, she points out to the sea. As I turn to follow her gaze, I see why she stands in such shock. The ocean has receded. I can barely see the shoreline.

7

I FIND MY MIND entirely detached from my body as I go into a full-on sprint to try and reach the water. I come to a sudden halt when someone grabs my arm. Vince.

"Adira, what are you doing! We don't have any idea what is going on!"

"They're in there, Vince! Liam and Avery! They're in there!"

"I understand that, but we have no idea what could happen to anyone that goes in there right now, Adira. It's not safe!"

"Exactly! There are two boys in there, and I'll be damned if I lose them to the sea too!"

As I'm screaming at him, his eyes turn from me to the sea. I turn to follow his gaze and find myself running with him in the opposite direction. The receding ocean is now in full charge back toward the rest of Maurea. The closer the wave gets, the taller it seems to grow. I feel as though my soul has jumped out of my body and I'm running on pure instinct. Vince grabs my arm again as we sprint toward land. I look up to see the rest of the Dorian running as well with the exception of my mother, who still stands in her same state of shock. Right before I am able to reach her, we're thrusted underwater.

The sheer force of the wave crashing into my back has knocked out at least six minutes of air. The wave caused Vince to lose grip of my arm, and we split off in opposite directions. I pull my head out of the water just as another wave hits and sends me turning forward. I've never thought in my life that I could possibly drown. But as I sink further into the ocean, I feel as though I am being abused by the sea. My body crashes into a sandy surface. I open my eyes to see I've crashed into someone's hut. I look up to see that there is still about fifteen feet before the surface breaks. All of Maurea is underwater. I try to train my eyes to see in the underwater madness. I see other people about twenty meters from me swimming for the surface. It's only then that I remember how my two brothers have been underwater this whole time. I count back in my head. It's been about ten minutes since they ran outside. Ten minutes? Has my world really gone to hell in less than ten minutes? The last time I gave the boys lesson, they were both able to stay under for twelve minutes. They're running out of time.

I discover that the deeper I go into the water, the less I can feel the effects of the waves. I make a break for the surface to get a full intercostal breath. As I once again plunge underneath, I go straight for the ocean floor before I start my search. Conserve energy wherever I can. Minute and a half. The ocean I knew is in chaos. Decorative shells and belongings that used to be in homes are now floating in the open water. As the mud from people's homes starts to fall apart in the water, the water turns a shade of brown that makes it hard to make out objects in the mush. Why is the water so cold? I push myself on. Grabbing onto anything I can to propel myself forward.

I look to my right and see a familiar shadow moving toward me. *Is that what I think it is?* Luna swims right past me from above my body before she quickly turns around without stopping toward the direction she came. My instincts tell me to follow her. Being that my instincts are the only thing I am able to go off on at the moment, I conform to their wishes and follow after Luna as fast as I can. I see them before she stops swimming. Avery is trying to break Liam free of some coral he seems to have gotten his left foot jammed into. No doubt from the force of the first wave. I quickly swim to them and push Avery toward the surface. He tries to stay and help, but I can see his lips starting to go cyanotic. I give him another push vertically, and he ascends toward the surface. From what I can see, the waves are coming in less frequently and with less force. Some land might be surfaced again. I say a silent prayer to whoever is listening that it's true.

I bring my head down to the piece of coral to better see what has his foot stuck. A rock has fallen over the branches of some pillar coral. With three pushes, I am able to move the small boulder. As his foot breaks free, I can see the bone sticking out of his skin. I take Liam by the arms and push off the ocean floor toward the surface. When I break, I can see that a small plot of land, no more than one hundred yards, has peeked out over the surface of the ocean. I position Liam on my back and swim on top of the surface as fast as I can toward the sand. Vince is helping my mother aid Avery when they spot us moving up the small island. Vince runs up to me and helps me in getting Liam off of my back and lying flat on the ground without causing further injury to his foot. It isn't until then that I notice he hasn't been breathing. Vince begins doing compressions on his chest and breathing air into his body every thirty seconds, just like we were taught from a young age. *Please don't take him. Please don't take him.*

By the fourth time he has breathed for Liam, I know he will never do it on his own. I want to cry. I want to scream. I want to run into the ocean and let it claim me as it has now claimed Liam. I reach toward my chest. I can't breathe. Vince stops the compressions once my mother walks to him and puts a hand on his shoulder. She cups Liam's head in her hands and kisses his forehead. She then brings his head to her chest and cradles him as she lets out a wail that sounds inhuman. I look to Avery and see nothing but shock on his face as tears stroll down his cheeks. He tried with everything he could to save his other half. I will myself to walk over to him. The moment I get to Avery, he collapses into me.

"I tried, Addi," he says between sobs. "I tried so hard."

It takes everything in me to not scream in this moment. I look around at what used to be my home. Where there was once numerous homes and signs of beautiful life, now there stands nothing but a small patch of sand surrounded by the ocean that destroyed it. Within less than an hour, Maurea has disappeared.

"I know, Avery. You did everything you could. This isn't your fault." *Please believe it is not your fault.*

We sit there in tears together as we watch our mother rock Liam back and forth as if he were just sleeping. In that moment, all I can think to do to console Avery is to sing the same lullaby that I sang to his brother the night before. So we rock there and sing "Lady Blue." Soon enough, overcome by the shock and exhaustion of the day, just as Liam did by the fifth line, Avery falls asleep.

8

IT TAKES NO more than forty minutes before the ocean has receded back to the point where everyone can fit on land and the aftermath of its destruction can be accounted. Maurea has been destroyed. Where there was once countless homes and halls, there is now only mounds of sand all around. Miraculously, all of the Dorian are accounted for. Those that didn't make it were brought in by different search parties who went out. By the time everyone is accounted for, twelve, including Liam, have died. Eight of those who passed hadn't even reached eight years yet. Three that didn't make it were of the elderly population. One of the most shocking deaths was that of Pandora. With the leader of the Legions gone, Simon has stepped into her place.

"Adira." It's Eliot. He keeps his composure well, but his eyes are swollen from recent tears. Without thinking, I wrap him in a tight hug. He hesitates for a moment before wrapping his arms around me and returning the gesture. I can feel him take a deep breath. No one should have to hide their mourning the way he feels like he needs to.

"I'm so sorry, Eliot. She was an amazing woman and leader."

"Thank you, Adira," he says while stepping back slightly.

"I'm sorry about Liam as well. I came to let you know that Simon is calling for all the Heirs." We walk toward the small meeting that seems to have already started without Eliot and me. When we join, there's a silence that falls over the small group. Simon is the first to break the silence.

"Adira, Eliot. I cannot begin to tell you how sorry we are for the loss of your family members. I wish there was time we could give you to mourn, but I'm afraid the day we thought wouldn't come for hundreds or more years has arrived." He turns to the rest of the group to address us as a whole.

"What we just experienced is something very similar to a natural disaster that the Earth has experienced many times outside of the ecospheres. Only, believe it or not, a much smaller version. I am then led to believe that this whole occurrence is related to the integrity of our ecosphere. The day in which our ancestors have always been prepared for has happened. The Legions have voted. Maurea is no longer safe. We need to gain intel on how we can fix our ecosphere, or we must find a new home for the Dorian to reside."

"Leave Maurea? That's a joke. How are we supposed to live anywhere else? Our bodies are acclimated to Maurea, Simon. You said so yourself. How are we expected to thrive outside of here?" Lane babbles on. The disrespect he veers toward Simon is infuriating, but his questions are legitimate. How are we supposed to survive anywhere else?

"I understand your trepidations," Simon continues. "But this is the reality of the situation that we've been put into. I never intended to ask more than what was expected of you Heirs, but now I must." He pauses and wipes a hand down his face like he's bracing himself to ask what he needs to. "We can't even consider leaving Maurea without an idea of where to go. We need someone to find a place for the Dorian to settle. I know it's too much to ask but—"

"I'll do it," I cut him off. I surprise even myself by what comes out of my mouth. All eyes turn to me. Lane is the only one who doesn't look shocked. Simon has a staggard look, but I notice a swell of relief behind his eyes as well. I know he doesn't want to ask this of us.

"And I'll join you." I turn to see Vince. The relief in Simon is quickly replaced by worry. But he knows he can't ask anything of us he wouldn't ask of his own kin. I turn my head to see that Leia won't look up from the ground.

"Well, in that case, why don't I tag along as well?" Lane says with his half smile. "After all, Adira and I were to be mated tomorrow, and it would be a shame if she were to go running off anywhere else without the sense to come on back," he states while staring down Vince. Vince stands up taller as if to challenge him. I shoot a look to Leia again to see tears welling up in her eyes as she stares at Vince.

"Actually," Simon cuts in. "We've decided that due to the circumstances, we will not be moving forward with the pairings of this year until we have established if there is a way to stay here in Maurea or until we find a new place to settle. Priorities have shifted." Lane hasn't broken eye contact with Vince.

"What *exactly* does that insinuate?" Lane asks.

"It *insinuates* that the second part of the mating ceremony won't be taking place until further notice. For now, all partners that were assigned earlier today are still valid. However, it is a fluid situation, and we will monitor it as the situation evolves." Lane and Vince still haven't stopped staring holes into each other.

"Is that going to be an issue, Vince or Lane?" They turn their glares to Simon.

"No," Vince states barely above a whisper.

"Of course not, Simon." Lane puts his charm back on as if on cue.

"Unless anyone else would like to join the three," he pauses. I hold out hope that Eliot or anyone else would volunteer. I can't imagine spending so much time alone with Vince and Lane of all people.

"No? Well then. Lane, Vince, and Adira. If I could have a word privately." Simon guides us three away from the others until we are completely out of earshot.

"I wish I had more to tell you as to what is out there. But our information is over a millennium old. I can get you out. But I can't give you any promises of what 'out' will be and what lies ahead for you.

"Think back to your lessons. If the other ecospheres are still intact, we are connected to two of them. The forest ecosphere, Tragdome, and the jungle ecosphere, Sentri. We don't know nearly enough on these two in order to make the decision as to which one you should attempt to travel to. If either of these places seems willing or able to support us, reason with whomever has taken charge of the land, if there still *is* anyone, and return to us so we can discuss if we start from scratch on Maurea or if we should settle elsewhere. If it seems as though no other ecospheres would be inhabitable for us, we will need to leave them altogether. The only way to leave the ecospheres completely is through Avil, the desert. If our intel is still correct, both Tragdome and Sentri will be able to get you there."

"Dad, slow down. You can't expect us to remember all—"

"We go to either Tragdome or Sentri in which we are connected to see if those places are fish dung or the people decide they don't want us hanging about, and if that's the case, we go on to Avil, which is connected to both Tragdome and Sentri, to get out of our little fancy bubbles and find somewhere else in the world in which our ancestors ran from. Oh, and no one has any accurate idea of what we're running into being that this information has been passed down for over a thousand years. Sound about right?" The three of us turn to Lane, who has a cheeky grin on his face as he stares back at our struck faces.

"Yes, sounds about right," Simon says.

"Brilliant! Where off to then?" Lane says half-heartedly. As frustrating as he is, for the second time now since we've met, I'm glad he's here. He's smarter than I gave him credit for, and him pretending like we aren't running into our certain deaths oddly makes it all a bit easier.

"I'll give you all the night to say goodbye to your families. Get your affairs in order and meet me at the north shore at first light. I'd give you guys something to take with you, but it appears the ocean has claimed everything for now."

"Wait!" We all turn to see Leia running toward us.

"I'm coming with you," she says between gasping breaths. Lane lets out a laugh.

"Wonderful! A double date it is." He walks off toward his parents, chuckling along the way.

"Leia, are you sure? This isn't something to take lightly. You could leave and very well not come back," Simon says. She looks down at her feet again before meeting Simon's eyes.

"I'm sure." I've never seen Leia in a determined manner before. But the look she gives Simon, we all know that she isn't going to be changing her mind.

"Very well. Vince, bring Leia up to speed on the situation. I'll see you all soon." Simon and I leave Leia and Vince to their conversation.

My mom is still sitting on the ground holding Liam. I gently rest my hand on her shoulder. She flinches at my touch and then looks up to see who has disturbed her deep thoughts.

"Mom . . ."

"You're leaving." I pause. I don't want to hurt her. But I know this is something I need to do.

"Yes. Tomorrow morning." She gently lays Liam's head down on the sand and puts her hand on his forehead before standing up and turning toward me. She quickly wraps me in a hug. I can feel tears threatening to come back as I cling to her. Having a mission is making this easier. Like muting the grief. But I can feel it starting to peel its way into the forefront of my mind the longer I stand on Maurean sand.

"Just come back, Adira. I know why you need to go, but we need you to come back." She pulls back to look at my face.

"I promise, Mom." She lets me go and tries to cradle Liam back into her arms. Tears run down my cheeks as I put my hand on her shoulder to stop her.

"Mom, he's gone . . . Let me—let me take care of him," I croak out. Her lip quivers as she bends down and gives him one last kiss on the forehead. She whispers something too quiet for me to hear into Liam's ear before she nods and turns to pick up Avery and walks away without another word. I stand there staring down at my beautiful brother whom I had just comforted the night before. A boy who had so much life in him, reduced to nothing. A strangled sound comes out of me as I fall to my knees in the sand next to his body and let myself break for a moment. At least I tell myself it'll be for just a moment, but once I start, I don't know how I'm supposed to put myself back together. There's a pain in my chest that feels permanent, like a scar that will never heal properly, and it'll take one bad movement, one bad moment, for it to burst open. All of a sudden, strong arms enclose around me. I look down, and I recognize the hands of Lane. I surprise myself by not pushing him away. I can't hold myself together right now. I don't know how, but Lane can see that. So I hang on to the tether that he's offered me, and I weep over my brother. All the while, he doesn't say a word. He doesn't need to. Eventually I move toward him to try and pick up his body to move it to his place of rest.

"Let me," Lane says in a soft tone. I turn my eyes and see his consoling gaze. Another tear falls, and he reaches up and wipes it away with his thumb before resting his hand on my cheek.

"I'm sorry you lost him, Adira. It is a loss I can't understand," he says barely above a whisper. I turn away from him after a moment and bend down to kiss Liam on the forehead. He's already gone cold.

"Say hi to Daddy for me. I love you," I whisper in his ear. Once I back away, Lane steps up and carefully cradles Liam to his chest before walking away. I give myself a moment before getting up and finding Avery and Mom. No one has blankets. No one has *anything*. I find them already sleeping, cuddled up against each other. I go to Avery's side and lie down and wrap my arms around him. I'll make it back. If not for myself, then for him. He lost a father and now his twin. I refuse to let him mourn one more person in his life.

"I'll always come back," I whisper.

I wake before first light, but I know that sleep will evade me for the rest of the night, so I slowly disentangle myself from Avery. The movement wakes my mom.

"I've gotta go," I whisper. She nods.

"Avery is sleeping. It may just be easier for the both of you if you let him sleep." I know she's right. Avery is the one person at this moment that could possibly convince me to stay. I kiss Avery on the forehead and give my mom one last hug before I head to the north shore. I'm not surprised that I'm the first one here. I sit, and I stare out at the ocean. Loving and hating it simultaneously. How can I feel so betrayed by something that isn't even a person? I stand, grabbing a handful of sand and chucking it into the water as hard as I can with a grunt. Not satisfied, I bend down and throw handful after handful at it, wanting to make the ocean hurt like it hurt me. As ridiculous as that sounds . . .

"Feel better?" Lane's voice comes from behind me. Without turning toward him, I drop my handful of sand.

"Nope," I respond. A light chuckle escapes him as he comes up beside me. The stars are starting to fade out of view as more light peeks through the sky. I stand there huffing, refusing to let the tears that are welling up spill over.

"You ready for today?" he asks. I shrug my shoulders.

"Can you know if you're prepared for something if you have no idea what that something is?" He lets out a small laugh.

"No, I guess not," he replies.

"I just . . . I'm good. In the water, I mean. I'm a good swimmer," I blubber. He nods. "But I feel like that's going to be useless out there. Who cares if I can swim well when you're nowhere near the ocean? I'm just starting to feel really stupid for signing up for this in the first place," I prattle on. A smile tugs at his mouth.

"You have skills far beyond the water that I believe will come in handy, Adira," he says matter-of-factly. We fall into silence for a while. Soon, the sun peeks over the horizon.

"I um . . . thank you. For last night," I mutter. Lane keeps his eyes on the horizon and nods.

"Why'd you do it?" I blurt. A startled look crosses his features as he turns to me.

"Why wouldn't I?" he counters. I shrug.

"I don't know. It just seemed out of character for you . . .," I say, hoping to not insult him.

"You might discover just how little you actually know of my character, Adira." He looks at me with such intensity. For the first time, I notice just how deep of a blue his eyes are. Not like the sea. Not like anything, really. It seems to be a color set aside just for Lane. Have I really never looked into his eyes before? Is he right? Have I been so blinded by who I thought he was that I never even bothered to look him in his gorgeous eyes and see there's something so much deeper to who he is?

The sound of footsteps walking toward us causes me to break the intimate eye contact. I can feel the blood rush to my cheeks as Vince, Leia, and Simon walk toward us. Lane smiles slightly to himself, pleased with the reaction he's pulled from me. I look to see if Vince saw the small interaction. His refusal to meet my eyes tells me he did.

"Last chance for anyone to back out," Simon says. We look around at each other silently. Determined but anxious looks across each of us.

"Well then." He dips down and starts to draw figures in the sand. He draws one large circle with parallel lines leading out of it on both sides with smaller circles attached.

"The circle is Maurea. The two tunnels on each side lead to Sentri in the east and Tragdome in the west. Maurea supplies whatever bodies of water the ecospheres have. There should be tunnels that lead to both. I hope you all have been doing your breathing exercises. I don't know how long you will have to be underwater for, but it's the only way out of Maurea. And as Lane so elegantly pointed out, this information is over a millennium old. I'm just hoping it's correct." He gives a short, concerned look toward Vince.

"Um, small thing. We haven't decided where the hell we're going," Lane states with a tone of annoyance. Vince is about to say something before I interrupt.

"He's got a point," I interject.

"If we're going to be under for a long time, it's best we make that decision now so we can adjust our path. Better to not waste time and air," I add.

"You see, the lady agrees. Now, if I can be so kind as to make a suggestion. I say we go to Sentri."

"Tragdome could have more resources," Vince quickly retorts. Lane turns to him and walks a step closer to be face-to-face with him.

"Ahh, yes, very possible. Except not. Lest you forget our lessons, my friend. In the old world, rain forests were home to about 50 percent of life on this godforsaken planet. Henceforth, even if the poor saps they put there have died off, I'd bet you something real shiny that there's still all sorts of goodies. Not to mention the climate in Tragdome is probably much colder than it is here, and thus our hairless bodies could freeze and, *henceforth*, die before your balls ever get the chance to drop." Vince's cheeks rise in color as he takes a step closer until he and Lane are nose to nose.

"Just a suggestion," Lane says with his cheeky grin. How he goes from one of the most consoling people to this cheeky personality in no time at all is beyond me.

"If you two are quite done," Simon interrupts the silent challenge.

"Lane has a point, Vince. Your bodies will be more acclimated to Sentri's climate. Although, Lane, I am surprised that you were paying such close attention during our lessons," Simon says what I'm sure everyone in the group was thinking. Lane doesn't say anything. He backs away from Vince and winks at me as he comes to stand between me and Leia.

"That settles it then. Let's get moving," I say, looking toward the rising sun. Simon gives me and Vince a hug as we walk toward the water.

"We will see what we can do here to try and make Maurea inhabitable. But the hope of our people lies in your hands," Simon says.

"No pressure," Lane retorts. I find myself snickering a bit. The seriousness of the situation is suffocating, and at the moment, Lane is the only one that seems to have a brighter effect. I close my eyes and start to home in on my breathing. Lane walks up to me from behind and bends over and exhales on my neck before whispering in my ear.

"Hold your breath, little fish, our first big adventure together. Better than any other couple's story so far, don't you think?" I feel chills go through my body. Lane chuckles and then starts walking into the water. I stop Vince before he follows after. I had a million words to say to him, but now that we're here, I feel as though I can't speak any of them.

"Good luck," is all I can manage.

"You too," he says without meeting my eyes.

I walk deeper into the water and breathe deep before I plunge underneath, leaving Maurea behind me.

9

THE WATER HADN'T yet settled to the point where we could all see clearly. Lane has taken up the position of leading the pack. I follow directly behind as Vince and Leia straggle from the back. We dive to the ocean floor and make our way across the coral reef. I try to keep Simon's makeshift drawing at the forefront of my mind as I rack my brain to figure out where the tunnel is that leads out of Maurea and into Sentri. Lane starts to lead us beyond the coral reef and toward the drop-off once again. I wonder if the whale knew that the world above it had just crumbled to pieces. I wonder if it would care if it did. I conclude that it would as I swim ahead of Lane. I look back to see that Leia is starting to straggle behind. A lot of good your singing lessons are doing now. We've been under for eight minutes now. I've got at least twelve left in me. But I know the others won't be as fortunate. We need to find the way out, and we need to do it fast.

We all tread off the drop-off looking around at each other trying to divulge some sort of plan when Luna comes swimming toward us. But instead of stopping at my side as usual, she swims right past us and deeper into the open ocean. She starts to plummet deeper to where I almost can't see her. Lane and I exchange looks before we turn to follow her as fast as we can without looking back to see if Vince and Leia are following. We trust that they are. We swim twenty yards before we lose sight of Luna. Ten minutes. I'm guessing Leia is starting to get uncomfortable. Where are you, Luna? Lane nudges and points downward. There's a streak of brighter blue in the darkness of the deep ocean. Floating in place where the mysterious tunnel of blue light seems to be starting, is Luna. We plunge directly down, trying to make up for lost time without exhausting ourselves out of any more held air we have left. We reach Luna once it's been about twelve minutes.

Lane heads directly into the tunnel with Vince close behind. I stroke my beautiful friend in thanks as I silently wish that this won't be the last time that we see each other. I turn to go through the tunnel when I look to see only two people swimming through. Where's Leia? I turn around to look past the drop-off, but the rest of the ocean is pitch-black. The sun is far set by now, and we are too deep underwater for the light to make it through if it hadn't. I swim out knowing I only have my sense of touch to guide me through the water. Luna has left her spot at the entrance and is nowhere to be found anymore. It's been beyond twenty minutes. I can feel my own chest starting to tighten as my lungs beg for air. Two of us can't die here. I start to turn back before I see a slight shimmer below the entrance. The light from the tunnel reflecting off of Leia's hair. I swim down and fight the pain in my head as the pressure of the ocean starts to compress on me. I grab her by the arm and use all the strength I have left to heave her up and through the tunnel. *Come on, Leia, give me something.* I can't do this on my own. I start swimming through the tunnel, dragging her behind me. The water starts to blur in front of me as I continue to drag her through what looks more to be a never-ending tunnel that will turn into our deathbeds. I feel myself fading. I want to let go of Leia and make a run for whatever is forward, but I know I can't. Vince would never forgive me. I could never forgive myself. How long have we been under now?

Twenty-five minutes? My body takes over and tries to take a deep breath. I feel the burning go throughout my entire body. Instinct telling me to cough until every drop is emptied from my lungs. I fight with every fiber of my being against myself. The pressure in my chest feels like my body is going to collapse in on itself. My sight quickly deteriorates as my peripheral vision blackens out. Just keep swimming. Just a little farther. Is my mind starting to deteriorate, or did the water change? The regular blue has turned a lighter shade of green. And it's so warm. So warm I think I could fall asleep right here. Fall asleep and wake up to Dad and Liam. I'm so tired. Perhaps just a moment. I will rest just a moment. Before I close my eyes, I see a hand reaching toward me.

~~~~~~

I wake to unbearable pain. I spurt upward as water comes forcefully out of my lungs. I try to take in the sweet air before my lungs take over and cough over and over again.

"Adira, breathe. Slow down, breathe." I turn over on all fours and clutch at the earth as my lungs try desperately to empty themselves. Eventually, the coughing slows, and I am able to take my first deep breath. It *hurts*. I have a few ribs that are bruised, if not broken. I take a few more breaths and eventually feel like the world comes into a little more clarity. It smells strange. It's only then that I realize the earth that I have been clutching isn't the usual coarseness of sand. Strangely soft. Moist. Almost sticky. I finally open my eyes and roll onto my back to suck in the air around me. I feel as though I've never breathed before. I don't know if that is due to going without it for far too long or if it is the difference the air seems to hold in this new ecosphere. I want to sit up and look around, but it feels too good to just lie here and breathe. I close my eyes and count my breaths. I open my eyes to see Vince staring down at me.

"Adira, are you all right?"

"Vince," my voice rasps out. The salt water must have affected my vocal cords. I suddenly remember who I was dragging through the tunnel. I shoot myself upward despite the pain that radiates from my chest and side throughout my body.

"Leia. What happened to Leia?"

"Adira, relax. She's fine. It took us a second to get her back, but she's all right. She's resting," he says while gesturing over to a sleeping Leia near a very large tree.

"But we were dead. I blacked out in the tunnel right before I saw a—"

"Before you saw me, darling." Lane walks up, clothes still dripping. "Little Vincey over here was still feelin' a bit beat, and so I went on down and grabbed ya. You're welcome," he says with a wink. Vince looks down at the ground. A look of anger with traces of shame lingers on his face.

"I'm going to go check and see that Leia is doing all right," Vince says while standing up. He pauses at Lane before looking back at me then walking on toward Leia. A pang of jealously shoots through me. How is it that I just saved her life, almost at the cost of my own, but he feels more need to tend to her? Part of me starts to wonder if we all would've been better off had I just left her. The moment the thought enters, I feel ashamed of it. Lane notices the change in my demeanor. He kneels down and comes face-to-face with me. I start to back away when he holds out his hand. I look down at it and then look up to meet his gaze.

"Come on," he beckons. "We've just wandered into another world. Care to take a look around?"

"Don't you think we should rest after that? That maybe this isn't the best time to be rummaging around in a place we don't have any familiarity with?"

"Absolutely," he says with a grin. "Coming along then?" His hand still extended. Against my better judgment, I take it. I waver as I stand. Lane holds me in place until I find my balance again. Once I feel that I can walk on my own, we set off.

I can't get over the smell of the air. The usual salty smell of the sea is replaced by a sweeter, more musky scent that makes me lightheaded until I grow used to it. The uneven ground combined with my ever-increasing fatigue and sore muscles makes it hard for me to walk straight. I look up again, hoping to glance a sight at the sun when I trip over what appears to be a group of vines. Lane doesn't catch me this time, and I go tumbling down.

"Well, little fish." Lane laughs while kneeling down once again to help me to my feet. "Looks like you might need to find your land legs."

"Lane, I need to go back. We don't know what we might run into here. I need to rest." I get a glimpse of his face and see dark circles under his eyes.

"You could use the rest as well." His gaze goes over my face and down to my knee, which is now bleeding from the fall. There's a look of amusement on his face that makes me suddenly angry. Suddenly, the sun seems to wink out of existence, and the jungle grows darker. I look up to see dark clouds through the breaks in the branches of the trees.

"Whatever, Lane. Go out and get yourself killed if you'd like." I turn around to walk away and back toward the small pond. He laughs but doesn't follow until a crack of lightning goes across the sky, and within seconds, rain starts pouring down. He trots until he's next to me as we make our way through the dense jungle back to Leia and Vince.

"What, not a fan of storms?" I taunt him. Play him in his own game, if I must.

"A little water never hurt anyone," he says with his signature grin. Even in the darkness from the storm, I can see all of his perfect white teeth. How invigorating. We pass a hanging cluster of vines before coming into the clearing of the pond. Leia and Vince have moved under a cave-like rock formation that's near the banks. We hurry there and soak in the warmth of the fire that Vince had started. Leia is lying closest to the fire, looking pale in the light the flames give off. Her breaths are shallow. I can see the pain in every breath she takes. I'm reminded of the ache in my own.

"How're you feeling, Leia?" Her eyes drag up toward me as though the act of bringing her gaze away from the fire is tiresome.

There's a twitch of a smile in one side of her mouth before she looks away again.

"I'm okay. I suppose I owe you a great amount of gratitude. Thank you, Adira. I owe you."

"You would've done the same," I respond while taking the spot close to Vince. He meets my gaze and gives me a warm smile. I look across the fire where Lane sits as he glares at Vince through the flames. There's a long silence that follows. The only sound being the lick of the flames and the pouring rain with the occasional sound of an unknown animal. The smell of the earth becoming more and more potent as the time goes by. A soft snoring starts coming from Leia after a while.

"We need to discuss what we should do about her," Lane breaks the silence.

"What do you mean 'do about her'?" Vince replies, anger immediately taking over his expression

"She isn't exactly in prime shape to go on a hike through the jungle. Don't pretend like you both haven't been thinking the same thing. We didn't come here to babysit. We run into something out there that is dangerous, we have to protect ourselves in whatever way we can. May I remind you, all of Maurea is counting on us to come back. And not empty-handed."

I look over to Leia's sleeping form. I don't know how long she was down before Lane and Vince got her back, but it must've been too long. She looks so breakable. I'm beginning to have the same worries Lane is. We're not off to a great start here. But we came together, we should leave together if possible . . . right?

"Lane, we can't just leave her here. Even if one of us who is perfectly healthy is alone out here, we would be doomed. If even half of the creatures that we've learned about exist in this ecosystem are still living, there's hundreds of things that can kill us." Just as I finish, as if on cue, we hear a quick rustling in the dense leaves before hearing an animal cry out in pain followed by a hissing sound that makes the hairs on my neck stand on end.

"That's my whole point, Adira. We come up against something

like *that*, I don't want to have to worry about carrying someone over my back while running for my own life."

"You really are a selfish prick, aren't you, Lane? Can't think about anyone but your damn self," Vince blurts out. I can see the tension in his neck and shoulders building. The calm Vince that I've always known seems to be disappearing in Lane's presence. Ever since we got the news, it's like anger has taken a hold onto Vince, and it just seems to be growing. Whereas Lane remains to appear completely calm.

"No. Not just about myself. Unless you've forgotten, Adira has almost died as well trying to save her because Leia decided to sign up for something she couldn't handle. I may be a prick, Vince. But at least I know what I'm capable of and what my limits are. Your *mate*, however, has proven herself incapable of doing so. So, unless either of you have any ideas, I suggest dropping the deadweight," Lane concludes. From a survival standpoint, what Lane suggests makes sense. I've already tasted death because of Leia, and it was before we had even reached Sentri. The ocean is the place where we are supposed to thrive in, and she had to be saved. What would become of her here? And who would she drag down with her? I look up to see Lane looking toward me. I meet his gaze as his facial expression acknowledges the conflict he reads on my face. But we are better, more evolved than this. And we can't make that decision for her.

"We know this small area. It has adequate shelter from bad weather and access to water. For this next week, we should just go out on smaller hikes getting to know the area and return here. If after a week she isn't looking like she's going to improve, we can discuss this again." No one responds. There's a silence that drags on until the rain starts to ease up. I can feel the fatigue growing inside of me. My eyelids start to droop before Vince snaps me out of my daze.

"She can't stay here alone. We don't know what's out there, and if something comes here, one of us is going to have to protect her."

"You've got to be bloody joking—"

"If we're going to give her a week, we give her a week with her best shot," Vince interrupts.

"Fine," I respond before they start screaming at each other and attract whatever is out there closer to us. "We will go out in pairs. Someone stays back every day with Leia. In seven days, if she isn't able to travel, we go without her."

"Works for me. Work for you, Vincey?" Vince looks straight into the flames, refusing to meet my or Lane's eyes.

"Fine."

"Well then. Tomorrow, you get the first round of babysitting duty." Lane pokes at the fire before lying on his side. Propping himself up on one elbow, he looks at me.

"Best get some sleep, little fish. Big day tomorrow." He winks at me before lying on his back. It can't be far into the day, but I feel like I really could sleep through the whole day and night. It isn't long before his breathing slows to the point where we assume he has fallen asleep.

"I don't trust him," Vince breaks the silence.

"I know you don't. I don't really either." I inwardly wince when I realize that's a lie. Lane can be a jerk, but he's never been less than honest. I do trust him. "But we're alive because of him. He's an ass. But he's an ass we need." He turns toward me and hesitates before reaching to cup my cheek with his hand.

"Adira, I want you to know, I would never put her life above yours." I want to believe him. I want to believe him so badly. I want to go back to the moment before our world cracked. When he held me and I felt wanted. Desired. Before it became clear whose life he was truly more concerned with. I move his hand away from my face and turn around to lie down on my side.

"Don't make promises you can't keep." Before long, I drift to sleep to the sound of the rain.

10

I AM RUSTLED AWAKE after what feels like being asleep for less than two minutes. I open my eyes slightly to see that it is the early part of the next morning and Lane is towering over me. I shut my eyes again, ignoring the annoying prodding. He nudges me again.

"What do you want, Lane?" I ask with my eyes still closed.

"Rise and shine, little fish. Big wide world for us to discover and all." I roll onto my back and feel a painful round of pinpoints go throughout my right arm accompanied by a sore shoulder. I must've slept on my side the whole night. The pain in my chest has turned into a dull ache. My ribs still feel sore, but not sore enough to be broken. It's the little things when you're stranded in a jungle. I stretch out my legs and try to shake out my arm to encourage the blood flow. Lane holds out his hand.

"I can stand on my own, thanks," I spit out, swatting his hand away with the back of mine. I look over to see Vince and Leia still sleeping soundly. I fight back against the jealousy that roves through my body, making my stomach churn. I turn and see Lane looking at me with humor in his eyes.

"Shut up." He puts his hands up in mock surrender.

"I didn't say anything," he says with a chuckle and his signature grin. We set off into the dense jungle. Everything is wet. I suppose I should be used to that, being that I've spent at least half of my life in the ocean; but even the air feels wet. My sore lungs work hard against the humidity in the air. Within a couple minutes of our trek, I can feel beads of sweat dripping down my temples and breasts. I look to Lane and see a ripple of sweat across his top lip. He stops by a tall piece of vegetation and grabs one of the huge leaves and brings it toward his mouth.

"Hey, what are you doing? We don't know if that's poisonous or not," I say as I pull him away from the plant.

"Relax. I'm just thirsty." He dips down again and takes the giant leaf and lets the fresh rainwater flow into his mouth. A stray drop runs down his chin as he motions toward another large leaf filled with water. All of a sudden my mouth feels extremely dry and parched. How long has it been since I've had a drink of water? Still, if this plant is poisonous, parts of it could be in the water. Lane notices my caution.

"Look, there's a waxlike covering on the leaf. Whatever is inside of this plant isn't going to be getting into the rainwater."

"And if there's some sort of poisonous . . . thing in it!?"

"Then we die here together. Romantic, right?" He holds out the leaf for me again. I hesitate. I touch my tongue to the roof of my mouth, feeling the dryness of dehydration. I resistantly bend down and open my mouth under the leaf. Lane gently tilts it until my mouth fills, and I stand up. He wipes a drop off of my lip, letting his fingers linger there for a beat longer than necessary. I look back onto the large plant and down at our bare feet. I tear off four of the largest leaves the plant has to offer along with some of the long, tough stems near the base of the plant.

"What are you doing?"

"I figured these would make good of shoes as any for the moment. We don't exactly have seal skin lying around," I say while handing him the two bigger of the four leaves. He wavers momentarily before kneeling over to mimic the way that I fashion my shoes. The leaves are big enough to wrap around our ankles and the tops and bottoms of our feet. The tops of our webbed toes stay exposed, but it's the best that we can do at the moment. I wrap the stems around my foot and ankle before braiding the last three together and tucking the braid underneath a cluster of makeshift straps. The wax feels strangely smooth and slippery underneath my feet. But it's better than the spongy, moist jungle ground.

"The wax on these should make them a bit more resistant, don't you think?"

"They'll do for now," he responds. We continue on, feeling a bit more energized after quenching the thirst of the night. If it weren't for the fact that our entire world has come crumbling around us, I might be giddy right now. Sentri is beautiful. It's as if the ocean has come above the surface with how many plants and colors are all around us. The trees are so tall they seem to disappear into the sky. Tiny animals have as many colors on them as royal angelfish. It's stunning. I find myself smiling as I observe everything around us.

It isn't long before rain starts pouring down all around us. Although it is annoying getting soaked when we haven't been dry all that long, the rain makes the thickness of the air thin out. Eventually it starts pouring so hard that any trek to scope out the area would be pointless. We can hardly see ten feet in front of us. We walk along on the jungle ground until Lane nudges me hard in the side.

"What is it?" He doesn't respond. I look up to peer at his face to see him staring, mouth ajar, at what looks to be a forty-foot-tall plant that has a rancid smell about it.

"Mushroom. I'm almost positive," he says as he walks toward the rank plant. Against better judgment, I follow. The smell doesn't seem to bother Lane in the slightest. After a few minutes without any sign that the rain would be letting up any time soon, I sit with my back against the stalk of the mushroom. I close my eyes, embracing the moments of rest as I start to feel the aches of my body settling in. I feel myself starting to doze when I hear Lane stand very slowly beside me.

"You're not trying to ditch me in the middle of the rain forest, are you?" I say with my eyes still closed.

"Adira . . ."

"Lane, it's still pouring. Give it a rest. Once it slows down, we can set out again, but there's no need to—"

"Adira, shut up and get behind me." I open my eyes to see a giant animal less than fifty feet away from where we stand. Covered completely with black fur other than the face, hands, and feet. Broad shoulders and a huge head compared to the rest of the body. There's what appears to be a child clinging to the back of the adult. I assume that the adult is a female at least. Possibly less aggressive. Though maybe more, due to the child she is protecting. I stand up slowly next to Lane, noticing her eyes follow me.

"What do we do?" I ask.

"You're the one with a wild animal for a pet. I thought you might have an idea," Lane croaks, his voice wavering.

"That was a manta ray. Not a-a—"

"Gorilla." How does he know all of this? We didn't talk about mushrooms or gorillas with Simon. I give him a skeptical look before returning my attention to the mother and child before us. With every huge breath she takes, I can see water spurting from her nostrils. The child that clings to her back is looking over her shoulder to peer at the strangers. I start shrinking down back to a sitting position.

"What're you doing?" Lane whispers a shout at me.

"Just sit down. Leave them be." Reluctantly, Lane lowers himself down and sits so close to me, I have to shift my leg to get him off my lap. After a while, the mother and child move on into the dense trees without looking back.

"How'd you know to do that?" Lane asks after a while.

"I didn't. I just gave it my best guess. I don't think she would have attacked unless we proved as some sort of threat to the baby." I pause, thinking of Liam. "I just did what I would want done if I was protecting someone I love." He stares at me for quite some time before looking back toward the trees that the pair disappeared into.

"Don't take this the wrong way, but you're actually pretty brilliant," he says incredulously. I smile and give a short chuckle.

"Wrong way. Wouldn't want anyone to think you were a decent person now, would you?" I say, nudging his side with my elbow.

"Well, I do have a reputation to carry on," he responds with his grin. We share a laugh together, and for a moment, I forget that we are in a foreign place with foreign creatures and unknowns behind every corner. It feels nice to laugh.

"Well, we should really try and get a bit farther before we head back for the night," I say as I head out from under the giant mushroom. Lane follows closely behind, and we set out once again through the dense forest. Sentri, although scary and daunting, is quite beautiful. I have never seen so much green in my entire life. It's as if the entirety of the world around me was a giant coral reef of green. I wonder if this is how it looks and feels for small animals that call coral reefs home.

After we break out of a particularly dense bush, we come into another clearing. But instead of giant mushrooms, there's these strange teardrop-looking plants with one giant hole in it, covered by a thin weaving of vines hanging all around us from high points of the trees. It actually looks quite cozy.

"All right, genius. What are those called?"

"That, believe it or not, I don't know," Lane responds. He looks up quizzically at the green teardrops all around us.

"What kind of animal do you think it's for?" I ask.

"I'm not sure. Something that can climb very high and has enough brain function in order to come up with something as sophisticated as that." We timidly continue forward until we are directly beneath the main cluster of them. Lane looks directly below them and continuously looks back and forth between the ground and the teardrops.

"What is it?" Curiosity in his face turns to panic as all the color from his face blanches.

"We need to go. Now."

"Lane, what—" He grabs me by the hand, and we're running

back into the dense forest from which we came. Lane continually looks behind his shoulder to look back toward the teardrops before heading into a faster sprint. One of my makeshift shoes starts to slip from my foot. Within a few more strides, I am down a shoe. I look down at Lane's feet and see that both of his have fallen off, and he is running with vines tangled around his ankles.

"Lane, what is going on!" He turns his head toward me, still in a deep sprint and holding my hand in his. For the first time since I've known Lane, there isn't a trace of the usual coolness in his face.

"Shut up, Adira. Move faster," he loudly whispers. I don't know why, but I listen. I pull my hand free of his, using both of my arms to propel myself faster to keep up with him. We run for what feels like at least five miles before Lane stops in his tracks and grabs my arm to pull me to a halt. Panting for breath, I bring my hands down to my knees, feeling the all-too-familiar ache in my chest.

"Lane . . . you have . . . to tell me . . . what happened," I say between heaves.

"Just listen for a second." For a moment, the only noise is our heavy breathing along with the calls from insects of the jungle. A few minutes into the silence, a rustling of leaves overhead make their way to us from farther back from which we ran. Lane starts frantically looking around until his panicked gaze rests upon what looks to be a cave.

"Come on." He takes my hand as we move, without much grace, over to the entrance of the rocky shelter. Once inside, we position ourselves to be out of sight from the entrance of the cave. The rocky floor gets drier the farther in we go. It feels nice to be treading on dry ground for the first time since we've arrived; but now that my feet are bare, the rocky floor isn't exactly inviting. My mind starts to wander back to Vince. He is probably starting to get worried about us by now. I would be if I were him and he hadn't come back yet. I wonder if Leia is starting to get a little stronger. If Vince is helping her. Taking care of her. The all-too-common fringe of jealousy starts to churn in my stomach. Get a grip . . . it's not the time for these thoughts.

"What was all of that about?" I ask.

"The ground beneath those things was completely clean."

"And?"

"And how many animals do you know of that pick up after themselves like that? Have a secret sea turtle at home that picks up his shit as he walks around, do you?" What is he getting at?

"Charming. But no, not exactly."

"No. But humans do. And I didn't feel like having some conversation with these people until we have a better idea of what we are getting into." It takes a minute, but it starts to click in my head. It makes sense. I wish it didn't. Damn, I really hate it when he's right. And that's an awful lot lately. All of a sudden, Lane starts taking off his shirt.

"Wh-what are you doing?" I ask while averting my eyes. Ignore the abs. Ignore the abs. Ignore the abs . . . He starts wringing out his shirt.

"I'm sick of feeling soggy. Don't get too excited," he says with a grin. He turns around and continues to wring out the water. My eyes start roving on their own volition and end up falling on a bruise that goes from the right side of his lower back onto his ribs.

"What happened?" I ask softly, reaching forward to touch the skin. He flinches back from my touch and puts his shirt quickly back on.

"Nothing, don't worry about it." Fine, if he doesn't want to talk about it.

I sit on the rocky floor, acknowledging that we will be here for at least a few minutes. Lane eventually relaxes and sits next to me. We stay silent for a while, straining to hear anything outside. After a few minutes without anything alarming, I break our silence.

"If I ask you something, do you promise to be honest?" A smile plays at the edges of his mouth.

"Always," he says it in his lackadaisical way, but there's a sincerity in his eyes that tell me just how much he means that.

"How do you know so much about this place? There are things that we haven't talked about that you just somehow know?" He nods as if expecting I'd ask eventually.

"That would be my good ol' dad. We were going to be learning all of this stuff eventually, but due to, well, you know"—he gestures around the room—"we never got the chance. Ever since Simon told us about everything, my dad has been giving me some extra lessons. He expects me to be the head Legion, and anything less is unacceptable." Lane looks away as if he's trying to hide something in his gaze from me.

"Your dad seems pretty intense," I prod. He gives a humorless chuckle.

"Yeah, you could say that." A tick in his jaw appears as he fidgets with his hands. I feel a pang of pity for Lane. I don't know the details of the conflict with his dad, but the relationship I had with mine was something so amazing that I have sympathy for anyone who has less than that. It seems Lane has far less.

"Let me know if you ever want to talk about it," I say. He looks to me and studies me for a moment.

"You actually mean that," he says.

"Of course, I do. As long as you continue to be honest with me, Lane, I'll return the favor." He nods after a moment, and then we fall back into amicable silence. After a while, I feel myself drifting in and out of consciousness, letting the fatigue of the day take over. When I wake up, it's gone dark outside, there's a fire crackling in front of me, and my head is rested on Lane's shoulder. I jump up, wiping some drool from my chin.

"Well, good morning, little fish. Nice little nap, had you?"

"Lane, what the . . ." I look outside to see that it's completely dark. "Are you serious, Lane! Vince and Leia are probably freaking out! Why did you let me sleep so long?" He chuckles.

"Who am I to deprive you of some apparently well-needed rest? And a bit of a cuddle as well," he says with a half smile. I feel the blood rush to my cheeks.

"That's not the point. We told Leia and Vince that we would be back before nightfall and—"

"Ah ah ah, we told them we would be back. We gave them no such promises as to when that would be."

"Well, you would think that would be at least partially implied."

"Relax, little fish. I'm sure your boyfriend is getting along just fine with Leia." I can feel my cheeks flooding with blood once again. This time, he notices.

"Oh dear, seems I hit a bit of a nerve," he says with another chuckle. He stands up and walks to peer out of the opening of the cave. It seems the old Lane is back.

"That's none of your business," I seethe.

"Oh, little fish, I think it is my business," he says turning back to me. "After all, we are still betrothed, in case you forgot."

"Hardly. You heard what Simon said. We have no idea how things are going to work out once we get back to Maurea." He takes a step closer to me.

"And I suppose you're hoping that they overrule over a millennium of tradition and rules so that you and Vincey can run off into the sunset?" I can feel the anger rising in my chest. I open my mouth to speak before he cuts me off.

"Well, I genuinely hope that works out for you." I take a step back. The mocking look on his face turns to one of solemn.

"Because why would I want to be with someone who so clearly wants to be with someone else?" There's a pain that goes across his eyes before he turns back toward the entrance of the cave and walks away. Before walking back into the forest, he turns back to me.

"I have more respect for myself than that." I falter for a moment before following. The rest of the trek back to the small pond is spent in silence with the occasional trip over a random vine or bush. The jungle floor gets so dark at night. Eerily dark. What feels like hours later, we finally emerge from the dense greenery into the small clearing. Vince looks up with fear and anger prevalent in his face as he runs up to us.

"Where the hell have you been?" he spits at us. I immediately go on the defense. The last time I saw him this worked up was when I had my encounter with the whale. Even in the dense darkness, I can see he is trembling. I look over to Leia, who has a look of relief sprawled across her face in the firelight. She was also worried about us. A fringe of guilt goes over me.

"Relax. We ran into what we think are dwellings where people have been living. We had to hide out for a while so we weren't found." Vince looks like he could punch either of us in the nose. Man, am I getting sick of this Vince that is somehow always pissed off. Lane explains everything in detail about what we saw that led to the conclusions that we did. Vince and Leia don't look like they were either catching on or that they were buying what Lane was telling them.

"What do you mean? How do you know it was for people?" Lane steps up and moves toward the fire where Leia is seated at.

"The homes were far too sophisticated and advanced for anything that is less than human. Trust me, mate. We aren't the only two-legged chums walking around Sentri."

11

I CAN FEEL MY body begging me to go back to sleep before I even reach the fire. I sit down across from Leia and Lane. Vince straggles over to the fire and sits by my side. I stare into the fire, avoiding eye contact with all three. I don't have the energy to argue with anyone else today. What was that about with Lane, anyway? Since when has he ever cared about anyone but himself? Now I'm supposed to believe that he has real feelings for me? I look above the flames to meet his eyes. Part of me wants to look away. To escape from the guilt I feel rising in my stomach. Why should I feel guilty for loving someone else? He doesn't really care. Not really. It's just another one of his mind games. He likes to play games. The same games that make it impossible to look away even when every part of me wants to.

I can feel my eyes growing heavier as I invite sleep to wash over me. I want this day over with. We learned enough about Sentri to know that we don't know nearly enough. This could take weeks. Months. Who knows if Maurea has that kind of time.

"Adira, could I have a word with you for a moment?" Leia breaks me out of my thoughts.

"Um, yeah, sure. Of course." I get up and walk over to help her up. Has she always been this skinny? I feel like I might break her as I help her up by her arm and waist. We walk over to the other side of the pond, out of earshot of Lane and Vince. I can probably count the number of one-on-one conversations I've had with Leia on one hand. If this isn't about Vince, what else could she possibly want to talk to me privately about?

"I wanted to thank you." Well, that's not what I expected.

"Oh, um, for what?"

"For saving my life yesterday. You put your own life in danger by doing what you did. I haven't had the opportunity to thank you properly yet." A sudden swell of affection for Leia wells up inside of me along with a swell of guilt. She really is one of the kindest people I have ever met.

"Like I said, you would have done the same," I say with a smile. She wavers for a second. I reach out to support her arms before her legs buckle slightly beneath her.

"Leia, come on. Let's go back to the fire. You need to get some more rest."

"No, listen to me. I need to tell you something, and I need you to keep it to yourself." I'm taken aback by the sudden change of tone in her voice. I waver for a second. When I look into her face, a strong expression of conviction stares back at me.

"What's going on?" She sits on the wet ground and takes a few deep breaths before continuing. She waves her hand to beckon me to come closer. I crouch next to her and lean in.

"I know you're tired after today, but I need you to go out with Vince tomorrow for the second round of scouting," she says barely above a whisper.

"Yeah, okay. Why was this something that needed to be said in private?" She looks toward Vince, and I notice tears falling down her face.

"While you two are out tomorrow, I will convince Lane to leave as well, catch up with you two, and move on. Vince can't know." I bolt upright.

"What the hell, Leia? Are you joking? Is this your idea of a joke?" We just saved this girl, which she *just* thanked me for, and now she wants to run off into the jungle injured and alone?

"Adira, be quiet! Sit back down!" Her voice is so quiet, but the sternness of it makes me obey. She takes another round of deep, ragged breaths.

"I'm dying," she says with a somber tone of finality. I had suspected it. I think we all have. You don't get to go that close to death and come back unscathed. Within the day and a half that we have been here, her eyes seem to have sunken into her skull, and the simple act of talking comes at great difficulty. But it feels as though you can only have so much death within a certain period of time. We had our fill.

"Leia, you just went through a lot yesterday. You were just knocked out from the lack of oxygen for—"

"I'm guessing around fifteen minutes." I don't need my reflection to know a look of shock has gone across my face. I don't know what to say. She really shouldn't have been able to come back from that. I guess she never really did.

"I-I didn't realize," is all I can manage to say. There's a long silence that draws out between us. I can see the acceptance in her face of the fate that she has been able to come to terms with, but she can't hide the sorrow I see in her eyes. Before long, I find my tears joining hers on the wet ground of the Sentri floor. I don't know her well, but she's too young.

"You don't even want to try? You could try, Leia. Try to survive. We would take care of you." At least for six more days.

"That's not what you came here to do. You three came here to pave a way for our people. You can't do that if you're just trying to drag me along to survive one day more." I'm at a loss for words. I want to comfort her. But where there used to be a girl that I looked at as weak and sensitive, I now see a girl with strong, beautiful conviction and bravery unmatched.

"I need you to go with Vince tomorrow. I'll suggest tonight that you two go farther out. Far enough that you can't make it back here in one day. Find a safe place to camp. By then, I'll have convinced Lane to go after you. He is a talented tracker. He will be able to find you. Do him a favor and make it easier for him if you can though. Don't try covering tracks or anything. And I know you won't like this, but Vince can't know." I consider what she's said for a moment.

"Leia, that's not a fair thing to ask. He's my best friend. I can't lie to him about this. If he ever found out, he'd—"

"He'd forgive you because he loves you." Shit. There it is. I look everywhere but her gaze. Shame floods over me until I feel as though I may as well be drowning for a second time.

"Adira, it's okay. Really. More than anything, I want him to be happy." That, we have in common. I finally meet her gaze.

"I don't know what to do, Leia. What do I do about all of this? This stuff with Lane and Vince?" I honestly can't believe it came out of my mouth like that. Why would she want to talk to me about my boy issues when she's talking about literally sacrificing herself to help our mission? When I look up at her again, though, all I see is understanding and perhaps a little bit of humor.

"I think you'll figure it out. Not that it isn't a tough decision. I mean, look at them." We both look over to the fire and find ourselves sharing a laugh.

"I suppose of all the problems going on right now, it's a great one to have, and quite minimal at that," I say between chuckles.

"Don't count it as minimal. They are both very handsome, but offer very different things. I think each one will bring out a different side in you as well. I guess it's just going to depend on who you turn out to be after all of this, Adira." The sudden seriousness of her tone brings me back to the harsh reality of the life I now live. I hadn't thought about that. In the last two days, I know I've already undergone enough change to prompt a metamorphosis of myself. I think of Liam. He'd tell me to ditch both of them and just live with him and Avery. I smile at the thought.

"We should get back to the fire. You have a big day tomorrow." I help Leia stand back up on her feet before pulling her into a hug.

She flinches at first at the sudden, unexpected spurt of affection. But soon after, she wraps her arms around me and returns the hug. Tears begin to fall once more, mourning a great friendship that never was because it never had the time.

We walk back to the fire and take our previous spots. Both Lane and Vince are wearing suspicious looks on their faces.

"What was all that about?" Vince asks.

"I just wanted to formally thank Adira for everything she did for me yesterday," Leia replies.

"Well, in that case, you're welcome," Lane says, leaning back on his elbows. I roll my eyes in response. Vince can't help but chuckle a bit. All the better. I prefer this Vince to the angrier version that seems to pop up around Lane.

"Anyway," Leia continues. "We also talked over strategy a bit." I can see the note of surprise go across their faces. I imagine mine would have mirrored theirs had I not just had the conversation with her a few moments ago. The girl who used to sing more than talk was all of a sudden calling the shots. Deadly ones at that.

"Adira has agreed to go back out again tomorrow. This time, with Vince." Lane props himself up from his elbows and opens his mouth to contradict. I shoot him a look, and somehow, he understands. He looks toward Vince and then back to meet my gaze. He closes his mouth and leans back onto his elbows once again. His apprehensive look is now geared toward me.

"Vince, we have both agreed that it would be best that you two go out and stay out for a night so you have the opportunity to go farther and maybe obtain more information about what and who exactly we're dealing with. You're wasting hours of the day to have time to come back here. Now that we have a suspicion—"

"It's not a suspicion, I know," Lane interrupts.

"Either way. We have to confirm and get more information." Lane quickly bolts back up again.

"And why, may I ask, is it Vince and Adira that are going? I'm the one who realized there are people there in the first place, so wouldn't it make more sense that *I* be at least one of the people that is going tomorrow for this extra little field trip?"

"I volunteered," I respond. "And it's Vince's turn to go out. One of us should get the chance to rest." Vince turns to me.

"Adira, I can't believe I'm saying this, but I agree with Lane. You went through a lot yesterday, and you spent the whole day out there today. Let me and Lane go." He peers into my face, trying to meet my eyes. I refuse to look his way. He knows me too well. He'll know something's up.

"Enough. It's already been decided," Leia breaks the silence. "Vince and Adira will leave tomorrow at first light. Lane will get plenty of rest and will be able to go out with Vince the following day." Leia looks at me, and I meet her gaze. Somber understanding between us. Vince and Lane once again look taken aback by the finality in the tone of her voice. I stand up and walk away from the others.

"Where are you going?" Vince asks.

"To sleep. We have a long day tomorrow. I suggest you do the same." I lie far enough away from the others that it'll discourage the others from continuing to try and converse with me on the subject, but close enough that the warm glow of the fire still reaches me. I lie on my side facing the large rock wall. My body aches. By the morning I'll have brand-new ones to join the old. What I would give to be back in my bed in Maurea. With Mom and Avery and Liam. I wonder if Liam is with Dad now. What happens after this all ends? If there is anything.

I wonder what will happen to Leia. What made the quiet girl who seldom spoke all of a sudden choose to risk her life to come on a dangerous quest, only to sacrifice herself so that we may have a chance out here. *Liam, Dad, if you're out there, be with her. Watch out for her. Help her survive this.*

Help *me* survive this.

12

SLEEP DIDN'T COME easily last night. Leia haunted my dreams with fragments of images of guilt and shame surrounding everything around me like a dark shroud. I wonder if I'll ever get a decent night's sleep while we are in Sentri. Likely not. In the end, it isn't the dreams but my stomach that wakes me this morning. Now that the general shock of the last few days has worn off, hunger has taken over my body. It's been three days since we've had anything to eat. The constant rain makes staying hydrated easy enough, but we need to find food. It would still be a while before hunger would kill us, but we need the energy, and my head is starting to feel light from the lack of calories. We won't make it very far today without some food. Not if we're going to make it far enough to not come back. There are tiny creatures crawling around on the ground all around us no matter where we go. I can't imagine they taste all that good, but food is food at this point. Even if it does have too many legs.

I'm the first one up. I stand up too fast and wait a while until I feel like I have my legs better under me. I look over and see the other three scattered around the rock wall, sleep seemingly undisturbed. I walk sluggishly over toward a muddy patch on the bank of the small pond to see what I can find for us to eat. I don't have to dig very far. I'm guessing the rain causes them to come out. Some are actually rather beautiful. I can't bring myself to think of the colorful ones as food. There are quite a few small, black, ovular critters that seem about as harmless as you can get eating from the dirt. As unappealing as they look, my mouth starts to water as I gather a few in my hand. *Don't chew* . . . I force them into my mouth and fight the urge to spit them immediately out. I swallow as quickly as I can manage. I swear I can feel them trying to crawl up my throat. My eyes start to water with the grotesque feeling. Within a few seconds, it stops, and I can feel my stomach groan with approval. I go find the largest leaf near me that I can reach to collect the night's rainwater to wash them down, hoping I didn't just ingest some foreign poison. I wait a few minutes to assess whether or not what I just ate will kill me. After only feeling my stomach begging for more, I make my way back to the same source. I dig a little deeper to find what looks like dozens of them. Good, enough for everyone. I take another handful and pop them in my mouth and immediately swallow, finding it much easier now that I knew to expect the crawling sensation. My stomach growls in approval once again. I give myself another two to three handfuls before grabbing another drink of water and using a large leaf to collect some to bring over to the group. I can't help but laugh at the thought of Lane waking up to a feast of critters. With the calories, I can feel my head starting to clear. Within an hour, Vince and I should have enough food and energy to start our trek onward.

"Rise and shine, Dorian. Grub is on."

All three rub the sleep from their eyes and take a couple of takes between me and the leaf full of crawling food.

"I'm pretty sure they aren't poisonous. If they were, I'd probably be dead by now. Had about seven handfuls myself." Lane lets out a chuckle and rolls onto his other side away from us. Leia is the first to reach out and grab one between her index finger and thumb. She watches it kick its legs around a few times before plopping it in her mouth and swallowing. I can see her wince at what I imagine to be the feeling of the feet crawling.

"Yeah, you'll get used to that," I respond to her look.

"Well, at least I can count how many legs this one has on both my hands," she responds. I wince at the thought of eating the long, eel-like creature with what looked like hundreds of legs sprouting out of its sides. I wouldn't want to feel that one going down. Vince is next to grab at the creatures. He decides to take a full handful and shove them in his mouth. He immediately starts to chew, and I worry that my own food will make a reappearance. He starts to choke on what I assume is the taste of a combination of mud, creature, and blood. He eventually swallows and looks up at us with water in his eyes.

"So, um, don't chew, right?" he says with a smile that shows off a nice chunk of critter stuck on his front tooth. Leia and I burst out laughing.

"Sorry, thought that was at least partially implied." He can't help but laugh as well. He goes to get himself a drink of water before returning to grab another handful and stuff them in his mouth. This time, without the chewing. Leia continues to eat them one at a time. I can almost see a little color returning to her face within just a few minutes. Vince seems to look a bit more energized as well. If I hadn't known that today might be the last day I'd ever see Leia, I would feel optimistic. Yes, we were eating bugs, but at least we got a bit of a laugh out of it from Vince, and we know now there is something in this jungle for us to eat. Hunger and thirst at least will not be the things that kill us.

"Lane, you need to eat," I say, nudging his back with my foot.

"Yeah, as scrumptious as that looks, darling, I'm not quite to a point where I am *that* hungry," he retorts. I turn to Leia.

"Can you make sure he eats today?" Leia smiles and nods in response. Part of me really thinks that she already looks a little bit better just after getting a few calories in her. The other tells me it could just be me wanting to see that color of hope. I'm not naïve enough to expect to see her again, but I can hope. At the very least.

We go on eating our tiny critters until the leaf is empty. Once they're gone, we split the leaf itself and munch on it. It's not as flavorful as seaweed, and the wax made chewing more difficult. No idea if there is any nutritional value in the vegetation as well, but we figured it was better than nothing. I show Leia where I collected the earlier batch so that once Lane gets over himself, he can eat.

"Well, we should probably get going, Adira. If we're going to do this whole overnight fiasco, we may as well get the most out of it," Vince says.

"I still think that whole idea is stupid," Lane retorts with his eyes still closed. I roll my eyes and meet Leia's gaze. With a slight nod, I beckon her over to the side while Vince busies himself with washing up before we head out.

"Are you sure about this? Leia, we can help you. It doesn't have to be like this," I say, once out of earshot of Lane and Vince. Leia gives me a half smile and pulls me into a tight embrace. I wrap my arms around her and fight back the sting of tears in my eyes, aware of the company we have.

"It's going to be okay, Adira. You're going to be a great leader someday. All of you are. Even Lane," she adds with a chuckle. She pulls back from our embrace. "I'm just sorry I wasn't strong enough to be able to be there to lead with you." I pull her back into our hug and let a tear fall.

"Leia, you are without a doubt the strongest person I've ever met. Never forget that. And don't talk like this is a life sentence. Please don't stop fighting. Promise me." I pull back and look her in the eyes. She nods once.

"Ready to go?" Vince calls from behind me. I take a deep breath to compose myself before turning around with a smile.

"Yep. Ready when you are." Vince smiles back at me, but it doesn't reach his eyes. He knows something is up. Luckily, he doesn't ask any questions. Not yet at least.

"I'll see you tomorrow," he says to Leia with a grin. She smiles in response. I turn to give one last wave to Leia.

"Goodbye, Lane!" I yell as we start to walk off. A half-hearted wave from the ground is all I receive in return. I chuckle in response.

Vince lets me lead the way since I'm the more experienced of us two in the jungle. I stop at the same plant I used to collect our food on to fashion us the same shoes as yesterday.

"Huh, smart," he says while inspecting his new footwear.

"Always the tone of surprise," I tease in respond. It feels good. After three days of awkwardness and guilty looks, it finally feels like Adira and Vince again.

As the walk goes on, it's easy to fall back into our usual friendly banter. What's even better is that the banter now has a flirtatious undertone to it. Or maybe it always has with Vince, and I never let myself fully recognize it. I let myself forget about everything else but Vince in that moment. Forget about Lane and Leia. I let it be us. As we're walking in the Sentri jungle, I imagine that it was *my* name he said at the ceremony. That it was me all along. That the kiss didn't end and that I could count on more in the future. Deep down I know it might end up hurting me more in the future when I come off of the high of the fantasy. But in that moment, I let it take the pain away. It isn't long before we start recounting some of our more embarrassing childhood memories, trying to one-up one another in who was the biggest idiot as kids.

"Really, Adira. You cannot compare the one time I got scared of an abnormally large crab, which are terrifying, by the way, to the time you stuck your hand in sea turtle dung thinking that it was a weird kind of sea stone," Vince says between laughs. I had hoped he had forgotten about that one.

"I guess I'll never live that one down, will I?"

"Absolutely not. I will be here by your side the rest of your life simply to remind you of that." I don't mind the sound of that. The laughter quickly turns into nervous chuckles before we fall into silence for a while. I realize I haven't been paying much attention to my surroundings, and we've been walking for quite a while now. But so far everything looks fairly familiar. As familiar as dense green can look. I'm sure the rest of the jungle pretty much looks the same. I'm pretty sure in a few hundred yards or so we'll be coming up on the giant plant that Lane called a mushroom.

"Rest of your life, huh?" I break the silence. Vince just grins. We walk another hundred yards or so before Vince responds.

"Mind if I ask you something? And you promise not to get mad?"

"Um, yeah, I suppose," I say with narrowed eyes.

"What's up with you and Lane? It's like ever since the ceremony, I don't know, you're different with him. Did the ceremony change that much overnight?" And the fantasy bubble goes *pop*. Of all the things to talk about, he wants to talk about Lane . . . But I guess I've been asking myself the same question. *How has it changed so much overnight?*

"I don't know, Vince. I'm supposed to be mated with him for life. Wouldn't it be a good thing if I didn't hate the guy?" I want to still hate him too. It would make it easier to love Vince.

"No," he responds.

"What do you mean *no?*"

"I mean no. It wouldn't be better if you didn't hate the guy." I'm so taken aback by his answer that I didn't notice we had come into the clearing with the mushroom. Have we traveled this far already? I look up to see if I can track where the sun is in the sky, but the canopy of trees has blocked most of the view. I imagine it's at least been a few hours. Maybe five? In another hour or so, we should come across the dwellings. Probably best to be quiet from here on out. Both for our safety, and because I have no idea what to say in response to Vince.

"The homes we were talking about yesterday will be coming up soon. Let's get out of the clearing. And stay as quiet as you can from here on out," I say. The looks he gives me is one of compliance, but I can tell he isn't going to drop the previous subject.

We run out of the clearing until we are back in the dense jungle. Even though there is covering all around me, I feel vulnerable. Naked. Out of my element. I know Vince and I don't have the advantage here the same way whoever lives in Sentri would be at the disadvantage in Maurea. We're a weapon in the water. In the open, we're a vulnerability. I can tell Vince feels similarly the way he walks in a crouch-like position. A lot of good holding my breath for a long time gets me here. Our golden-white hair makes it hard to blend in with anything in the jungle as well. As we trek forward, I find myself fighting the urge to run in the opposite direction. Vince is a good talker. If we run into people, he'll be able to negotiate better than anyone. He is Simon's son, after all. It isn't long before we come to the place where the homes are. I was about to walk into the clearing to get a better look before Vince pulls on my arm, pulling me back into the camouflage of the greenery, and puts a hand over my mouth. I'm about to slap it away when he puts his finger to his lips and then points toward the clearing. A little boy, can't have reached more than three or four years, walks from the opposite side of the jungle into the clearing. He's absolutely . . . beautiful. He has darker skin. Brown, but almost looks like there could be a hint of red. I would have never seen that color and imagined it as skin, but it's beautiful. Flawless. A full head of straight, black hair is cut short. His eyes are rounder than any child's I've seen, and darker. Perhaps a similar shade to his skin. I would have to get a closer look to know for sure. Not too long after, a child that looks to be in her thirteenth or fourteenth year enters the clearing. She has the same beautiful skin and eyes. Her straight hair falls just above her shoulders. Shorter than Vince's. As I further inspect, I notice that her arms and legs seem abnormally long compared to the rest of her body. Out of proportion. And I can't quite be sure, but—

"They have an extra finger on each hand," Vince whispers to me. I hadn't noticed it on the boy. But when I look, I can see it. Right before their pinky, there's an extra finger. I would imagine it aids in climbing. The arms and legs must aid in that as well. They've adapted. Evolved. Just like the Dorian.

"Unbelievable," Vince breathes out.

"They're beautiful," I whisper in response. I can't take my eyes off of the boy. Everything about him is enchanting.

"We need to move, Adira. We're too close to this clearing. Anyone could come and see us," Vince says barely above a whisper.

"Well, you've got that right." I freeze in place at the foreign voice. Trying to think back through months of training with Simon on diplomatic speaking. What do I say? Do I run? I see my panic mirrored on Vince's face. We both turn in sync to look at a man dangling from one arm by a tree before he hops down. I'm sure on anyone else it would have looked graceful. But his scraggly hair combined with the overly disproportionate limbs makes it look almost animallike. We can hear people drop behind us, but don't turn around to look. Three? Maybe four?

"What, do I have something in my teeth?" The man picks at his tooth with his extra finger. He has a strange accent. I try to move my mouth to speak, but nothing comes out. I can hear Vince take in a deep breath to finally speak before the strange man cuts him off, "So listen, normally we'd probably go about this in a bit more of a 'professional' manner, but being that you two were kind of just spying on us—very rude by the way, where are your manners? And no offense, you guys look sort of . . . unusual, so we're going to go about our tactics the old-fashioned way." I feel a strong blunt to my head before everything goes black.

13

I WAKE UP TO the smell of embers and a throbbing pain in the back of my head. It takes me a moment to remember what had happened. As soon as reality hits me, I shoot up and immediately lose my balance and fall back over. When I open my eyes again, there are black dots scattered across my vision. I'm alone in what looks to be a dome-shaped hut. *Wait a minute, I'm alone. Where's Vince?* I look around to get a quick inventory. My kelp blouse and trousers are nowhere to be seen. I'm in a softer set of clothes that fit my bodice well enough, but the sleeves on both the pants and shirt are far too long. I roll them a few times so that I can stick my hands and feet out easily. My makeshift shoes have been replaced with what appears to be some sort of animal skin. Quite comfortable actually. There's a mud-like substance on the back of my head. Afraid to inspect further, I just hold on to the hope that it's helping heal the wound back there. I twist my hair up into a knot on the top of my head and stand slowly this time. Nothing in here gives me the impression I am a prisoner of any sort. I take comfort in that. But where is Vince? I hear a child's laughter from outside the hut. Brief memories flash before me. Could it be the same child as before? Fear is suddenly replaced by curiosity. Another laugh joins in. A laugh that I would love any day but now is the sweetest sound imaginable.

"Vince!" I scream without thinking twice. I run out of the hut, moving too quickly. How hard did they hit my head? I trip and fall over what appears to be my and Vince's clothes right outside the hut.

"Adira! Hey, you okay? Slow down a bit, you hit your head pretty hard," he says as he helps me get back up to my feet.

"*I* didn't hit my head?" I say through my teeth.

"HAHAHAHA! I like this one. Sorry about that, love. Nothing personal, just business. I mean, think about it. You could have been a *crazy* person or something." Such an ironic thing to hear from such a crazed-looking man once again dangling from a branch. I don't know why, but I like him so much immediately against my better judgement. Even if I am slightly annoyed. Maybe that'll go away with the headache.

"Right. Suppose I can understand that," I respond. Some apprehension is soothed away by the ease I see in Vince. He looks comfortable. Happy even. He sees the questions in my eyes and nods. I turn to the other man.

"I'm Adira."

"I know. Vince here has told us all about you. And your cool little water land you came from. All that fun shit. Too bad about your world falling apart though, real bummer. I don't know why you all didn't just come and *talk* to us. Had to be all weird and stalkery about it," the strange man says, all the while swaying by his left hand and foot on a low branch. I thought about trying to explain to him about why we would want to gather intel before we made communication, but I gather that Vince has already had all of those baseline conversations.

"Right, um, so what was your name?" I ask.

"Oh shit, sorry." He swings down from his branch and lands in the same strange way perfectly on his feet. "Name's Lonny. But don't call me Lon Lon. I don't care what these assholes tell you, it's a stupid name." Some of the others around start chuckling. "Shut up, or I'll have your tongue. Do not give the shiny people any ideas. So, Lonny." Yes. I definitely like this Lonny.

"Lonny, nice to meet you. Formally this time," I respond. Vince smiles down at me. More than anything else, I find comfort in this. I suppose it's better that I was passed out through all of the hard parts of the conversation. I'll have to get a play-by-play later once we're alone.

We spend the rest of the evening being a part of the lives of the Amoran people. Hearing stories and learning as much as we can around the huge fire in the center of the clearing. Lane was right about the teardrop-shaped dwellings. It's where they sleep. The huts, however, are for living. Extended families all live under the same roof and never have to leave. Whenever a new pair is bonded, they will simply choose a household to belong to. Apparently, more often than not, the male joins the female's family. But once a new pair is made, they work together to make their own dwelling, and it's where they spend every night privately as a pair. The children stay with their parents until they are weaned, and then they go to sleep in the children's hut, which is watched over each night by a different member of the community. It's actually something that's been beautiful to watch. Having a mate solely for love, not just about having children. It's clear that love is the binding factor of this group of people. I'm having a hard time differentiating between who each child belongs to because everyone treats them like they're their own. They drop formalities and are just with each other fully in each moment. The same little boy from earlier, who I learned is named Matty, comes and sits with me for a while. I realize their eyes aren't brown like their skin, but a very dark green. Not like my brighter green that looks like light seafoam, but a deep, dark, forest green. They're mesmerizing. He finds my long, light hair to be something very fun to play with after I wash all of the muddy substance out of it. Vince does most of the talking when it comes to explaining Maurea and the Dorian. They ask a lot of questions but are willing to answer some of our own in return. It turns out that Lonny's father, Abe, is the person who's considered in charge. However, he doesn't receive his position through birthright. They do it by vote every decade or so, unless they really like who is currently calling the shots. Abe has been in the position for thirty years now. They had no idea about anything regarding the ecospheres and what lies beyond. Somehow, they don't seem all that bothered about the shock of information. Definitely surprised, but it seems as though they are perfectly content with Sentri and all that it entails. It's interesting that they've evolved without consciously determining who can pass along genes. They've done it naturally, without any dumb ideas of "responsibility." The little boy tugs twice on my hair.

"Hey, is it true that your toes are funny?" Both Vince and I let out a chuckle.

"Would you like to see?" I ask. He nods enthusiastically. He reminds me so much of Avery and Liam when they were his age. I slip my feet out of the comfortable new shoes and spread my toes as wide as I can in front of the firelight so that they can all see clearly. Vince does the same. All at once there are dozens of "WOAHS," and then tiny hands are touching our webbed toes. Some of the younger ones look afraid to touch them until an older child does it first, and then they enthusiastically jump in and have their turn.

"Hey! You're also missing a finger!" another little girl exclaims pointing at Vince's hand.

"Haha, well, to us, you all simply have one extra," Vince responds with his brilliant smile. The little girl blushes in response. Matty lets out a huge yawn, which is quickly caught on to about every other child that was sitting around the fire.

"All right, time for bed," declares Abe. His statement is met with a roar of tiny disapprovals but are quickly silenced by Abe simply raising his hand. A collective groan comes from the kids as they follow the person who I would assume is up for their turn to babysit for the night to the children's hut. Lonny turns to me and Vince.

"So, uh, what's the deal with you two? Sorry to be blunt and all, but we only got one extra dwelling, and I mean we can try to work something out if it's like a brother-sister situation or something, but can I be honest? You two give each other *weird* looks if you're brother and sister. Like is said, none of my business, but erm—"

"We will take the dwelling," Vince responds smoothly. I try to ignore what feels like my heart beating out of my chest and keep my face smooth. I suppose Lonny didn't buy it fully.

"Rrrrrrright. Well, it's the lowest one. Even with your weird-ass feet, you should be able to climb that far to get in." With that, Lonny and the rest of the Amoran get up and start making their way to their own dwellings. I slip my shoes back on as fast as I can before Vince offers his hand.

"Shall we?" I take his hand, hoping he doesn't notice that mine is trembling. We make our way over toward the direction Lonny pointed us in. Our definition of easy to climb is clearly vastly different from Lonny's. I'm glad that the Amoran are much better climbers than we are and are tucked into their own dwellings, so they don't see how hard it was for me to get up there. Vince has an easier go at it than I did, though. He's able to make it up and in and then helps pull me up the rest of the way. Right before I make it up into the small teardrop, a small piece of wood jams into the palm of my hand. Once inside, I can see why these are really only meant for two people plus an infant. They're small, but very cozy. A sheath of leaves and vines covers the entrance to each one to give the inhabitants privacy. I run my hand around the walls of the teardrop before it catches on the small piece of wood in my hand.

"Damn it, stupid tree . . .," I mutter under my breath. Vince takes my hand and inspects it closely before gently probing out the small piece. He lets his hand linger on mine. His gaze goes up to meet mine for a moment before I avert my gaze down. I feel blood rush to my cheeks. For a moment, Leia's face comes blaring into my mind, and guilt settles into my stomach.

"Adira . . . I know there are a million more important things going on right now, but I would really like if we could talk about what happened after the ceremony. And perhaps continue the earlier conversation," he adds with a smirk. I don't move my eyes from the floor. After a long pause, he takes his finger under my chin to force me to meet his gaze.

"What're you thinking?" he whispers.

I'm a terrible person. I love you. You chose her, but now I can't hate her because she's the most selfless person I've ever met. Your moods go back and forth so much lately that I can't keep track. You've never been an angry person before, and it now seems like you're angry more often than not. I take a deep breath to try and settle the sudden flutters in my stomach. Settle on one.

"I can't keep track of what *you* are thinking, Vince," I respond. "It's like one moment, you think of me as nothing but a friend, the next you're calling Leia's name at the ceremony. Then I open my big mouth, and you just kiss me." I blush again from the memory. "And then it seems like you were far more concerned with Leia after we got through to Sentri the other day, and now you don't want me to like Lane because what? You want to be with me again? You're also angry *all the time*. What is it about Lane that makes you so upset? I can't keep track of where your head is, Vince, and it's not really fair," I blurt out the last part. He wears almost an amused look on his face. He lets me calm down before responding.

"Adira, Leia was in far worse shape than you were when you two came around the other day. I was worried she wasn't going to make it through the night. My concern for her was far more about my trepidations for her health rather than my feelings for her compared to mine for you," he explains softly. "And like I said after the ceremony," he continues. "I can't know what you're thinking. Of course, I would have wanted to say your name that day, but I had no idea you felt that way. None at all. I didn't want to put you in a position that would make you question our friendship and would end in us not being able to be happy together as mates, so I chose Leia," he says matter-of-factly. "And on the subject of Lane, it's been a matter of frustration to me similarly to the way my relationship with Leia has been to you. I can't keep track of whose side you're on. I'm not usually an angry guy. You know this. But seeing you with him just makes me so . . . irate. Adira, despite everything that has happened in the last week, in the last *twenty years*, it has always been you," he concludes. I take a moment to let everything sink in. I really did just let jealousy seep into my mind and discolor everything going on with Vince. But I can't ignore that he is right about Lane. Feelings for him have morphed in the last few days. But with Vince sitting here in front of me, the choice seems so obvious. So undeniable.

"It's not about sides, Vince. But he's the one according to Maurean law that I am bound to." I look back to my feet, tears starting to tingle in my eyes. Vince moves closer to me and wipes away a fallen tear before cupping the side of my face and bringing my gaze once again up to meet his. In the green light of the dwelling, his eyes look a glorious gray. Mesmerizing. Like I could stare into them forever and not get bored.

"Adira," he whispers. "We are not in Maurea." The next moment, his mouth is on mine. Again, without thinking, my lips start moving with his. I start to close my eyes before Leia's face comes to the forefront of my mind again. I put my hand against his chest to push him back. Tears start to flow as I look up to meet his confused gaze.

"I can't," I whisper. He clenches his jaw as confusion gives way to anger.

"Because of Lane?" he asks between clenched teeth. I let out a frustrated sigh.

"Not everything is about Lane, Vince. I'm just tired. Can we please just go to bed?" The look in his eyes softens as he takes in my defeated form. He lets out a sigh.

"I'm sorry, Adira. I've just missed you. I've missed us. And I feel like I've messed everything up, and I'm a bit confused on what to do at this point."

"Well, we aren't going to figure it out tonight," I say with a small smile. He gives me one in return.

"No, I suppose not," he says as he gathers up the blankets. I lie down facing the entrance of our teardrop. Moments later, Vince's arm goes around my waist as he pulls my back to his chest. I relax into his arms and can feel my fatigue pulling me under.

"I love you, Adira," he whispers.

"I love you, too."

14

WE WAKE TO the feeling of swaying as the dwelling leans back and forth. I look up and see what looks like the indents of two feet on the ceiling. Vince follows my gaze.

"What the . . ." Before Vince can finish, Lonny's dangling body is in our doorway.

"Gooooood morni—HOLY SHIT! I DIDN'T SEE ANYTHING I SWEAR!" Vince and I jump as Lonny continues to ramble on. My face burns with his implications.

"Lonny, we weren't doing anything, we were just sleeping," I say with a yawn.

"Well, that's incredibly boring," he replies as he starts swinging down. "Better get down before the grub is gone!" Vince and I both laugh at our arboreal friend's retreating figure.

"Good morning, Adira," he murmurs with a smile.

"Good morning, Vince." I return a smile. It's not like we did anything other than sleep last night. But we slept *together*. It feels oddly intimate, and I feel more well rested than I have since we got to Sentri. Good thing too. There will be a lot to do today, especially with Lane supposed to be finding us by tonight. Lane will be *here* . . . I feel my face drop, and Vince notices my change in demeanor.

"What is it?" he asks, touching the frown lines on my forehead. I try to smile, but I know it doesn't reach my eyes.

"Nothing," I reply. "Just don't want our perfect little bubble to pop." He chuckles and pulls me into an embrace.

"Then don't poke it," he murmurs, then kisses my forehead. We will have to discuss what was said last night and what that means from here on out . . . But first things first, food. I lead the way out of the teardrop. It's much easier getting down than it was getting up. Once we get within a safe distance from the ground, we jump. As we walk toward the main huts of the village, we hear Lonny's continued laughter. Vince grabs my hand as we come to where the fire was last night. I guess he's feeling *very* "couisly." I smile at the small gesture. Lonny hears our footsteps and turns around to face us, a look of betrayal in his eyes.

"You owe me the next capuchin you bring in. Bet's a bet," Lad, one of the hunters we met yesterday, says as Lonny rolls his eyes.

"What bet?" Vince asks as we join them.

"I bet that you two wouldn't be able to help it but boink last night. You two just lost me a perfectly good couple meals," Lonny replies with the continued look of betrayal. I roll my eyes and find a spot to sit.

"What's a capuchin?" I ask.

"Monkey we've got here," Lonny replies. "They're adorable *and* delicious," he adds with a smile coming back to his face. I remember learning about monkeys with Simon. I hope I get the chance to see one alive.

"Speaking of which," Lonny interrupts my thoughts. "You two must be getting hungry." I am, now that he mentioned it. I don't relish the thought of eating a monkey, but it sounds better than what was for breakfast yesterday.

"You lovebirds just hang tight. I'll rustle up some grub," Lonny says as he walks toward his family's hut. I know that I have to let someone know that Lane is going to come poking around, and I have to do it without Vince around. Now seems as good a time as any.

"Hey, Lonny. Wait up, I'll help you out!" I call after him. Vince thinks nothing of it and makes himself at home by starting up a conversation with Lad. Lonny's hut is very similar to the one I woke up in yesterday. I can smell food already cooking. It's completely foreign, but my mouth starts to water immediately.

"Go ahead and grab some of those herbs over there." He gestures by a large wad of greenery. I don't know which ones he wants, so I grab a large handful and bring them over to him.

"Sure, that'll work," Lonny says with a shrug as he begins to tear them apart, adding to the concoction that's cooking over the small fire.

"Lonny, I needed to talk to you about something," I begin.

"And here I thought you just wanted my charming company," he teases. "What can I do for you, gorgeous?" I smile at the compliment.

"There's another man that we came into Sentri with. He's going to be tracking us to catch up and find us today," I say.

"Say no more, my lady. One swift ass-kicking to the afterlife coming right up."

"No no no! That's not at all what I mean." I ignore the disappointed look that crosses Lonny's face. "I was wondering if you could send someone out to help and bring him here. He's a decent tracker, so if you guys go around the same area that you found us, it shouldn't be too hard to find him," I finish.

"Uh-huh. And I'm guessing that this is the same fellow that you came out with a couple days ago that bolted after he saw our dwellings, yeah?" I try to hide the shock on my face, apparently not well. "Ha, yeah, we saw that whole ordeal. Kind of impressed if I'm being honest. Vince said he figured that out just by noticing we don't leave our shit around. Pretty smart, that one is," he adds.

"Um, yeah, that's the one. But, Lonny, there's something else . . ." He sticks his finger in the concoction and then puts it in his mouth while looking up at me with a curious look across his face.

"Vince can't know." He gives me a wary look. "Lane will explain everything once he gets here, but until he does, Vince can't know," I say barely above a whisper. He says nothing for a while, looking back and forth between myself and the food he's cooking.

"Listen, beautiful. I may not have the *most* experience with relationships, but I'm at least like 90 percent sure that honesty is kind of important," he says while continually licking bits of the food off his finger.

"It's complicated," is all I manage to say. He looks at me with food dripping from the same finger he has licked at least ten times now.

"All right, all right. Not like it's any of my business anyway. I just like you two, ya know? Even if you did lose me a capuchin. So just in case you're keeping track, I'm team Vince." Blood rushes to my cheeks.

"It's not like that," I mutter. He gestures to my burning face.

"Clearly." *Pop* goes my bubble. "Well, anyway, if your friend got freaked by just seeing proof of our *existence*, he probably isn't going to be too psyched to see us. Is there anything we can tell him that may convince him that we haven't actually killed you?" It takes me all of a couple seconds to know exactly what will make him trust them.

"Tell him that 'little fish' sent you," I respond. He gives me another wary look before turning back to his pot.

"Grub is done."

We dish up the food and bring it out to everyone. Vince and some of the other Amoran men seem to be getting along well in their conversation. I sit next to Vince as Lonny hands me a bowl and sits next to Lad and whispers something in his ear. Lad looks toward me, and I drop my gaze to my food. I see him nod slightly in my peripheral vision and look back up to meet Lonny's gaze. He shoots me a wink before turning to Vince.

"So, how long have you two known each other?" Lonny asks nonchalantly.

"Long as either of us can remember, really," Vince replies, a smile tugging at his lips. All of the Amoran have started digging into their breakfast. Vince and I haven't taken a sip. I take the stone spoon in my hand and scoop up some of the liquid and bring it to my mouth.

Its foreign and intoxicating smells hitting me again. I take a small sip and have to practice every bit of my restraint to not throw away my spoon and suck down every last drop of the food directly from the bowl. I have never tasted anything so full of flavor. *Delicious* would feel like too grand of an understatement to suffice how phenomenal this food was. The meat doesn't have much flavor on its own. It's very chewy and seems to have a weird layer of some oil over it. But the rest of the food makes up for it.

"How is it?" Vince whispers to me.

I finish my bite and swallow before I say with a smile, "If you don't start eating that, I'm taking your portion, and I will not feel bad about it." He responds with a laugh as he picks up his spoon and puts a huge bite into his mouth. I can see the pleasure light up in his eyes as all of the flavors hit him. None of us talk until all of our bowls are clean. Lad collects all of our bowls to go get second helpings for everyone.

"So, long as you can remember? Your families live together then?" Lonny asks. Do families that aren't related live together in Sentri?

"Not exactly," I respond. Making a note to inquire later about the complicated living situation here. "Our dads were a part of the previous generation's Legions. They were best friends. Me and Vince being the Heirs to pick up their titles for our generation, we quickly became best friends as well." Lad returns with our second helpings, and I dive right in.

"*Were?*" Lonny asks.

"I'm sorry?" I reply.

He takes another huge spoonful of food and asks with his mouth still full, "You said *were*. They *were* best friends." I immediately feel Vince's gaze on me as I try not to choke on my bite of capuchin.

I swallow hard before answering, "My dad died." Silence follows. No one even takes another bite of food, as if it would be disrespectful to the memory of a man they never knew.

"What happened?" Lonny asks in a tone he tries to keep conversational. He puts his bowl on the ground next to his feet. Vince grabs my hand and squeezes just to remind me that he's there. I have never really talked about what happened to Dad. Not even with Mom or the boys. I can't explain why in that moment, surrounded by people who were strangers to me yesterday morning, I feel able to tell his story.

"You don't go into the water after dark, especially when there's a storm. It was past midnight, and it was the worst storm we'd had in years. People's homes were caving in, chaos was everywhere, no one in all of Maurea was asleep." I pause to take another bite of the soup. "Someone had gotten hurt. Some object fell on them, and they were bleeding fast. Dad and I ran to their home. I had been training with him for a while on some of the medicinal parts of the job that come with being in the Legions. There's a specific kind of seagrass that can stop heavy bleeding like that, but you can't store it. You have to get it fresh. It's only good for about twenty minutes after it's torn from the sea ground.

"We tried everything. I tried packing the wound with anything I could find, but it wouldn't stop bleeding. There was blood everywhere, and it was so dark, but I could feel it . . . the artery was shredded. It just wouldn't stop bleeding." My eyesight starts blurring as Vince rubs soothing circles on the back of my hand with his thumb. "When I looked up to ask him what to do, he was gone. Running toward the ocean. I screamed at him to come back. To go into the ocean when it was that angry was suicide. I didn't know what to do, so I just continued to try and hold pressure until Dad would come back. I knew he would. If anyone could survive that, it would be him.

"So, I stayed. And I held that man's leg as his blood washed over my hands and pooled at my knees until the storm gave up and first light started peeking into his home. I knew he was gone when the blood went cold, and I felt it starting to get sticky on my hands. I stood up and walked out of their home. I could barely hear his mate screaming behind me as she bent over his body. I looked out to the ocean, and for the first time in my life, I hated it. Because I knew, even if I didn't want to admit it, I knew it took him." I set my half-eaten bowl of food onto the ground beside me. I know that my face is covered in tears, but I can't bring myself to care. After all, it is the first time I am able to say the entire story aloud. I turn to Vince to see his own tears streaking down his face. He leans forward and kisses each tear from my face, and the rest of the people around us seem to disappear. It's as if it is just him and me again.

He holds my face in his hands and whispers, "It's not your fault he died. It's not your fault your dad died. You are so *good*, Adira. And he would be so proud to see you where you are today." A sob escapes my throat as I crush myself into his shoulder and just let him hold me. He brushes my hair in soothing motions, rubbing his hand up and down my spine until my sight clears and I feel I'm able to breathe normally again. Once I do, we both seem to remember that we are, in fact, not actually alone. I look up to meet Lonny's gaze.

"What was his name?" he asks.

"Daniel," I reply. "His name was Daniel."

15

A FEELING OF DREAD begins to fester in my stomach as it sinks in how different the rest of this day will look compared to the peace and comfort of the morning. After some further discussion, it was decided that I would be going along with the group that goes to get Lane. Him actually seeing me unharmed might be the only thing that keeps him from getting himself hurt in his attempt to take down the Amoran people. Because he would try. Even though there's a part of me that dreads when he will show, knowing that I will face the ramifications of the secret I've kept from Vince; each hour that goes by has me feeling more anxious when Lane doesn't arrive. None of us has ventured into Sentri alone, and we've seen enough to know that it has dangers that not even Maurea possesses. If anyone can handle it on their own, though, I suppose it's Lane. I don't know why, but in the time that has followed our coming into this new world, I have found that I perhaps enjoy his presence. Maybe that's going too far . . . I tolerate it. I'm dreading the moment that Vince will realize what we did. I also don't want Lane knowing about the moment Vince and I shared last night. I don't know why I care. I shouldn't. *I don't.* At least that's what I keep telling myself on repeat as Lonny and I gather up the supplies we will need once we receive word from his scouts that Lane has been spotted. Vince went off with Abe to help wherever was needed and to continue to observe and learn. Soon, we decided, one of us will have to go back to Maurea to check and see that everyone is still all right. That there even still is a home. Make sure that the Legions are aware of what's here and the possibilities. Having our people coming to live in Sentri hasn't been discussed yet. It seems evident that the Amoran people are waiting from us to hear what we need. Vince and I decided that we would wait to discuss it with the rest of the group before mentioning it to Abe and Lonny. Little does he know that only includes one other person at this point. Guilt starts to eat away at my stomach again until I feel like I'm about to hurl.

"From that greenish tint on that pretty face of yours, if you're about to blow chunks, do it outside please," Lonny says while pointing toward the opening of the hut we're currently occupying, gathering some dried plants and nuts to take with us in case we get hungry on the trek.

"Sorry," I mutter. He waves his hand in dismissal. We continue to collect what will be needed for the day. Lonny continues to give me sideways glances until I can hardly stand it anymore.

"What? What is it, Lonny?" He puts both of his hands up in mock surrender and quickly averts his gaze.

"Just here if you need to talk some stuff out, that's all," he responds. After a few minutes, he starts his glances again and I take the satchel he has in his hands to halt him in his work.

"Out with it." He snatches the bag back from me before sticking his tongue out at me. The action reminding me an awful lot of Liam and Avery. Love and pain radiate through my chest for a split moment. Lonny takes a deep breath before finally speaking up.

"I'm just thinking. Maybe you should go and speak with Vince about the situation before Lance shows up and—"

"Lane."

"Huh?"

"His name is Lane." Lonny studies my face before continuing.

"Right. Perhaps you should speak to Vince about everything with the other girl before *Lane* shows up. From what I've gathered, those two don't have the most positive of relationships. Don't think you really want *Lane* to be the one to break the news to him." I roll my eyes at each over pronunciation of his name. But I know he's right.

"I know . . . Can you continue to collect everything else without me so I can go find him?"

"You realize I've been living without your assistance for many years before you and your shiny hair came into my life, right?" I roll my eyes again but can't help the half smile that tugs at my lips as I turn toward the entrance of the hut. Just as I leave, a man I haven't officially met yet, but remember from the ambush yesterday, runs into the tent panting. He nods to me before turning to Lonny.

"We've spotted him. And he's moving fast." Shit.

"Well, princess," Lonny says, closing up the satchel and swinging it over his shoulder, "looks like you're out of the difficult conversation woods for a few hours longer." I dart for outside and barely make it before I heave up the breakfast we had this morning. I hear Lonny mutter a curse under his breath as he hurries to my side and holds back my mane of hair. His voice drops low enough so that the other man can't hear.

"Hey, it's going to be all right. No matter what happens, it'll work itself out. I believe that." Just as I start to catch my breath, another wave hits me until the entirety of my stomach feels drained. Lonny pats my back lightly until I am able to stand upright again. I look up at this man who was a stranger to me no more than forty-eight hours ago. A man who knows more about my story than even the man who I am going to go meet who I am engaged to be *mated* to. I don't know why I feel compelled to do so, but I pull him into a bone-crushing hug. After a few moments of what I imagined to be him being stunned, he puts his arm over my shoulder and squeezes back. After a few moments, he pulls back and picks out a leaf from his bag.

"Chew on this. Your breath smells like ass." I take the bitter leaf and chew on it as we follow the man into the dense forest. With their extremely long legs, it doesn't take long for beads of sweat to start dripping down my body as I try to keep up.

"You know, this trip would go a lot faster if we could travel up there," Lonny says, pointing toward the trees overhead.

"I'm not exactly built like you," I respond with a smirk. Lonny lets out a low laugh.

"No, I suppose not. But you could always learn some things while you're here." I give him a shrug of my shoulders as a response. Swinging through trees isn't something that sounds particularly enjoyable to me. My tongue starts to tingle from the leaf in my mouth enough that I decide to spit out the remnants. My mouth does surprisingly taste much better after the bitter plant. My stomach feels a bit eased as well.

"Can you fight?" the man leading our hike, who I learned is called Zander, asks.

"Fight?"

"Yeah, fight," he says with a sort of swagger that reminds me of Lane.

"Um, no, not exactly. I can hunt. Underwater, that is. I'm handy with the spear that we use for that. But as far as using the weapon outside of the water, I would imagine I'm pretty useless," I respond. Lonny slowly looks me up and down.

"You're built like a fighter. And if you can use a weapon like a spear underwater, I imagine you'll be even quicker with it outside of the water if you can get yourself coordinated enough. And from that suffocation of a hug earlier, it's easy to discern that you're strong too. You may be a decent hunter and warrior outside of the water, princess." Zander nods in agreement. I smile at the thought. The only fighting I had ever seen on Maurea were petty fights that almost always involved two men. But there was never any art to it. To learn something like that would be extremely helpful. Especially if this may be a place where we call home someday soon. I turn to Zander.

"Would you be willing to give some lessons?" A smile spreads across his face, showing off every one of his white teeth.

"If you think you can handle it, *princess.*" I roll my eyes but smile at the yes he just gave me. We continue to trek on until I get to a point where I am about to ask for a quick break when Zander quickly brings up his hand in a fist. Whatever he detected is something beyond my senses. I strain to try and hear whatever it is that caused the sudden stop and change in demeanor from both Lonny and Zander. The latter turns toward us, putting a finger to his lips before moving us into thicker greenery.

Before I am able to react, Zander scoops me up and puts me onto his back. I almost let out a yelp before Lonny's hand goes over my mouth and whispers in my ear, "We have to go up. Just hang on. He's close now. There's more of us up in the trees." He lowers his hand as I look up and find what looks to be about a dozen men and women scattered throughout the lower branches. Some that I recognize from our ambush smile and wave as if also thinking of the same memory. As Zander climbs up the tree with expert precision and speed, I cling for dear life as he shimmies up as easy as if he was walking on the flat ground. Once he stops and finds his comfortable balance on a thicker branch that is covered with enough greenery to make us barely visible, I make the mistake of looking down. The world starts to spin, and my grip loosens on Zander's chest. He grabs at my arms with one of his ginormous hands and turns to whisper in my ear, "Relax. Breathe. You'll get used to the heights." I chuckle softly at the impossibility of the statement and try to focus on breathing in through my nose and out through my mouth until the world starts to hold still again. Instead of looking down, I look across to the other Amoran people gathered whose gazes are all facing south. It's so dark down here on the forest floor that I have a hard time seeing much of anything. I make a mental note, adding another trait to the list of ways the Amoran people have adapted and evolved. After a few minutes, I hear a twig break. I flinch slightly at the sound. Zander nods his head in confirmation. Sure enough, a few seconds later, a familiar head of golden white starts creeping into my vision on the forest floor. I let out a tension I didn't know I was holding at seeing him safe and, what appears to be, unharmed. Lane continues to tentatively move forward until he is a little more than twenty yards away. Zander turns around to whisper, "All right, your move, princess. The rest of us will come down once he sees you." With that, Zander moves to the other side of the gigantic tree trunk to shimmy down in expert quiet stealth. Once we hit the forest floor again, I take a moment to breathe, making sure I am not about to throw up anything else even though I'm fairly sure my stomach is completely empty at this point. Zander gives me a crooked half smile before I walk around the trunk to face Lane.

He hears me before he sees me and starts to turn to find cover.

"It's me," I say, voice trembling. I swallow once. Twice.

It takes him a moment before he runs up to me and looks as though he is about to pull me into an embrace before he stops himself, throat bobbing, and croaks out, "Are you hurt?" My eyebrows knit together in confusion. I guess I sounded pretty pathetic and might still be a little green from this morning.

"No, no, I'm fine. I'm good. Great, actually." He looks at me like he is about as convinced of that as I would be if the situation were reversed. I take another deep breath and look away. He grabs my chin firmly and, with a touch surprisingly gentle, holds my gaze.

"Adira, what happened? Where is Vince?"

I swallow again, trying to make my thoughts into something coherent for me to say. Not being able to come up with anything better, I mutter while still holding his gaze, "Just don't freak out, okay?" His eyebrows knit together as branches start to ruffle overhead. I suppose they've had enough of my pathetic attempt at an explanation. In a wave, each of the Amoran people drop from their places in the trees to surround us in a circle. Panic replaces confusion in Lane's face as he takes my arm and waist and pushes me behind him in a protective stance. I see his fists starting to ball together and realize I need to start explaining now before he gets himself hurt.

"Lane—"

"Shh, Ad. When I tell you to run, you run like hell. Got it? Do not look back. And keep one eye on the ground as you run." I don't know whether to roll my eyes at the command or to be taken aback by the self-sacrificial statement and physical stance he is in that shows he would fight for *my* survival over his. I gently press my hand against his back and notice him tense at the contact.

"Lane, it's okay. They're friends." Confusion crosses over his expression, but he doesn't ease up from his stance. I step around him to face him. He tries to pull me back, but I grab the hand that he tries to pull around my waist and hold it in my own and squeeze.

"Please, just trust me." He freezes at that. He doesn't even seem to breathe. He looks down at our hands before straightening and then moving me partly behind him before dropping my hand. Lonny is the last to drop down as he meanders closer to Lane and me. Lane starts to stiffen as I'm sure he's making the same assessment I did of Lonny initially.

"Relax," I whisper.

"Well, well, well. *You*, I must say, had a much more realistic and appropriate reaction to seeing us than Adira and Vince did." Lane jolts at what I imagine to be the familiarity that Lonny speaks of me and Vince already. "You should have seen them. They just stood there with their mouths open, gaping like fish." Lonny brings his hands up in mock surrender and opens his mouth in fake terror. A rather comedic imitation of what I'm sure we looked like. Something similar to a growl comes out of Lane.

"You and I will talk about *that* later." I roll my eyes at him but can see some of the panic still written on his face.

"It really is okay, Lane. They're friendly. And more than willing to be compliant with us." Lane slowly looks around the group that surrounds us before meeting my gaze again in the end.

"You have some explaining to do."

16

WORDS AREN'T EXCHANGED as Lonny turns with Zander to lead the way back to where we came from. Lane follows after I start moving. Those that surround us give us space as Lonny and Zander slowly make their way far enough ahead to give Lane and me the privacy that we need. Lane never relaxes his rigid stance. Seeming to try and establish every threat around us, including the friends that he still sees as anything but. After what I gauge to be about an hour of walking, he turns his gaze to me.

"So, what should we talk about first? The new band of brothers you seemed to have made or Leia?" Lane says as if it's just another day.

I don't know why, but I can't keep myself from asking, "Were we wrong? Am I terrible for allowing it? For basically forcing you and Vince along with letting her . . . I don't even know . . ." Lane is staying uncharacteristically quiet. I expected to be chastised or some sort of retort or joke at my expense. I don't know if the silence is better or worse.

He swallows hard, not bothering to look at me as he finally replies, "Leia is her own person. Capable of making her own choices.

You are not in charge of her. You don't have the right to *allow* her to do anything. You respected her enough to let her make her own choices. Don't put blame on yourself where it is not due." I try to keep the shock off of my face. No quips, no smart-ass remarks. Just stark honesty layered into his words. A small part of me eases at the release of guilt that I have been harboring.

"From a survival standpoint, what Leia decided to do was what was best for us. For Maurea. She was a deadweight at this point." I turn my head sharply toward him.

"Don't say that," I say quietly, but not weakly.

"It's the truth, Adira. And you know it. And so does Leia. There's a reason she made the choice she did." I have no response to that. I know he's technically right, but there's something about the word *deadweight* that makes me want to punch him in the throat. Honest. One thing Lane will always be.

"So, are you going to catch me up on what I've been missing, or leave me out to dry here, little fish?" I would never tell him, but I'm beginning to grow fond of the nickname. I hide my grin as I launch into my explanation of what we have learned so far about Sentri and the Amoran people. I tell him about the culture, the homes, the people, the little things I've observed, and every impression I've made so far. He stays silent the whole time, nodding passively here and there, eyebrows shooting up when I explain what the leafy teardrops were that he had seen previously. By the time I finish my explanation, his posture has relaxed a little. His eyes not darting from person to person.

"So, you've been busy it seems. Anything else I missed while I was away?" I turn my head away from him to hide the redness that suddenly flushes my cheeks. Now is not the time to explain what happened with Vince. I don't know why I feel so guilty anyway. We just slept. Well, we cuddled . . . and kissed again . . . and told each other that we love each other . . . Not that I owe him an explanation in the first place.

So instead I ask, "How was Leia when you left? Do you think she might stand a chance?" I can tell by the apprehension in his gaze that he knows I'm hiding something—but seems to think now isn't the time to pry. Where was this semi-considerate Lane back in Maurea?

"The little food we were able to get seemed to help. She had color back in her cheeks before I left, but not enough for her to change her mind and come with me. I don't think we know enough about Sentri in order to make the call of if she will survive or not." He is right, we don't know nearly enough about this strange world. But . . . with that, an idea pops into my head, and I nearly sprint to Lonny and grab onto his arm.

"Lonny. Tomorrow. Can you spare a few people for another scouting?" Zander turns with Lonny to stare at me like I sprouted another head. Lonny looks down at the arm I'm holding.

"Um, ow." He pries my hands off, and I offer no apology as I ask again. The whole group has stopped now. Some taking the small break as a chance to rest against the many trees that surround us. "But yeah, I don't see why not. How many, and why?" I feel so incredibly stupid to not have thought of it sooner. So incredibly stupid. Lane walks up behind me at that point and looks like he realizes the plan that has formed in my head. I wait for a nod from him in confirmation before I turn back to Lonny.

"Leia. You guys have food and shelter and possibly ways for her to heal, right? What if we went back, found her, and brought her here?" Lonny looks to the forest ground for a moment, considering. He then turns to Zander; the latter nods and then turns to me.

"We can't leave until morning, and it's too far to get there and back in one day, so we will have to camp wherever it is that you all found to stay at the entrance to Sentri. It's too dangerous at night to risk leaving sooner, or to try doing this all in one day." Zander pauses, as if trying to find a way to sensitively say what he would next.

"You had mentioned that you do not go in the ocean after darkness." Both Lane and I nod at the statement. "Consider Sentri the ocean. With no land to escape to." My legs suddenly feel wobbly. What have I done? Leaving her and not having the sense to know to go after her the second we could have when we realized who the Amoran people were and what they provide. Lane notices my unsteadiness and sets a hand on my lower back to study me. I don't brush off the contact. Zander continues, "She is injured, alone, and near water. She is not the only one who gets thirsty. We will try. But understand that in Sentri, nothing is certain, and the only times when one can be considered safe is when they are surrounded by others. At this moment, she is not." Self-loathing takes root in my chest. While I was caught up having my moment with Vince, with Leia's intended mate, I've further risked her life. Stupid. Idiotic. Selfish. I don't think I could be more furious with myself than I am in this moment. How am I supposed to be a leader for the Dorian people when I couldn't see past my immediate surroundings to protect *one*? Tears start sliding down my face. I can't bring myself to care that everyone here is seeing it again. Something in Lane's gaze shatters at seeing it. Zander places a broad hand on my shoulder.

"We will *try*, Adira. The past is over with. Leave it there. We will set out in the morning." With that, he turns back around and starts walking once again. Lonny gives me an understanding half smile as he turns after him. The rest of the group waits for me and Lane to move before they get up from their places of rest to follow. We walk in silence for another few miles until I start recognizing parts of my surroundings better. We're getting close. Lane keeps making sidelong glances at me as we continue on. I can't bring myself to be embarrassed that he had seen that moment of weakness. Or think about how he doesn't have some remark about it. I couldn't even bring myself to think about how Vince was going to react once he realizes what I've done. The stupidity of what I didn't realize being too caught up in everything else. Too caught up in *him*. I shiver at the thought. Lane catches the movement.

"Don't go there, Adira," Lane says, breaking the silence.

"Go where?"

"To wherever it is that your head has been since you realized what we can do for her. That we might be too late." I cringe at the last sentence. "*Might*, Adira. The broad one is right. It does you no good to dwell on it. You made a mistake. Move past it, and do what you can to fix it." I contemplate his words for a moment. Let the honesty of them wash over me. Not being able to think of anything else to say, I ask the question bobbing around in my mind.

"Why aren't you being your usual self?" He crunches his eyebrows together at the question.

"What's that supposed to mean?" he asks with a crooked grin.

"Well, you're usually . . . less pleasant." His eyebrows shoot up. "I mean, did you leave the asshole Lane in Maurea? I don't get it." He chuckles softly to himself.

"And in what ways, little fish, am I such an asshole?"

"Well, you're arrogant, seem to always pick fights because anything else will bore you, and I must add, you don't exactly make it subtle when you check out my breasts every single time that we have an interaction, Lane. Some—no, most, would consider that slightly piggish." He lets out a burst of laughter. Lonny turns around for a second with an amused look on his face before turning back toward Zander.

"Well, first of all," Lane says after he gets over his fits of laughter, "of all the males in Maurea, I am the best hunter, have been training hardest, and let's be real, I have some pretty noticeable genes."

"Wow, and you're super humble," I snip back.

"Some would just say it's the truth. I'm a very honest man, Adira. In case you hadn't noticed yet." I have. "As for the picking fights, I'll have you know, I am rarely ever the one that tries to start them. Though I've rarely tried to dissuade them from happening. Things can get pretty boring in Maurea." I roll my eyes. "And as for you." My heart seems to start galloping so hard in my chest I think anyone within ten feet would be able to hear it. "You yourself have simply *glorious* genes, little fish. And I've never noticed anyone else giving them the appreciation they deserve." I bristle at the compliment. He leans over and whispers in my ear so that no one around us can hear, "And that includes the assets that so often capture my attention," he states softly. His voice gone husky, I feel my face burn as my core heats. I move a pace away from him as we continue on. The grin that lights up his face tells me he noticed.

"Do I make you nervous, Adira?" I turn to him with an incredulous look on my face.

"What would I have to feel nervous about?"

"About the way you feel about me." My mouth drops open, and I take another exaggerated pace away from him. His grin widens.

"You're delusional," I say, voice cracking on the last word, making all of his teeth show in the full smile he now displays. I can feel how hot my face is burning.

He licks his bottom lip before chuckling and saying, "You keep telling yourself that, little fish." I sharply turn my head toward Lonny and Zander, both of their shoulders bobbing up and down in laughter.

"You two got something to say up there?" I ask loudly. Lonny turns around and starts walking backward. His face is red with what I imagine to be concealed guffaws.

"I have so many," Lonny says as he and Zander burst into bounds of laughter. Lane laughing with them. I shoot all three of them the most pointed of glares I can manage.

"And for the record," Lonny continues, "I do agree that you have very nice assets." With that, Zander completely loses it and clutches at his stomach. Okay. Heightened hearing added to my mental list of Amoran traits. I pick up the nearest rock I can find and throw it with all the strength I have toward the pair. Lonny dodges it, but it hits its mark on Zander's side. Barely. He turns toward me, and I see actual *tears* streaming down his face from laughing so hard.

"Ow!"

"Brutes!" I exclaim back. This sets all three of them into even more laughter. "I do not know either of you well enough for you to joke around with me in this kind of way, pricks." Zander wipes away his tears and says, "Adira, I think you and I will be very good friends." He turns back around, shoulders still bobbing with Lonny's. I'm conflicted between throwing another rock at him or copying the sentiment. It's true. Something about these people made it so easy to trust them. To want to be friends. Family even. It's a good thing that Lane has come in. Perhaps we could use some skepticism. It isn't my or Vince's strong suit. Lonny and Zander are still laughing as we step into the clearing. Abe's booming voice is what greets us.

"I was beginning to get worried. It's nearly nightfall," Abe says, embracing his son.

"Sorry, Pops, not our fault that flippers don't move as fast as feet." I give Lonny a vulgar gesture in response. Amusement lights up his face. I look toward Lane to see him staring at something with a gaze that looks like something crossed between a predator marking its prey and sizing up a threat. I follow his gaze to see pure fury laced across Vince's face with his fists balled up so tightly at his sides that every knuckle has turned white against his tanned skin. The man I had grown up with seemingly nowhere in sight.

17

EVERYONE AROUND US seems to notice the unsaid dispute, and the clearing goes dead quiet. I look between them both before taking a step toward Vince.

"Vince, I—"

"Where is she?" he says with a quiet that is so unsettling, I feel my stomach drop. I turn back to see that Lane hasn't changed his stance at all. His hands loose at his sides, his face unmoving. I avert my gaze to Vince again and take another tentative step. Vince doesn't even seem to notice my presence. Every part of him solely focused on the male behind me. I try again.

"There's a lot we need to talk about, Vince. If you would let us explain—" Something like a growl cuts me off.

"Where. Is. She?" At the tone, Zander straightens along with Lonny and a handful of the people behind Lane and me. This is it. This is the apex of the anger in Vince that has been growing and festering for weeks. I don't think I've ever seen *anyone* so angry. Lonny looks to Abe, and Abe gives him a slight nod as if saying, *This is all you.*

Lonny takes a step toward Vince and says in a voice that sounds like it would coax a wild animal, "Look, Vince, hear them out. Don't make any rash—" A quick look toward Lonny cuts his sentence off. Lonny puts his hands up and retreats his step back. It looks as though the Amoran are going to let us deal this out on our own. No interference. The look Lonny gives me confirms this much. Vince inclines his head toward Lane.

"You. Start explaining." Lane is the picture of ease. Completely opposite of Vince at the moment. The only sign of any tension coming from the complete focus he seems to be honing into Vince.

"Leia made her choice," Lane says gently, but firm. No apologies in the tone. I didn't even see what happened in the mere seconds that followed. One moment, Vince was standing a good fifteen yards from us. The next, Lane is pushing me out of the way just before Vince forces his fist into Lane's face so hard, I hear his nose crack. I thought it would knock him out cold. Lonny rushes to get me on my feet to pull me away from the fray. Everyone else takes a step back. I can't help the scream that erupts out of me. I fight against Lonny to make my way toward them. Begging them to stop. It's not until Lonny pulls me a good five yards away and tells me to shut up and look that I realize the one punch that Vince got to Lane's face was simply because Lane had taken that moment to push me out of harm's way. For every hit that Vince tries to land, Lane evades and answers with one that hits home. Vince moves to hit him in the same spot. Lane ducks and delivers an uppercut to Vince's shoulder, causing him to take a step back. Vince rushes forward again, this time going for the groin before Lane evades once again and answers with another hit to the same spot on his shoulder. The dance continues, Vince never hitting and Lane continuing to hit only in his punching shoulder and opposite thigh. Zander maneuvers his way over to where Lonny and I stand, wide-eyed, stuck in a trance at the horror in front of us. If I have anything left in my stomach, I have no doubt it would be on the forest ground by now. Tears flow down my face freely as I try to think of how to stop what is happening. I feel so useless. So utterly useless and foolish.

Zander whispers in my ear, "It's genius . . . Lane is tiring him out. Notice he isn't giving him any hits that would seriously damage anything. He's hurting the things that could hurt *him* and nothing more. It'll be over soon." Yes, Zander will be the best to train me after this hell ends. I will never feel this useless again. Finally, Vince takes a step back. Humiliation and undiluted anger rippling across his features. He spits on the ground at Lane's feet. Lane spits the blood pooling into his mouth from his nose to the side of him. He might as well have spit it directly into Vince's face from the icy rage that followed. I take a step outside of Lonny's grip toward Vince. Lonny lets go of me but stays beside me, Zander flanking my other side.

"Vince," my voice cracks out. His hard gaze turns to me. "Vince . . . she was dying. She asked that we leave. This was all her plan. For us to come farther and do it without having to worry about keeping her alive along with surviving ourselves."

"And you just *let* her?" he asks me in a voice I've never heard before five minutes ago. Never heard directed at me. He doesn't even let me respond before he's screaming at me.

"You just *let* her leave. Knowing she would die. And didn't tell me, likely because you knew I would tell you it was so incredibly stupid, so incredibly cowardly, so incredibly *pathetic*, that we *don't* leave our people behind for *convenience*." Each insult he hurls at me brings him a step closer. Lonny and Zander are now inches in front of me and slowly closing me off entirely from him. A glance at Lane, and I see his nose still freely flowing blood. His hand clamped over it, trying to stop the bleeding. It would need be reset. And soon.

"It wasn't about convenience, Vince," I mutter, tears still freely flowing. "It was her choice. The entirety of the Dorian are relying on us to make it back. She did what she thought would give us the best shot at *saving* our people." Vince stops dead in his tracks and seems to consider something for a moment. Every eye in the clearing is on him.

"You disgust me," he says barely more than a whisper. I swear I could hear my heart break. The man I'm looking at is a complete stranger. I try to picture the man who held me that morning. The man who kissed me and held me last night. This man in front of me is an empty husk of a shell to that man. Sadness makes way for anger to creep into my blood.

I say between clenched teeth, "So what, everything you said this morning was bullshit? Everything we've ever been—nothing because of this? I *disgust* you enough for you to throw that all away?" My lip is quivering madly as I try to steady my tone.

"Forget what I said this morning, and forget last night. As far as I'm concerned, forget it all, Adira. You might as well have put a knife into her heart. You're as good as a murderer, and I'll have nothing more to do with the bullshit that is your cowardice and hypocrisy." Murderer. Coward. Hypocrite. Pathetic. Disgust. The words echo through my soul as the man I love turns around and stalks toward one of the huts, nursing his bad shoulder and limping. I had seen the anger brewing but had no idea how deep it went. How far into the chasm of Vince's soul his fury took him. The man I have known and loved my entire life is nowhere to be seen. Murderer. The word rings through me. I feel part of myself go completely numb. I start toward the hut that he retreated into. Zander and Lonny cut me off, pity written all over their faces.

"We leave at first light," Zander says simply and puts his hand on my shoulder in a reassuring touch. As Zander walks away, Lonny comes and grabs my hand.

"I haven't known you long. Or Vince. But I think that is why you should take what I am about to say even more to heart. Because you know I am not being biased." He waits for some kind of acknowledgment from me. A blink was all I could manage. "I don't know you well enough to tell you a good many traits about you, but I can tell you that none of the words he used to describe you are accurate due to the situation. Everything that just came out of his mouth was coming from a place of anger. Never trust words that come from anger. Give him time to cool off. I'd bet my next five capuchins he will be begging your forgiveness by morning." Another tear streaks down my face. Lonny gives me a sympathetic grin before wiping it away. The sound of Lane's approaching footsteps tears my attention away from my new friend. Still holding his nose as blood drips from his hand that is holding it. His face is far paler than what I would deem safe. He's lost too much blood. I turn to Lonny.

"I need hot water and bandages. If you happen to have any herbs for pain, that would be appreciated as well." My voice comes out in a rasp. He nods and stalks off to find what I asked. I lead Lane to the nearest hut, guiding him as quickly as I can. I sit him near the fire so I can have the most light to work.

"All right, move your hand. I need to see." I take some comfort in this. Healing, I can do. Something to distract me from the hell unravelling in my mind. He moves his hand, showing me his now crooked nose. I must have made a face because he chuckles once.

"That bad, huh?" I give him a grin that doesn't meet my eyes.

"No. Luckily it's only broken in one spot. I'm more concerned about the bleeding. It'll hurt like hell when I reset it though." He lets out a sigh. Lonny comes rushing into the hut with everything I asked for. He hands me the bandages and hot water and hands a plant to Lane.

"You're gonna want to chew on this for a second, mate. Might make you feel a bit out of it, but you'll be grateful in a minute." Lane immediately takes the leaf and starts chewing on it, the movement aggravating his broken nose. After about a minute, Lonny nods to me.

"Ready?" He takes a couple quick breaths.

"Just do it." So I do. Before he can think twice, I grip his nose in the exact way my dad taught me, and I flick my wrist until I feel the pop I'm looking for. Undiluted pain breaks across Lane's face as he doubles forward. I catch him by the shoulders and sit him back up. A curse I've never dared utter in my life comes out of him. I immediately dip the bandages into the hot water and begin wiping away at the blood on his face. I've done my job well. His face is thoroughly swollen, but his nose is straight again. It'll barely be noticeable when it's completely healed. The bleeding stops. I slow my actions, trying to make them more soothing, gentle. After I've washed away most of the blood, Lonny hands me two other leafy plants. One green, the other a bright-reddish orange.

"Wet these and put them all over his face. Especially the nose and by the eyes. It'll help speed along the healing process for both the swelling and the bruising." I nod my thanks, Lane mutters his. "You two can stay here tonight. Everything that you will need is in the corner over there," he says pointing to a pile of what looks like blankets and other means of comfort. "I'll bring some food in for the both of you. Try to eat something before you go to bed." Neither of us say anything in return. I want to thank him for everything. He deserves a monologue of it. But I only find it in me to smile up at him. He smiles back and leaves us to it. I pick up the leaves and start soaking them in the water.

"Well, the good news is that due to my perfect reset and these fancy plants, your face will be back to its normal, pretty self in no time," I say, my voice coming out hollow and flat.

"I knew you thought I was pretty," he says with a sly grin. I can't help the one that tugs at my own lips as I lightly punch him in the gut.

"Excuse me, do you not think I've been punched enough tonight?" he asks, familiar amusement making its way into his eyes again.

"Clearly not," I snide back. Lonny comes back in holding two bowls of what smells like the same thing we had for breakfast. Perfect.

"Eat. Then sleep. I'll see you two in the morning," Lonny says as he turns to leave. I grab his hand before he gets too far.

"Thank you. Genuinely. I don't have other words right now. But just . . . thank you."

He smiles down at me. "If you're going to go completely soft on me now, princess, I'm not going to have nearly as much fun in this friendship as I thought I would." I can't help but let out a chuckle. Friendship. Yes, it seems that in the short time I've been here, I've made friends. Even if I had lost the most important one today. Lonny struts out of the hut then, screaming good night as he walks toward Zander and Abe. I wave to them both. They wave back before turning back to whatever it is that they are working on, and I turn back into the warm hut. By the time I sit back down, I realize that Lane's bowl is completely empty. I look at him, question in my eyes.

"That—was delicious. Much better than your bugs." I snort at him and go to work on my own. Letting the spices sooth out the jagged edges of my icy stomach. After I finish, I take both of our bowls and set them beside the fire and go to reach for the now thoroughly soaked leaves. Lane grabs my hand before I can reach them. I meet his gaze.

"Don't be stupid enough to believe a damn word he said." No wavering in his voice. Just the brute honesty that is always there. And I believe he is being honest. He truly doesn't believe anything that Vince said. Even if they were true. I offer him a half smile before ordering him to tip his head back as I set each plant across his face. Focusing heavily under his eyes and on his nose. Once I finish, I set up his bedroll on one side of the fire with mine on the other.

"Did you need me to get anything else for you before we call it a night?" My voice is rough with fatigue and sadness. He notices easily enough.

"Not a damn word, Ad." I nod in response. He pulls up his covers before turning toward the fire and shutting his eyes, letting his exhaustion take over. I lie back on my own roll and close my eyes, trying to quiet my mind enough to get rest. Trying not to think of where I was at this time last night. What I was doing. After seeing his reaction today, I have to come to another staunch reality. Vince loves Leia. I don't know where that puts me or why he did what he did last night. But I suppose it doesn't even matter anymore . . .

Murderer. Coward. Hypocrite. Pathetic. The words echo through me like a sick melody meant to torture. Murderer. Coward. Hypocrite. Pathetic. I don't know who hates me more. Myself or Vince. Murderer. Coward. Hypocrite. Pathetic. Murderer. Coward. Hypocrite. Pathetic.

I don't know how long I lay there singing the demented song in my mind before the plan formulates in my head. Logic taking the wayside. She might not be dead yet. I look over to Lane. Perfectly passed out. Likely aided by whatever plant he had chewed on for the pain. I pick up the satchel near the entrance of the hut and collect the leftover bandages and leaves that brought pain relief along with filling a canteen with water before moving out of the hut. Right outside, I grab a spear rested with its head pointed upward. It isn't nearly the same as those in Maurea. The one I know I'm skilled with. But it'll do. I may be hunted tonight, but I'm also a hunter. Looking both ways, making sure that the village is asleep so I can get away undetected, I slip into the night. I don't know my way around Sentri well, but I've now made this trek two and a half times. I'll prove one of those statements wrong tonight. I am not a coward. Night envelops Sentri. But I can't find it in myself to be afraid as I step out of the clearing into the dense forest and fight my way through the dark. First light might be too late. I made a mistake, it's time I own it. I send up another silent prayer to whoever might be listening. That she is still alive. That I'll make it back to Leia on time. That Sentri won't take us forever in its ocean of darkness.

18

VINCE'S WORDS CONTINUE to ring through my head as I walk through the blanket of dark, doing my best not to stumble across anything that would make enough noise to let the more dangerous predators of Sentri know I stalk through their home. I shift the weight of the Amoran spear in my hand, finding comfort in the likely delusion that with it, I might stand a chance. I just have to keep walking. One foot in front of the other. My heart is pounding so hard and fast, the sound of it fills my ears. After far too long of stumbling blindly through the dark, my eyes finally adjust to the point where I can make out vague shapes and objects. I try to ignore the rustling that occasionally comes from overhead. One foot in front of the other . . .

After a while, my breath starts coming out in pants. The dampness that settles over the air is heavy compared to that of the comfortable mist of Maurea. My best guess is that I have been walking for around five to six miles at this point. Fatigue starts to wear in on my body, and each step begins to become more and more difficult. I imagine Leia lying by herself near the small pool, and the image keeps me trudging forward. My steps progressively becoming louder as my energy depletes.

Gosh, how did things change so drastically in twenty-four hours? I was in a place of utter bliss in the arms of a man I love, and now . . . well, now I'm stalking through the rain forest in the middle of the night alone. I can't help but huff out a laugh at the irony of it all. Whatever higher power controls all of this has a terrible sense of humor. I wait twenty-two years for him, and I get no more than twenty-four hours before he's ripped away. Worse yet, I have no one to blame but myself. I did this. I made the huge mistake. The logical part of my brain is screaming at me that this is yet another one, but I keep moving forward. I think one of the absolute worst parts of Sentri is the tiny *bugs* that seem to want to bite you everywhere that skin is revealed. I don't even want to see how bad I'll look once daylight returns. I don't think about the possibility of me not even making it to daylight.

The rustling overhead starts to pick up, and I glance up to see monkeys moving forward quickly across the branches in the moonlight. There has to be at least a dozen of them moving increasingly faster. They're soon too far ahead of me to hear the rustling of movement. I didn't realize that the constant noise they were making in the trees had turned from a source of disquiet to a comfortable background. Now that they're ahead, the silence in their wake is chilling. My racing heart banging in my ears now deafening. My body starts to react before my mind does. My palms sweat as I grip the spear in my throwing hand to a defensive position. The silence is broken up by a sound so soft I try to talk myself into thinking I imagined it. I slowly turn to check behind me and am stopped in my tracks by two glowing eyes. The monkeys weren't moving toward anything but running *away*. Without breaking eye contact, I turn my body fully and start walking backward. A small break in the branches gives me a chance to see the full body of the creature that stalks me. It's not tall, maybe a couple feet tall, but it walks on four legs and is built like it could run for days without stopping. Spots cover its entire body, and a deep rumble sounds from its chest. My mind starts reeling in the ways I might survive this. Fight and flight in complete conflict with each other. I can tell now that there's no way I can outrun this thing. I don't let the small frame fool me as I take in just how muscled the creature is. How sure its movements are. I don't know if my aim is good enough out of water to simply throw the spear and have enough luck to kill it in one throw. Unlikely. Very unlikely. My mind starts slowly coming to the realization that the only likely way out of this is for the creature to decide he's not hungry enough for this meal. And the way that he keeps stalking forward at a faster pace makes me think that *that* possibility, too, is unlikely. I start to reconsider my previous option of just taking the risk and throwing the damn spear when my foot catches on a vine on the ground, and I spill backward. The creature takes his opportunity and is pouncing before I hit the ground. My body takes over, and fight wins over flight. I use my left hand to catch my fall while thrusting forward with my spear in my right. The spear hits home in his shoulder, but so do his claws that dig into my chest and down my abdomen. I let out a yelp at the same time that he lets out small roar at the pain. I quickly get to my feet, and the dance starts. I make a small assessment of my injury and wince as I touch where it went deepest. Right above my heart. I move down to my abdomen. Nothing deep enough to spill anything. Not yet at least. But soon, my shirt becomes drenched with my own blood at the cuts that run down my front. I can see a slight limp in the way the creature stalks in his circle. Good. Maybe I'll have a chance. I can feel adrenaline taking over, masking enough of the pain to clear my head. This time I make the first move and force my legs forward in a run, making myself as large as I can get as I aim for the same place I hit before. But he's fast, and each movement causes more blood to gush out of my own wounds. He moves out of the way easily enough but doesn't attack in response. He instead resumes his stalking. The pain in my chest starts to overtake my senses, and soon, the sight of the creature trying to kill me starts to blur. He didn't spill my guts, but he knows he'll win. He's waiting for me to bleed out enough to be an easy kill. Clearly the injury I caused is enough to make him weary to fight me head-on, and yet, I'm still going to die here. I can feel my body slowly draining of any and all energy that I have left.

I hear rustling coming from the trees as I begin to picture every person I've ever loved to say my silent goodbyes. Perhaps wherever I go after this will be with Liam and Dad. Maybe Leia will already be there. The rustling behind me turns to thuds, and all at once, screeches boom out from behind me, turning my blood cold. My predator averts his gaze to behind me and, slowly, reluctantly, turns his back and runs toward the direction I was trying to go. I turn around to face the new predator that was bad enough to scare off the creature and am instead met with the most overwhelming sense of relief as Zander walks up with Lonny beside him and what has to be at least a dozen other Amoran people. Zander's furious gaze with his hand reaching out toward me is the last thing I register before the rest of the world goes black.

~~~~~~

The first thing I am able to register is a hard chest that my head is resting on. Or I suppose bouncing might be a better word. We're running. A second later, the pain manifests. I can't help the small noise that comes out of me.

"Hang on, Adira. We're almost back. Just hang on." Zander. It's Zander's chest I'm being carried away on. I try to distract myself from the pain by focusing on my other senses. My eyes feel too heavy to open. But the smell of fire and earth that comes off of Zander is grounding. I breathe deep, wondering if it will be the last thing I smell before moving into whatever life happens after I lose this one. I can tell we've broken into the clearing when I see orange light through my eyelids.

"Adira!" A distant panicked voice gets closer to us. I want to open my eyes, but it would just be so much easier to go back to sleep. I'm so tired. Another pair of hands is on me in a moment, and I hiss at the pain from the contact. They quickly move off.

"I've got her. We've got her," Zander tells the familiar voice. The voice was so nice, I wish he'd speak again. I start to shiver. When did it get so cold?

"Ad, what the hell were you thinking?" Lane. It's Lane.

"Lane?" I croak out, straining to open my eyes. I turn toward him to reach out my hand, causing more pain across my chest in result. I let out another involuntary groan as he comes into view. He took off the leaves and his eyes are lined with silver as he takes my hand, and Zander leads us into a hut.

"Lay her here," a soft female voice commands. Zander lies me on a soft bed, and as I straighten out my abdomen to lie down, I feel fresh blood warm my stomach and chest. The wave of new pain brings back a little more clarity. Lane curses under his breath and grabs my hand tighter. I feel my shirt being torn off by delicate hands. Once my entire abdomen is revealed, I hear more curses and deign not to look down to assess the damage. Throwing up over it probably wouldn't help anything. The pain is enough to make me not care about the blatant exposure of my body.

"I'll need more hot water, rags, bandages, and plenty of kanduli," the soft female voice says again.

"On it." Lonny. That's right, Lonny is here too. I open my eyes again to look at the women hovering over my body. She looks to be well past fifty years. Her long hair mostly black with silver streaked throughout. Her jawline is sharp and cruel, but her eyes are so soft that it makes up for it. She's beautiful. I turn toward Lane and see that his face is moist with tears. I try to give him a half smile.

"What were you *thinking*, Ad?" his voice breaks. I swallow hard before trying to speak.

"She's alone, Lane. I . . . I made a mistake . . . I had to—" A stinging pressure to my abdomen stops me short. I hiss at the pain as water runs across me, washing away the blood. I look to the ground to see it running red. I force my eyes up to meet Lane's once again.

"I killed her . . . didn't I?" A tear escapes down my cheek, and Lane stops it with the pad of his thumb. He keeps his hand there and rubs soothing circles on my cheek.

"What did I tell you? I told you not to believe a damn word of it, Adira. I meant that," he says, continuing the soothing motion. Lonny then runs back into the hut, followed by *him*.

"Vince," I wheeze out. Shame floods my stomach once again, and Lane immediately goes still for a moment before he removes his hand from my cheek and turns around to face Vince. The woman throws a bandage over my chest to give me a semblance of modesty.

"What the hell are you doing here?" Nothing but pure, quiet, promising rage is laced in Lane's words.

"What happened?" Vince asks, barely above a whisper.

"I'll give you one guess." Furor coating every word. I see Vince look down at me before his eyes move to my injury and stay there for a moment before meeting Lane's gaze again.

"I didn't ask for this. I didn't ask her to go anywhere," Vince says defensively. Lane takes his time taking deep breaths and turns around to look at me again. Concern, pity, and something else I can't name goes across his eyes before rage replaces it once again as he turns back to Vince.

"No. You just *spit* on the last twenty-two years of friendship you two had over a girl you've been betrothed to for *four days*. You just called her a *murderer* despite the fact that all she did was respect Leia's decision. You've known Adira better than anyone your whole life. Did you really think that if you convinced her she *killed* someone, she wouldn't do everything she can to undo it? No. You knew exactly what you were doing. You may not have asked her to do shit, Vince. But you all but threw her into that jungle." Everyone in the hut seems to freeze. Even the hands roaming over my stomach pause. Vince seems lost for words until he looks back at us and seems to finally notice Lane's hand still holding mine.

"And you all of a sudden care so much after having been betrothed *only four days*?" Vince demands with more bravado to his voice. *Seriously?* That's what he cares about right now? Lane drops my hand to stand and walk up to Vince. Even though the two are almost exactly the same height, Lane seems to tower over him.

"You. Do not know anything. About what I feel for her," Lane says in a voice so calm, it's more threatening than the rage. A sudden warmth floods my chest as his words register.

"Perhaps you also don't know anything about me and Leia," Vince retorts. The woman's hands start their work again, drawing out another cry. Lane comes back to my side and takes up my hand again.

Without looking back toward Vince, he says with the same deadly quiet and calm, "Get out." Vince looks toward me, and I open my mouth to ask him to please stay, but he turns quickly and turns out of the hut.

"That's enough excitement for her," the woman murmurs. She takes my head and lifts it up slightly, putting a cup to my lips.

"Drink this, dear." I obey immediately. By the third gulp, the world starts to blur again. Cobalt-blue eyes are the last thing I see before I slip into oblivion.

19

SEARING PAIN IS the first thing that registers as I crawl my way into consciousness. I reach my hand toward my stomach and feel a sticky substance. I open my eyes and try to lift my head to inspect it further when a dull ache throbs throughout my skull.

"You're up," Zander says softly. I manage to turn my head as he gets up from where he must've been resting and walks up to my cot.

"How do I look?" My voice comes out in a rasp. Zander gives me a half smile with a slight wince.

"Well, I wish I could say I've seen worse, but that would make me a liar. And I don't lie to friends." I smile at that.

"Does that make us friends?" He lets out a large laugh that makes me feel a little more at ease.

"I only carried your half-dead body and fended off a jungle cat for you, Adira. One would think that would make us friends." I let out a small giggle. Having another friend right now sounds kind of perfect. He gives me a knowing smile.

"Well, the good news is that your insides are still inside of you. Barely, but they're still there. Kira was able to stop the bleeding on time. Again, barely. You're going to be healing for a while. One doesn't face death herself and get up to go frolicking in the jungle the next week," he says matter-of-factly.

"I don't frolic," I tease. He lets out another booming laugh.

"You could have fooled me." I can't help but laugh along with him. After a moment, his face turns serious.

"So, since we have established that we are friends. Why don't you tell me what was going on in that little gold head of yours that night," he says while pulling a leaf out of my light hair. Already I feel tears welling up in my eyes.

"Did you find her?" I ask. He looks down at his feet for a moment before meeting my gaze.

"No. We found where you guys came in, but she wasn't there." Tears spill over.

"I made a mistake. I should have argued more with her about it. We shouldn't have left her. Vince was right, I—"

"All right, I'm gonna stop you there. I talked with Lane in more detail that night after everything settled. Let me see if I got this right. Leia was sick, she tried to get better but didn't, she then came up with a plan to save you other three and the rest of your people that involved her being on her own and you guys moving on. Did I miss anything of importance?"

"Uhm . . . no, I guess not."

"Well then, last I checked, you are an adult, Lane is an adult, and this Leia is as well. To me it sounds like she did what was best for your people. And unless you're leaving the part of the story out where you beat her with a rock over the head or something, *you didn't kill her.* And I really hate to point out the obvious here, but you don't even know if she's dead. And neither does Vince. Until we find her, one way or the other, don't assume anything."

"Zander, I was out there for one night and would have died if you all hadn't come in time."

"The jungle is a mysterious place, Adira. It holds a million different fates. None of which we can control." His eyes turn sympathetic. "None of which *you* can control." Right then we hear some muffled voices outside the tent. I can make out the voices of Lane followed by Lonny and Vince. Zander turns back to me.

"You ready to deal with all that?" he asks.

"Not even a little bit." Since we're being honest as friends and all. He gives me a knowing smile.

"Pretend to be asleep. It works with my lovely Elise all the time when I want to avoid conversation or confrontation."

"For friendship's sake, I'll pretend I didn't just hear that," I whisper. Zander winks just as the three walk into the hut. I close my eyes and hang my mouth slightly open to feign sleep.

"She just fell back asleep, it's best to let her rest," Zander says.

"She's been asleep for almost three days. Shouldn't she be eating something? Drinking? Shouldn't she just be awake by now?" Lane's voice is thick with worry. Three days? No wonder everything feels so stiff along with all the pain of my injuries. A rustling noise comes from the front of the hut, and I hear another set of footsteps come in.

"You'd be sleeping a lot too if you lost as much blood as she did. She's lucky to be alive. And she's fine. We've been getting sustenance in her." That must be Kira. I almost wish I wasn't fake sleeping. I want to thank her properly.

"It might help us relax if you guys would have let us see her more than once a day," Lane retorts.

"Yeah, because what Adira really needs for healing is you two alpha males having their phallic measuring contests," Lonny spits out. Zander lets out another bellow. I just hope that they don't notice the blush rising to my cheeks.

"All right, all of you out. Let me tend to her," Kira shoos out all of the males. "They're gone, you can open your eyes now." I can hear the smile in her voice even before I open my eyes.

"What gave me away?" I ask.

"You flinched a bit at Lonny's last comment. Then I noticed the blush. Otherwise, very convincing work," she says to me with a grin. "How're you feeling today?"

"Everything hurts, and I'm stiff all over. But I'm alive. And I guess I have you to thank for that. I can't even begin to thank you enough—" She holds out her hand, motioning me to stop.

"It's what I do. And from what I've heard, you would and have done the same. No thanks are required." She gives me one of the warmest smiles that's so large it crinkles the corners of her eyes. She starts organizing her tonics and supplies and begins her work on tending to my wounds. I look up at the ceiling, deciding that I'll give myself a few more days before I let myself see just how close I came to death. Kira gives a satisfied hum at the progress she seems to see and goes about replacing the bandages.

"It'll be a few days before you can get out of this bed yet, but you're healing even better than I could've hoped. You're a survivor, Adira," she says.

"Thank you, again." She waves her hand in dismissal at my gratitude.

"Can I offer you a piece of advice? As an old lady who's seen more things than I honestly care to?" Her question surprises me, but she radiates wisdom in a way very few do, reminding me of Simon.

"Of course," I respond.

"I believe every heart has a light. And that it is in the hardest of times in which the true nature of one's heart comes to its light. When that light comes, one might find that the one who shares the same light as yours isn't the one you expected," she says with a knowing smile. Without warning, tears start flowing down my face. I am so damn sick of *crying*. Kira oddly reminds me a bit of Geode. Although he would tell me to put on my "big girl flippers" and just do something about it, Kira seems to have a more delicate way that she goes about giving advice. Maybe that's why I feel like I can confide in her.

"I don't know what to do," I whisper. Kira grabs a rag and wipes the tears from my face.

"Don't let your head take over your heart. Follow its light, and you will find the one who shares that same in their own."

~~~~~~

Three more days pass before Kira lets me try to sit up and walk. It's a week before I can do it on my own. I'm tired enough to not need her brew that knocks you out, but it keeps the nightmares away. They seem to alternate between seeing the jungle cat jumping toward me and Vince's face and words of betrayal. Kira knows which one it is by whether I wake up screaming or with silent tears running down my face.

Lane and Vince come and visit once a day, every day. After that first day I woke up, it's never been at the same time. Vince never says much. He hardly looks me in the eye, and his visits usually don't last more than a couple minutes. I try to tell myself that it's a good thing he visits in the first place and that they aren't just because he feels guilty and responsible for me almost getting killed, but I'm not that naïve. I know that if the situation were any different, he'd be far away from me. I thought time might heal the cavern that's replaced the closeness that we shared, but it seems like he grows further and further out of my reach every time I look in his eyes. Every day that passes, he distances himself from me, and I can't help but do it in return. It feels as though I've just lost another part of my family. Vince is alive and well, but it seems I'm good as dead to him. I've tried bringing up our one night together and everything that was said, but every time I bring it up, he tells me it was a mistake and that we should pretend it never happened. That he never said what I've been waiting to hear for twenty-two years. I can't decide what pain in my chest is worse. The one from that horrible night in the jungle was at least just once, and it heals more every day. But with Vince, it's like every time I see him, I can see those same words reflected in his eyes. Murderer. Coward. Hypocrite. Pathetic. Disgust. And it feels like a wound that keeps getting torn open over and over again. I started out with a hopeful outlook on his visits, but now I've grown to dread every time that he comes by.

Lane, on the other hand, stays until Kira kicks him out with demands to leave me be so I can rest. I find myself looking forward to his visits. What I used to see as blatant cockiness has turned to a witty banter. Sure, he thinks pretty highly of himself, but he kind of has a good excuse . . .

"What're you staring at?" he asks. I drop my spoon into the bowl of stew, realizing I've been blatantly staring at him.

"Nothing, um, I was just . . ." He raises an eyebrow, and a cocky half grin tugs at his lips.

"Look, I wasn't—"

"Yeah, sure you weren't, little fish," he says with a male satisfactory look about him. He finishes off the last of his meal far before I'm even halfway done with mine.

"You gonna finish your stew, or are you too busy checking me out?" I choke on the bite currently in my mouth. Lane laughs while I cough out a lung.

"No, I will finish it. Keep your grubby hands to yourself," I say between coughs.

"I won't make any promises," he says with a heavy-lidded expression. I feel my face heat up and quickly shove more stew into my mouth. We fall into amicable silence while I finish my dinner. It feels good to no longer feel obligated to fill every silence with Lane anymore. In a way, he's become somewhat of a comfort to be around. But I also can't help but feel like my body goes on supercharge whenever he's around. Like I'm hyperaware of him whenever he and I are in the same space. The way I see him looking at me sometimes makes me think that it's not one-sided.

"You feeling up to going out to the community fire with everyone tonight?" he asks. After being stuck in this hut for the last thirteen days, it sounds really nice.

"Yeah actually, that'd be great." I position myself to get up before Lane quickly stands up and basically carries me to a standing position. Once I have my feet underneath me, I look up, and his face is inches away from mine. My tongue goes out to wet my lips on its own volition, and I can see him swallow as his eyes track the movement. All of a sudden I'm all too aware of how he holds me. His arms encircle me around my waist, and his chest is pressed up against mine in case I fall over. He moves his face impossibly closer to mine until he's a breath away.

"Um, we should probably, uh, get going?" I say barely above a whisper. He pauses for a moment and steals another glance down to my lips, his hands unmoving.

"No, I don't think we should, Adira," he says in a gravelly tone. He starts to tilt his head toward mine.

"Hey, are you two coming or what?" Lonny barges into the hut. We quickly jump apart from each other, and I wince at the tug I feel in my abdomen. I turn quickly so they can't see the blush that's overtaken my face. Lane sighs loudly.

"Yeah, we're coming," he says. He gives me one last look with a heated gaze before turning and heading out of the hut. I feel out of breath. I can't believe that almost just happened . . . I collect myself best I can before I head toward Lonny to leave the hut. He raises his eyebrows at me as I approach him. We head toward the fire together.

"Any idea what you're doing here, princess?" Lonny asks.

"Not a clue."

20

LONNY AND I are the last to arrive at the community fire. Vince is on one side of the fire and Lane is on the other. There is a place to sit next to each of them open, and I look back and forth several times before Zander calls out to me.

"Look who finally decided to get off of her ass!" I give a nervous chuckle and decide to go sit between him and Lonny. A look of disappointment crosses over Lane's face. Abe sends all the children off to bed, and then it's just all of the adults of the Amoran people.

"You have been here for a while now," Abe begins. "We've heard what happened to your home. I'm assuming you need our help for something." I look over to Lane.

"You guys haven't talked to them about it yet?" I ask.

"We thought it would be best for us to discuss it once you were better and able to chime in." All eyes turn toward me, and I realize that I've kind of become the unofficial leader amongst our little quartet that came into Sentri. Some leader I am . . . One of us is either roaming the jungle alone or dead, and I went about roaming in the jungle alone until I was *almost* dead.

"Um, okay . . . well, as you guys know, Maurea was basically washed away in a big storm that came out of nowhere," I begin. "Since, well, the beginning, there's never been something like that happen. At least not that the Legions have been taught. Our homes can withstand a lot. We've made sure of that. But the force of the waves eventually had all of Maurea literally underwater. People died." I stop to swallow the lump in my throat. I look up across the flames and meet Lane's gaze. He gives me a small nod of encouragement. I look over to Vince, and his eyes are down staring at his feet.

"Maurea is nothing but sand and water now. I don't think that it's possible for the Dorian to continue to stay there. There's nothing left and not enough land for all of us. The water never receded all the way back to its original shoreline, and the amount of land we have is a fraction of what we had." There are looks exchanged across the Amoran people.

"Isn't this exactly how your Originals came to Maurea? With just sand and the ocean? They figured it out. Why can't you all?" A woman who I haven't met yet speaks up. Lane answers before I have the chance to.

"There were five of them. It didn't take long for them to build what resources they needed in order for them to survive. Our current population is around one hundred fifty at this point. And it's not just able-bodied adults. There are children and elderly. The amount of land that has been exposed since the storm is so minimal that people are piling on top of each other. We need space."

"That's what concerns me," Abe speaks up. "Your friend almost died trying to get here, and she is in her prime. How do you expect children and the elderly to get here?" I look across to Lane. There's no way. Only the best swimmers would be able to get through.

"What if only some of them came here?" Vince asks.

"Vince, we can't just leave the others behind," I say.

"Really? It seems you have no issue with that," he rebukes, tone cold. I snap my jaw shut. Shame overwhelms me once again. Lane is staring daggers at Vince, and I'm starting to worry that another fight might break out.

"Your problem is resources, yes?" Lonny breaks the silence and the tension along with it.

"And space, yes," I respond.

"Take Vince's idea, but less . . . assholey. Some of you can come live here in Sentri to free up space, and some of them will stay over in Maurea. If we can fashion something to strap supplies to your back, your best swimmers can deliver what would be needed to help make settling back down in Maurea easier."

"Wouldn't the supplies get ruined during the swim?" I ask.

"Uhh, it's a rain forest. Literally everything is wet anyway," Lonny says with an embellished sigh.

I exchange looks with Vince and Lane.

"It could work," I breathe out.

"Hold on, we're just going to let them come in here and take over? How is that fair for us?" The same Amoran woman speaks up. Abe stands.

"Cena, we will adjust. That's what our people are all about anyway, yes? Adapting." He turns to me. "I will not, however, make my people feel like strangers in their own home. I know there are certain things we do differently here than the Dorian do, but they must be respected." I nod slowly.

"I'd expect nothing less," I say with a smile. "And I have a feeling that we could both learn something from each other if given the chance." A pleased smile spreads across Abe's face.

"I do believe we can, Adira. But I will allow my people to speak for themselves. Those who feel we should allow some of the Dorian to come live with us, please raise a hand." There's a moment where no one moves, then Lonny raises his hand, and Zander soon follows. Eventually all of the hunters have raised their hands, and it spreads around the circle. Cena and a few others keep their hands down, but the vote is strongly in our favor. I exhale out the tension I was holding. A plan. We have a real plan. One that can possibly benefit both groups of people.

"We are forgetting one thing." Vince speaks up. Abe sits down and turns to him, gesturing for him to continue.

"Leia. She could still be out there. We're just supposed to move on like she never happened?" he asks with ice in his tone. Zander shifts in his seat.

"We're sending out search parties every day, Vince. This will not stop when your people come. We're doing everything we can," Zander answers.

"You've been searching for weeks," Vince seethes. "What is the likelihood that she is even still alive?" I don't miss the look that Zander and a few of the other hunters exchange. The only thing breaking up the silence is the sound of the crackling fire and the soft rain hitting the barrier above us.

"We're doing the best we can," Zander answers solemnly. Vince stares into the flames for a few more moments before abruptly standing up and storming away from the fire and into the rain.

"Vince," I get up to try and follow.

"Just don't, Adira," he bites back. I slowly sit back down. Lonny taps my knee with his hand a few times in comfort. I don't know why I even try anymore. Abe breaks the awkward silence.

"Within the next couple of days, we shall discuss the timing of these events. For now, I am going to retire for the evening." He turns to me and then to Lane.

"I look forward to seeing what our people can do together." With that, he walks off toward his own teardrop. Everyone starts picking up their own conversations. I look into the fire, grateful for the progress we've made in so little time. I'm relieved that the Amoran have turned out to be such accepting and peaceful people. That they're willing to help us. I wish I could soak in this moment of triumph, but Vince's face as he stalked away is stuck in my head. I look up from the flames and see Lane staring back at me. I feel like I blinked, and my life got a million times more complicated.

"You wanna talk about it?" Lonny asks.

"No, I'm good," I reply. Zander and Lonny prop their elbows on a knee and rest their chin in their hand as they stare at me with expectant gazes.

"Really?" I ask with my eyebrows shooting up. They don't say anything, but just continue to stare at me in anticipation. I groan and look down at my feet. It would feel nice to get some of these thoughts out into the open. I don't exactly have Geode out here to confide in at the moment.

"Vince never talked to me about his feelings for Leia. He said he felt like he *could* fall for her. Not that he already had. It wasn't until he blew up about her being gone that I realized the extent of his feelings for her. And I know he feels betrayed. He has every right to. But I can't help but feel a little betrayed as well . . . Our first night here, he told me that he loved me. But his actions have shown that he's been in love with Leia. I guess I'm trying to figure out why he would even say it to me in the first place." Zander and Lonny exchange a strange look.

"What's that look for? What is it?" I ask. Lonny takes an exasperated breath.

"Look, princess, I think that out of anyone, you should know that it is completely possible to love two people at the same time." I'm completely bowled over. *Love?* I've known that I've loved Vince, but loving Lane?

"You're insane," I whisper. Lonny rolls his eyes.

"Fiiiine. Deny it out loud all you want, but I know love when I see it." *No, no, I can't be in love with Lane.*

"Lane is egotistical, self-centered, arrogant, bigheaded—"

"Adira," Zander tries to cut me off.

"No, I'm serious. He doesn't care about anyone but himself and is more concerned about the way his *hair* looks that day than he is about anything important."

"Adira, seriously, shut up," Lonny says between his teeth.

"Oh no, please continue." My heart drops to my stomach. I slowly turn to see Lane behind me with hurt in his gaze.

"After all, since I'm so self-centered and egotistical, I should love hearing all these things about me, right?" he says before stalking away. Well, that's great. Maybe I'll get every Dorian to hate me by the end of the week. I throw my face into my hands. Lonny lightly taps my back.

"That was . . . well, that was embarrassing. Not gonna lie," he says. I moan into my hands. "You must feel pretty crappy right now."

"Gee, you think, Lonny?" I snap.

"Don't get mad at me, princess. You're the one in denial deeper than any abyss I've seen." I refuse to start crying again.

"I should go talk to him," I say between my hands.

"Uh, yeah." They both say in unison. I roll my eyes as I stand.

"Any last advice?" I ask.

"Perhaps, and I'm just throwing this out there," Lonny starts. "Start off with a compliment. You know, just to even it out a bit. At least don't throw out another insult."

"Thanks, that's really helpful," I mutter.

"Aim to please, princess. Oh, and in case you're wondering or keeping track, I've switched teams."

"What are you talking about?"

"I've switched teams," he says nonchalantly. "I'm team Lane now." I scoff and walk toward the direction Lane left. I look around for a while with no luck finding him. My guess is he doesn't want to be found. Stupid. I am so, utterly stupid. Did I used to think those things about him? Absolutely. Is it fair for me to call him those things now that I've seen his true nature? I just . . . love? Lane? A few weeks ago, I couldn't stand being in the same room as him. You don't grow to love someone in a few weeks. That takes time. Years. It took years for me to love Vince. How did everything get pushed so much faster with Lane? I think back on the last few weeks of our lives. How much has changed. I try to pinpoint the moment that things flipped in my head. When did Lane go from the arrogant jerk to someone I've come to trust in? Find comfort in?

And then it comes to me. That moment on the shore when we were about to leave. Vince was off with Leia, and Lane let down his mask amid my grief to reach out and console me. Be there for me when no one else was. When Vince wasn't . . . I reach up and touch my cheek in the exact spot he did in that moment of comfort. Who's the asshole now, Adira . . . I decide to give up for the night. He can't hide from me forever. I'll find him tomorrow, and we'll talk.

I head back toward the hut I've been occupying the last couple of weeks. I'll take an extra dose of Kira's brew tonight. I don't think sleep will come any other way. My wounds start to ache the longer I walk. I'm thinking about going to grab Kira for some more pain leaves when I walk into the hut and see Lane sitting there facing the fire.

"I didn't think you'd be coming back," he says, still facing away from me. I shuffle forward slowly until I'm beside him. I sit and keep my eyes on the flames to avoid looking him in the eye.

"I was out looking for you," I say. He lets out a humorless laugh.

"Well, you found me," he says while throwing more kindling into the fire. I look toward him.

"Lane, I'm . . . I'm so sorry. I didn't mean it." He keeps his eyes forward.

"I think you did. You wouldn't have said it if you didn't mean it. We promised to be honest with each other, Adira. That was the deal. So don't go lying to me now." He finally looks at me, and I can see the depth of pain in his eyes.

"I used to," I whisper.

"You used to what?" he asks. I take a deep breath to build up my nerve.

"I used to think those things. Lane, you drove me crazy. You had this mannerism about you that just bugged me. The only thing you ever seemed interested in was my body, and I just . . ." I stand up, needing to pace out some of the nerves coursing through my body. "I don't know. I don't know what to do with this Lane. The old Lane—I could scoff at and walk away, and I wouldn't think twice about it. But then we come here, and you're funny and witty and painstakingly honest and . . . and you're comforting and vigilant, and I just . . . I don't understand." Lane slowly stands and leans against the wall.

"There are things that you just don't know, Adira. Things that no one does." He pauses and picks at his nails. A nervous habit of his. "There are expectations on me. I am to be envied. I am to be the best at everything without exception. I am to be *feared* by my competition." I see tears building up in his eyes.

"What're you talking about?" I ask. He looks away and rubs at his eyes. Then realization hits me, and I remember the bruise.

"Your dad," I whisper. He nods and then turns back toward me.

"Yeah, Dad has a way of teaching lessons that stick with you. And I hate—*hate* that I've let who he is and what he's done affect the way that I was with you." My heart breaks at the tears that start to overflow down his cheek.

"As for you, Adira," he says, moving slowly toward me. "You are, without a doubt, the most beautiful woman that exists. And not just in Maurea and Sentri. But every world beyond. And it's not just because you are so physically flawless that I want to get down on my knees and worship every inch of you." My stomach heats at his words as he continues to prowl closer. "But also because you are so smart. Headstrong, but in the best way. You are talented. You have so much compassion, Adira. You care so much. And you are so damned *brave*. Have you done stupid things with that bravery? Yes. But, Ad . . . you'd do anything for anyone that needed you. Adira, you make me want to be someone who is worthy of you. You make me want to be better. You *do* make me better." He comes and stands before me and reaches up a hand to cup my cheek and wipes away some of the tears that have started to flow freely.

"You don't have to say it right now, because I know the truth. And I also know there's a million other things going on in your head right now. But I'll say it because I mean it, and I've meant it from the moment that I knew you, little fish."

Don't. Don't say it.

"I love you."

A sob escapes me, and I'm done fighting instinct. I crush my lips to his. His arms immediately go around me as he kisses me back with fervor. I dig my hands into his hair as he runs his hands up and down my back. I feel intoxicated. Like I'm having a kiss for the first time. My whole world seems to implode and starts to circle around Lane. I am screwed. So deeply screwed. Because I can't say it yet, but I do. I know I do. And loving this man is just as terrifying as it is exciting. Our kiss deepens as my hands start to roam down his torso. I let out a small whimper when he tilts my head back with his hand and his tongue glides over mine. Bliss. This is pure bliss. One of his hands moves to my stomach, and reality comes barreling back in the form of sharp pain. I wince at the contact with my injury, and he immediately drops his hand. He leans back to look at me in the face. Both of us are breathing heavily as if we just ran for miles. He moves his hand back to my cheek and leans in to softly kiss it. He puts his forehead to mine and whispers, "When you're fully healed and we are finally mated, I will worship every inch of you in the way that you deserve." My core heats again, and I bite my lip as I look up and meet his eyes.

"Is that so?" I ask.

"Little fish, I would never lie."

21

LANE AND I spend the rest of the night talking in the hut. I tell him about my dad and brothers, and for the first time since Liam died, I feel like I'm able to fully grieve. He sits and listens and wipes away the tears when they come. He's always touching some part of me. Whether that be playing with my hair or rubbing his hand down my arm or resting it on my knee. It's like he's trying to convince himself that this is real. That *we* are real. I lean into every touch that he gives, basking in the comfort of it. Eventually I end up practically sitting in his lap while his hand runs through my hair. It's so . . . peaceful. Like I can finally breathe. Whenever I find my mind drifting to Vince, I leash it in and just let the guilt and shame take a break for the night. Vince obviously isn't thinking of me, so why should I waste my thoughts on him when there's a gorgeous man that can't keep his hands off of me right here?

Lane doesn't say much about his dad. Or his mom for that matter. From what he does divulge, I can gather that she knew about the abuse. She either didn't care enough to do anything about it or simply thought that Paul's way of "encouraging" Lane to be the best was a suitable way to go about it. Kira comes in when the first light starts to peek through the entrance of the hut. I move to quickly disentangle myself from Lane, but she just smiles and tells me not to move and gives me more leaves for the pain before giving me a secret smile and subtle wink before leaving. I recall our conversation when I first woke up and can't help the smile that pulls at my lips.

"What is it?" Lane asks with a smile of his own.

"Nothing. It just seems I've found my light," I respond. His eyebrows crinkle in confusion, but his smile just grows.

"Should I know what that means?" he asks with a laugh. I laugh along with him.

"Not exactly, no." He moves a piece of hair behind my ear, and some of the happiness leaves his face.

"What's wrong?" I ask. He sighs and kisses my cheek.

"Not a damn thing, Ad. But we should probably talk about what this means. What this'll mean for Vince and you too." I see a flash of jealousy go across his gaze. I look down at my hands in my lap.

"Um . . . you first?" He laughs at my attempt at avoidance.

"Okay, well, I'm ready to shout to the entirety of the jungle that you're mine. But I have a feeling that you wouldn't be comfortable with that quite yet." I snort humorlessly.

"I don't know, Lane . . . This is real. I want you to know that," I say, putting my hand on his chest. "But my feelings for Vince don't just go away overnight. Even if his did seem to." I expect to see anger in his eyes, but instead he just looks at me with understanding and expectantly to continue.

"There's a part of me that doesn't feel like I can tell him because it'll ruin our friendship. And then I remember that the friendship is basically ruined anyway, and so I wonder why I should even care . . ." I bring my gaze up to meet his.

"Give him time, Adira. How Vince has treated you since coming here is awful. Inexcusable. But I try to see it as if you were in Leia's shoes and he knew about it all and I'd have to assume you were dead. I'd probably be acting very similarly if not worse than the way he is." Okay, so add empathetic and understanding to the new Lane traits.

"Even if he did love Leia, he loves you too. One way or the other. Twenty-two years doesn't disappear overnight." Everything he is saying makes sense, but there are things that happened even before we got here that haven't been adding up.

"You know, Kira gave me some really great advice. She told me that it's during the hardest times that people's real selves will come out."

"And?" he asks.

"And ever since that day that Simon told us about everything— the ecospheres, earth, all of it—Vince has turned into this angry guy that I don't even recognize . . . On that day that me and Vince went out and found the Amorans, things started to feel like how they were before. And then literally the next day, the angry Vince came back in full force. I just . . ." I bite my lips to hold back my tears. "I don't know. I just feel like I don't know him anymore." Lane nods in understanding.

"So that begs the question. Do we tell him?" I take a moment to consider.

"I can't walk on water around him for the rest of our lives. I don't think it would help anyone for us to keep another thing from him. But, Lane, this might send him over the edge. He's been jealous about you for a while now, and . . . well, I've been denying it from the start. He's going to look at this as another betrayal." Lane puts both of his hands on either side of my face and forces my gaze to his.

"No more hiding, Adira," he whispers. I give him a small smile.

"And if Vince wants to fight, I'll kick his ass again." He shrugs nonchalantly.

"Please, please don't fight him," I implore. He lets out a heavy sigh.

"Fine. But only because you said please," he teases. Then he leans forward and presses a soft kiss to my lips, and I melt into him. I don't think I could ever get tired of this. Suddenly, we hear muffled voices coming from outside the hut. Kira's voice comes through.

"Lonny, you leave them alone, or I swear I'll—" and then Lonny is bursting into the hut. A wide smile breaks across his face before he lets out a huge guffaw.

"Oh, Zandeeeerrrrrrr!" he yells while turning around and leaving the hut just as fast as he came.

"How on earth did he—"

"I've been staying in his family's hut," Lane explains. "When I didn't come around last night, I'm guessing he put two and two together."

"Well, it's a good thing that we decided to tell people. Between Lonny and Zander, all of Sentri will know by dinner." Lane laughs and presses a kiss to my hair.

"You hungry?" he asks.

"Starving." As if on cue, an obnoxiously loud rumble sounds from my stomach. Lane chuckles and disentangles me from his lap.

"I'll go see what I can find for us."

"I'll come with. I'm not going to be able to wake up if I don't get moving, and the inside of this hut is starting to get real old." He smiles and reaches for my hand. For a second, I flinch back from it. Vince will be out there. There's no going back from this. I know that by taking his hand now, there will never be a point where I will ever be with Vince. I take a second to mourn the life that I've wanted for twenty-two years. It's okay to be a little sad in this moment. I look at Lane's hand still stretched out toward mine. The last twenty-two years is in the past, and I can't help but get excited thinking about the possibilities of my future with this man. I slowly take his hand and take a deep breath for nerve. We walk out of the hut, and Kira is there mixing something in a stone bowl.

"Good morning again," she says with a huge smile.

"Good morning, Kira," I respond with my own smile. She gives me a knowing look as we walk toward the main firepit. It's not raining this morning, so the sounds of the rain forest are amplified without the constant noise of the water. All of a sudden, a loud howl comes from the distance. Lane and I must look freaked out because Kira chuckles before explaining,

"It's a howler monkey. Quite obnoxious, but harmless toward us."

Lane and I nod and continue walking. I think I'm going to enjoy calling Sentri home. There are so many things to learn. So many things to do. Speaking of which, I turn back to Kira quickly.

"Kira, when do you think I'd be able to start physical training?" She stops her mixing momentarily and stands to walk over to me.

"May I?" she asks, motioning toward my shirt. I nod, and Lane releases my hand while Kira lifts up my shirt to inspect my wounds. I'm all too aware of Lane's gaze on me, and my cheeks heat. She lowers the shirt.

"You're healing extremely quickly. I'll bring in some more healing tonics that should help the process move along even quicker, and in about a week, you should be okay to start. But start *slow*, Adira. I will talk to Zander myself about it. He doesn't have a bone in his oversized body that understands *slow*. In the meantime, try your best to only rest in the evenings. I know it seems counterintuitive, but walking around and doing regular activities will help your body heal faster." I beam down at her and look to Lane to see him smiling at me.

"Thank you. Thank you, thank you, thank you." I pull her into a crushing hug. She doesn't hesitate to wrap her arms around me and return it.

"Now go get some food, you two. You must be hungry after last night," she says with a wily grin.

"Oh, no, we didn't—"

"It's none of my business," she says as she starts back up with her mixing. Lane chuckles beside me and takes my hand back in his, and we head toward the smell of food. Lonny is cooking some sort of meat over the fire, and Zander is sharpening one of his many spears.

"Good morning," I call out. They both turn toward us and break into huge smiles.

"You two are obnoxious," I mutter.

"I'm not even going to deny that," Lonny says as he turns back to his cooking. Zander lets out a booming laugh.

"What're you cooking, Lonny?" Lane asks.

"This, my friend, is something very similar to what almost killed princess," he states. "Obviously, they aren't easy to hunt, and so we don't have them often. But I thought that this was something to celebrate," he says with a waggish shimmy.

"What're we celebrating?" Vince comes up and asks. My heart drops to my stomach and my mouth suddenly goes dry. Lane drops the food he was holding onto the ground, and Zander stops his movements midstride. Lane is the only one that seems to be at ease. He looks to me and gives me a small, private smile. I can do this. I can do this. I stand and face Vince.

"Lane and I are . . . um, well, we're together." No one moves. Vince's eyes go to Lane for a moment before he turns his glare to me.

"Well, you two certainly deserve each other." Underneath the anger in his voice, I can see the hurt. He turns to leave, and I start to follow him.

"Adira—" Lane tries to stop me.

"No. He doesn't get to keep avoiding these conversations just because he's pissed. We've all been through crap the last few weeks," I seethe. "I'm popping the damn self-pity bubble," I mutter as I stomp toward him.

"Hey!" I yell at his retreating figure. Vince doesn't respond and just starts walking away faster. I trot up to him and grab him by the arm to spin him around.

"You don't get to ignore me forever, Vince!"

"I can sure try," he retorts.

"Honestly, Vince, what is your *deal?*"

"You betrayed me!" I freeze where I'm standing. Vince is panting, and I can see tears welling up in his eyes.

"You don't get to say that," I whisper. "You've been in love with Leia since the beginning, and you still took me up into that teardrop. You still told me you loved me. You kissed me *twice* and spewed lies at me that you would put me first. That you cared about me *more*. You don't get to be betrayed by this. You don't get to spew hateful words in my face. I did what you could never do. I put Maurea first. I put *Leia's wishes* first. You are not her keeper, Vince. And I'm done being the person that you blame all your issues on. You want to be mad at someone? Be mad at Leia. She signed up for something she couldn't handle, and she made the decision to stay behind." I feel slightly guilty saying it, but it's true. And I feel like I weigh twenty pounds lighter. Even if he takes none of it to heart. I've said my peace. He stares at me, and his eyes go from angry to desolate, and a lone tear falls down his cheek.

"I do love you, Adira," he whispers. "I just... I love her more." I thought that when I heard that out loud it would break my heart all over again. But Lonny is right. I know that I understand how you can love two people at once. But you'll always love one more.

"I'm sorry, Vince. I'm so sorry she's gone." The dam breaks, and Vince collapses in tears to the ground. I hesitate before wrapping my arms around him. He doesn't push me away, and I let out a sigh of relief.

"It's easier to be angry, Adira. Because unimaginable pain is the only other option," he says between sobs. I start stroking his back in comforting caresses.

"I know, Vince. I do." Because it's obvious that Leia and Vince really did have a relationship. If Lane were to go missing today, I'd lash out at the whole world too. My heart breaks for my friend. So we sit there in the middle of the Sentri jungle, and I just hold him and let him cry. I don't know how long it is before he finally stops, but my legs went numb a long time ago from my awkward position.

"Do me a favor and don't make out with him in front of me at least for a little while," he says. I snort.

"I promise," I respond. He laughs a little with me. It feels *so* good. It feels like we're moving on. I don't know how our relationship is going to look from this point on. Now that I'm with Lane, I'm not fawning over Vince all the time. And even though this is the first step to moving past this, I know he can forgive me for what happened with Leia, but he'll never forget. There are some things that will never change though, romance not even a part of it.

"I love you, Vince." He sniffs and sits up straight and looks me in the eye.

"I love you, too." I pull him into a hug. I don't know what moving on will look like, but I'm so glad we're doing it. We start to head back toward the fire. My stomach is loudly protesting the fact that I still haven't had a bite to eat. When we get back to the fire, more of the Amoran people have arrived. Most people give us a pleasant smile and turn back to their conversations. Vince goes to sit next to Zander, and I take up my spot next to Lane. He immediately wraps his arm around me.

"How'd it go?" he asks. I give him a bright smile.

"We're moving forward." He smiles and presses a kiss to my hair. Then he gets up and grabs me some food. I take a huge bite, starving. The meat is delicious. Lonny really knows his way around some spices.

"Lonny, this is amazing," I say with my mouth full.

"Thanks, princess," he says with a grin. He looks back at Vince for a moment before turning to me and giving me a not-so-subtle thumbs-up. I roll my eyes but can't help the smile that plays at my lips. I turn to Zander.

"So, Zander, are you still up for training me?" A devious smile lights up his face.

"Oh, hell yeah."

"Relax. Kira said we have to start slow. And she seems super sweet, but I don't want to be on the receiving end of one of her lectures." Zander swallows, and his face blanches slightly.

"Dang it," he mutters.

"Would you mind if I joined in on that?" Lane asks with his usual bravado. Zander's face lights back up.

"Oh, do I have things I can teach you," he muses. Lane chuckles. Abe saunters over and picks up some of the meat.

"I'm glad you three are here," he says. "We can further discuss timing of bringing your people here." He starts digging into his food.

"It might be beneficial for one of us to go back to Maurea just to see how everyone is doing and also to give an update on the situation before we start any actual movement of people or supplies," Lane says. Abe nods as he eats.

"So, which of you flipper feet are going to go?" Lonny asks.

"I would but—"

"No way, Adira. If you can't train for a week, you sure as hell can't do that swim." Lane cuts me off.

"I'll go," Vince speaks up. I see Lane sag slightly in relief.

"I don't think you should go traipsing through the jungle alone, though," I mention.

"I can send some of the hunters to escort him. They can stay there a few days and wait at the pool for him to come back," Zander says. He turns to Vince. "How long do you need there?" Vince considers for a moment.

"Give me three days. That should be enough time to get some sort of organization going over there. My dad and the rest of the Legions should be able to take care of the rest in our absence." Zander nods and stands to leave. I assume to talk with whatever hunters he'll assign to accompany Vince. Abe nods.

"You'll leave in the morning."

22

VINCE LEAVES AT first light the next morning with three Amoran hunters accompanying him. They'll take the whole day to travel to the entrance pool, and Vince will do the swim the next morning into Maurea. After the three days, he'll make the swim back, and they'll spend one more night at the pool before heading back. I have a feeling that the next five days are going to crawl by at an infuriating rate. In the meantime, I have to play catch-up. While Lane and Vince have been learning more about the Amoran culture and the jungle, I've been stuck in a hut healing. After we see Vince and the others off, my first stop is with Kira. I was the best healer out of the Heirs in Maurea, so I figure I should learn the medicinal practices here as well. I find her coming out of someone else's hut. She flashes me a smile when she sees me approaching.

"Look who's up nice and early," she says, wiping sweat from her brow.

"Ha, yeah, I'm actually wondering if you wouldn't mind having an assistant for the day. I was kind of the main healer back in Maurea, and I'd like to learn how to be one here." Her smile broadens.

"You've come on the perfect day. Lexa is well on her way in her labor. It'll probably be a couple hours yet, but an extra set of hands would be wonderful." I've done a few births on my own back home. Luckily, all of mine have been uncomplicated and were rather quick labors being that none of them were first pregnancies.

"Is this her first?" I ask.

"It is. But she's handling it very well. I was just going to find some more water to boil. Would you mind?" She holds out three canteens. I jump at the opportunity to work.

"Not at all. Just give me a few minutes, and I'll be right back." She gives me a smile before ducking back into the hut. I turn around and head back the way I came. Water. Okay. It's a rain forest, right? Shouldn't be hard to find water. I do the only thing that I've done on my own here to get water so far and start finding large plants with water resting in their leaves. I start filling up one of the three canteens, and I realize very quickly that this is going to take way too long. I huff out a breath of frustration.

"Are you lost, little fish?" Lane's voice startles me, and the leaf I'm currently emptying slips out of my grip, and the water falls to the ground. I mutter a curse as I straighten and face Lane.

"What're you doing?" he asks with amusement written all over his face.

"Well, I was *trying* to get water for Kira. I'm helping her with a birth today, and she needs me to fill these." He grins and holds out his hand.

"Come on," he says.

"No, Lane, I really need to get the water." He just laughs and takes my hand.

"I know. I'm going to show you a much quicker way so you're not *foraging* for water." He leads me in the opposite direction I was heading, back toward the main firepit. We go behind it and into a hut, and there in the middle is a giant pool of fresh rainwater. I quickly bend down and start filling up my canteens. The hole in the ground has layers of the waxy leaves all along it that seem to be intricately sewn together. I look up to see no roof.

"The tree above serves as a nice fountain when it rains. They've had to dig it deeper and deeper over the years so it doesn't overflow. This way they never worry about water," Lane explains. I think about the long and tedious process of having drinking water back home. This is *luxury*. Once my canteens are filled, I quickly stand and give Lane a peck on the cheek.

"Thank you!" I shout as I run back out of the hut. I hear his laugh as I make my way to Lexa and Kira. By the time I arrive, Lexa is in the middle of a contraction. Kira is holding her hand and wiping her brow. It's so hot in here, and I can feel sweat building on my brow already. The contraction passes, and Lexa takes a few deep breaths. Kira turns to me and points toward the fire.

"Go ahead and get two of those canteens boiling for me, Adira. Bring me the other." I do as she says and then go to kneel at Lexa's other side.

"Hi, Lexa, my name is Adira. I'm going to be helping Kira today if that's all right with you." A panicked look crosses her face.

"Is something wrong?" She turns to Kira. "Why do you need help? What's wrong?" Tears start welling up in her eyes, and Kira shushes her like you would a small babe.

"Don't be silly, dear. Adira is just trying to learn how to be an Amoran healer." Relief goes across her face. She turns to me.

"Sorry about that," she says. "I can't stop freaking out and crying all the time, it's so embarrassing." I take her other hand in mine.

"You're doing amazing. I've seen mothers who were in a far worse state than you are right now." I give her a reassuring smile. She starts to smile back, but another contraction starts, and her hand tightens on mine.

"That a girl," Kira croons. She moves away from her side and goes to check how dilated Lexa is. A smile breaks across her face.

"All right, dear. Now's where the fun begins. At the next contraction, you're going to push. Listen to your body. You push for however long and hard you feel you need to. If we need to adjust as we go, we will." My own heart is starting to quicken. Births were always something that I loved and hated going along to with Dad when he was training me. I was lucky that there were so few births after he died that I had to handle on my own. Birth is a beautiful thing, but one of the most unpredictable as well. Anything can go wrong in a second. Lexa's grip tightens on my hand, and I know that it's time. I lean forward to help her sit up and give her best push. I support her back with one arm and let her clutch my other hand as hard as she needs. She lets out a scream as she pushes with everything she has.

"Good push, Lexa, good push!" Kira praises. The contraction passes, and Lexa sags. I grab the wet rag that Kira was using and dab at her brow.

"Are you hoping for a boy or a girl?" I ask. She looks up at me and smiles.

"I want a boy. And I want him to look just like his dad. Same crazy curls, same goofy smile, all of it." She beams.

"Where is he?" I ask.

"Oh, he was one of the hunters that went off with Vince. He's going to be so upset he missed this. I'm a little early." She gives a shy smile. What a lovely surprise for him when he gets back, though. I hold her hand through the next contraction and whisper encouraging words into her ear as she gives everything she has into it. I look down toward Kira after the contraction passes and see a worried look furrow her brow. Her gaze meets mine, and I see panic in her eyes. My stomach drops. I keep a brave face on, and I pat Lexa's hand.

"Would you mind if I take a look down there?" I ask.

"Not at all," she says. I drop her hand and go take a look. My heart drops when I see that the baby is breech, coming out bottom first.

"How many breech births have you done?" I ask in a whisper.

"None that survived," she whispers back. I've only seen this once, and it was when Dad was still here. It was rough, but mom and baby made it. I can see the usual calm Kira falling apart at the seams.

"Okay, Lexa. We're going to have to do things a little different," I say in the most reassuring tone I can manage. Lexa sits up quickly and looks between me and Kira.

"What is it? What's wrong?" she asks.

"Lexa, I know this is scary. But the calmer you are, the better this can go. So, take a couple of deep breaths for me." I demonstrate for her to breathe in through her nose and out through her mouth. She gets in a set of a shaky breaths.

"Baby is just coming out bottom first. Since he wants to be in a different position, we're going to have to do the same, okay?" I look to Kira, and she nods, giving me the right of way to take over. I have her grab a chair for me, and we hoist Lexa into it.

"Scoot all the way to the edge for me. Kira will sit behind you and hold you up so you don't fall, okay?" They both follow my instructions.

"Okay, Lexa. I need you to follow my directions on the pushes until baby arrives. Your body might be telling you something different, but I need you to trust me. When the next contraction starts, I need you to push as hard as you can. Give it everything you've got." Tears stream down her face, and she takes another couple of deep breaths. She nods to me, and I grab some of the hot towels and lay them below her. The next contraction starts up, and Lexa starts screaming. Kira and I yell our praises to her through the whole contraction, and by the time it passes, the bottom is delivered. My mind goes through all of the things that my dad said during this part. I start quoting him word for word.

"Your little one has the cutest little cheeks, but we need to get the rest of him out, okay? I need you to do a couple of little pushes. Kind of like pulses." Lexa does exactly as I instruct, and Kira helps her breathe through it all. After a minute, his legs pop out and his torso along with it. All that's left to deliver is the head.

"You've got a boy on your hands, Lexa. We're almost done, okay? Now, I'm going to do something that may seem weird, but again, I need you to trust me. I'm going to let his body hang until your next contraction. Once you feel the contraction starting, tell me, and give me your best push yet." Determination goes across her face as she nods. I gently let his body go and hold my breath. A few moments pass before she starts groaning.

"It's coming!" she shouts. I grab a clean warm rag and cradle the boy's body as Lexa gives one last monstrous push.

"Here he is!" I exclaim as his head is delivered. I wrap him quickly and start rubbing at his back to get him to cry. Nothing. As I'm flicking the bottom of his foot, he starts to turn blue. I quickly grab the knife next to me and sever the cord and lay him flat on the ground.

"What's going on? Why isn't he crying?" Lexa demands.

"He just needs a little encouragement, that's all," Kira croons. I start to panic. I need to clear his air passage, but I don't have anything that I usually use.

"Kira, I need something to suck the mucous out." She helps Lexa lie down and runs to her things and comes back with a straw-like plant and bends over the baby and starts using her mouth to suck everything out. She turns to me after a minute.

"There's nothing left in there, I got it all." More color is leaking from the boy's body. I put two fingers between his armpit and elbow and try to feel for a pulse. Nothing. I can feel myself shaking. Lexa is bawling behind me as I start giving him tiny compressions and breathing for him. Kira is silently crying as well, and Lexa starts screaming.

"Come on, little guy. Come on," I mutter over and over again as I pump his heart. After what feels like hours, a tiny wail escapes him. Everyone lets out a collective breath of relief, and I wrap up the tiny boy and hand him to his mother. She has snot and tears all across her face with a look of utter reprieve in her eyes. She puts him to her breast, and he immediately latches. Tears of terror turn to tears of happiness right before my eyes. She continues to feed her son while Kira and I pick up everything from the birth and get to cleaning. It's another hour before we are done and are able to leave mother and baby alone to have some privacy.

"We will be back to check on you in the morning," Kira says. Lexa looks to both of us, and her gaze locks on mine.

"Thank you," she mutters with fresh tears spilling down her cheeks. I give her the best smile I can manage in that moment before exiting the hut. I didn't realize how much time had passed. It's gone dark. Kira and I walk in silence for a while on our way back to the main fire.

"I really don't know what I would have done if you weren't there today, Adira. How'd you know to do that?" she asks.

"My dad. Almost everything I said in there was verbatim of what he told a mom back home who was delivering breech. Everything that I know is from him." She gives a contemplative nod.

"He must be very wise."

"Yeah, he was," I mutter. She looks to me but doesn't say anything. Some things don't need to be said. We're almost to the fire, and I see Lane is there laughing with Zander and Lonny. He looks up, and concern goes across his features. He must see the exhaustion written over my face. He gets up and walks toward me.

"Hey," he says with his usual smile. I try to smile back, but I know it doesn't reach my eyes.

"Hi," I respond. He looks at me worriedly.

"How'd the birth go?" Before I can even turn away, bile crawls up my throat, and I bend over to retch. Lane curses and goes behind me to hold my hair back. Once it starts, it seems it doesn't want to stop. I end up kneeling on the jungle ground while Lane holds my hair in one hand and caresses my back in soothing strokes with the other until my body is shaking and my stomach is even more empty than it was to begin with. Once I'm positive that there's nothing else that's going to come up, I try to stand on shaky legs. I don't get far before it feels like my legs collapse underneath me. Lane catches me and, in one swoop, picks me up and holds me against his chest. He carries me past the fire and the concerned looks from Lonny and Zander to the hut. He sets me down gently on the bed and rests a hand on my cheek.

"I'll be right back," he says and then kisses my forehead before leaving the hut. In a few minutes, he's back with the same leaf Lonny gave me for nausea and a bowl of stew.

"There's nothing but the broth in here, but I don't think your stomach can handle more at the moment." I try to grab at the bowl and spoon, but he holds it away from me.

"It's fine, I'll feed you. You just rest."

"Lane, don't be ridiculous. I'm not a child, I can feed myself," I say reaching for the bowl and spoon again. He holds it out of my grasp.

"I know. I know you can take care of yourself, and you'll take care of everyone else too while you're at it. I know it seems inane." He leans over and kisses my hair. "But today, you spent all day taking care of someone else. Please, just let me take care of you," he murmurs. So, I do. At first it feels silly. But after a while, it feels oddly intimate. Between bites, I tell him about the birth. He doesn't say anything, just nods and gives me spoonful after spoonful. After the bowl is empty, I chew on the bitter leaves until my stomach feels settled. Lane makes sure that I drink some water too, and before long, my eyes start to droop. Lane gets under the blankets and pulls me so I'm lying on his chest.

"Every time I think that you can't surprise me, you pull out something else. You saved a life today, Ad. I am so proud of you." I lean my head back. He knows what I want and leans down to kiss me.

"Thank you," I mutter, "for taking care of me." He holds me a little closer.

"Always, little fish. I will always take care of you."

23

I SPEND THE NEXT few days with Kira. She shows me how to differentiate different plants and their healing properties. Lexa heals more and more every day, and her little boy who she decided to name Arthur hasn't had any issues since his birth. Right now, we're working on stripping different plants and mixing others into salves, teas, or brews. As we work, Kira tells me about her life here in Sentri. Her mate died a few years back, and she's poured her everything into her healing since then. They tried, but never ended up having children. But they loved each other enough that she says just having him was more than enough.

"Our mating ceremony was very special. Probably one of the best days of my life. What are the mating ceremonies like in Maurea?" she asks.

"It's actually not very personal. Everyone who's in the pool that year takes part in the ceremony. It's split between two days. The first day is when mates are chosen and pairs are made, and the second is when the match becomes official to the eyes of the Dorian," I explain.

"You mean to say that people aren't paired until the day before they're mated?" she asks with a furrowed brow.

"Well, some come to the first day with a preconceived match. They have to also get the Legions' blessing that day, but only some end up doing that. Three couples out of our group came as pairs." She nods.

"And then the rest of you talk amongst yourselves as to who goes with who?" I can't help the laugh that escapes me.

"No, not exactly. We're each given a number. That tells us our order that we get to select. So, whoever draws a one gets their first pick out of the others for who will be their mate. And so on and so forth." Kira presses her lips into a fine line.

"What is it?" I ask.

"It just seems a strange way to go about it, is all. I mean, what if you're chosen by someone you hate? And how is it fair for the last two people to be paired with no choice in the matter?" Another giggle escapes me.

"Lane chose me. And I was not fond of him when he did. I had every single thought that you just said coursing through my head when he said my name." She nods with a smile playing at her lips.

"Well, at least one pair worked out."

"How does it work here? The ceremony and selection," I ask. She hands me a bowl with some dried leaves in it, and I start grinding them down.

"Well, all matches are made on their own and in their own time. As long as they have lived for eighteen years, they are permitted to find a partner. A tradition that started a few generations ago was that before a pair could be mated, one of them asks by hunting down a jungle cat and offering it to him or her." I stop what I'm doing.

"You mean the women go and hunt those things down as well? I haven't seen any female hunters."

"Oh, you have. They're just not as obnoxious about it as the boys are. Some of our best hunters are female," she muses. I wonder if I'll ever get to a point where I could be helpful on a hunt. I'm not exactly built like an Amoran, but that doesn't mean I can't try.

"So, what happens after they accept?" I ask. A smile broadens her face.

"Joy spreads across all of the Amoran people. We celebrate all through the night. The next day, all nonessential jobs are put on hold to prepare for the following day in which the main ceremony will take place."

"And what happens at that ceremony?"

"The woman and man prepare separately. Part of the ceremony is them preparing their dwelling in which they will reside. They work together to form a home that will continue to be sustained until the day they both are gone from this life. Once that happens, it is cut down. There is dancing and singing as you prepare your dwelling. Once you are finished, the tribe will have a chance to voice the things that they see in you and your partner that will make your partnership strong and fruitful. Then, you go before the tribe leader, and you declare your intent for one another and any other words you want to share in front of all of the Amoran. The tribe leader then declares you as mated." I smile at her.

"That sounds really beautiful," I murmur. I can see her gaze travel to another time.

"It is," she replies. She takes the bowl back from me and starts packing everything into a sack before hoisting it over her shoulder.

"Well, I think that's enough for the day. Vince and the others should be getting back soon. Why don't you go check in with everyone beforehand?" I give her a hug before turning to leave.

"I'll see you tomorrow!" She waves as I run off. It's felt so good to be useful lately. While I've been with Kira, Lane has been off learning something different every day. Yesterday he came into the hut covered in blood from skinning different animals all day. He's also already started some lessons with Zander. There's been a few bruises that he's come back with, but I notice that Zander always has one or two as well. They seem to have formed a really close bond through their fists. I'm excited to get my own training started.

"Hey, princess!" Lonny shouts before he drops out of a tree no more than three feet away from me.

"You ever thought of getting around using the ground? Seems much simpler," I tease.

"Well, let me ask you this. Would you rather walk or swim?" Swim. What I would give for a nice long swim right now. I miss Luna. I'm starting to grow to love Sentri, but I miss the water.

"Swim. I miss swimming so much."

"And I would rather traipse through the trees," he says with a grin.

"Any news on Vince and the others?" I ask.

"Nothing yet, but they should be back soon." Right then, Zander comes running to us.

"They're back," he pants. We follow him until we get back to the main firepit. All four of them look like they could use a long night's rest. Vince has a look of defeat spread across his face.

"How'd it go?" I ask, afraid of the answer. Vince looks around before murmuring,

"Maybe we three should talk in private." I lead them toward the hut that Lane and I have been occupying. As soon as we're inside, Lane turns to Vince.

"What is it?" he asks. Vince starts nervously fidgeting.

"Things are . . . fine. They aren't great. I wouldn't even call them good. They're just, fine. The water hasn't receded any farther, so they're all pretty condensed."

"Okay . . . so what's the bad news?" I ask. Vince looks toward Lane.

"When I discussed the plan and everything over here in Sentri, there was a particularly vocal antagonist to the idea." Lane huffs out a breath.

"Let me guess . . ." Vince nods.

"Your dad stirred up a lot of unrest with the idea of moving and separating our people. The idea was catching for a while, but you're going to hard pressed to find someone that is willing to go."

"How is that possible?" I muse. "There isn't room for everyone to live there. They can't possibly sustain life at Maurea for much longer." Vince starts pacing around the hut.

"I know. I do. And my dad is doing his best to turn some of it around, but there's only so much that he can do now that all of this doubt has been planted. Paul has basically taken his job. He's in charge now. He also went and told everyone about where we were and all about the other ecospheres. He's set the narrative for everything. My dad had a plan on how to break the news, but Paul got to everyone first." Lane curses under his breath. "And that's not all." We look up at Vince. "Your dad insisted that you come back to Maurea immediately," Vince says. Lane lets out a small chuckle. That chuckle quickly turns into raucous laughter until he's bending over and wiping at his eyes. Vince looks at him like he's gone insane, and I'm starting to worry.

"Of course, he did," Lane says after catching his breath. "The bastard has no control over this whole situation. I honestly wish I could say that I was surprised by any of this." Lane's mirth quickly turns to anger. I reach out and take his hand. Some of the tension in his shoulders seems to relax.

"Are you going to go?" Vince asks. Lane lets out another humorless chuckle.

"No. Last I checked, I'm a grown man who's fully capable of making my own decisions." He looks to me and squeezes my hand. I offer him a small smile.

"I thought you might say that," Vince mutters. "You should know, if you aren't in Maurea in the next five days, he plans to come here to get you." Quiet rage takes over Lane. I can see him falling apart at the seams.

"Vince, can you give us a moment alone, please?" I ask. He nods and quickly leaves the hut. Lane lets go of my hand and starts pacing the hut.

"Hey, talk to me. What's going on in your head?" I probe.

"He can't come here, Adira . . . He's small-minded. He's angry. He's incapable of change. He's controlling. He single-handedly turned the whole of the Dorian against coming here. It would take him all of a day to turn the Amoran against all of us." He starts moving around frantically. "He can't. He can't come here . . .," he keeps muttering over and over. I walk up to him and put my hands on either side of his face.

"Hey, breathe, baby. Breathe." He looks back at me with tear-filled eyes. After a few moments, he takes a few shaky breaths. He brings his forehead down to mine. I stroke his face with my thumbs until his breathing slows.

"I won't let him hurt you again," I whisper. A tear falls down his cheek.

"Why?" he asks. As if the thought of someone being there for him, *loving* him, caring for him is such a foreign thought.

"You promised to always take care of me, so it's only fair. I will always take care of you." He leans down and kisses me softly on the lips. Then he kisses my nose and forehead before wrapping me in an embrace. I inhale the scent of sweet saltwater and earth that I've come to associate with Lane.

"I love you," he whispers.

And because I know it beyond a shadow of a doubt, and I know that more than anything, he needs to know it too, I respond, "I love you, too." He freezes for a moment before disentangling his arms from around me to look me in the face. A huge smile spreads across his lips.

"You said it back."

"Well, we promised no lies," I respond with my own smile. He kisses me again, and for a moment, we're just there with each other in this moment. After a while, I know that we have to discuss the subject at hand.

"What're we gonna do," I murmur. He lets out a heavy sigh.

"Would you come with me? Maybe with us two there, we can work on convincing people to come back with us. We can even go with supplies so that they see that the Amorans are friendly and that there are means to survive here."

"Lane . . . I think that I should live here. I've learned a lot from Kira already, and I think it would be helpful for at least one of us that was here in the beginning to be here to help the Dorian acclimate."

"Ad, I will not be leaving your side. If this is where you want to stay, then here is where home will be. But I have to go back to deal with my father. I can't run away from this." I take a moment to consider.

"We have five days until he threatened to come here. So give me a couple more days to heal, and we can get some stuff together before we head out." He nods and presses a kiss to my hair. Then he leaves the hut to go find Vince. Lonny comes in shortly after.

"So, what's the plan, princess?"

"Me and Lane are going to be going to Maurea for a short trip in a couple days. We'll take some supplies with us." Lonny must notice something in my expression.

"Anything else you wanna talk about?" A grim countenance crosses over my face.

"It's not my thing to tell," I say. He nods in understanding.

"I'll get some supplies together. Will you two need escorts to the entry pool?"

"No, we'll handle it on our own." He nods and turns to leave.

"Lonny." He turns back toward me. "Thank you," I mutter. "For being a friend to a stranger." A goofy grin spreads across his face.

"We didn't stay strangers for long, princess. I'm glad your weird feet came trekking through our home."

"Our?" I ask. His smile broadens.

"We both know this is your home, too, now." I smile back at him. He turns and leaves the hut. Over the last few weeks, Sentri has turned from a strange and foreign land to something that has become comforting. Every turn I make, I see something new to discover, and there is *so much* to see. I know in my heart that part of home will always be the ocean. My body was made for it. But Sentri has become a new home with possibilities that go beyond the water. I know that I will protect my new home from all forms of threat. If one of those threats happens to be Lane's father, then so be it.

24

WE DECIDE THAT it's best not to waste time. As soon as Kira checks me over and deems me well enough for the hike and swim, we make plans to leave. Zander plans to be a part of the group that takes us to the pool along with two other hunters. We'll leave tomorrow morning at first light. Lane has been more quiet than usual since hearing the news of his father. I try not to pry. There's a lot to unpack in his relationship with his father, and I know that when he's ready to talk about it, he will. I'm helping Lonny prepare all of the supplies that we'll be taking with us. He chats on and on about random thing after another, not at all bothered by my lack of responses. I find myself getting more anxious the closer that we get to going back. I wasn't nervous to meet his parents when we were first paired. I didn't care much about the way that Lane thought of me, nevertheless his parents. Things have changed so drastically since leaving Maurea. I'm not even sure *why* I'm so nervous being that I definitely don't want the approval of his abusers. I think I just want some sort of confirmation that I'll be good for him. Lane pushes me.

He does so in a way that forces me to grow and own up to myself. I just want to be the same for him.

"Where'd you go, princess?" Lonny is waving a hand in front of my face.

"Sorry. Just lost in thought." I tie up the package I'm working on.

"What're you thinking about?" I hand him the finished package and turn to start another one.

"I'm nervous about this whole thing. Nervous about seeing his parents. Nervous about seeing Mom and Avery. Nervous to see my home look more foreign to me than Sentri." He nods in understanding.

"Yeah, that's a lot. Any idea how you're going to convince your people that moving is a good idea?" I drop the materials I'm holding.

"How do you know about that?" I ask.

"I am an excellent eavesdropper," he says with a tone of pride. "Relax, I didn't tell anyone. Well, except for Zander. But he doesn't count." I roll my eyes.

"You are unbelievable," I mutter. He puts his hand to his chest.

"Why, thank you, princess." I toss a heavy root at him, and he catches it and sticks his tongue out at me.

"Very mature," I chide.

"I aim to please." He tosses it back to me, and I add it to the bag.

"You never answered my question. How're you going to do it? Because I don't need a bunch of hostile and crabby webbed toes coming in and ruining what we've got here." His tone goes serious.

"Honestly, Lonny, I'm still figuring it out. I need to see the situation for myself before I can really see what might work. I'm hoping that bringing these materials is going to be a good first step." He nods and ties up the package he's finished working on.

"You'll figure it out. There's a lot of brainpower between you and Lane." I smile at him.

"We'll do our best." He gets up and walks out of the hut. I put the last few materials into my bag and head out. I make my way toward the main fire and do my best to shake off the anxiety about tomorrow. Let tomorrow worry about itself. I see Lane before he sees me. There are two little girls who are braiding his hair.

He's laughing and talking with them as they pull his hair in one direction or another. A smile breaks across my face. I think back to how scared I was of Lane being around my brothers. I was afraid he wouldn't be a good influence and that he wouldn't be someone they could look up to as a man. How wrong I was. I make my way closer, and when he sees me coming, he flashes me a smile that I've started to recognize is specifically for me. Every time he smiles is drop-dead gorgeous, but when he's smiling at me, his eyes have a shimmer to them, and I can see the adoration, the love. I don't know what I did to deserve this man.

"I like your hair this way," I say, suppressing a laugh. His hair is sticking out in a dozen different directions. I can tell it's going to take a while for him to get all the knots out that have undoubtedly formed. He gives me a look that tells me he knows exactly what condition his hair is in at the moment. I reach up and undo my hair that's thrown into a knot on my head and let it fall.

"Can I have a turn?" The girls look to my hair, and their mouths drop open at seeing the golden-white locks that reach my lower back. They let out a giddy scream and tell me to sit down. As soon as I do, four hands latch onto my hair, and they start playing. Lane gives me a grateful glance. I motion for him to sit at my feet. He does, and I get to working at pulling out the braids and trying to smooth out some of the knots with my fingers.

"How'd training go today?" I ask. His shoulders bounce as he chuckles.

"Zander never takes it easy on me. Not that I want him to. I'm learning a lot, and *fast*. We have fun and all, but he's actually a great teacher." I hum in response.

"Did you and Lonny get everything packed up?" he asks.

"Yeah. Everything is ready for tomorrow." His shoulders tense up. I move my hands down and start massaging at his neck and shoulders.

"It'll be okay," I whisper. He grabs my hand and kisses the palm.

"I love you," he whispers. I stroke his face with my thumb before brining my hands back to their task of his hair.

"I love you too," I say in a soft voice. After a few more minutes, I've finally gotten his hair back to its usual perfection and mine is thoroughly styled. A shocked gasp sounds behind us. I turn to see Lonny gaping at me. He looks to the two little girls.

"Oh no no. This will not do," he mutters. He comes up and shoos the little girls away. They wave as they run toward the other children. Lane and I wave back.

"If you wanted your hair done, princess, all you had to do was ask. Look at this, this is a mess," he says as he starts pulling at my hair. "I've been dying to get my hands on this hair, and you just let two hooligans come in and botch it," he chastises.

"I didn't realize you were so into hair, Lonny." I laugh.

"Are you kidding? Half the time you see anyone here looking halfway decent, it's because of me." He pulls at a particularly large knot, and I wince. I start running my hands through Lane's hair as Lonny works. Eventually, I see all of the tension leave his shoulders, and he rests his head on my knee. Zander comes up and sits next to me.

"Everything is ready for the morning," he says in greeting. Lane and I nod. After a few more tugs on my hair, Lonny finishes his work.

"Much better," he self-praises. Lane turns around and looks up at me. A sultry smile tugs at his mouth.

"What?" I ask defensively, bringing a hand up to feel at my hair. There's a large braid that goes across the top of my head with two smaller ones on each side of it. All of my hair is pulled into one tie with the braids reaching to the end of it.

"Nothing," Lane says as he stands up. He leans down and presses a kiss to my cheek. "It's sexy," he purrs in my ear. I bite on my bottom lip as my face reddens. Lonny makes a gagging sound behind me. Zander laughs.

"Get a room," Lonny mutters as he and Zander waltz away. Lane chuckles as he sits down next to me. I rest my head on his shoulder, and he puts his arm around me. We sit in silence for a while, just watching the flames dance.

"I miss the water," I mutter. He sighs.

"Me too. I wish we weren't going back to it under such unpleasant circumstance." I hum in agreement. He kisses the top of my head.

"Lane," I look up at him.

"Hm?" He locks eyes with me, and for a moment, I totally forget what I was going to ask. Other than me, everyone in Maurea has blue eyes. But not like his. Not the deep cobalt that makes you feel like you're drowning in an ocean of Lane.

"What is it?" he asks. I shake my head and let out a giggle.

"Sorry, you just have really pretty eyes," I say with a blush. He laughs and cups my cheek as he dips down and presses a kiss to my lips. I open my mouth, and the kiss deepens. Part of me knows that a lot of other people are around right now and can see me making out with Lane, but it's like the rest of the world disappears when he kisses me like this. His touch is intoxicating. The moment it starts, I just want *more*. He breaks the kiss, and I have to actively try not to pout.

"There isn't a soul that I've met whose eyes have compared to yours, Adira. Not one." Another blush rises to my cheeks. He smiles and runs a finger across my cheekbone.

"You have no idea how adorable that is," he says. I turn away to hide my smile.

"What is it you wanted to ask me?" Oh, right.

"Look, I know that there are expectations on us just like there are on everyone. But now that things are changing so drastically, I figure we can make our own rules . . ." He nods and waits for me to continue. "Do you want kids?" I ask. He looks taken aback by the question.

"Do you?" he counters. I look down at my hands in my lap.

"I think so," I say. "I always knew it was expected of me, and so I never even considered *not* having them." He hums in contemplation.

"I do," he says resolutely. "But not for some bullshit of passing down favorable genes. But because I love you. And I want a family with you." I look up at him and offer a small smile. "But, Adira, if that isn't what you want, then all you have to do is tell me."

"You'd give up having kids just because I didn't want to?" A staggered look crosses his face.

"Of course. Why wouldn't I?"

"How would that be fair?" I ask. "For me to get what I would want and for you not to." He gives me a small smile.

"Adira, I need you to understand something," he says as he puts both of his hands on either side of my face. "I will *always* put you first. Always." I lean into his touch and smile.

"And I will always put you first. You're just lucky that I also want kids." He exhales in relief and presses a quick kiss to my lips before crushing me into a hug. I let him hold me for a minute as we sit there. After a while, most of the Amoran have gone off to bed for the night.

"We should get some rest," I murmur. He nods and stands up, holding his hand out to me. I take it, and we walk back to what has become our hut. That night, I fall asleep without anxiety and fear. Because I know that no matter what tomorrow brings, I have someone that'll have my back. And I'll have his.

~~~~~~

We make it to the pool in decent time, only stopping every few miles to give myself a chance to catch my breath. Being inactive for those few weeks that I was healing affected me more than I thought. I'm even more anxious to get my training started once we get back now. It was strange spending the night back at the pool where all of this began. I keep thinking that I'm going to look up and see Leia. They haven't stopped searching for her, but the search parties are becoming few and far between. If they haven't found her yet, it's unlikely that they ever will. Part of me is hanging on to this hope that she's still out there. That she's okay and the whole situation will just become a bad memory.

Zander is strapping supplies onto our bodies as we prepare to make the swim into Maurea. I had wondered how we were going to carry that much supplies on our backs, but he's also attaching them to our calves and arms. It'll be a more difficult swim with them, but as soon as we're out of the tunnel, we can break for the surface, so we don't have to worry about running out of air.

The nerves have caught up to me at this point. I've been fantasizing so much about getting back in the water again that I didn't even think about how the last time I was in the ocean, I almost died. I'm also swimming into a situation that is completely unpredictable where we will be not only confronting Lane's father, but also possibly seeing Leia's parents. Not to mention, I'll be seeing Mom and Avery again.

"All right, you two are strapped up and ready to go," Zander says after tightening the last strap on my right calf.

"Hey," Lane whispers from behind me. He wraps his arms around me and bends down to kiss my shoulder. "We're going to be fine. I've got you." I turn around and wrap my arms around his neck.

"And I've got you," I whisper back. The smile that he saves just for me lights up his face as he bends down and kisses me like we're the only two beings in Sentri.

"Euch. All right, all right. Save it for the fishes, you two," Zander says as he feigns gagging. Lane throws his arm around my shoulders and leads me toward the small pool. I start homing in on my breathing. Lane gives me one last look, and together, we dive down into the pool. Lane leads the way, and before I know it, the water changes from a green tint to crystal blue. It takes less time than I anticipated for us to be out of the tunnel and into the open ocean. I forgot how dark it is this deep down. It's been about ten minutes, and I can tell that I'm not going to make it to twenty. This much time out of the water has done more damage than I thought it would. Lane angles toward the surface, and we begin or ascent. We stop at certain intervals in order for the pressure to regulate in our bodies before we continue up. It's been fifteen minutes now, and my lungs are starting to scream at me. I can't even think about how good it feels to be back in the ocean because everything hurts. The injury on my stomach is starting to sting with the excursion. The packages attached to me feel like they gain more weight with every stroke. By now, Lane and I can see each other clearly through the sunlight that breaks the surface. A concerned look crosses over his gaze as he notices my struggling. Lane swims down to my legs and undoes the straps attached to them and holds them in one arm. I don't even try to stop him. He continues his swim toward the surface, and I follow with a little bit more ease now that I'm not weighed down as much. I start to feel dizzy right before we finally breach the surface. I tread water for a while and greedily gulp down air until it feels like my head is firmly back on my shoulders. Lane wouldn't ever admit it, but I can tell that he's exhausted too. He's down an arm now with holding my packages in the other.

"Let's go," I pant.

"We can rest for a minute more if you need, Adira," he says between huffs. I shake my head at him and start swimming toward the shore. We've arrived exactly where we left off all those weeks ago, on the north shore. There's no one over here at the moment. We lie on our backs as we wheeze in air.

"Are you okay?" he asks after a few minutes. I nod.

"I think so." I tentatively bring my hand down to prod at my stomach and can't help the small wince that escapes me. Lane notices and instantly sits up.

"What is it?"

"Nothing. It's just a little sore. I knew it would be after a swim like that being my first one back." He gives me an unconvinced look as he carefully lifts my shirt to check the injury. He curses under his breath. I look down and see that the edge of my deepest gash has started bleeding.

"Damn it," I mutter. I start holding pressure to it, and Lane starts rummaging through the different packs we brought.

"Which one of these do you need?" he asks as he frantically looks through each bundle of greenery.

"I don't need it. That's for the people here. I'll be fine." He looks up at me.

"I'm not letting you leave this beach until you take one of these plants to fix that, Adira. And don't even think about trying to run away, I'm faster than you, you know," he adds with a grin. I chuckle and point to the darkest plant in the bundle he's holding.

"Hand me that one, please." He does, and I put it in mouth and chew until I know it's in a paste form. I spit in into my hand and laugh at the look that crosses Lane's face. I smear it on the wound that's reopened and lay it there for a moment to let it dry.

"You really got good at that stuff, didn't you?" Lane says as he wipes the rest of the paste off my hand.

"I like it. It keeps my brain and my body busy." Lane nods.

"You're just a badass," he says with a smirk. I nudge him playfully and take his hand as he helps me stand. We walk hand in hand across the sands of Maurea. Of all people, Geode is the first to see us.

"Ho! Adira!" He stands on wobbly legs and moves toward us. I'm surprised he survived the disaster, but so glad. Once we make it to him, I let go of Lane's hand and wrap Geode in a hug, ignoring the pain in my stomach. The last time I talked to him, he was encouraging me to go after Vince wholeheartedly. Seeing him brings back a perspective of just how much has changed in the last few weeks. I can't think of anyone more perfect to run into first. Geode, being the gossiper that he is, will know what's been going on in Maurea better than anyone. After he steps back from our hug, he extends a hand toward Lane.

"Lane, good to see you, lad. I'm glad you both are all right."

"It's good to see you, Geode," I say with a warm smile. "How've things been?" I take a look around and feel my stomach drop at the vast nothingness that Maurea has become. Geode is the closest thing to remote that you can get on the island now. There isn't room for privacy. All across are families bundled together with occasional makeshift tents popped up here and there. Maurea has turned desolate.

"Not great, kiddo. Lucky the storm never came back, but whatchu see here is whatchu get. We eat fine, and they've been able to rig up the water system again so that we're fed and hydrated, but that's as far as it goes. The soul of this place is gone," he says gruffly. No tears spring forward, but he sniffles like he's holding them back.

"And the unrest about moving to Sentri?" Lane asks. Geode glances at him before quickly looking down at his feet.

"We know about the ecospheres. But your father, well, the idea is not a popular one," he says while continuing to keep his gaze down.

"I have a really hard time believing that being that *this* is the alternative," I say. Geode looks nervously toward Lane.

"Please, speak freely. I am not my father," Lane says with a sympathetic glance. Geode offers him a small tight-lipped smile and glances around.

"There's been rumors," he whispers.

"What kind of rumors?" I ask. He glances around to make sure no one is listening.

"Your father has been claiming terrible things of Sentri. Both about the place itself and the people that live there. Things I will not repeat in the presence of a lady." He looks toward me. Lane and I glance at each other, and I see my own confusion mirrored in his gaze.

"Didn't Vince tell everyone the truth about it? The jungle is dangerous, yes. But the Amoran people are welcoming and kind and can teach us how to navigate it," I say. Geode nods vigorously.

"That's the part that gets even more fishy. He's off claiming that Vince was 'turned' or something by the people and that we can't trust nothing that he says. He mentioned that if any of the rest of you came around, we couldn't trust you neither. I figured it was all scuttlebutt, but for a while, he even had me wondering. Convincing way of talking your father has," he says gesturing toward Lane. This is worse than I thought. Being apprehensive is one thing. Full-on lying and making up stories and accusations is another. Why is he so against this?

"What has Simon done in all of this?" I ask.

"All of the parents of you kids that left have been staying pretty tight apart from Lane's folks. Been staying real quiet. I hate to tell you, but you two aren't going to be met with a lot of trust here. Simon, Leia's parents, and Lana have become the gossip of the island ever since Vince came." Lane curses under his breath.

"Thanks, Geode. We'll get something figured out." He gives me another hug before Lane and I set off to see the rest of the Dorian.

"This just doesn't make sense. Something isn't adding up," I mutter. I look to Lane and see shock sprawled across his features.

"I can't believe it took me until now to realize something," Lane says with a staggered look.

"What?" He looks around and slows down so that no one will hear us.

"Did you ever think about how weird it is that over a millennium has passed and the information we got in our classes about the other ecospheres and Earth is somehow accurate and up to date?" I shake my head. "The detail that is discussed. I mean, Sentri was *exactly* like it was taught to us. Obviously, we don't know how the rest of Earth is now and can't know if those histories are true, but think about it, Adira. There's only one way that we can be getting such exact information about outside of Maurea." Shocks rolls through me as realization hits.

"Someone's been in contact with the outside this whole time."

25

WE QUICKLY DISCOVER just how true Geode's words are as we make our way through the mass of people. Skeptical gazes follow us as people stop what they're doing to whisper to the person next to them. Anger rolls through me at Lane's father for the amount of damage that he's managed to do in such a short period of time. He took advantage of the fear of our people and used it to manipulate. I don't know what his endgame is with this, but I'm determined to find out.

"Addi!" I turn to see Avery running toward Lane and me. I bend down just in time for him to jump into my arms. Avery's shoulders start shaking with sobs. I bury my face into his curls and hold back my own tears as I squeeze him as tight as I can.

"I missed you," he says between sniffles. I look into his face and wipe away the tears on his cheeks.

"I missed you, too. How're you doing?" He looks to both sides of us and bends closer to whisper in my ear.

"I know you're not crazy, Addi. I've been telling all the other kids that you're too smart and that Paul is a big fat liar," he says with trembling lips. I give him a hard kiss on the forehead.

"Thank you, Avery. We'll get everything figured out, okay?" He sniffles and nods. "Where's Mom at?" He wipes his nose before taking my hand and silently leading me. Lane follows beside me. Every time someone gives us a wary look, Avery glares back at them in the most obvious way he can. I can't help the smile that comes to my lips at his blatant display of loyalty. I missed him much. He's such a smart kid. We come up to one of the makeshift tents, and Avery lets go of my hand to run inside. No more than a couple seconds later, my mom comes bursting out of the tent and freezes for a moment when she sees me. She comes out of her trance after a moment and rushes toward me and pulls me into a bone-crushing hug. After a moment, she leans back to look at me from head to toe.

"Are you hurt at all?"

"I did something stupid at one point and got hurt. But I'm okay now. They took really great care of me." She hushes me and looks around to make sure that no one heard.

"Let's talk inside." She gestures toward the tent. We make our way into the tight space and sit on the sandy ground. Lane takes my hand, and my mom notices the gesture. A small smile tugs at her lips.

"I'm so happy to see you two. But things are . . . complicated here," she says.

"Geode filled us in on most of it. My father seems to have started up quite an unrest." Lane's jaw tics, one of his signs of his growing frustration.

"That's one word for it. Simon and I seem to be the only ones that haven't believed a word of it," she says, taking my other hand.

"Hey!" Avery shouts. My mom smooths the hair out of his face. "And you, darling."

"Can we leave these packages in here for now? I know there isn't much room, but we need them somewhere safe in the meantime." She gives our packages a skeptical look before nodding. We pile all of them into one corner of the tent. I role out my shoulders now that the weight is finally off of them. Lane and I exchange glances before I look back to Mom and Avery.

"Mom, we're going to need to speak to Simon privately." She nods and starts fidgeting.

"What is it?" Lane asks.

"Is it true? What Vince said? Is there a place for us to go?" she asks barely above a whisper. I smile warmly at her.

"Yes. It is a dangerous place with all the different creatures that are there, but the Amoran are *good* people. And they've been able to keep us safe and are willing to teach us how to be safe there as well. They're different than us in some ways, but they're very kindhearted. As long as we respect their culture and values, there would be no issue with some of us moving there." A tentative smile goes across Mom's face.

"I'll take you to Simon," she says as she stands and leaves the tent. I give Avery a kiss on the top of his head before following after her. Lane follows close behind me as we weave around tents and people until we come up on one slightly isolated from the rest. Mom gestures toward it and takes my hand and gives it a slight squeeze.

"Let me know if you need anything, okay? And I mean anything." I wrap her into a hug.

"I will, Mom." She clutches me tight and whispers in my ear, "You will tell me about you and Lane later." She lets go of me and gives me a subtle wink before walking back the way we came. Lane and I exchange glances before slipping into the tent. Simon startles at seeing us.

"Hi, Simon," I mutter. He quickly stands and wraps me in a hug. All of these hugs are starting to irritate my injuries, but I won't complain.

"Vince had told me you were hurt. I'm happy to see you both alive and well." He takes Lane's hand and gives it a firm shake. The formality of it seems strange to me in a moment like this.

"I'm glad you feel that way. We know you're in the minority," Lane says. Simon releases a heavy sigh.

"I'm afraid your father has made quite a mess of things."

"We know all about that. That's not why we're here," I say. Simon gives me a contemplative look before gesturing to continue.

"We need to know how you know all of the information about outside of Maurea. There's no way that with no means of recording the information, that we've been able to have as accurate of information of the outside world that we do." Simon nods.

"I was wondering when one of you would ask. You're a smart group, and I wish I had a better answer for you. Paul's father was the one who passed our group the information that we received that we have, in turn, passed to you. I, too, was suspicious of the amount of information that was passed along for a millennium. But that wasn't the only thing that stood out during my time of coming into the Legions." His voice drops lower. "We were halfway through our lessons of the outside world before one day, Paul came in claiming some of the information was wrong. Nothing terribly far off. Just little edits here and there. Things that could get construed with the test of time."

"Like he was told information by someone else," Lane utters. Simon nods.

"After that, Paul was the one that passed on the information to us. He claimed his father had told him everything else and that the responsibility of teaching it had fallen on him. He tried to use this as a means to become head Legion, but the rest of us decided against it and chose Pandora." Lane lets out a humorless laugh.

"I'm sure he loved that."

"Quite the opposite. He distanced himself from the rest of the Legions after that. Showed up for his base duties and did nothing more. Never weighed in on big decisions and acted as if he didn't care whether or not the Dorian thrived. Daniel and I tried to talk to him, but he wouldn't hear it. He kept saying that 'none of this matters anyway.' We were never able to change his outlook." I look toward Lane and can see the gears working in his mind.

"What're you thinking?" I ask.

"I'm thinking it's time we had a conversation with Dad."

It isn't hard to find where Lane's parents have decided to set up their own camp. They're right in the center of what is now Maurea and have twice as much supplies as everyone else. Their tent is somehow larger as well. As we get nearer to the tent, Lane reaches forward and grabs my hand. His grip is tight, and his hand has a slight tremble to it. I squeeze him back and rub my thumb across the back of his hand. He stops in front of the entrance to the tent.

"I've got you," I whisper. His grip loosens slightly, and he gives me a half smile that doesn't meet his eyes. He bends over and kisses my cheek.

"Thank you." I give his hand one last squeeze before he pushes the tent flap aside and walks in. Paul and Camille seem to be in the middle of their dinner. Camille startles at the sight of us, whereas Paul behaves as if we are expected visitors.

"Lane, darling! You've come home!" Camille shrieks as she runs to her son and throws herself at him. I make to let go of his hand so he can properly embrace her, but he squeezes my hand tighter, so I stay where I am. Camille notices and looks down at our entwined hands and puts on a broad smile, but not before a look of contempt briefly crosses over her features. Paul slowly stands from his seat and saunters over to us as if this is the most casual of meetings. I have to remind myself that punching him in the throat wouldn't exactly do us any good at the moment.

"Adira, son, it's good to see you," he says as he outstretches his arms and moves toward Lane to embrace. Lane steps back.

"Oh, is it?" Paul's smile faulters for a moment before he regains his composure.

"Of course. We've been terribly worried about you," Paul says matter-of-factly.

"I bet. What with us being brainwashed and having to live with savages in a terrible and hostile world." The same jaw tic that I see in Lane appears in his father. He quickly glances toward me and down at our hands before looking back at his son.

"Perhaps we should speak privately, son. You needn't worry your bride on such things."

"Oh, this bride is fine hearing of such things," I quip. I see his hand twitch, and I can tell he's not used to being talked back to, and he's itching to use his hand for other things. Lane notices the movement, and I see his shoulders tense as he grinds his teeth together. We aren't off to a great start.

"Paul, we wanted to reiterate what Vince came and told you. Sentri is a safe place for our people to go. There are things we would need to learn, but the Amoran people are welcoming and willing to teach us everything we need to know on how to survive," I state. Camille goes from over-expressive to seemingly trying to disappear into the tent wall. My statement is met with silence. Paul eventually cools his face back to a look of indifference.

"And I am so happy to hear that, Adira. But I'm afraid without any sort of proof of this, we have no way to confirm this as truth."

"Why isn't our word enough?" Lane asks. Paul's jaw ticks again as he averts his gaze toward his son.

"The word of any man is just that. A word," he says between clenched teeth.

"It seems as though your word was enough to convince the entirety of the Dorian that Sentri isn't safe and that we are untrustworthy. What makes you think that your word is so different from mine?" Lane challenges. Paul's mask of indifference faulters further.

"Because, son, you are an *Heir*. And I am *Legion*. There is no—"

"One of the Legions," I interrupt. His eyes widen at my intrusion, and Lane shifts his body slightly to stand between me and Paul.

"I'm sorry?" He seethes. I don't back down.

"You called yourself *Legion*. It's not a thing. You are a part of *the* Legions." I note a small look of panic before he gives me a guise of irritation. He opens his mouth to speak, and I cut him off again.

"It's clear we aren't getting anywhere here. We'll leave you be." I look over toward Camille and see blatant shock. I turn to leave, and Paul grabs me by my arm. His grip is so tight that pain immediately shoots up to my shoulder.

"I don't believe this conversation is even close to over," he says between clenched teeth. Lane grabs Paul's arm that is squeezing me.

"Let. Go of her," he says with a soft voice that promises violence.

Paul's grip tightens on my arm as he turns toward his son and challenges, "And what exactly are you going to do about it?" For a moment, I can see the little boy that Lane was, cowering before his abusive father. For just a moment, there is fear in his eyes. It's enough that Paul notices, and his mouth lifts in a sneer. But almost as quickly as the fear came, determination and rage replace it. Sweat starts to bead on Paul's upper lip and forehead as he stares Lane down. He finally notices that there is more to the Lane standing before him than there was when he left. Physically and mentally. He hasn't been training long enough for there to be obvious differences, but if you look closely, they're there. There's more definition to the muscles he already had, and new ones that weren't in as much use before are becoming more prominent. Lane tightens his grip so hard that his knuckles turn white.

"I said. Let go of her," he says in the same quiet voice. Camille is sobbing in the corner, and it takes everything in me to not scream at her. Where was this sadness and panic when Lane was being beaten? All of a sudden you're a concerned wife and mother now that Lane might have the upper hand? My hand is slowly turning purple from Paul's grip on my arm. Finally, he releases it. After another moment, Lane releases his own grasp. He goes to stand toe to toe with his father.

"If you ever lay a hand on her again, make no mistake. I will kill you." I turn toward the entrance of the tent to hide the smirk that lights up my face. We leave Paul and Camille behind and head toward my mom and Avery.

"Well, that was quite the threat," I muse. He grabs my hand as we continue forward.

"It wasn't a threat. I would tear apart every world for you, Adira." I swallow the lump in my throat and look up at the man who I've grown to love more than anyone. We're surrounded by skeptical gazes, but in that moment, I don't care. I stop us in our tracks and throw my arms around his neck and bring his mouth down to mine. Lane picks me up, and I wrap my legs around him as he holds me up with one hand and plunges his hand into my hair with the other. After several gasps and even a few whistles, I break our kiss and rest my forehead against his.

"I love you so much," I whisper. A soft chuckle escapes him.

"You don't know how long I've waited to hear those words from you."

"You'll never stop hearing it," I say as he sets me down. "Till this and every other world burns."

26

BY THE TIME we make it back to Mom and Avery's tent, the whole of Maurea has heard of our arrival. I do my best to ignore the apprehensive gazes that follow us, but I can't help but feel betrayed. These are people that I took care of, people I was friends with, people I grew up with my entire life. One word from someone who doesn't seem to care the least bit about them has completely derailed the way in which they view me. The way they view *us*.

When we make it back to the tent, Mom is cooking fish over a fire, and Avery is sorting through some shells and has them organized into two piles. I sit on the ground next to him and pick up a shell that I recognize as the last one I most recently gave him. I'm surprised he was able to find it after the storm. I set it back down in one of the piles, and he quickly picks it up and moves it to the other.

"What're the piles for, Avery?" He points toward the one closest to him.

"This one is Liam's. The other one is mine." My mom flinches slightly, and my stomach drops. I can't imagine how hard it has been for Avery with losing his other half. I've had things keeping my mind and body extremely occupied that made it easier to cope with the loss of my brother. Avery has had very little. With nothing around, I can't imagine the dark places my mind would've wandered to. In that moment, I'm extremely grateful that Avery isn't older than his six years. The obliviousness that comes with youth is something to be envied. Lane plops down next to Avery and picks up one of the shells in Liam's pile.

"Ahh, a junonia! A good find. One of my personal favorites," he says examining the shell. Avery smiles up at him.

"That one was Liam's favorite. It has exactly twenty-seven spots on it." Lane nods and sets it back down. His eyes meet mine, and I give him an appreciative smile. Mom takes the fish off of the spike and serves it out to each of us. As I chew on the savory meal, I can't help but miss the many spices that come with a meal in Sentri.

"So, are you going to tell me what is in the packages you brought?" my mom asks in a hushed tone.

"Supplies, medicine, things to help everyone here. While we're here over the next few days, I can teach some on how to use certain herbs for different ailments, and Lane can show people how to use the other materials to help fortify the shelters you've already put up." She nods and glances around, always making sure no one is listening.

"You'll have to go about this in a smart way, Adira. You know that people don't exactly trust you right now. I have a hard time believing that anyone here is going to just use a medicine from a different world when there's already been a speculative narrative set when it comes to you two and this *other* place." She has a point. This had been nagging at the back of my mind. There are things at play here though that take precedent. I can teach Mom how to use the herbs and plants easy enough in case there is an emergency, and she can work at divvying out supplies as people become less apprehensive. For now, my focus is on Paul. All we know is that it was Paul who's had contact with the outside. I plan to find out who that person is, and what the outside even *is*.

We have two days before we need to be headed back to Sentri. I can only hope that in that time, Paul decides to make a move.

Lane and I gather our own supplies and set up our own camp that is close enough to Paul and Camille's that we will be able to keep watch to see if he tries to sneak off anywhere. The hard part is making it look like we aren't watching him, which is particularly difficult when every pair of eyes within a fifteen-foot radius seems to be on us. We can assume he's been talking with someone on the outside. The question is how.

"What do we do if he doesn't go anywhere before we need to head back?" I voice my concerns.

"I think he will," he says matter-of-factly.

"How do you know?" He glances at my arm where finger-shaped bruises have started to form.

"We both stood up to him today. That isn't something he's used to. He needs to be the one in power, the one in charge. We took that from him today." He looks toward his parents' tent. "He'll take back that power in one way or another. In some way, he'll act on that urge before we leave. Of that, I'm positive." A grim look crosses over his features. I bring my hand up and press my thumb to the crease between his eyebrows. He looks down at me, and his gaze softens.

"Today was the first time you stood up to him," I whisper. He puts his hands on my hips and pulls me in closer.

"Yes," he says in a gravely tone.

"*Why?*" I finally ask the question that has been burning in the back of my mind ever since I found out about the abuse. Ever since I can remember, Lane has been one of the most physically fit males that I've ever seen. My guess is that by his fifteenth year, he could've stood up to his father's hand.

"There's an inherit fear that he was able to put into me. Part of me knew when I would be able to best him in a fight, but it was like he could see that in my eyes every time the thought came whenever he would . . .," he chokes off. I nod and wait patiently for him to continue on his own time. "Anyway . . . it's like he could tell, and he had a way of crushing the notion right then and there. After a while, it was just easier to shut down. Go someplace else for a while and pretend it wasn't happening. He made sure I felt nothing for myself.

He made sure I never had a *reason* to stand up to him." His hands squeeze tighter on my hips. "Then he touched you." His eyes darken. I put my arms around his neck and pull him close until we're pressed up against each other.

"Lane . . . I know what he did to you your entire life has made you think terrible things about yourself. But from here on forward, I need you to fight for yourself as hard as you fight for me." My bottom lip starts quivering. "Because you aren't nothing. You're *everything*." My voice breaks. He tilts my head up by my chin with a gentle hand until I meet his gaze.

"I promise," he whispers before bending down and brushing his lips against mine. "Why don't I take the first watch. You get some sleep." I know there's no point in arguing, so I nod and make my way into our small, temporary home and do my best to get comfortable. The fatigue of my body takes precedent over my rushing thoughts, and it isn't long before I slip into blissful oblivion.

When Lane nudges me, my first thought is that he's tired and it's my turn to be on watch. But he puts a finger to his lips, telling me to remain silent, and points toward his parents' camp. Paul is casually standing outside of his tent and coolly looking around as if he's just checking on all of his people. He takes a step toward the nearest tent to him and listens for a moment before moving on to the next.

"He's checking to see that everyone is asleep," Lane whispers in my ear. Just then, Paul turns in our direction, and I quickly pull Lane down next to me. He lies on the ground and puts his arm around me as I lie on his chest. We both pretend to sleep as I strain to hear Paul's footsteps. It's subtle. So subtle that if you weren't actively listening for it, you wouldn't know that it was there. But I track his movements around us for what feels like over an hour before I hear the steps progressively coming closer and closer. It feels like my heart is beating out of my chest. It must be, because Lane starts to rub small, soothing circles on my back with his thumb to try to relax me. I focus on my breathing until I hear the footsteps stop right outside our tent. I fight the urge to hold my breath. Sleeping people don't hold their breath, Adira. Even with my eyes closed, I can feel the loathsome stare that he glowers into me. Can he hear how hard my heart is pounding? I feel the strongest impulse to fidget under his odious stare. But luckily, after what feels like a lifetime, he turns and walks away. Lane and I wait another minute before we open our eyes and dare to sit up. Right as I peek my head out of the tent, I see Paul look both ways before heading toward the north shore. Lane and I exchange a glance before he nods, and we're off on silent feet. We hop from tent to tent, making sure that we keep our distance. Once Paul gets to the waterline, he takes off his shirt and plunges underwater without a second glance. Lane and I straighten.

"Do we follow?" I ask. Lane shakes his head.

"If he were for some reason to turn around and see us following, we'd be screwed."

"Why would he turn around?"

"Because he's careful. Calculated. He took his time making sure the whole of Maurea was asleep before he snuck away. It's too big a risk." Lane lets out a curse. Then, an idea comes to me. I grab his hand and turn him toward me.

"What if he *was* being followed but didn't think twice about it?" He looks at me in confusion. "Do you trust me?"

"Always," he says without hesitation. I quickly peck him on the cheek and run toward the west shore, where I know there are a large population of crustaceans not too far. I breathe deep and plunge under the water and wait for my eyes to adjust to the darkness of the ocean. It isn't long before our salvation comes floating up to my left side. Without pause, I start swimming toward where Paul went under. Luckily, he hasn't gotten far enough to be out of the light of the full moon that breaks the ocean's surface. I turn toward Luna and point toward him. I make the gesture multiple times and will her to *please* know what I'm trying to ask of her. After a moment, she leaves my side and drifts toward Paul. A triumphant smile breaks across my face, and I quickly turn around to get out of Paul's line of sight. When I break the surface, Lane is already waiting for me on shore. I run up to him and give him a hard kiss, thoroughly soaking him.

He doesn't seem to mind. A smile lights up his face when he sees my gleeful expression.

"What is it?" he asks.

"We humans don't deserve animals." The answer seems to placate him enough for now. He wraps his arm around my shoulders as we make our way back to our tent. When we get back, Lane immediately lies down and looks like he could fall asleep any second. I give him a kiss on his forehead.

"I'll take over watch for the rest of the night." He takes my hand and pulls me down next to him. "Lane, I'm soaking wet."

"Well, I'm flattered, darling." I swat at his arm and sit up.

"One of us should stay on watch. What if he comes back?" He sighs louder than needed.

"If he wanted to kill us, he would have earlier. But he didn't. Because he's not *that* stupid. Come here," he says tugging on my hand again. "Rest, baby." I heave a twin sigh and lie down next to him. He pulls my back into his chest, and it isn't long before his breathing becomes even with the rhythm of sleep. As I feel myself drifting off, I reflect on how much has changed since the last time I slept on Maurean soil. I think of the way I viewed the man who now holds me. My last thought before I drift to sleep is of the utter gratitude I have to have been so completely wrong.

27

LANE AND I wake up early the next morning. Lane stifles a yawn while I stretch out my tense muscles. I start to rub out a knot in my shoulder before Lane replaces my hand and starts working it harder. It feels so good that a small noise escapes me, and he chuckles.

"Don't tease me this early in the morning, love," he says in a low gruff. I laugh and turn around to pull his mouth to mine. His tongue teases on my lips, and I laugh and pull away.

"Don't *you* tease me this early in the morning," I snide. He laughs and gives me a quick peck on the nose before stretching and leaving the tent. I follow close behind. Most of Maurea still sleeps.

"When do you want to try and see where Dad went?" he asks after surveying around. I look toward his parents' tent. Neither of them has come out. I'd guess that Paul would probably be sleeping in later due to his late-night activities.

"Maybe we should go now. While everyone else is asleep?" He contemplates for a second before shaking his head.

"It'll raise too much suspicion. We clearly aren't welcome here. We'll make an excuse to leave, and we'll make a quick pit stop before heading back to Sentri." I nod and turn to break down the tent. I have to give Mom the instructions on how to use everything that we've brought.

"Let me go talk to Mom and Avery. Can you give me a couple hours?" He nods and kisses my forehead before I set off toward their tent. Mom is awake and making breakfast while Avery is still fast asleep.

"Good morning," I say softly as I walk into the tent. She gives me a bright smile as a greeting and gestures for me to follow her outside.

"Me and Lane need to leave today. We might be able to figure out some things. We need to go over everything that I've brought so that if an emergency comes up that you guys can't handle, you have some backup for it. If people ask where it comes from, make something up. I don't care. Just get people the help they need." She nods sympathetically.

"I'm sorry they don't appreciate everything that you've done and are doing for them," she says, taking my hand. I give it a squeeze.

"I think I can survive without the fawning of our people," I say with a chuckle.

"Well, some people can't," she says looking toward Paul's tent. I duck inside to grab the packages we brought, and then we spend the next hour and a half going over every plant, root, and serum I brought. I make Mom repeat everything back to me three times before I deem she knows everything well enough. By the time we're done, most of Maurea is awake, and Avery is munching on some dried seaweed. I ruffle his hair, and he gives me a broad smile with plenty of green interspersed throughout his white grin. A laugh bubbles out of me, and I give Avery a kiss on the top of his crazy hair. His grin falters for a moment before he takes another bite of his food.

"Do you have to go, Addi?" he asks after a minute. When he looks back up at me, I can see his eyes have started watering. I wipe the hair off of his forehead and give him a sympathetic smile.

"Not much longer. We'll all be living together again soon."

"Aren't you going to live with Lane?" My smile turns more genuine.

"Yeah, I think I will. But we're going to be real close. Close enough that we will get to see you every single day if you want," I add with a wink. His smile plasters back onto his face.

"I like him. He helped me with my swimming a lot," he says, fidgeting with the food in his lap. My brow furrows as I look over to where Lane is helping Mom reorganize the supplies.

"When did he do that?" He shrugs.

"When me and Liam started getting to do the longer swims." My breath catches in my throat. Once we reach four years is usually when those more extended swims start happening. He's been tutoring my brothers for two years, and I had no idea.

"He even asked me and Liam if he could ask you to be his person," he says matter-of-factly.

"What do you mean?" He shrugs again.

"He says he would have asked Dad, but Dad wasn't around. So, he asked us." I feel tears sting from behind my eyes. He let me treat him like a glorified man-whore for our entire lives, and here he was, helping my brothers for years without any sort of recognition.

"Why didn't you ever tell me?" I ask. He looks up at me with a mischievous look.

"He said it was our little *secret*. He said we were the only two people in Maurea that knew an unmatched pair before the ceremony." I can't help but chuckle at the hilarious craving that my brothers always had to be special and different in some way possible. Little did they know that they are the most special young boys out there just by being their crazy selves. As I look down at Avery, I'm overwhelmed with grief for Liam. Part of me feels like I'm looking at a ghost when I see him. The two looked so alike; but with every year that they got older, their own differences stood out more. Avery is missing the freckle that Liam had on his left cheek. Avery has a brown spot in one of his eyes that was visible in the sunlight that Liam didn't have. I just now realized that Liam's hair was curlier too. The tears spill over, and I crush my beautiful brother to me.

"I love you," I say between sniffles. He hugs me back and squeezes as tight as he can.

"I love you, too, Addi." Lane comes ambling over and concern crosses his features when he notices my crying. I just wave it off. If I get into it right now with him, I will fall to pieces, and we've got things to do. He gives me a soft smile.

"Ready to go?" I nod and give Avery's curls one last kiss before standing and heading over to hug my mom again. As I separate from our embrace, I see Paul and Camille sauntering over toward us. I try to drop my face into the mask of indifference I've seen Lane don so many times.

"Leaving so soon?" Paul asks with feigned pleasantness.

"We know when our presence is unwanted," Lane replies indifferently. A flare of anger flashes in Paul's eyes.

"I thought that Vince had passed on that we wanted you here. Back *home*." His jaw ticks. Lane remains a pillar of coolness.

"Yes, well, being that I'm a grown-ass adult, we've made other plans. But I'm sure we'll see you around soon, Dad," he says with a grin that doesn't meet his eyes. Paul's mask faulters, and Camille puts her arm through Paul's and does her best to diffuse the anger she sees brewing in her husband.

"Do come back soon, darling. We miss you." Her gaze shoots to me, and I see real malice. I can see how badly she wants to be rid of me. She really thinks it's all my fault that Lane has decided to step away from his parents. As if it had nothing to do with her husband's abuse and her allowance of it over the years. I give her a spiteful smile in return.

Try me.

We waste no time as we head toward the shore and dive underwater. It doesn't take long for Luna to find us. She pauses for a moment on my left before swimming on as we follow close behind. The water cools as we swim deeper and deeper into the ocean. The deeper we go, the darker it gets; and within ten minutes, Lane and I are swimming close enough to feel the movement of each other's strokes rather than relying on our eyes to both watch each other while trying to keep an eye on the slight glimmer of Luna's skin. Five minutes later, it's getting to a point where I'm having a hard time following. Right when I'm about to stop Lane to turn around, Luna swims back toward us and stops. Lane grabs my hand as she swims around us and heads back the way we came. I try to look around, but with barely any light leaking through this far down, it feels practically helpless. I reach down and feel mushy sand. We've reached the bottom of this part of the ocean. Without letting go of my hand, Lane swims forward slightly and reaches out with his other to start feeling around. I don't know what he's expecting to find other than open water, but I mimic the actions. After seventeen minutes, I'm starting to get uncomfortable. We're going to have to pause on the way up, and we just screwed ourselves out of the time to do it. I expected too much of Luna. We should have just followed the night before. I start to panic and flail my other arm around hoping to feel something. *Anything.* All of a sudden, my foot rams into a hard surface. I tug on Lane's arm, and I feel him reach forward and find the surface I'm touching. He feels around it before he pauses and squeezes my hand once before letting go. After a moment, a large groan sounds, and what seems to be a door swings open from the ocean floor. Fear paralyzes me for a moment. If we go down there and there's nothing but water, we're dead. But going up is hardly an option anymore either, so I reach out for Lane's hand again, and we sink down into the hole the door left. Lane reaches up and closes it behind us, and light fills the small space. The water starts draining. The second my mouth is clear, I start gulping in air. Lane does the same. Once all of the water is drained, the light starts to flash red for a few seconds before another door we hadn't even noticed pops open. Lane and I exchange a glance before creeping forward on silent feet. It feels like we've walked onto another planet.

Everything is hard and cold. The ground we walk on, the walls we pass, everything is a shiny variant of gray. Long pathways split off every few dozen feet, and we have no idea which way to go. After five minutes of going straight, Lane decides we should make a turn. The second we do, we see two people walking toward us with their heads down looking at what looks like another gray object that has light coming up from it. We quickly backtrack and run down another path until the couple passes. We aren't going to get answers by avoiding where people might go, so we go down the hallway they came from. We pass through two doors that swing open on their own volition, and I try to suppress the dread that is rising in my chest. We go farther until some of the walls start being replaced by something see-through. I run my fingers across it and is surprised to see my touch make a mark. When I try to wipe it away, a larger smudge just replaces the small one that was there. I make a mental note to *not* touch anything else as we continue forward, peeking into each room through the see-through walls. Whenever we hear voices coming near us, we head to another break in the path to hide on the other side until they pass. Lane is about to go forward down the path we were hiding on, but I stop him as I hear the voices come in more clearly.

"Phase two is almost ready to begin. Paul has ensured that he has the situation under control, and the timeline doesn't need to be adjusted."

"He can't possibly know that," seethes a second voice. "With the damn primates tampering with our surveillance in Sentri, we have no way of knowing what's going on there, and the tsunami took out all of the surveillance in Maurea. So, please. Enlighten me about how he possibly has things under control." The first man stutters for a moment before finally being able to speak.

"W-we were able to give him a camera to attach to his tent tonight. He's assured us that it will be up by tonight. A-and he said that his son has recently returned from Sentri." Lane flinches beside me. "He's confident that he can get everyone from Maurea back to where they belong."

"And if he can't?" the second voice spits.

"He's assured us that he'll take care of the problem either way." I feel myself pale as I realize exactly how he would intend to "take care of the problem." The one who is obviously in charge scoffs.

"I don't like balancing this many years of hard work on one man's ego. Sentri wasn't scheduled to undergo any sort of disturbances for another decade, and those brats being there is continuing to *disturb* plans that have been in motion for a millennium." The first man audibly swallows.

"Sir, the experiment was an enormous success. Surely you see that? And with the girl, we can gather more information. More research on the genome," he says in a hopeful tone.

"So, we just stop then? Say good enough is good enough? Phase two of this has been riding on the backs of scientists for generations. Know this. I will personally throw you to the ravagers if this project gets blown to hell. Consider Paul's mistakes your mistakes. Get those kids out of Sentri and get things moving on time."

"Yes, yes, of course, sir," the first man says with a wobble to his voice. I hear his footsteps starting to retreat before the second man stops him.

"I want more progress on the girl. Things are moving too slow with her, and if you think I'm rough on you about this, Williams, you do not want to see what *my* boss will do to you if he is unsatisfied."

"But-but, sir, she's barely recovered from all of her previous injuries. With what we're taking now, if we increase the tests and extractions, it could kill her." Something akin to a growl comes out of the man.

"Keep. Her. Alive. I don't need her sane, I don't need her happy. But if what we think we're seeing on her recent readings is correct, we need her heart beating. Do I make myself clear?" There's a short pause.

"Do I MAKE MYSELF CLEAR!" Williams drops whatever he's holding in his hands and blubbers out apologies.

"Yes. Crystal. Absolutely clear." Without another word, the terrible man's steps start retreating in the opposite direction. Williams gathers his things and hurries off down another pathway. I don't realize my hands are shaking until Lane grabs hold of them and kisses them silently before giving me a smile that doesn't reach his eyes. I feel like we just got some of the answers we were looking for, but somehow it left even more questions in its wake. Lane stands up, and we take the other path that neither of the two men went down. When we pass through another set of doors that opens on their own,

I automatically start looking around into the rooms on each side. We're about to turn down another way before I stop in my tracks and all the blood drains from my face. I feel myself faulter and my legs give out. Lane grabs me before I fall and takes my face in his hands.

"Baby? What is it?" I look beyond him toward a glass room. He turns to follow my gaze. His body tenses the moment he sees. Silent tears stream down my face.

"Leia?"

28

MY STOMACH DROPS, and for a moment, I'm worried I'll vomit all over the cold floor. Lane's face turns a shade of gray. My feet move on their own volition toward Leia. Once I get to the door that separates us, I try to pull it open, but it stays firmly shut. At the noise, Leia's eyes open, and I watch them shatter as she sees us. Tears immediately well up in her eyes and pour over. That's all she can do with all of the . . . things sticking out of her. Small, sturdy tubes are coming out of every place that they could manage. One is stuck down her throat. Two more are sticking into each arm. One of them looks to be putting stuff into her while another is taking blood out. There's a gray, circular device that's attached to both of her hips and both of her kneecaps. They look to be driven all the way to her bone. I want to scream. I want to tear this cold, gray prison to pieces until it burns. Never in my life have I ever wanted to harm someone; but as I think of the man who probably just ordered for whatever they're doing to her to be increased, hatred pools in my stomach and manifests into something dark inside of me that I've never experienced before. I think back on his words . . . "I don't need her sane. I don't need her happy. I need her heart beating." My fists clench at my sides, and I count to ten. Hunting him down and doing any of the number of things running through my head right now isn't going to help Leia.

I try the door again, but it still doesn't budge. Leia's eyes look behind us, and panic takes over her features. We turn to see the man who I imagine is Williams is staring at us with wide eyes and trembling from head to toe. Luckily, Lane is smarter and quicker than I am and lunges forward before Williams can scream. He quickly puts his hand over his mouth and taps at a pressure point with lightning speed. Williams goes slack, and Lane catches him. He looks up at me and blows a lock of hair out of his eyes.

"Well, shit," he mutters. I turn back to Leia, and I see her try and reach her hand up. She starts weakly gesturing to her chest. I get as close as I can to the see-through wall to try and see what she's showing me. Is there another tube there that I can't see? I shake my head in frustration, and she feebly points beyond me toward Lane and Williams and then gestures back at her chest. I look toward him and then back at Leia. Her eyes widen. She points more aggressively at her chest and then back at Williams. I look down at the spot on his chest that she's pointing to on her own. There's a small white thing with a depiction on it that looks exactly like him. I snatch it off of his clothes and hold it up so Leia can see. Her eyes widen even more, and she points toward the door. Is this a key of some sort? There's no hole to put it into. I start muttering curse words under my breath, and Lane comes over to try and help. He takes notice of a small black part of the wall that has a red light into it. He takes the key from my hands and gestures it toward the light. It beeps and turns green, and I hear a click on the door. Elation floods through me, and I push the door open. I give Lane a huge peck on the cheek before running in. He grabs Williams and tosses him over his shoulder before following after me.

I approach her quickly, but I stop before I touch her. I'm afraid I'll break her. My hands hover as I take inventory of her condition. She's so skinny. Her collarbones are sticking out of her, and if I move the small dress covering her, I can see her ribs sticking out of her sides. Tears well up in my eyes again.

"I'm sorry. I'm so, so sorry, Leia. We never should have left you. I'm so, so sorry," I blubber over and over again. She grabs my hand and squeezes it. Her eyes soften, and she nods. I look at all the tubes surrounding her, and I worry that if I pull any of them out, something bad will happen. This is beyond my capabilities as a healer. I don't know what to do with this kind of technology. I turn toward Lane, who is still holding an unconscious Williams. I eye the bed next to Leia's.

"Put him on the bed," I order him. He flops him down as I scramble around the room looking for something to tie him down. I find some tubes that look to be similar to the ones that are in her arms and deem them as good as I'm going to get in here. I only have two, so I tie his hands to an opening in the bed. Lane can handle holding down his feet. I pick up some sort of cloth that was lying next to the tubes and shove it in his mouth. I find a small, thin knife on top of a small table grab it.

"Can you wake him up?"

"He should wake soon anyway. He was starting to stir a little bit starting about a minute ago. I was about to hit him again." I nod and stand by his head, holding the small knife to his throat. After about another minute, his eyes flutter open. There's a moment of peace, then replaced by confusion. When his eyes focus on me, utter terror. His legs start to kick, and Lane grabs on to them and holds them down to the bed.

"Let me make myself completely clear," I say in the same quiet voice promising violence that I've learned from Lane.

"If you scream, or in some way make our presence here known, I will not hesitate in the slightest. Do I make myself clear?" I apply enough pressure with the knife for the smallest trickle of blood seep out. His eyes water, and he nods slightly. I take the cloth out of his mouth, and he starts whimpering. I stifle the sympathy I start to feel for him and focus.

"How do I take these out of her?" I gesture toward the tubes connected to Leia. He swallows once.

"I can do it. I can get her out if you—"

"If you think for a second I'm going to let you touch her, you're out of your mind." He blinks and swallows a lump in his throat.

"Okay . . . Go get some gauze from the cabinet and hold it over where the needle is going into her skin and just pull it out gently. Keep the gauze there for the blood," he says in a trembling voice.

"English, asshole," Lane seethes. He looks between us with a gaze of confusion for a second before realization hits.

"Right. Of course, you don't know what a gauze and needle and all of that is. Um . . . okay, go over to that cart right there." He gestures his head toward the small table. I walk over to it and look back toward him.

"Okay, open that top drawer. Good, now start from the left and go over three dividers. You'll see white squares. Grab two of those." I do as he instructs. "Now, carefully take off the tape covering the needle, hold it there and gently pull out the tube by the top of it." I take a couple deep breaths to try to stop my hands from trembling. I take hold of it and pull out gently. The second it's out, I put the gauze on it and hold pressure. I move her arm up so that it will keep the pressure without my having to hold it. I throw the tube on the ground and head over to the one on her other arm and repeat. She gives a resemblance of a sigh and bends her arm up on her own. I look toward Williams.

"The one down her throat?" He looks nervously toward something that has flashing colors all over it.

"Same sort of thing. You'll have to use an empty syringe to deflate a small bubble at the end of it. Then you just gently take it out, but . . . that's the ventilator. It's helping her breathe . . . I was going to try to take it out today, but she might die if you do." My stomach drops. We can't leave her here. I look to Leia, and she nods and gestures with her hand, telling me to take it out.

"For your sake, let's hope she doesn't." I find the empty syringe he speaks of and follow his directions to take out the bubble. Once done, I start pulling slowly, and she immediately starts gagging. I flinch back to stop, but she grabs my hand and nods, urging me to continue. Quicker is best. I grab a hold of the tube again and pull as gently but quickly as I can. She gags until it comes out and coughs for a while before she starts gulping in breaths. I give her a few minutes to breathe as I take her wrist in my hand to feel her pulse.

"You don't have to do that. The monitors will tell you. Her SpO$_2$ is steady, as is her blood pressure and heart rate." I glare over at him and keep my fingers on her pulse. After another minute, she grabs at my hand.

"Hi," she rasps out. Part of me crumbles, and I fall into sobs and hug her the best way I can. Her sobs join mine, and I sit there with her in my arms with guilt and relief flowing through me with even intensity.

"Love, we can't stay here. People are going to come back. We need to go." I wipe at my nose and sniffle before standing and giving him a nod. I turn to Williams.

"What do we do with him?" I ask. Lane looks down at him for a minute, contemplating before going up to the side of him, and he starts undoing his bonds on one hand.

"What are you doing?" I seethe. He ignores me and gets an inch away from Williams's face.

"Congratulations, you're finally going to get to see Sentri." His face blanches, and he starts blubbering.

"I-I-I'm not like you. I can't hold my breath that long. It's impossible for me to get there without drowning." Lane doesn't buy it for a second.

"I think your boss mentioned something about 'surveillance' that kept getting messed up in Sentri. I don't know what the hell that surveillance is, but there has to be a way you're putting it there. And I'd venture that you know exactly how to get there. If not, I'm pretty good at compressions. Maybe you'll get lucky and live," he says with a vengeful grin.

"They'll know. They'll know something is wrong. That someone broke in and took me. They'll know."

"Yeah, well, we'll know a hell of a lot more once we get you talking. But I don't feel like doing it here. You have two options here, Williams. I'm pretty sure you're gathering what the first one is, I suggest you take the second." His face gets impossibly whiter as he considers his options. He eventually nods, and Lane immediately starts undoing his other bonds.

"Where is everyone anyway? We've run into maybe ten people so far," I demand. His bond breaks, and he starts rubbing at his wrist as he sits up.

"It's Christmas today. Only core staff." The three of us exchange looks of confusion. Later. We can ask questions later. I turn to Leia and help her swing her feet off the bed. She tears off the remaining tubes that were sticking to her chest.

"Can you walk?" She nods and tries to take a step before immediately falling. I grab her before her knees hit the ground. Williams curses.

"The marrow collectors. They're in her bones, she won't be able to put weight on her knees." The look he gets from Lane and me is enough to get him trembling again. Lane comes over and bends by Leia as I help her climb onto his back. After he nods, I turn back to Williams, flashing the knife.

"Your show now. Let's go." He swallows another knot in his throat and nods before leading us out of the room. As we run, he checks at every intersection before continuing forward. Whatever this *Christmas* is, I'm grateful for it. Luck was on our side today. We walk down path after path until finally, we come to a dead end with a door that has a similar look to it as the one we came out of. He gestures his key toward a similar red light we saw earlier, and we walk in. Once inside, a red light flashes for a moment before we hear a distinctive *click*. Williams climbs up a ladder and wrenches a door open on the ceiling. The familiar damp, rich smell of Sentri hits me, and I can't help the smile that lights up my face. We all crawl out and find ourselves in a part of Sentri I haven't seen yet. Once we're all out, Williams shuts the door, and it disappears into greenery. If you didn't know it was there, you never would've seen it. Luck continues to be in our favor as it isn't raining. Not yet at least. Lane takes in his surroundings and looks up toward what he can see of the sun through the canopy of trees. After a minute, he starts walking. I don't hesitate to follow.

"Where-where are we going?" Williams wobbles after us.

"Toward our escorts. We aren't far from the pool. We should get there in a few hours," Lane replies dryly.

"Ahh, yes. The pool. The only part of Sentri we really know about. I still can't believe you found the only other entrance in." He gives a humorless laugh.

"What do you mean?" I ask.

"We haven't had a read on Sentri for almost half a decade. We've tried editing the cameras. Making them smaller, making them waterproof, nothing worked. Some creature always found them and either *ate* them or broke it. All except for the one that we put into the stone wall above the pool. That's the only way we knew you all went here, and how we found Leia." He shakes his head. "Hundreds of thousands of dollars lost. The focus shifted to Maurea since we had the most surveillance and control over what was going on there." Lane and I exchange a glance. It's hard to get a real grip on everything he's telling us when we only know half of the terminology he's using. I turn back to him.

"Why are you surprised that we knew about the underwater tunnel to get here? Isn't that part of the knowledge that whatever person you have on the inside has been telling the new Legions every five years?" He shakes his head again.

"A statistical anomaly . . . The five scientists we sent into Maurea knew about the tunnels because they knew *everything*. They were a willing part of the experiment. Whoever was in charge back then didn't clarify that they shouldn't pass on that information. But of all of the original people that were put into each ecosphere, Maurea was the only one that passed on the knowledge of the experiment. We never gave them those updates or reminders as to where they were. Somehow that information got passed down from generation to generation without more than a couple bits of misinformation. Like

I said, statistical anomaly . . . Absolutely fascinating." He babbled on. As he prattled on, he studied everything around him. To his own chagrin, him not keeping an eye on the ground caused him to stumble and fall multiple times. We kept our pace and walked on and let him run to catch up. After an hour, it started to rain, much to Williams's dismay. We stopped by one of the waxy leaf plants to get Leia some water. After having some ourselves, we went on. A couple hours later, the pool comes into view. Williams steps on a twig that snaps, and Zander's head shoots in our direction. His eyes widen when he sees Leia clinging to Lane's back. He starts jogging toward us and pauses when he sees Williams come into view. He trots the rest of the way to us and moves to take Leia off of Lane's back.

"I've got her," Lane says with strained voice. He must be tired by now from carrying her for so long. I offered to take a turn, but he adamantly refused. Zander nods and looks toward Williams for a moment before turning and walking with us toward the pool. Lane walks to the fire and drops down to help Leia off his back. Zander takes most of her weight and lightly lays her down.

"Thanks, Lane," she mutters. She doesn't seem at all shocked or concerned to see not only Zander, but the other Amorans around us. She rests her head on her hands and, within seconds, seems to fall into a deep sleep. Zander looks down at her for a moment before turning toward us and eyeing Williams suspiciously.

"So, uh . . . what the hell happened?"

29

LANE AND I tell Zander and the others everything that happened from the moment we got to Maurea to our arriving back in Sentri. Every once in a while, they'd shoot Williams a hateful glare. After we recalled everything, I went over to Leia to inspect her further. I carefully maneuvered her onto her back so I could check her hips and knees easier. She didn't even stir. I glare over at Williams.

"I need to know everything you did to her." His face pales again. This man doesn't have an ounce of bravery in him. I have to fight against instinct to take pity on him. He's the enemy even if he is a pathetic one.

"Where do you want to begin?" he asks barely above a whisper.

"The tubes in her arms. What were they for?"

"One was taking blood in intervals. The machine connected to her right arm would go off and take blood from her whenever her body had remade enough of it for us to take more without—without killing her." Every pair of eyes was on him. And each one promised violence. He looked around, and his brow started visibly sweating.

"And the other?" I prod.

"The-the other was an IV cocktail of sorts. That's how she got her nutrition and fluids and anything else that we might need to inject her with. There was also a mild sedative in it. Oh, um, a sedative is—"

"I know what a sedative is," I cut him off. He swallows and nods before continuing.

"Between the sedative and the consistent blood loss, we didn't bother with restraints. We figured there was no way for her to escape."

"Looks like you figured wrong," Lane says with feigned coolness. Williams looks nervously toward him.

"Yes. Yes, I suppose so." I stare at him and say nothing until he visibly becomes more uncomfortable.

"And the tube down her throat." He looks down at her.

"She was hours away from death when we got to her. Her lungs were so shot from the combination of fresh and salt water that they didn't work on their own for a while. They might have had a chance, but Stroft insisted upon starting the marrow and blood extraction for studies immediately. We placed the tube on her third day in the lab. As I said earlier, today was the day we were going to try to take her off of it." Silence falls over the camp.

"What is in her hips and knees?" Lane asks in the same cool voice. There's a moment of guilt that flashes in Williams's eyes.

"It was easier to put those in to collect her bone marrow. We would alternate sites. Hip, knee, other hip, other knee. The metal that you see is a guide for the—for the needle to go through for the extraction."

"Needle?" I ask.

"Yes. The small metal tip that you saw at the end of her tubes that you pulled out of her arms. Those are called needles," he explains.

"So, you used a similar needle," I prod. The guilty look flashes in his eyes again.

"Well, n-no. To get to the bone marrow and manage to actually extract it, a larger one was needed." The guilt suddenly made sense.

"What, you could sedate her to keep her from running but couldn't sedate her for you to suck out her marrow like a leech?"

I seethe. His hands start shaking more as he looks around at the furious gazes being shot at him.

"It-it wasn't my choice. They said we had to ration the sedative we had. Our funding wasn't prepared for additional experiments. Leia was a surprise to us all. We couldn't give her more, or we might run out before our fiscal funding came in. We've lost over 90 percent of our financial partners since this project began. Conservation had to be considered," he blubbers.

"Right. Humanity apparently didn't," Lane accuses. Tears start welling up in Williams's eyes. I ignore it and move on.

"Can we take them out?" He sniffles and wipes at his nose and nods.

"Yes. Yes, you can. You'll need a way to keep it disinfected for a few weeks until everything can heal, but I can do it with perhaps the right tools. But it'll hurt. The extraction will hurt. The recovery will hurt."

"Well, unlike you, we aren't monsters. We'll knock her out for the removal and give her what we can for the pain," I retort.

"Yes. Yes, of course." He keeps his chin lowered, hardly ever meeting my eyes. I look to Lane and Zander.

"I want Kira there when we do it. We'll take turns carrying her back to camp tomorrow." They both nod.

"What're we doing about him?" Zander nods toward Williams. He seems to stop breathing at the mention of him.

"We need more information. He comes with."

"Right, but what are we supposed to *do* with him?" I look at him for a second and then back down at Leia. Anger takes precedent over every emotion running through me.

"He doesn't need to be sane. He doesn't need to be happy. I just need his heart beating."

I leave Williams as a blubbering mess as I stand up quickly and stalk away from camp.

"Where are you going?" Zander asks.

"To forage for some things to help Leia in the meantime until I can get back to my own stash at camp." I trudge forward through the rain. Every drop that rolls off of me feels like it falls to the ground contaminated by the rage emanating off of my skin. As thunder rolls and lightning strikes in the sky, I imagine Sentri fuming with fury alongside me. After a few moments, I hear footsteps rushing behind me. I turn to see Lane coming after me. I wait a moment and let him catch up. Once he does, I turn and continue forward without word. He says nothing as I forage. He just holds whatever leaves or roots I hand to him without question. After an hour, we turn to head back so that we return before dark. We're less than half a mile away when he suddenly takes my hand and drags me to a stop. I wipe at my eyes and look up at him. The rain has calmed to a drizzle, and tiny water droplets stick to his long eyelashes. He looks at me for a moment before bending down and dropping everything we just foraged on the ground and standing back up.

"What are you—" he cuts me off with a kiss. It starts out hard and unrelenting but softens after a moment. When he breaks the kiss, he rests his forehead on mine.

"Don't go where you're going, Ad," he mutters after a moment. I look up at him.

"What do you mean?" He cups my face in his hands and runs his thumb over my cheekbone.

"That dark place. You're so undeniably *good*, Adira. Don't let them take that from you." I step away from his grasp.

"What, like they don't deserve it?" I seethe. "They tortured her, Lane. Tortured her. They've basically controlled our entire lives for some bullshit experiment. We're expendable. I'm allowed to be upset!" He nods and takes a step closer to me.

"I know, baby. Really, I do. But it takes so much out of you to work your way back from that dark place if you stumble too far." He takes another step closer. "It wasn't until you came along that I even had the ability to step back into something that felt like light." Tears start welling in my eyes. There's a dam that's about to break that I'm not ready for.

"Talk to me, Adira. Don't go there, just talk to me," he pleads.

"I hate them," I whisper after a moment. It was enough. That one statement was enough to blow up the dam.

"I hate them," I say through clenched teeth. "I hate how violated I feel right now to know that they've been watching me my whole life. I hate them for what they did to Leia. I hate Leia for getting caught in the first place and being stupid enough to think she could handle coming to Sentri. I hate Maurea for not being what it was supposed to be. What I thought it was my entire life. I hate Simon for keeping this from us. I hate Dad for never telling me *anything*. I hate Vince for making me choose. I hate him for hating me when I only followed what Leia wanted. I *hate* your father for what he did to you. I hate your mother for allowing it. I hate *you* for letting it go on so long. I hate Sentri for being the only place where no one is watched. How is that fair? How is *any* of this fair?" I scream. "But most of all, I hate myself. For all of it. I hate that I fell in love with my best friend. I hate that it was my fault that anger took him over and it'll never be the same with us again. I hate myself for trusting Simon. I hate myself for not going after Dad. I hate myself for not getting to Liam in time. I hate myself for being such a bitch to you before we came here. I hate how fast I fell in love with you. I hate that me loving you comes at the price of my best friend. I hate myself for letting Leia stay behind. It's my fault, Lane. It's all my fault." The sobs crescendo until I feel like I can't breathe. I collapse to the jungle ground, and Lane pulls me into his chest and starts making shushing noises and running his hand through my hair like he's trying to calm a panicked child. Minutes go by with him making calming noises and alternating between running his hands through my hair and rubbing soothing circles on my back. Once my sobs turn to hiccups, he pulls back from me and puts my face in his hands again.

"You don't hate, Adira. You're just so angry at the world right now. You've got so much anger, and you don't know what to do with it. And you have all the reason to be. Don't bottle this up anymore. You can talk to me. You can always talk to me." I freeze in his gaze for a moment and look down at his lips. I crush my mouth to his in the next second. He hesitates for a moment before kissing me back.

I don't waste my time with the sweet kisses. I want to claim. Mine. He's mine. This world took enough from me. It wouldn't take him. I push him down onto the ground and move my mouth down to his neck and nip lightly between his neck and shoulder. A small shiver rolls through him, and he grabs my hips. I bring my mouth back to his and roll my hips. A small groan comes from his throat, and I take it as encouragement. I bring my lips back to his neck as I reach down to undo the clasp on his trousers. He freezes and grabs my hand.

"Ad, what are you doing?"

"What does it look like I'm doing?" I say between kisses. I try to wrench my hand free, but he just holds it tighter. I freeze for a moment before I roll off of him. My cheeks color in humiliation. He notices and runs a finger over my face.

"You're extremely vulnerable right now, love. And we're soggy and wet on a jungle floor. And you just told me you hated me," he adds with a grin.

"I don't hate you," I say quickly. His smile broadens slightly.

"I know, love. I know." He kisses my forehead. "This isn't how I want our first time to go. And I'm sure it's not what you want either. I'm already not a man who's worthy of you. I would go even further into that category if I took advantage right now," he says wistfully as he puts a stray hair behind my ear. Tears threaten to reemerge.

"I'm sorry," I mutter. He gives me a soft smile.

"Don't be." We stand up, and I try to dust off some of the mud all over my clothes. It started pouring enough again that by the time we get back, hopefully most of it will have washed off.

"You're wrong, by the way," I say as we continue our walk to the pool.

"Unlikely. But wrong about what?"

"You not being worthy of me. You're better than you let anyone see. Avery told me about how you've been tutoring them all this time. Every time I think I know every part of you, something else pops up that makes me love you even more." He grabs my hand and intertwines his fingers with mine.

"I loved working with your brothers. They were both hilarious.

And quick learners. Liam especially. He was well on his way to being able to best you and I someday," he says in a sad voice. I smile at the thoughts of racing Liam in the water. He was always so competitive.

"Thank you. For being there for them in a way I couldn't after Dad died." He gives my hand a squeeze. We come up on the pool, and I let go of his hand to go check on Leia. She's still sleeping. I don't know how long it will take for her to have any semblance of energy between the marrow and blood loss and the sedative.

"Zander, get some water boiling for me." He stands up and does as I ask. I crush a combination of two different leaves and a root into as close of a powder as I can manage with the ground and a round rock and scoop it into my hand. It looks more like squashed mush since I didn't get a chance to let them dry out. Zander hands me one of the cups he brought in his pack after filling it with the hot water. I toss the ground ingredients into the water and wait for it to cool enough to drink. After I test it, I do my best to rouse Leia. She does slightly, and I position myself behind her to help her sit up.

"I need you to drink this. It's going to taste awful. But you need to down it. All of it." She nods weakly and does as I ask. It takes her at least twenty minutes before she's able to finish it all. Once she does, she lies back down and falls asleep promptly.

"If you don't mind my asking, what was that?" Williams asks.

"It should help her body replenish her blood quicker and also help her fight infection." He nods with a look of wonderment. I take another one of the leaves and chew on it until it's a paste, and I spit it out into my hand. Williams winces slightly, and his mouth dangles open as he watches me put it over every "metal" opening in both her hips and knees.

"And-and what's that for?" he asks with unbridled curiosity.

"Hopefully it'll keep the open wounds from getting too infected before we can get her back to camp."

"Fascinating," he whispers. I have a little bit of leftover paste, so I turn to him.

"Where's the thing that's able to watch us right now?"

"The camera?" he asks. I nod. He shifts uncomfortably.

"I obviously wasn't there when it was installed, but from the angle it gives, somewhere in the center of that rock wall." I look toward where he's pointing and walk closer to it. Lane joins me, and we browse over the entire surface.

"Here," Lane says, pointing to a small, black spot that is perfectly circular. I have to get onto his shoulders to reach it. I smear the leftover paste onto the "camera," and Lane lowers me down.

An hour later, some of the hunters come back with a fresh kill for dinner. Zander cooks it up, and I tear Leia's portion into tiny pieces so it's easier for her to swallow. Before I help her eat, I take another portion and walk over and hand it to Williams. He takes the meat and mutters his thanks and immediately starts eating. I stand there for a moment more.

"I'm sorry," I say. He stops chewing and looks up at me in bewilderment. After a moment, he swallows his food and clears his throat.

"Whatever for?"

"For what I said to you. You may be a prisoner, but you're a person. And you'll be treated as such. Even if you and your people couldn't extend us the same courtesy." With that I walk back toward Leia and catch Lane's proud grin. I smile back. I rouse Leia again and help her eat her food one tiny bite at a time. We give her stomach five minutes between every three bites to settle and acclimate to food being in her for the first time in a while. After a moment, I feel Williams's gaze on us. I look up and see him studying Leia with tears streaming down his face and a look that shows a feeling I've become all too familiar with. Crushing guilt.

30

WE HEAD OUT promptly the next morning. Having Williams and carrying Leia is undoubtedly going to make the trip back go a little slower. Zander takes the first shift in carrying her. She does her best to hide her winces from the pain of being moved and jostled, but at least her color looks better today. I make some more of the same tea and have her sip on it as we travel. By five miles in, she finishes it. Apparently, my apology to Williams last night encouraged his curiosity even further. The entire walk he was asking question after question until Zander finally shut him up when he asked him if he was trying to attract every deadly predator directly to us. His face turned white, and he promptly shut up. I stifled the laugh that was bubbling up, and Zander gave me a wink. At ten miles in, one of the other hunters offered to take Leia. He ended up taking her the rest of the way. I could smell camp before I could see it. Lonny must be cooking. When we break through the trees, the kids are playing one of their favorite games, and most of the village is seated around the main fire. When one child yells out "They're back!" everyone turns to us. Lane and I are the first seen, and Lonny throws both of his hands up and screams, "Hey heyyyy! Look who's back!"

I giggle under my breath. I missed him. Zander follows us close behind followed by Williams. Curious gazes follow him, and he looks around with unconcealed wonderment. He pays particular attention to the teardrops. Vince stands and waves. I wave back. I can tell the second that he sees Leia as she emerges from the trees in the hunter's arms. He sucks in a breath and freezes where he is. He doesn't move an inch. Leia is fast asleep in his arms, so he moves at a slow easy pace. Whatever trance Vince is in breaks, and he's sprinting toward us. The hunter hands her over to Vince when he gets close, and I see Vince's hands trembling as he carefully cradles Leia in his arms. Tears start streaming from his face as he strokes her face. I look down at the pair sitting entwined on the ground. I gaze at my childhood best friend. He can say that he loved me more, but he's never looked at me like that. He never would have. He was meant for Leia the same way I was meant for Lane.

Her eyes flutter open after a minute, and he starts crying harder. Her tears join his on the Sentri floor, and she reaches her hand up and cups his face. He takes her hand and kisses her palm.

"Don't leave me again," he whispers over and over again.

"I won't."

"Vince, let's get her in a hut by a fire," I say. He looks up at me and nods quickly. He gingerly picks her up and brings her to the same hut that I spent all of my time healing in. He gently sets her down on the cot. I turn and leave, giving them an opportunity to reunite in private. Lane is waiting outside for me when I come out.

"They make a cute couple," he says, taking my hand.

"Not as cute as us," I say tipping my head up to give him a kiss.

"Obviously. That goes without saying." I laugh as we walk hand in hand toward the main fire. When we get there, it's mostly silent. Williams sits with Zander standing right behind him. He looks incredibly uncomfortable. Lonny is staring at him like he's some sort of strange anomaly. Williams's eyes dart from place to place, and sweat beads on his forehead. When Lonny sees us, he casually points to him.

"Care to explain our newest visitor, princess?" Lane chuckles.

"Lonny, meet Williams." Williams stands awkwardly and holds out a hand toward Lonny. Lonny looks down at it, and his eyebrows shoot up. He looks back into Williams's eyes, and I have to stifle my laughter at his reaction. I honestly think he might pee himself. After a moment, Lonny looks back toward me and Lane.

"You lovebirds have some explaining to do." He turns without another word, and we head toward Abe's hut. Once we're all inside, we all take a seat, with the exception of Zander, who remains standing behind Williams. Abe barely glances at Williams and gestures for us to continue. We relay everything from start to finish again about our time in Maurea and after. When we finish, Lonny looks more confused than he did before we started. Abe keeps the same look of contemplation on his face from start to finish. After a long stretch of silence, Abe turns to Williams.

"Your people are not watching our village at the moment, correct?" Williams shakes his head quickly.

"N-no. We've tried over the years through droids and other means to replace the cameras, but Sentri apparently did not want to be seen," he says with a tone of wistfulness. Abe hums in agreement and looks back to me.

"I'm going to leave everything that happens to him in your care, Adira. They obviously haven't had much to do with our people here. I imagine this is a bit more . . . personal for you, Lane, and Vince."

"About that," Lane chimes in. "I think we need to keep a watch on him at all times." Williams blubbers.

"Surely you don't think I'd honestly try to escape. I-I-I could barely tell up from down in that jungle, how could I—"

"I didn't say it was to keep you from escaping." Williams swallows.

"Then what for?"

"If I saw Adira in half the condition that you left Leia in and I knew that you had something to do with it, you wouldn't be breathing right now. I imagine Vince is having similar convictions. We need information from you, and I don't need his temper getting in the way of that." Williams turns a shade of green. I turn to whisper in Lane's ear.

"What happened to not letting the darkness in?"

"It's too late for me, darling. I revel in the dark," he says with a smirk and a wink. I elbow his side softly, and he lets out a husky chuckle.

"We will rotate people to keep an eye on him. We're more than happy to help in whatever way you need as long as it doesn't interfere too severely with the work needing to already be done," Abe says. Lane nods.

"Thank you, Abe. I think we're all tired enough from the day." He turns toward Williams. "Tomorrow we'll start the interrogation." Williams nods and looks around at everyone.

"I can take the first watch," Lonny says with a mischievous grin. Williams pales.

"Keep him in one piece, Lonny," I say with a grin and turn to leave, Lane following close behind me. I almost run straight into Vince on my way out.

"Where is he?" he demands. I put a hand on his chest.

"Lonny is taking the first watch of him tonight. You go back and be with Leia. I'll be there with Kira in a second." His gaze is still at the entrance of the hut, as if he can see Williams through the door.

"Fine, I'll take the second watch," he says with forced calmness.

"No, you won't." Lane steps in front of him. Vince's nostrils flare as he stares him down.

"You don't get to tell me what to do," he says in a clipped tone.

"I get it. Really, I do. But we need information more than you need revenge. Do everyone around you a favor and *think* for a second before you do something stupid that could mess this up for all of us."

"They could have killed her!"

"We know, Vince. We know. We were there," I say in a tone analogous to coaxing a wild animal. "But he has so much information that we could use. We're in real danger. There are things we found out that you don't know yet. Please. *Please* just trust me." His eyes suddenly flash down to mine, and for a moment, I swear I can see anger boiling his irises.

"Trust you? She never would have been in that situation in the first place if you wouldn't have left her!"

"Are we seriously back to this?" Lane jumps in. "I thought we were over this. Also, explain to me why you seem to just blame Adira when it was a decision that *three* people made."

"I expected nothing less from you. I expected more from the person who claimed to be my best friend for my entire life." Just like that, the knife goes back into my chest. It's not like I haven't been thinking everything that he's saying since we found Leia, but it's different hearing the accusation out loud. That part of me that thought Vince and I might be able to go back to where we were before all of this with Leia returning is being promptly squashed. Obliviated. It seems we're just going back to him blaming me for the whole thing.

"Move. The hell. On, Vince," Lane seethes. Vince stands there in frozen rage for another minute before promptly turning and going back to Leia. I release the breath I didn't know I was holding, and Lane wraps his arms around me from behind.

"You're not about to go traipsing through the jungle again, are you?" he whispers in my ear. I can hear the smile in his voice. I elbow him, and he chuckles.

"That's not funny."

"It's a little funny." I try to conceal my smile. I turn around and wrap my arms around his neck.

"I need to go find Kira so we can take a look at Leia tonight before we go to bed." He nods and kisses my forehead.

"I'm going to go track down a place for us to sleep tonight since our old place is now occupied."

"I'll come find you in a bit." He smiles and softly kisses me before turning back into Abe's hut. I go on the hunt for Kira and find her checking in on Lexa and her newborn.

"How're they doing?" A smile breaks out on her face when she sees me.

"Adira, you're back! Little one is doing fine. I'm a little concerned about Lexa. She's growing pale and now seems to have picked up a fever. I've been able to keep it under control for the last couple days, but it isn't letting up yet." Likely an infection of some sort. I make a mental note to check in on her the next time I do rounds.

"I know it's getting late, but I have one more patient that needs some attention tonight."

"Lead the way." I fill her in on the situation as we make our way toward Leia. The second we walk in, Vince shoots up as if expecting an intruder. Leia offers a weak smile.

"Hello, Leia. My name is Kira. I've been working with Adira since she came here. Would you mind if I take a look?" She nods. I grab my own bag of supplies from the corner of the room where I usually keep it, and we carefully approach. Kira keeps a suspicious eye on Vince.

We make quick work of a head-to-toe assessment before checking all of the interventions I did before coming here.

"Smart work, using the Kanduli paste to keep the wounds from infection," she says, checking over her hips and knees. Vince's eyes flash to me for a moment before settling back on Leia. "The man who you brought back. He knows how to take these out safely?"

"Yes."

"Absolutely not," Vince says through his teeth. "He isn't getting anywhere near her. You fix her." Anger boils in me at the way he's speaking to Kira, but she keeps the same calm effect as she turns to him.

"I understand your reservations. But this isn't something that I am familiar with, and if I take them out, I could do more damage than good. It is safer for us to supervise while he does the removal." Vince stays silent for a moment before nodding. Kira offers a smile in return. After applying fresh Kanduli and wrapping her knees and hips, we brew her some more tea and help her finish it. Kira then pulls out an already dried and crushed plant and adds it to some water and hands it to Vince.

"What's this?"

"Something to help you," she says sweetly.

"I'm fine. I'm healthy. You should be focusing on her." Leia looks at him with a surprised face and opens her mouth to speak before Kira raises her hand to silence her.

"I've done everything I can for her tonight. This will help you feel better. It might even help you get some sleep."

"I don't—"

"Take it, Vince," Leia cuts him off. He grinds his teeth for a moment before reluctantly taking it. Kira stares at him until he finishes every drop. She takes the cup back and puts it in her bag.

"We will be back to check on you in the morning."

"Thank you. Thank you, both." I give her hand a squeeze and turn to leave.

"Adira," Leia calls out.

"Yes?"

"I'd do it all over again. For you guys to get to where you are with these people. I'd do it all over again." Rage flashes in Vince's eyes, but I know it's not directed toward Leia. It's all for me. One step forward, five steps back. I look at the man in front of me and can hardly recognize the boy who had been my best friend my entire life. The one who I could tell anything to without having to worry about judgment. The one who would move the world for me, and I would do the same for him. But then that world broke. Those two people seem to be from another life. Like two stars caught in an orbit of something greater than themselves that are destined to follow each other's path without ever meeting again.

"I wouldn't," I whisper. I turn to leave Leia and the man who's become a stranger behind.

31

I FIND LANE CONVERSING with Zander by the fire. Both are eating whatever it was that Lonny had cooked up. Lane hands me a bowl as I take a seat between them. They both take notice of my fallen expression and offer their comfort with a sympathetic smile from Zander and a comforting arm from Lane.

"Do you want to talk about it?" Lane asks. I give him a small smile that doesn't meet my eyes.

"No. Maybe later." He nods and kisses my forehead.

"Well, we have one extra dwelling available that we can give you two. They're normally reserved for pairs that are already mated, but being that we're kind of out of options," he shrugs.

"We will be soon enough, anyway," Lane says with confidence. Zander lets out his low, throaty laugh and stands to leave.

"I'll see you two in the morning for the interrogation. Try to get some sleep." We bid him good night and fall into amicable silence while I finish my food. I didn't have Lonny's cooking for a few days, and I felt deprived from it. The man has a gift.

"You sure you don't want to talk about it?" I choke back a sob.

"You know that feeling when you're holding yourself together until someone asks you if you're okay?" My bottom lip starts quivering. Lane scoots closer and wraps his arm tighter around me.

"I miss him," I whisper. He kisses the side of my hair.

"I know, love." He sits there rubbing a soothing hand up and down my arm and lets me cry and grieve for my lost friend.

"I'm so damn sick of crying," I mutter after a while. He laughs and squeezes me tighter. "I'm tired." He hums in agreement.

"Let's go to bed." He stands and holds out his hand for me to take. We make our way to the same dwelling that Vince and I shared. The climb tugs on the scars covering my abdomen, but at least I can do physical activity now without wincing in pain. I lie down in the firs, and Lane tugs my back to his chest. I let all thoughts of the last arms that held me in here float away in the Sentri wind as I drift to sleep.

I wake to the feeling of lips on my neck, and shivers roll down my spine.

"Good morning to you too," I say in my morning rasp. He hums to himself, and I turn around to bring my mouth to his. He settles over top of me, and I wrap my legs around his hips. His tongue caresses mine as I weave my fingers through his hair.

"We should go," I say between kisses.

"Mhmm," he hums, deepening the kiss.

"Wakey wakey, lovebirds! We've got shit to do that doesn't involve you two fondling each other!" Lonny screams from below. Lane growls, and I huff out a breath of frustration as I lower my legs.

"Hold that thought," he murmurs against my lips. I giggle as he maneuvers off of me and uncomfortably shifts his trousers. I laugh a little harder.

"You'll be the death of me, woman," he says in a low gruff. Damn, there's just something about this man's voice in the morning . . .

"You started it," I retort. He bends down and gives me another peck.

"Guilty," he says with his signature smirk. I throw my hair in its top knot, and we climb down to make our way to Abe's hut.

Williams is awake and fidgety already. I swear this dude doesn't ever just turn off.

"You need something to eat?" He flinches at the sound of my voice. I nod at the hunter currently watching him. He nods back and heads out of the hut. Williams looks nervously between Lane and me.

"No. No, I'm fine, thank you." Lane looks at him suspiciously.

"You know we aren't going to poison it. If you really want to make sure we won't, I'd eat before we start the interrogation and get everything we need out of you." I elbow him.

"Stop, you're gonna make him piss himself, and then I'm going to have to clean it up," I mutter. He grins and asks him again if he wants something to eat. He decides he does, and Lane leaves to go grab something for him.

"Take a seat, we'll be here a while," I say gesturing toward one of the logs around the small, dwindling fire. He reluctantly sits but keeps his rigid stance. He starts picking at his nails, and I see some of them are already bloody.

"That's a bad habit," I comment nonchalantly. He looks down at his hands like he doesn't realize he's been doing it this whole time.

"Yes. Terrible habit. Just a-a nervous tick, if you will." I hum, and he sits on his hands and starts bouncing his leg instead. I quirk an eyebrow at him.

"You always this nervous?" He looks surprised at the question.

"Not *this* nervous. But I suppose I am in a very unique situation." I nod.

"You seemed pretty freaked out when you were talking to . . . what did you call him?"

"Stroft," he says in a quivering voice. "He's not the most . . . understanding of bosses." Lane comes in holding three bowls of stew. Lane and I immediately dig in while Williams stares down at the bowl. Lane scoffs and rolls his eyes. He goes over and dips his spoon in Williams's bowl and takes a bite.

"See?" When he sits back down, Williams takes his first tentative bite. He looks pleasantly surprised by the flavor and starts eating like he hasn't had food in days. We wait for him to finish before we start asking questions. By the time he's done, Abe, Lonny, and Zander have joined us. He sets his bowl down once he's done.

"Okay, what do you want to know?" Right then, Vince walks into the hut and cuts a glare toward him. Everyone in the hut tenses, and time stands still for a second. The look in Vince's eyes promises violence, and Williams can see that. After a minute, Vince moves to stand on the opposite end of the hut, leaning against the wall. I step forward.

"Let's start at the beginning. What do you know about the experiment?" It takes a moment for him to take his frightened gaze off of Vince. Eventually he turns to me and swallows the lump in his throat.

"There has been an ongoing debate amongst the anthropological field ever since Darwin's theory of evolution was established."

"Again, English, asshole," Lane says impatiently.

"I'm sorry, let me start over . . . Darwin was—*is* a very famous scientist who came up with a theory on evolution. That theory was—and I'm oversimplifying here—that evolution was a product of adapting to one's environment and survival of the fittest. This theory explained the fossil findings of humanoid bone fossils found across the world. Basically, how humans *became* humans. We have become the most evolved of any creature and, thus, the top of the food chain." He looks to me, and I nod for him to continue.

"Part of the debate was about whether or not modern technology and medicine had come so far that humans could no longer evolve. After all, if you have no harsh environment to adapt to, why adapt? And-and if someone is born with a deficit but can still pass on those genes because of modern medicine, survival of the fittest is all of a sudden moot.

"There was a society started by a very wealthy man. Extraordinarily wealthy. He became obsessed with this idea that you could almost *force* evolution if humans were once again in an environment without modern technology and medicine. He started raising support for an experiment from other anthropologists. Of course, there were debates on the ethics of such an experiment, but the ecospheres were eventually created. Some of the anthropologists that supported this eventually became what you know as the Originals. Of course, you think there was only five."

"What do you mean we *think* there was only five?" Lane asks.

"Well, it wasn't plausible to create a whole society of people with only five people to . . . well . . . procreate. The five Originals that you know of were the five anthropologists that were put in charge to be what you now know of as the Legions. They believed so strongly in the work they were doing, they wanted to be a part of it. Written into history," he says in a wistful tone. "Anyway. There was actually twenty-four people per ecosphere. We put out word about an experiment being done and asked for volunteers. Those that agreed to the program would gain a lifetime of funds for their family in exchange for taking part in the experiment."

"You tore people from their families?" Vince asks in a dead voice.

"Tore? No no no. We didn't force anyone."

"No. You just exploited their poverty for the sake of an experiment."

"For the sake of *science*."

"We can argue over the lack of morality later. Continue," I say. He stares at Vince for another moment before turning back to me.

"As I said, five anthropologists were put into each ecosphere in a position to be in charge. After the ecospheres were created and the people were dropped into their environments, there was no interference from the outside. They watched from afar. As you can imagine, the first generation was the one that had the hardest time with survival. I mean, imagine trying to survive on nothing but the ocean and sand without the ability to swim as you do. People died. Unfortunately, that *is* a necessary part of survival of the fittest. Only the fittest survive." Silence fills the hut as we all glare daggers into Williams's skull.

"They knew what they were signing up for," he says barely above a whisper.

"Continue," I demand. He clears his throat and starts picking at his nails again.

"The way they envisioned for the society to run only ended up being carried through in Maurea. Somehow, the group democratic system that was set up in the very beginning continued on until this day. Remarkable really . . . The other three went off in their own directions. Sentri became more egalitarian, Tragdome eventually separated into different tribe groups, and those that went to Avil died out before the second generation could even be born."

"Why wouldn't you go in and save them if it was still the original group?" Lane asks.

"That's against the whole point of the experiment. Survival of the *fittest*. That means without modern medicine." Lane's jaw ticks. I nod again for him to continue.

"With the way that the society was set up in Maurea, they started passing down all of the information about the rest of the world. This wasn't something that was planned, but again, they wouldn't intervene. At five years in, the information they were passing was getting . . . messy. Not entirely accurate. So, we decided that every five years, we would reach out to one of the Legions and give them updated information. Like I said before, we never mentioned the original experiment. Statistically, the information had to fade away over the years, that's why I said it was such an anomaly. *It didn't.* Other than the misinformation about there only being five people in the experiment to begin, everything else was accurate. To this day, it's one of the topics most discussed with potential sponsors. Generation after generation, it was the one thing that was discussed that stood out so prevalently that you were able to pass it down to the next group of Legions. It's one of the reasons that we became more invested in Maurea above the other ecospheres. There were social anomalies present in your society we weren't seeing in others. The fact that you were *controlling* procreation was something we didn't even think of."

"How much good could it possibly have done?" I ask. Williams gives me a confused look.

"Look at you. You are overweight, short, have sandy-brown hair, and five fingers and toes. Now look at Lonny and Zander." Lonny grins widely as Williams's eyes turn to him. "Extra finger, longer limbs, climbing abilities—all things you don't have. They've clearly adapted just as much to their environment as we have to ours. So, what was the point of making people live alone if it didn't do shit in the first place?" A flabbergasted look crosses his face.

"Surely you see there's a difference in the evolutionary level . . ."

"Watch yourself, fat man," Lonny says.

"I-I mean no disrespect. I'm sorry, I should clarify . . . The ocean has a lot to offer, but *your* ocean is a very small percentage of what the entirety of the Atlantic Ocean is. The Amoran had more resources available to them, such as all of the healing herbs, plants, roots, and venom they've been able to procure."

"Get to the point," Lane clips.

"Your ability to avoid disease and heal from injuries." The hut goes silent again.

"What are you talking about?" I ask.

"Your selection process made it impossible for people with any disease that could later be life-threatening carry those traits. The Dorian did what no one thought would be possible. You eliminated disease." Silence falls again.

"That's bullshit," Lane exclaims.

"I would have thought the same thing! But when we acquired Leia, it was confirmed in her DNA. Not a trace of any gene that could later lead to any disease. No Alzheimer's, diabetes, heart disease, cancers—nothing. And the only reason we were able to collect as many specimens as we did is because her body rejuvenated itself at a speed that was unprecedented. I mean, have any of you been injured and it took far less time to heal than you would have thought?" My hand impulsively moves to my stomach.

"Let's take a break," Lane says all of a sudden.

"Why?" Zander asks.

"Let's let everyone get a breather." I look over and see Vince fuming. I figured as soon as Leia's name came up, we'd get a reaction like this.

"Good idea, let's take a short break." Lane and I turn toward Vince and wait for him to storm out of the hut. He starts stalking away back toward Leia.

"Vince, wait!" I shout out, running toward him. He quickly turns around, and I almost run into him.

"The second. *The second*—that he is done giving us information, I am going to kill him." He turns back around and storms the rest of the way to Leia. I stare toward him in shock.

"He doesn't mean it," Lane says from behind me. "He just needs some time to cool off."

"I don't think it's him needing to cool off. I'm starting to think it's just him."

32

VINCE IS THE last to return back to the hut. Williams may be a blubbering mess, but he's not an idiot. He sees the subtle change in Vince. He looks to me with pleading eyes. I look away from his gaze and say nothing. None of us know exactly what to do in this situation.

"Okay . . . so, the experiment was a success, and you pay the most attention to Maurea. What does Lane's dad have anything to do with this? What can he possibly be getting out of it?" I start us back up. Williams starts fidgeting again.

"Like I said, we've lost most of our funding. We've received a very obvious answer to the original question that the experiment was intended to answer. The human can indeed evolve and will do so according to their environment. But now that we've answered the question, the people who provide money to keep this experiment going are less interested. They need a new question to answer. Being that your evolutionary progress was indeed impacted by something enacted in your society, it only made sense for us to go with something that leaned more toward a social experiment rather than a biological one. We had a foothold in Maurea already with Paul, so it was in Maurea that we decided phase two should take place in."

"And what exactly is phase two?" Lane asks.

"Well, we've seen how things work in a group monarchial society with democratic methods, an egalitarian society, and a secluded tribal society. There's one that hasn't been considered . . ." He goes silent.

"And?!" Lonny yells. Williams flinches.

"A dictatorship. A society run with a sole person in authority over all else with the ability to make all of the decisions." I feel my face pale.

"Does that for one moment sound like something that would succeed? Your own history suggests otherwise!" I shout. His leg starts tapping anxiously.

"Yes, well, we have more reason now to get a good idea of all of our options . . ."

"Why?" Lane asks. Williams seems to try to find the right words.

"This experiment took a decade to be launched. And, as you know, has been going on for over one thousand years. One generation after another of scientists. To get a spot on the team was something amongst all scientific fields that was envied ever since the beginning.

"Anyway, when it was launched all the way back in 2024, the world was in a different place. The year is now 3061, and we've used up most of the Earth's resources, and nations are falling apart piece by piece. Enough so that a more global government has been established, and there has been some . . . disagreements . . . as to what kind of a government should be run. Word got out about the details of the experiment, and if we start on this phase, we might receive full funding once again and possibly gain the opportunity to *expand*."

"You can't keep your own world's natural resources alive, what makes you think you can add something useful onto ours?" Lane snaps.

"Well, that's the thing, we've been able to create some nature reserves since the global directive was put into place. Enforcing rules seems to be the main issue."

"Which is where the Dorian people come in," I conclude.

"Exactly. There are just too many cooks in one kitchen. A major potential sponsor is willing to provide us with funding to keep this project going if we provide him with evidence that a dictatorship would be in the best interest of mankind."

"And I'm guessing he wants to be the man in charge?" Lane asks. Williams nods.

"How do you plan to get evidence in such a short period of time? Maurea isn't going to just switch from the way we have been running things to this bullshit overnight." Williams starts biting at his lip.

"Yes, well, we have figured out ways to incentivize a want for change . . ." He stops meeting my eyes, and his foot starts tapping even faster.

"And how have you managed that?" I ask, thinking I might already know the answer. He swallows a lump in his throat and still doesn't meet my eyes.

"Historically, after some sort of disaster, people become vulnerable to change. Willing and eager to have some sort of certainty amongst the chaos." I feel my heart pounding in my ears. Lane reaches down and grabs my hand.

"So, you're telling me that you created that storm with the purpose of wiping Maurea out to so *Paul* could manipulate them into letting him be our dictator?" I ask barely above a whisper. My voice sounds foreign even to myself. Forced calmness laced with the promise of violence. My free hand rolls into a fist that turns my knuckles white. Williams is visibly shaking, and tears well up in his eyes. I can see realization dawn on his face when he notices his habitual need to ramble without thinking twice about his words has suddenly caught up to him.

"We didn't have a choice," he cries. I feel my blood pumping in my head to the point of being deafening. Every ounce of sadness I've had suddenly turned to anger.

"You killed my brother," I mutter. He starts sobbing.

"I had no say in it. I had nothing to do with it!" he babbles on.

"Get him out of my sight before I kill him," I say to no one in particular. Abe picks him up by the arm and carries him out of the hut. The five of us remaining in the hut stay silent. Unchecked hate rolls through my entire body to the point where I feel as though I could run and fight forever and I still wouldn't be able to get this energy out of my body. After a moment, I turn to Zander.

"Now seems as good a time as any for you to start training me." His eyebrows shoot up in response. Lane tugs on my arm.

"Adira, maybe now isn't—"

"Now is a great time actually," Zander interrupts. "You'd be fighting on nothing but rage right now. Pure instinct. I've gotta know what that is for you to properly train. Let's do this," he says with a smirk. He walks out of the hut, and I drop Lane's hand and follow close behind. We get to the same place that Vince and Lane had their fight, and Zander posts up on one side of it. He puts his hands forward and uses his fingers to beckon me.

"Come on, princess. Show me what you've got." I've never fought without a weapon before. I've never actually *fought* before. Unless you count a little tussle I had with a shark once, but that barely counts. You give them a hard tap on the nose, and they leave you alone. Zander is a beast in and of himself. I have a feeling I could break his damn nose, and he wouldn't even flinch. The anxiety takes over the rage for a moment before I stuff it down and let fury take over again. I charge at Zander with a cocked fist and drive it toward his head. He ducks and maneuvers away with little effort. He doesn't touch me yet. I take another breath, and I attack again, this time followed by my second fist shortly after. Rather than ducking out of each punch, he blocks each one with his forearms. This goes on for a few minutes with little grace. The fact that he isn't even breaking a sweat when I'm already panting is only adding to the fury boiling inside of me.

"You've got legs too, princess. Use them," he says between blocks. I follow his direction and start working up to a pattern. After a while, I stop focusing on trying to fight and just let the tension ease out of me as my energy dwindles through each punch and kick. Suddenly, Zander moves, and I punch open air and almost fall over before he catches me from behind. At this point I'm gasping for air and my muscles burn. It feels good. Really good.

"Better?" he asks, still holding me. I nod, and he drops me.

"You have no idea what you're doing, and you've gotten out of shape," he says, appraising me.

"Gee, thanks, asshole," I retort.

"But you have good instinct and a skill set that'll make it easy for you to learn. I look forward to our next tussle, princess," he says with a wink. He turns and starts walking away.

"Zander," I call out. He turns back toward me.

"Thank you." He gives me a smile and keeps walking on. I turn back toward the main fire to see Lane staring at me. I make my way to him and try to ignore the smirk playing at his lips.

"Don't. Say. Anything. I've never fought before . . . Was it that bad?" He grabs my hand and kisses the back of it.

"It was kinda cute," he says, barely concealing a laugh. I punch him in the side.

"Shut up," I mutter. I start walking toward the stream where most of us do our bathing. I can smell myself, and it isn't a good thing.

"Do you feel better?"

"Well, I'm not going to hunt him down and kill him. Not yet at least." He hums. We walk in silence for a while.

"I don't know who I am anymore," I mutter. Lane's eyes shoot to me.

"What do you mean?"

"What I said at the pool, what I said today . . . I never would have said those things before. I never would have *meant* those things before. But for a moment back there, I honestly thought I could. I imagined myself . . ." Nausea pools in my stomach.

"No one is perfect, Adira. We all have a little darkness in us. You just can't let it take over. Don't let it be who you are." He caresses my cheek. I do my best to shake off the conversation in the hut, even if just for a moment. We approach the stream, and I turn to give him a sultry look.

"Are you planning on joining me?" His eyes darken as they travel down my body and back up. He bites his lip and gives me a pained look.

"Perhaps it wouldn't be the best idea . . ." I give him a sultry smirk.

"Perhaps not." We stand there staring at each other for another moment before he hastily turns around and heads back the way we came. A laugh bubbles out of me as I turn around, strip my clothes, and dive into the cool water. As I scrub the dirt, sweat, and blood off of my skin, I imagine scrubbing my soul free of the darkness that's seemed to take hold of it. I know that Lane is right. I know that no one is perfect. But lately, it feels like it might feel so much easier to just let that darker part of me take over. She wouldn't feel this much. She wouldn't experience the heart-wrenching grief every time she thinks of her father and brother. She wouldn't care that she's lost her best friend. She wouldn't care that her whole life has been formulated and designed by someone else. She wouldn't care that she's been watched since the moment she was born. She wouldn't care . . . She wouldn't care. How much easier it could all be if I wouldn't care.

33

BY THE TIME I finish washing up, my mental exhaustion has caught up with the physical. It feels like there's a part of me that wants to just scream and cry, but the other part has smothered any ability to feel in that magnitude. Like I've been muted. Who knows, maybe everything has finally caught up to me, and I'll have the reprieve of going insane. Though I seriously doubt it.

I change back into my clothes and make my way to the dwelling in something akin to a trance. A few people smile and wave and shout out greetings. I'm surprised with how much it takes out of me to simply raise a hand and fake a smile. Lonny steps into my path.

"So, I was thinking of some more questions we ought to ask little fidgets. Woah, you look terrible," he says when he finally looks up at me.

"I'm going to bed, Lonny," I say as I step around him. He continues to follow me.

"This early? You've still got a good few hours of daylight left. You haven't even eaten!"

"I'm tired. I'm going to bed," I drawl. He continues to follow me.

"Are you okay? I know that was a lot back there if you—" I hold my hand up to stop him and take a deep breath.

"I'm tired, Lonny. I'm going to bed," I repeat in the same, dead drawl. Worry covers his face, and he nods. I climb into the dwelling with additional effort due to my sore muscles. The second I step in, I lie down on top of the furs, not bothering to burrow under them, and let the temporary numbness that's taken over my soul carry me into restless slumber.

I'm back in Maurea. I look around, and I see our homes all perfectly intact, as if the storm never happened. It's starting to rain, and everyone is rushing inside.

"Adira!" I turn to the sound of my name, and shock rolls through me.

"Daddy?" I cry out.

"Come on!" he shouts, beckoning toward the hut he's about to enter. I run toward him as fast as my legs can manage. He disappears into the hut before I have a chance to hug him. For him to hold me. As I step inside, there's a child crying in the corner and a woman wailing over her mate, who is currently bleeding out on the floor.

"Come hold pressure, Adira." I do as I'm told and drop to the floor. Dad stands and turns to leave.

"Where are you going!" I shout, tears starting to run down my face. I can hear the wind picking up outside, and it's gone dark.

"I'll be right back."

"Don't leave me!" I shout and let go of the bleeding leg to reach toward my father.

"Keep holding pressure, Adira! I'll be back soon." And he leaves. A sob escapes my throat, and I push harder on the leg. The child starts crying louder and louder, and the woman is begging me to save her mate.

"He'll be back. He'll be back," I mutter over and over again. After a while, the blood runs cold, and I stand with rain, blood, sweat, and tears drenching me.

"No!" the woman shouts. I exit the hut without another word. The storm is still going.

"Adira!" I turn to the sound of my father's voice. He's entering another hut. I run after him.

"Dad, wait!" I run into the hut, and Lexa is in the middle of labor. Dad turns and holds out a squirming infant for me to take. He's blue and not moving. I rush to his bag and find the instrument I'm looking for. I suck the mucus out of his throat, and he gives out a wail.

"Give him to me," Lexa says barely above a whisper. She's turning paler. I hand her her little boy and turn to see Dad walking out of the hut.

"Dad, wait! I think she's—"

"There's no time, Adira! Come along!" I give an apprehensive glance back to Lexa before following him back out into the storm. As we enter the next hut, we walk into a room of hard gray with blinking multicolor lights coming from all around us. Faceless bodies lie on tables. Dad walks past all of them until he gets to one. He looks at one of the surfaces with blinking lights before looking down at our newest patient. Leia. He takes out all of the tubes attached to her and turns to leave.

"No, Dad! We can't leave her here!"

"There is more, Adira! We do what we can, and we move on! Come!"

I feel my throat constrict. I turn to Leia and bend down to whisper in her ear, "I'll be back for you."

She gives me a look of desperation as she follows my retreat out of the gray room. The storm is picking up now to the point where it's hard to see more than a few feet ahead of me. My dad reaches back and grabs my hand; a sob escapes my throat at the first contact I've had with him. He leads us into the next hut, and I recognize the interior of my old home. There lying where we usually would eat is Liam. His face ashen, his lips blue, and his bone sticking out of his leg. Avery is holding his hand and pleading for him to wake up while Mom wails over his chest. Tears prick at the back of my eyes, and Dad turns without a second glance to head back into the storm.

"*What* are you doing!" I shout.

"To save the next."

"But, Daddy, Liam—"

"Is gone!" He turns to me with a shout. "There's nothing we can do, so we move on to the next!" I'm openly sobbing at this point. He ignores it and moves on to the next hut. We walk into another room of gray and blinking lights. This time the bodies aren't faceless. Horror grabs at my chest as I look around and see so many . . . too many. All with the same tubes that Leia had in her. I first pass Geode, and he grabs onto my hand as I pass without even opening his eyes. I start blubbering with tears and snot running down my face.

"Daddy, please," I beg. He moves on without looking back. I pass Walter, Eliot, Pandora, and Avery. In the next row, I pass Kira, Zander, Lonny, and Abe. Desperation builds in me with each face that comes into view. I've lost sight of Dad. All of a sudden, a scream erupts out of an all too familiar voice, and I feel my stomach drop and my face pale. I run toward the scream and come up on another see-through wall that is impossible to get through. On the other side is Lane, lying on a table with all the tubes except for the one down his throat. Paul is standing over him with a large needle and gives me a sinister smile before stabbing it into his son's hip. The scream that bubbles out of Lane sounds inhuman. Like anguish given form. I scream and pound on the glass as hard as I can. I feel my hand break as the wall fractures, and I continue anyway. I scream until it feels like my voice is going to break. I don't care. I'll scream my way to silence.

"Come back, baby," a voice whispers behind me. I try to ignore it, but it comes again stronger. "Wake up, Ad."

All of a sudden, I'm launched back to Sentri. I'm in the teardrop, and strong arms are holding me. I intake a rough breath and smell the familiar scent of Lane. I relax into his embrace, and he gives a sigh of relief. A dream . . . It was just a dream . . . I repeat over and over in my head. I open my eyes to see Lonny, Zander, and Kira shoved into the small space. Kira carefully approaches me and takes my wrist in her hand. She counts for a moment before dropping my hand.

"Take some deep, calming breaths for me, Adira." She imitates the same breathing technique we use for all of our anxious patients, and I follow her direction. After a minute, she grabs my wrist again. She looks to Lane behind me and nods.

"Better," she says with a soft smile.

"I just—" My voice comes out in a rough, raspy sound. "I was having a nightmare." The three nod, and Lane squeezes me a little tighter. The image of him being tortured comes to my mind, and I squeeze him back. He's fine. He's here. It was just a dream. Kira hands me a tea, and I take it without question. After the first few sips, my throat feels a little less raw. I nod at her in thanks. She gives me a smile in return.

"We'll leave you two be," she says as she gestures for Zander and Lonny to get out. They reluctantly do, and after a moment, it's just me and Lane. He maneuvers me so that he can look at my face. Worry is sketched all about his features. I run my hands over every inch of his face before moving down to his arms and down his torso.

"You're okay . . .," I whisper. It seems that's all my voice is capable of at the moment. He cups my face and wipes away a tear I didn't even realize had fallen.

"Yeah, baby, I'm okay. Are you?" I almost instinctually blurt yes. But as he looks at me and I see the love he has for me glowing in his gaze, I'm done lying. To him and to myself.

"No," I whimper. His eyes soften further, and he pulls me to his chest.

"That's okay, Ad. It's okay to not be okay right now." I nod and look back at him.

"I just don't know what I'd do if something happened to you. If I ever lost you," I rasp. He leans forward and kisses my forehead.

"You'll never have to know. My soul is entwined with yours in a way that is uncapable of unraveling. From now and through whatever life comes next, I am yours."

34

WE DECIDE THAT it's in everyone's best interest that we hold off on any more information dumps from Williams. After he successfully removed the pieces from Leia's hips and knees, Vince went from looking like he was going to kill him to looking like he would only seriously maim him. I can't be with him in a room for longer than ten minutes before Liam's face repeatedly flashes through my eyes, so over the next few weeks, we build up a pattern. A routine.

Zander has me working on getting my body stronger every morning. His workout routines are far from easy, but it's a nice way to start the day. I'm so exhausted that it's almost impossible to think. We run and climb, he has me lift something heavier every day until my muscles feel like liquid, we do pushups until I eat dirt, and then we run some more. It's grueling. I love it.

After I wash up, I go on my rounds with Kira. We check in on Lexa and her gorgeous baby, Arthur, every day. He seems to be thriving. He hits every developmental mark and overall seems like a happy little boy. Lexa is a different story. It seems like every day we come back, she is more skinny, more ashen, more sad. I know this can happen with some moms, but I've never seen it to the extent that it's showing up in Lexa. Kira and I have tried to talk to her about it and give her possible herbs to help with some of the symptoms, but the harder we try, the more she refuses. At this point, half the reason we check in on them is to make sure that Arthur is being properly cared for. Her mate is as doting as ever on her and Arthur. We see his worry intensify with every visit. We always leave wishing we could do more.

After rounds is when we go to interview Williams. His nervous energy never subsides. He's constantly on edge, always looking over his shoulder. He has good reason. He has nothing but enemies here. His fear is useful at least. He hasn't hesitated to give up an ounce of information as if he can buy his way to understanding or forgiveness. It seems the only loyalty he has is to himself and science.

We've learned that we at least have time. Well, Sentri does. Things will quickly devolve in Maurea until it gets to a point where Paul has ultimate control. We've started working on a plan to help get people out, but we're stuck with the same issue that we had in the first place—only the strongest swimmers will be able to get here. We also learned that their loss of Leia is going to be an even bigger piece of damage to the USDF. The United Science and Discovery Foundation. Lonny's reaction upon hearing the name was, "They're about to discover the foundation of my foot up their ass." I can't say I disagreed.

Apparently, they were starting research on how to use the Maurean genes that allow for faster healing and elimination of genetic diseases. They were getting close to figuring out how to make them into an immunization of some sort. The *one* question he refused to answer was when he was asked how they planned to get enough of the bodily materials needed in order to create a mass supply of these immunizations. His silence was answer enough. Since then, we've been in meeting after meeting about what to do with the information we have. What the best way to go about the crisis would be. We have yet to agree on anything.

Once the interrogation and meeting concludes, I continue training with Zander. Lane comes in and joins every once in a while.

The training in the afternoon consists of me actually learning how to fight. At first, I honestly felt like a fish out of water. Slowly, he taught me to use my shortcomings as my own weapon. We were four weeks into the intense training by the time I was able to best one of the hunters who Zander had recruited as a test. Once he deemed I was well enough at hand-to-hand combat, he taught me how to use a spear, daggers, and bow and arrow. The spear was easy enough for me to get used to outside of water, and then it was easy work transitioning those skills to knife throwing. It was the bow and arrow that took lesson after lesson after lesson just to hit the damn target. Eight weeks in, I was in the best physical shape of my life. I was no longer panting for breath on the runs, I was keeping up with Zander on the climbs, I had yet to beat Zander in a fight, but I at least was making him break a sweat right now, and he had to *work* to beat me, and I was one of the best spearmen in Sentri. I think I will always have a proclivity for the spear. It's a way for me to bridge my Maurean roots to my life in Sentri, but I've come to prefer and rely on my knives more than the spear as I start joining the hunters on their trips out. Kira made me two holders to keep them always on me. One is strapped to my thigh with the other on my forearm. Feeling physically capable of taking down any adversary has helped me get into a better mental and emotional space. As my body strengthens and my skills hone, I feel my vulnerability melt off of my bones. Part of me welcomes a real fight. Let them try.

Leia has improved drastically with Kira's medicinal aid and Lonny's cooking. She still has pain and a bit of a limp, but she's at the point where she's able to be an active member of the Amoran now. She mostly helps watch the children, and they ask her to sing for them every day without fail. Vince's countenance improved along with her health. He isn't openly glaring at me anymore, but he still won't meet my eyes for longer than a second. I try not to let it bother me. I *know* it bothers Leia. She's apologized on his behalf numerous times and has chastised Vince on multiple occasions for the way he treats me when it was her decision. He just won't hear it.

"*Men.* As if I'm incapable of making my *own* decisions. He has to blame someone else. I don't understand why he doesn't just yell at me and get over it," Leia rants. I snort at her.

"You're sleeping with him, Leia. Of course, he isn't going to yell at you." Her face turns red, and she playfully smacks my arm.

"Oh my gosh, Adira." I openly laugh.

"What? It's true! He's absolutely smitten with you. I'm pretty sure he's incapable of even being mad at you." Her cheeks darken further.

"You know, we never really talked about everything with you and him. Last time we talked boys, you were pretty torn up between Vince and Lane." I drop my eyes from her gaze. No one really fully filled her in on Vince's blowup when he first found out about what we'd done. What Leia had instigated.

"Me and Vince were never meant to be. I know twelve-year Adira would wholeheartedly disagree," I add with a smirk. "But everything happened exactly as it should." I look across the fire to where Lane and Lonny are joking around with one another.

"I found my soul mate," I say wistfully.

She groans, "You two . . . I'll never have it, I'll never understand it, and I'll always be jealous of it." My eyes shoot to her.

"What do you mean? You and Vince love each other."

"We do. *I* do. I love him. And he clearly loves me. But . . ." She gazes around to make sure no one can hear. "I don't think you can love someone the way you and Lane love one another with so much . . . anger in you. He never used to be like this . . . Back home, I don't know. He was funny, easygoing, just . . . *Vince.* I still love him, but it's like he's a different person." I know exactly what she's saying.

"There was a moment a few weeks back . . . back around when we first got you back that I had so much anger and resentment that I honestly thought I could kill Williams." She looks hardly surprised and nods for me to continue. "I still loved Lane. More than anyone. He just was one of the people that helped me see through the haze of anger. That and working my ass off until I didn't have the energy to be angry," I say with a laugh. She chuckles along with me.

"But you let him help you through it. I've tried with Vince. I've tried to help him move on. I mean, if anything, he should be able to get over his weird resentment toward you. You two were inseparable for the longest time. Best friends. I feel terrible. I feel like—" Her voice catches. "I feel like he doesn't know how to really love anymore, Adira. Like I'm something he possesses. Owns. Something he's responsible for." I reach forward and squeeze her hand.

"I've found ways to cope, Leia. He hasn't yet. You just need to give him some time."

"I don't have more time and energy to give. I love him, Adira. I really do. But I deserve more than someone who just sees me as something to protect. I deserve more than fleeting moments of passion. I deserve more." Tears start rolling down her face. She hurriedly wipes them away. I soften my gaze.

"You do. You do deserve more. I just think Vince will eventually be able to give that to you. But you're right. You've been through enough. You deserve to just have a little happiness." She gives me a soft smile. I turn to look back over the flames and find Lane gazing at me. A sensual smirk plays at his lips when my eyes meet his.

"Don't let that go, Adira," Leia says. I catch Zander walking away; an idea comes to me. I get up to go chat with him.

"I won't," I say as I walk away. "We'll talk later!" I shout as I continue on. I catch up to him and pull at his arm.

"I need a favor," I say in greeting.

"When don't you need a favor, princess?" I roll my eyes, and he laughs.

"I want to go on a hunt." Confusion creases his brow.

"You've been on, like, twenty."

"No, I want to go on a very specific hunt." Realization dawns, and his face breaks out into a huge grin.

"We're hunting wild cat tonight."

Zander goes off to assemble the best Amoran hunters for the night after telling Lane that he'll be stealing me tonight for additional training. We've done so many crazy things for training that he doesn't even second-guess it. The same way I used to home in on my breathing before a big swim, I do now as I check the knives already attached to my thigh and forearm and attach an additional two to my waist and fasten two spears along my back in the shape of an X. I'm dressed in the traditional clothing worn by the Amoran women who complete this ritual. It takes me a moment to get used to how much skin is exposed. A piece of fabric goes around my breasts and is secured in place with a strap around my neck and one that goes around my torso, about a hand's width above my navel. Most of my stomach is exposed, showing off my scars that have healed by now but will forever be etched in my skin. There was a time when I shied away from them and tried not to look, but in this moment, I wear them proudly. The skirt goes to the jungle ground with a slit that goes all the way to my hip, exposing my dagger strapped to my side. At least it's my color: green. Kira had come and done my hair for the occasion. She did something similar to what Lonny had done previously. One giant braid went over the top of my head with three smaller braids on each side of it were all pulled back and bound together with a tie. Even up, my hair falls to my lower back. I can feel the adrenaline kicking in as my blood pumps in my ears. Lonny rushes toward me with a frantic look on his face.

"Oh, please please pleeeaaaassseeee let me come, princess. I've been waiting for one of you to *finally* do this hunt I swear I'll help—" He pauses and looks me up and down before blinking exaggeratedly. "Sorry, for a second there, I forgot you were about to propose to someone." He shakes his head out like he's trying to clear it. "Anyway, PLEASE let me come, I've been working on—"

"Lonny. Shut up. Yes, of course, you can come. I figured my best friends would be there." The words come out before I can even think twice about it. We both stand frozen for a moment, and Lonny looks like he's about to cry. I feel like I might. I didn't even realize that spot was really and truly up for grabs until Lonny and Zander took it over. They stepped up the second that Vince stepped out without a second thought. Lonny pulls me into a bone-crushing hug. After what feels like five minutes of him squeezing the life out of me, he hurriedly lets go and wipes at his face and shakes out his whole body.

"Dammit, woman. Making me cry when I'm about to go kill things," he mutters as he walks toward the rest of the hunters. I chuckle and follow. Zander gives me another huge smile as I walk up in my getup.

"Damn, princess! Who knew you could pull off the Amoran look like you invented it?" I laugh along with all of the other hunters present.

"All right, you all know how this goes. We can aid her in whatever way she needs, but this is Adira's kill. Adira, which four of us do you want on the ground with you?" I look around at the assembled group. I know I want Lonny and Zander with me down there, now I just need to pick the other two. My gaze settles on Zafira and Lily, two of the best hunters in Sentri. A smirk grazes both of their faces as I glance between them. I match their grin.

"Will you join me?" I ask.

"It'll be our honor," Zafira answers for them. I turn to Zander and Lonny.

"Don't act like you didn't know you guys would be with me." They give me twin smiles, and Zander turns to the rest of the hunters.

"All right, the rest of you, to the trees." And with that, we're off. The other five start climbing, and we take off on a run. I let adrenaline and instinct take over. A smile breaks across my face as my heartbeat matches the pounding of my feet on the Sentri jungle floor. After we're about a mile in, I hear the sound of a howler monkey coming from above us. I recognize the tone. Ajax has spotted something. We slow to a crawl and drop to our stomachs to creep up on the creature. After crawling for a few minutes, the soft call of the myna reaches us from farther ahead. Another comes from slightly to the west. They're closing in on the perimeter. I look to Zander, and he nods to me. This is my hunt. My call. I look to Lily and use the hand signals I've learned to send her east toward the first call. I turn to Zafira and send her west toward the second. I check to make sure that we're still downwind. Lonny and Zander flank me as we prowl forward. The song of the cotinga comes at me from directly ahead. We have it surrounded. I put my hand up to halt Lonny and Zander, and they freeze, waiting for my direction. I strain my ears to hear the creature walking. The rhythm is slightly off, suggesting a possible limp. I exchange a smirk with Zander and Lonny before mimicking the call of an oropendola. All at once, the other five hunters drop from the trees, filling in the holes that are left open by us on the ground. The creature startles and immediately gets into defensive position. I feel the air deflate out of my chest at the sight of the creature. Of course. Of course, it would be the same cat that gave me the scars I now proudly display. I don't know if it's possible, but for a moment, I swear recognition flares in his eyes.

"Hello, handsome," I say as I reach back and grab hold of one of my spears. He growls and prowls back and forth, only turning around when he gets too close to one of the spears on the perimeter. The other hunters have created a fighting ring, and I'm alone inside of it with the beast of the jungle. We do a similar dance as the last time we met, but this time I'm surer on my feet. Fear doesn't roll through me, anticipation does. He is the first to lunge. I forgot how quick he is, and he catches my skirt, tearing it to the knee.

"Come on, Adira!"

"You got this, Adira!"

Encouragements fly at me from all around the circle in a mixture of words or just yips and chants. The cat lunges again, but this time I'm ready for the speed and jump out of the way, using my spear for balance as I vault over his shoulder. Before I land, I grab the dagger attached to my thigh and unsheathe it to stab it into the leg that I injured all those weeks ago. He roars out and slashes with his paw. I duck out of the way at the last second. My blood is pumping in my ears as adrenaline courses through my very bones. The jaguar starts pacing closer and closer to the perimeter. I eye his back legs, noticing the blood slowly trickling from one of them. A satisfied smirk graces my lips, and he snarls at me again. I see his muscles coil to pounce toward me. I ready myself for attack, but not for him to go for the perimeter. He leaps toward Ajax. It would've been an easy kill for him, but they're saving him for me. Ajax ducks away at the last moment, and the cat takes off into the jungle. I secure my spear behind my back and sprint after him. I can hear others following me, but all my focus is on not losing him. I might have a chance of gaining on him with his injured leg if fate is on my side tonight. The full moon peeks through the trees, and I see the flash of a tail plunge into a thick wall of foliage. He stops running, and I stop in my tracks. I hear the treads of the other hunters halt behind me. My shoulders heave with every breath as I strain my ears toward the bush.

"Is he gone?" Lonny asks. I put my hand up to shush him. He's here. I know it. I can feel it. *Come on, handsome . . . come out and play.* A low rumble emanates from the foliage, and a smile tugs on my lips. I reach back for my spear on instinct, and the whole jungle seems to go silent. A second later, he pounces from hiding and comes right toward me. I stab forward toward his heart. He moves at the last second, and I miss, hitting somewhere in his stomach. He bites down on the handle, breaking it with ease so it's not dragging on the jungle ground. I reach to grab the other spear right as he jumps at me once again. I hear Zander's and Lonny's shouts of warning and thrust the spear into the beast's heart right as he falls on me. I feel his last couple of breaths as his body sags against mine. Dead. Zander is the first to get to me. He rolls the jungle cat off of me, and my blinding smile is the first thing he sees. A booming laugh erupts out of him, and Lonny comes running up.

"Holy shit! Holy shit, that was amazing!" He joins in on the manic laughter. Zafira walks up with a triumphant grin and offers a hand to help me up.

"Well done. I look forward to seeing the proposal." Lily gives me a hug, and the others gather around to offer their congratulations and inspect the kill.

"Want me to carry him back, princess?" Zander offers. I shake my head.

"No. I want to finish this." I look down at the beautiful beast. Never again. Never again will I feel powerless. A proud grin splits Zander's face. Zafira and Lily help lift my kill onto my shoulders, and we head back to the village. By the time we make it back, all of the Amoran are asleep. Lonny has a look on his face that suggests he's contemplating the audacity of people being asleep in the middle of the night.

"Lonny, don't—"

"HEY! EVERYONE GET YOUR ASSES UP!" The rest of the hunters join in on the shouting to rouse everyone. I roll my eyes and chuckle. I should've expected this. People start emerging from their dwellings with tired looks of annoyance that turn to expressions of excitement as they peer out and see the jungle cat on my shoulders. Leia peeks her head out, and a smile breaks out on her face. I had told her that I would eventually be doing this, I was just waiting for the right time. Vince follows her with his usual broody look. Finally, I catch the eye of Lane. He wears a look of tired, gleeful confusion. Once everyone notices our gazes on each other, they go silent and open a path for him to get to me. His eyebrow quirks, and he slowly saunters toward me. Nervous energy flows through me, and I feel my hands starting to shake. I take tedious steps forward until I'm in front of him and bend down to drop my kill at his feet. I swallow the lump in my throat.

"Lane," my voice croaks. He gives me his signature smirk. I clear my throat and try again.

"Lane. You're literally the last person that I ever thought I would fall in love with. But . . . then the world fell apart. And life just started to feel like it was all superfluous. You came in, and you showed me that even as worlds collapse, even as everything that could go wrong, does, even as people abandon you, you would be a constant. Always there.

"When the days came where it felt so much easier to just stay in the dark and let it take over, you gave me a reason to reach for the light. To continue to *be* a light. I'm sorry I've so strongly misjudged you most of our lives, because you are so *good*. You are kind, funny, compassionate, and you love with everything in you. I know you say that you revel in the dark, but you illuminate my life in a way I didn't know was possible." I look down at the jaguar at my feet.

"I offer you this kill to symbolize a promise. I promise to always take care of you as I know you'll always take care of me." Tears start flowing down his cheeks. "I wanted to ask you . . . to please be mine. In every way. Be my mate. But not as a duty to Maurea, but as a duty to our souls. Because my very *being* burns for you. And there's no one I'd rather have alongside me as we take on these worlds broken."

35

FOR THE SECOND time tonight, the jungle seems to go completely silent. A lone tear falls down my cheek. Lane steps up and cradles my face in his hands.

"You," he says barely above a whisper. "You gorgeous, unbelievable"—he looks down at the jaguar—"badass woman. You amaze me more and more every day." He wipes the tear away with his thumb, and I hold my breath. "Yes." I gasp out a sob. "A million times, yes." I throw my arms around him and pull his lips to mine. He picks me up, and I wrap my legs around him as the whole of Sentri erupts into cheers and celebrations. My tears mix with his as he rains kisses on every inch of my face. Lonny starts shouting loud enough for people all the way back in Maurea to hear. Lane rests his forehead on mine, and laughs bubble out of us. For a moment, time seems to slow. I realize that this is quite possibly the happiest moment of my life so far. Pure, unadulterated joy floods through my very being. Lane looks back down at the kill.

"Are you hurt?" I shake my head and give him my most dazzling smile. He sets me down, and I rearrange my skirt. It seems he just now notices what I'm wearing. His eyes darken, and he swallows a lump in his throat.

"You evil little thing . . ." He eyes me up and down. Heat pools in my stomach and drops lower as I give him a smirk.

"You like the outfit?" He lets out a humorless laugh. I bite down on my bottom lip, and a sound akin to a growl comes out of him.

"Lonny!" he yells without breaking eye contact with me. Lonny trots up and stops short when he sees our gazes on each other.

"Umm, do you need me for this?" he asks with a knowing grin. Lane ignores his question.

"When is the soonest we can do the ceremony?" His hands ball into fists at his sides. Lonny looks back and forth between us and does his best to hold back a laugh. Unsuccessfully.

"Tomorrow," he says between cackles. "We can do everything tomorrow. I'll get Kira and Zander's help on everything, and this ridiculous tension can finally be over with." Lane's eyes finally leave mine, and he gives Lonny a smile.

"I appreciate it, friend." Lonny lets out another laugh and pats him on the back before going to find Kira and Zander. I close the space between us again and interlock my fingers with his.

"Think you can make it till then?" I ask. He groans and kisses my forehead.

"I can try." A laugh bubbles out of me. He lets go of one hand and leads me toward the horde of people.

"Let's go let people congratulate us," he says with a chuckle. I laugh along with him. Kira is the first to get to us. She wraps me in a warm hug and gives a kind smile to Lane.

"A beautiful kill, Adira. One worthy of the proposal. You make a perfect match."

"Thank you, Kira." She smiles and nods before leaving us be to converse with others. Leia runs up to us with Vince slowly trailing behind her. She wraps an arm around each of us until we're bound in a group hug.

"I'm so happy for you guys. I can't even begin to express it." She separates and takes a step back as Vince comes up. His expression is one of indifferent boredom, but his eyes tell a different story. There's the usual anger there, but something else lies underneath as well. It takes me a minute to recognize it, but when I retake Lane's hand, it flashes into more prominence. Sadness.

"Congratulations," he says softly. Lane must see my face drop. He gives my hand a tight squeeze. I see Leia try to hide the pain in her face by turning away and feigning interest in the fire across the way. When she turns back and I lock eyes with her, I give her a tight smile. I meant what I said earlier. She deserves all the happiness in the world.

"So," Leia breaks the awkward silence. "When's the big day?"

"Tomorrow," I answer with a grin. I see Vince flinch slightly before he tries to scold his features back into indifference.

"Why so soon?" he asks between clenched teeth.

"Why wait?" counters Lane. Vince just nods in response. Leia takes both of my hands in hers.

"You must sleep with me in the hut tonight. I know you aren't having a Maurean wedding, but there are at least some traditions we can uphold." Vince shoots his glare toward her.

"I'm just supposed to sleep in the dirt?" Leia and I flinch at his tone. I narrow my eyes at him, and he avoids my gaze. Where the hell does he get off talking to her like that?

"Don't worry about it, Leia. I can find somewhere to stay so you and Vince can—"

"No," she cuts me off. She turns to Vince and takes a deep breath. "I would like Adira to stay with me tonight. I'll talk to Lonny about finding a place for you for the night. I don't think that's too much to ask." Vince flexes his hands three times before he lets go of the breath he's holding and his eyes turn to me.

"Fine," he mutters. He turns and walks away, leaving us three alone.

"Are you okay?" I ask. She waves her hand at me.

"Tonight isn't about me. Or *him*. I'll see you soon, yeah?" I nod. "*Soon.*" She gives a knowing glance at Lane. He chuckles and repeats, "Soon." She smiles, satisfied, and walks away. We spend another hour or so conversing with the Amoran people and accepting congratulations. Upon news of the ceremony tomorrow, most run off to bed to get adequate sleep for the big day. Finally, it's just Lane and I left lingering by the fire. Well, the last ones awake. Lonny fell asleep on one of the logs around the fire and is snoring loudly with his mouth wide open in what looks to be a very uncomfortable position.

"So, what do I need to know about this ceremony that's happening tomorrow?"

"Just go with the flow," I respond. He nods and leans down to brush his lips softly against mine. After a moment, he deepens the kiss, and I lean into it. Right then is when Lonny lets out a particularly obnoxious snore. I laugh and lean away. Lane groans as I back away from him.

"One more damn day," he mutters. I nod and look away for a moment to hide the sadness that I know is written on my face. He catches it and grabs my chin between his fingers to bring my gaze back to his.

"Tell me," he implores.

"There are just people I wish could be here for this."

"We can wait, Ad."

"No," I say quickly. "No. I want to be with you. In every way that I can be," I say with a blush. "Besides, there's no way that everyone I want there can be there. Kind of impossible . . ." He nods in understanding.

"They'll be there, love. Your dad and Liam." I look up at him through my eyelashes and crinkle my brow.

"What do you mean?" He shrugs.

"I'd like to think there's another life after this one. One where we can check in on the ones we love who we left behind." I tilt my head and lift my eyebrows. "What? Is it so dubious to think something like that might be waiting for us?" I give him a smirk.

"No, I guess not. I like the thought of them being there," I say, intertwining my fingers with his. His fingers stroke my cheek.

"I love you," he whispers. I stand on my toes and kiss him.

"I love you too." With that, he turns and leaves to spend the night in our dwelling. I head toward Leia's hut, practically giddy. I'm also plenty exhausted. I'm about to walk in when I hear arguing from inside.

"I can't live like this, Vince! This constant anger . . . the resentment! I just . . . I don't know you!" Leia's voice rings.

"I did everything for you, Leia! Gave up everything! Do you know what I've lost? Out of respect for you?" Vince's anger radiates.

"Respect for me?" she seethes.

"She left you out there! She left you, knowing you could die! And I distanced myself from her, I lost my *best friend* out of respect for you!"

"Adira has respected me more than you ever have, Vince! Gosh, you think I always need a man running around deciding what's best for me? I made a decision based on what would be the best for our people. She respected that. *You* decided that I wasn't capable of making my own decision and took the entirety of your anger out on your best friend. Do you want to know why her and Lane work so well together? They're equals. She takes care of him just as much as he takes care of her. Did you notice he didn't say anything about how *she* proposed to *him* instead of the other way around? He said nothing because it was something to be expected of that relationship. It's give-and-take, Vince. What every relationship should be. And you don't seem to have a singular idea of how that could possibly work." A silence follows. I really should go. This conversation isn't meant for my ears . . .

"You know what I think?" Leia says. "I think if this was really just about my safety, you would've been over this anger by now. But it's not."

"What're you talking about?"

"You resent *me*." Another silence. "You resent me because if I never would have made the decision that *I* did, you never would've gotten mad at your best friend, you never would've screamed at her enough to send her into the jungle—yes, I know all about that, and you would still have your best friend." I can practically hear Vince's teeth clenching.

"Get over yourself, Vince." Leia seethes. "Adira has apologized about her involvement in the plan. I've apologized. Ironically enough, you're the only one who hasn't taken any responsibility for your actions. You might not have had any control over what we did, but *your* reactions are your own. You don't get to blame Adira for your relationship being destroyed, and you *sure as hell* don't get to blame me." My stomach drops. I can see now that the Leia that Vince fell in love with is likely gone now, too. The timid, shy, and quiet Leia was left back in Maurea with the kind, patient, and benevolent Vince. They're staring at familiar strangers trying to find people that don't exist anymore.

"Where does this leave us?" Vince asks after a while.

"I just . . . need some time," Leia responds. A moment later, Vince bursts out of the hut. Luckily, I'm hidden enough in the shadows that he doesn't even notice me as he storms away toward Abe's hut. I enter a second later and find Leia in tears. I run up to her and wrap her in a hug. She sobs for a minute longer before wiping at her eyes and fanning her face.

"Oh my gosh, I'm sorry. Tonight is totally not about me."

"Don't be ridiculous, Leia . . . Do you want to talk about it?" She looks at me and gives me a knowing smirk.

"You heard." One side of my mouth tilts into a smile, and I shrug.

"Just the end of it." She nods. "Do you want to talk about it?" I ask again. She shrugs.

"I just think that we need some time apart. Maybe once you're officially off the market and he has some time to work through everything in his head, we can work back to something, but for now . . . I don't know. This isn't working for me. I don't think it's working for him either, but he gave up everything for the mere notion of me. I think the idea of losing me after everything seems inconceivable to him. That's all I really want to say about it for now." I nod and consider something.

"You're really good at that, you know."

"Good at what?"

"Analyzing things, wording them in eloquent ways. Advice. I

think people would feel better just talking with you about some of the things they're going through." Her eyebrows crunch together.

"Would you mind talking with someone for me? You can say no, obviously. But I have a mom who's having a hard time adjusting. She had a pretty traumatic birth, and I'm worried she isn't connecting with her baby as much. Me and Kira have tried, but we don't have the same way with words as you do. Could you give it a shot?" She considers for a moment.

"I'll try. I can't promise anything." A smile lights up my face, and I pull her in for another hug.

"Thank you, thank you, thank you, Leia!" She laughs and hugs me back.

"Obviously not until *after* tomorrow. We have a long day ahead of us."

"Hopefully an even longer night," I murmur. She bursts out laughing, and I join her. Damn, it feels good to laugh. I change into something more comfortable to sleep in, and Leia pulls out a bowl with some thick, red liquid inside. She grabs my foot and drags it onto her lap.

"What are you doing?" I ask with a laugh. She grabs a tiny bundle of grass and dips it into the mixture before painting it onto my toenail.

"Some of the little girls discovered that if you mash some colored berries with a certain liquid that's found in one of the roots of a random plant I can't remember, it stains your nails," she says, flashing her beautifully painted toenails. "Not that I think Lane will be paying any attention to your toes tomorrow," she says with a quirked eyebrow.

"I don't know," I say with a smile. "He did say after we were mated that he would worship every *inch* of me." Leia swoons.

"Girl!"

"I know!" We burst into another round of laughter.

"I meant what I said. I'm unbelievably happy for you two. Although it's a little hilarious how much your opinion of him has changed since he proposed to you back in Maurea." I shrug.

"That was different. The whole thing was different. He was asking out of obligation to bullshit Maurean ideals. Not love." She lets out a humorless laugh.

"Adira, that boy has been in love with you since you two first raced as six-years." I can't help the blush that comes to my cheeks. We fall into amicable silence as she paints all of my toes. Another idea comes to me.

"Will you sing tomorrow?" I ask as she sets my foot down off of her lap. A smile lights up her face.

"Of course! What did you want me to sing? I know a few of the Amoran songs but not all of them."

"Actually, since the whole day is going to be one of Amoran traditions, I was hoping you'd sing a Maurean one to bring in a little piece of home."

"I love that idea. Which one would you like?" I give her a small smile.

"Lady Blue."

36

I DON'T KNOW WHY I bothered even trying to fall asleep last night. I do my best to stifle my yawns as Kira and Leia prep me for the ceremony today. Kira looks like she got as much sleep as I did. Today would have been a day full of preparing for the mating ceremony tomorrow, but we promptly decided to skip that step, so Kira has been working tirelessly to do a day's worth of work in one night. I try multiple times to apologize for the inconvenience, but she won't hear it. Since Lane and I also already have a dwelling, we're also skipping the part of the ceremony where we'd create it. I really don't mind; if I'm being honest, I don't need a big, flashy ceremony to know that Lane is mine. We've belonged to each other longer than I've been willing to admit. I'm eager for it to be official. Everyone is buzzing with excitement. I can hear people running around doing last-minute preparations outside the hut. Kira is helping me put on the elaborate ceremonial gown while Leia does my hair.

I'm grateful for Kira's help with the dress. It looks like a rough combination of the one I wore yesterday and the one I wore for my ceremony in Maurea. This one is held together with different straps and ties that delicately cover my bodice while still exhibiting my curves. The fabric feels so soft and delicate, making the gown extremely comfortable. The neckline takes on the likeness of my mother's dress with the looser fit that falls low on my chest. The skirt of the gown has slits up both legs that go to my hips. The color is one that I haven't worn often, but as I look down at the black fabric, I decide I should wear it more often. It's a dress that makes one feel beautiful and powerful. Leia decides to keep my hair down for the day, letting its full length fall to my lower back. She puts in a couple small braids interspersed throughout it with some vines and beautiful black flowers weaved in.

"All right," Leia says as she steps back, appraising me. "You're ready." A huge smile lights up her face. Kira gives me an approving nod.

"Oh, wait! I almost forgot," I say as I turn to look for what has become my favorite accessory. I attach the strappy holster to my upper thigh and sheathe my dagger.

"Okay, now I'm ready." Lonny comes bursting into the hut, freezing when he sees me. His eyes lock on the dagger for a second before continuing up to finally meet my eyes.

"How do I look?" I ask with a chuckle.

"If looks could kill, princess." I flash him a grin as I pass him on my way out. I wonder what Lane will be in today. He looks good in anything. I mean *anything*. Really seems kind of unfair. Zander meets us outside and gives me a similar appraisal to Lonny's.

"You two realize that you can't gawk like that once I'm a mated woman," I say with a smirk.

"Says who?" Lonny asks with a look of dread. I laugh openly at his expression and leave his question unanswered.

"So, what happens now?" I ask Kira.

"Everything should be ready. We'll go to the clearing where the ceremony will be held, and you and Lane will hear from the Amoran people why you do or don't make a good match."

"Or don't? You didn't mention that people speak of different reasons couples don't work well together . . ." I try to not look toward

Leia, thinking of Vince. If he wanted to make a scene today, that would be the time to. Kira gives me an understanding smile.

"It rarely happens. Only once in my lifetime has a couple ever gotten . . . discouraging feedback. You and Lane are a smart match. I don't think you will have anything to worry about." I try to shake the dread building in my stomach. Leia grabs my hand and gives it a squeeze.

"It won't be an issue," she reassures me. I give her a nod and a grateful smile.

"Shall we?" Lonny says, holding out an arm for me. I interlock mine with his and walk toward my future. I can feel my heart beating in my fingertips, and my stomach is a mess of nerves. All of Sentri will be here with the exception of one person who's having to keep watch on Williams. I'm sad that Mom and Avery can't be here for this, but I'm glad that my Amoran family is here to witness it. This is going to be our new home. It makes sense for us to have this ceremony here.

We break into the clearing, and the breath gets knocked out of me. Flowers cover the Sentri floor in a myriad of colors. Everyone present wears at least one black flower somewhere on their person. The same flowers that are woven into my hair. There is a singular path where the flowers don't lie that leads straight to *him*. His eyes glisten with unshed tears as he gazes at me. He wears the same shade of black in the form of a loose, long-sleeve shirt that cuts almost to his navel in the front, tucked into trousers that hug every muscle of his toned legs. His hair is pulled back into a bun that sits near the top of his head. Don't get me wrong, I love it when he leaves his hair down; but having it pulled back brings out his strong jawline and brings more focus to his piercing eyes. I'm practically drooling. Lonny clears his throat. I hadn't realized I'd stopped walking to gawk at Lane. Leia starts singing, and I continue forward, doing my best not to run straight to him. We finally make it to where he and Abe stand, and Lane leans down to whisper in my ear.

"I like that you kept the dagger." I can hear the smirk in his voice. I give him one of my own before we turn toward Abe. Leia finishes the lullaby, and he gives us both an approving smile before speaking to all of Sentri.

"Lane and Adira have made their intentions known to be mated. We ask that you speak your thoughts on their intent." Silence falls across the crowd. For a moment, I wonder if no one is going to say anything. What happens if they don't? Lane reaches down and grabs my hand, giving it a reassuring squeeze.

"I've seen the way you are apart, and I've seen the way you are together. Together, you are more sure of yourselves, as if you've found confidence in your individuality through your union. A good match." A voice shouts from the back of the crowd. A smile lights up my face, and Lane tightens his grip on my hand. Another voice speaks up.

"You both seek to assist in whatever ways you are able. You'll be of good service to each other and to your community. A good match."

"You know how to laugh with one another. Never lose this. Humor is one of the best remedies of all. A good match."

"You can see the passion that lies underneath the love. A good match."

"You always make sure that the other is taken care of before you worry about yourself. A good match."

Tears start freely flowing down my cheeks. I sneak a look toward Lane and see him crying as well. One after another, people speak out on the different reasons and ways that Lane and I make a good match. If I had any doubts about mating this man before, they would be thoroughly squashed. I suppose that's probably the whole point of something like this. To help solidify the decision one way or the other. Leia says something similar to what she said to Vince last night. That we are equals and that's why we'll work. Lonny exclaims, "Since no one else will talk about, you're both hot as hell, that's bound to work out." We laugh along with the crowd. We're about to wrap up that part of the ceremony before a voice rings from the very back.

"Adira, you care about people more than anyone I've ever met. You speak out for the voiceless, and you respect people's wishes above all else. You always search for the light in people even if they don't deserve it. You are a lot of things, but above all else, you're brave. But not for yourself, you're brave for others. And that makes you someone who could be the best match for any bastard lucky enough to have you." My breath catches, and I try to hold back a sob. "Lane, you're one of the smartest men I've ever met. I see the way you care for her. I see the way you love her. And I think you can really take care of her even though she'll never need it." He stops to clear a lump in his throat. "There's not a man that exists that deserves her or will ever be worthy of her. But you come the closest." The clearing goes quiet once again. "I'm sorry for the hurt I caused you," he concludes. I let go of Lane's hand intending to run to my childhood best friend, but he turns and walks away back toward the rest of camp. I turn to Leia and see her in tears.

"Let's continue," Abe's voice rings out. I turn back to Lane, and he gives me an encouraging smile.

"We'll talk to him after," he mouths. I nod and face Abe.

"Now you'll have a chance to speak vows to one another before this audience. Lane?" He clears his throat and grips my hands.

"There aren't words that can adequately describe what you mean to me, Adira. From the day that the little six-year girl beat me in that race, I was infuriated and smitten." The crowd laughs along with us. "I hope to someday be a man that is worthy of you. I look forward to trying to be that man for the rest of this life, and whatever comes next. I love you." A sob escapes me, and he wipes the tears off my cheek. I can hear Lonny loudly sobbing behind me and even see water welling in Abe's eyes.

"Adira?" Abe motions for me to speak. I do my best to swallow down the lump in my throat without a lot of success.

"Well, I kind of gave this big romantic speech last night . . ." Laughs teeter out of the crowd again. "You have nothing to work toward, Lane. You're a man who's worthy of me and more, and I'm sorry I ever made you feel like you weren't. Thank you for being there not only for me, but for my brothers. As we prepare for this life as mates, I promise to love you every day for the rest of forever. I will be a woman for our future daughters to look up to as I know you will do the same for our sons. I will fight alongside you as warriors for Maurea and Sentri. And I will make the conscious choice every day to wake up and choose you. Choose us." New tears spring to life in his eyes and fall down his beautiful, perfect face. "I love you." I conclude, barely above a whisper.

"If no one objects," Abe says loud enough for everyone to hear, "I present to you two persons, now become one soul." Lane tugs me to him and crashes his lips to mine. The jungle erupts into cheers as I melt into my mate. Lane picks me up, and we deepen the kiss. The rest of the world fades for a moment as I drown in the joy that I have found the soul akin to my own. As we separate, the rest of the world bleeds back in. We turn toward the crowd to see people dancing and singing. Lonny and Zander are bawling as they hop up and down like small children. I laugh through the tears streaming down my face and look around to see if I can find Vince. I don't see him anywhere, but the crowd is so heavy now that I doubt I could even if he was standing ten feet from me. I turn to yell in Lane's ear over the noise.

"Have you seen Vince?" He shakes his head.

"No. He might need some time to process this. We should let him have that." I nod. He's right. I'm sure Vince will come to us when he's ready to talk about it. I can't help the relief that flows through me. I didn't realize I had been holding out for *some* kind of support or approval from Vince for my relationship with Lane. Him giving it during the ceremony means more than he probably knows. I look forward to telling him.

Lonny and Zander are the first to wrap us in eager embraces. Leia and Kira are close behind. By the time we make it out of the clearing, I'm pretty sure we've hugged every single Amoran in Sentri. Within no time at all, music erupts, and the dancing goes from senseless to bordering on choreographed. Lane wraps his arm around my hip and bends down to whisper in my ear.

"Dance with me." His breath tickles my neck and sends shivers down my spine. He takes my hand and leads me into the drove of bodies already dancing. It takes me a moment to get into the choreography of the dance, but once I do, I fly. My heartbeat matches the beat of the drums, and my blood flows with the melody of the music. Halfway into the next song, a downpour starts. The music stops for a fraction of a second before starting up again, and all of Sentri dances in the rain. After a while, the tempo slows, and Lane pulls me in closer. We sway to the sound of the music and the wind, and I find myself in pure bliss. One of his hands leaves my hip, and he drags it slowly up my body before stopping to cup my cheek, bringing my lips to his and kissing me with all the reverence in the world.

"Have I told you how incredible you look?" he asks in a gravelly voice. A sultry chuckle escapes me.

"I was going to say the same to you. I like the hair. A lot." I look up at him through my lashes.

"Black might be one of my favorite colors on you."

"Hmm," I say as I step back, appraising him again. "I'd say the same for you." He flashes his signature smirk before tugging me to his chest and leaning down to whisper in my ear.

"I'm thinking I'd like to have a more private celebration with my mate." His mouth moves down my throat, stopping where it meets my shoulder. His lips lightly graze there, a promise of a kiss rather than a proper one. A small whimper escapes my throat, and I feel his mouth pull into a smile. I ignore the fluttering in my stomach as I take his hand and lead him toward our dwelling. People give us knowing smiles as we pass. I climb up first, and Lane follows close behind me. The party is still in full swing, but at least some of the sound is muted out inside of our little teardrop.

I wring out my hair, trying not to disturb the beautiful flowers too much. Lane comes up behind me and starts picking them out one by one and placing them carefully on the floor. When the last one hits the ground, his hands go to my shoulders and slowly move down my arms. Goose bumps spread across my skin, and I feel my heart rate speed up. He takes a hand and moves my mane of hair to one side. He feels where my pulse is racing with his fingers and takes a step closer so my back is pressed against him. His lips replace his fingers, and he kisses my pulse. Softly at first, like he's testing waters. Savoring. Like he's tasting the finest nectar. I move to turn around, but he pulls my hips back against him, keeping me in place.

"Do I not get to kiss you as well?" He gives a low laugh.

"Let me touch you, Adira," he says in a husky voice. I swallow and nod, letting him have control. For the moment at least. His hands start a gentle exploration, giving certain areas more attention than others. He gauges my reactions, figuring out what I do and don't like. Only problem is that I love all of it. I could drown in a sea of Lane's touch and die happy. Without even realizing it, he's maneuvered the different straps and clasps so that with one single *snap*, the dress pools to the floor. There's a single moment. A second of hesitation, insecurity. For one moment, I almost reach to conceal the scars that cover my torso. Lane catches the movement and turns me around. His eyes darken impossibly further as he drinks the image of me in.

"This hardly seems fair," I say motioning to his fully clothed stature. I try not to fidget. He doesn't break eye contact as he undresses. For a moment, we just stand there. Then he takes a confident step forward, pulling me into his arms.

"Don't you ever think that you are anything but stunningly, magnificently, and extraordinarily beautiful, Adira." I feel my cheeks redden. He takes a hand and strokes my blush. "Now, I believe I made you a promise." I crinkle my brow and look up at him.

"And what promise is that?" He scoops me up, ignoring my small squeal of surprise, and lays me on our bed.

"To worship every inch of my stunning mate."

Lane never breaks a promise.

37

I WAKE UP FEELING sore and satiated. Well, as satiated as I can get. I don't think I can ever get *enough* of Lane. We spent the night "privately celebrating" our union until the early hours of the morning. I can tell by his even, deep breaths that he's still asleep. I do my best to stretch out my sore muscles while my back is still pressed against his bare chest. He shifts slightly, and I freeze, hoping not to wake him up. After a moment, his breathing picks up the rhythm of sleep again. I smile to myself and snuggle in closer. I could use at least another couple hours of sleep. I feel myself falling to sleep when suddenly, a high scream comes from outside. Lane and I are up in a moment. We make quick work of redressing and head out of our cocoon of solitude.

We see multiple people climbing out of their dwellings and all heading toward the same direction. We follow the crowd, making our way to the west side of the forest. Lane takes my hand and guides us through the thick cluster of people. It's like you can feel the shock reverberate as people behold what's lying there. We're almost to the front when Lane abruptly turns around and blocks me from moving any further. His face pales, and I see horror in his eyes.

"Lane? What is it?" I ask as he continually tries to bring me back the opposite way, blocking my view. As people retreat from the site, looks of pity shoot toward me, and dread builds in my stomach. I can feel my hands shaking as I push back on Lane's chest.

"Let me see, Lane."

"Baby, please trust me. You don't want to see that." He looks down at me with pleading eyes.

"See *what*?" I can see his instinct to protect me fighting the instinct to trust me to make my own decisions. The latter wins out, and he leads me back to the front of the crowd. The second I see it— see *him*—I almost wish I hadn't. My whole body goes numb, and the only thing keeping me standing is Lane's arms holding me upright. A terrible sound emanates from the crowd, and Lane tightens his grip on me. I see two bodies in my peripheral vision emerge from the horde of people. They move toward me, but I bat them all away as I collapse to the ground next to my childhood best friend. Next to his body. The same sound erupts again, and Lane is back at my side. He's saying something . . . I can't hear him. The other sound is too loud. Too consuming. I stare at Vince's face, devoid of any color. His eyes. His beautiful eyes that you could read every emotion in, now staring lifeless into nothing. The sound grows louder and louder. It takes a few minutes for me to tear my eyes away from Vince to look at my mate and understand what he's trying to say to me.

"Baby, baby, shhhh . . . Breathe. Breathe." Oh . . . that sound is me. Lonny and Zander are here. And Kira. Kira is looking over Vince. She's feeling for a pulse that I know won't be there. She's inspecting his bloody wrists and taking away the knife that colored them. I can't breathe. I can't breathe. He can't be gone. He's always been there. Even when he wasn't, he was still around. There was still a chance. We were starting to work things out. He had moved on. What happened? This can't be real. I'm sleeping, and I'm going to wake up, and this will all be gone. This isn't real. This isn't real. I take Vince's hand in mine, and I try to breathe through clenched teeth. I feel empty, like part of me just died. Ceased to exist. Kira comes back again. I didn't realize she had left. She puts a covering over Vince, but I refuse to let go of his hand.

"Adira, let us take care of him," Kira croons in a soft voice. I ignore her and grip his hand tighter.

"Adira—"

"Give her a damn minute," Lane snaps. She reluctantly nods and stands to give me a semblance of privacy. I turn to see half of Sentri still standing around, staring at us. At him. Anger takes over, and I stand on unsteady feet.

"Leave him alone! Get out of here!" I scream over and over again. People quickly scatter, and then it's just me, Lane, Zander, and Lonny. I turn back and kneel by his body. One of his hands is outside of the cover. I move it underneath and feel myself break. I sob over him. Over another body. Another person gone.

"Why, Vince?" I choke out between sobs. I don't know how long I stay there. No one tries to rush me, and I find it in myself to be grateful for that. I woke up this morning happier than I had ever been in my entire life. Maybe this is just how the universe works. There must be a balance. For every overwhelming joy, there must be an overwhelming tragedy. How . . . poetic. How filthily poetic. When I finally stand, it's pouring rain. Sentri washes away the blood of the first man I ever loved as if it was never there. I turn without word and walk back toward the main fire. I'm cold. Someone put a blanket around me at one point. I don't remember when. I sit on the ground before the fire and gaze into the flames. I know people stare. I know they whisper about him, but I can't find it in me to say anything. So I sit, and I stare at the dancing flames.

Some unintelligible amount of time later, food is put in front of my face. I'm not hungry. Or maybe I am, but it feels good to be hungry. The physical feeling of emptiness feels akin to the emptiness of my soul at the moment. Lane kneels in front of me and lightly puts a hand on one of my legs while the other holds the stew.

"I need you to eat, baby." It takes me a moment to respond.

"I don't want to." I hardly recognize the coarse scratch of my voice. Lane sits down behind me and pulls me into his embrace. A part of me that's been frozen melts. He takes the bowl in one hand with a spoon in the other and feeds me the broth one small spoonful at a time. Part of me thinks that I should be embarrassed that I'm being fed like a child, but I can't find it in me to care. He promised to take care of me. I know that right now I need to be taken care of. By the time the broth is gone, night has fallen. I feel so tired. Like I could sleep for years and it wouldn't be enough. I look up from the flames and see that most of Sentri has gone to sleep. Lonny and Zander sit across from us, and Kira sits with Leia, comforting her the best that she can. I stand slowly and go over to her. She looks up at me with tired, anguished eyes.

"I'm tired," I scratch out. "Let's go to bed." After a minute, she nods and takes my hand. We silently walk to what has become her hut. I know that of all the people in the world right now, we are the ones who best understand what the other is going through. We lie down in the firs next to the fire that Lane adds kindling to. He gives me a kiss on the forehead and promises to be just outside if I ever need him tonight. Leia and I lie there in each other's arms and draw strength from shared tears. I know it will be a long road to find peace with the death of a man we both loved. For now, at least we have solace.

38

THE NEXT WEEK passes in a blur of grief. I give myself those days to mourn. Kira handles the body. Everyone walks on eggshells around Leia and I. No time will be enough to mourn the loss of Vince, but now it's time to make a plan. To move on. We aren't sure what to do with Williams at this point. We have to formulate a way to help the Dorian without bringing too much attention to the people running the experiments. The problem is, we have no idea how to even begin to do that. I haven't seen Williams for weeks. From what I've heard, he continues to talk a *lot* and asks plenty of questions. Lane and I make our way to the hut he's currently staying in. Before we go in, Lane gently grabs at my arm.

"Are you sure you want to deal with this right now, Ad? I can handle it. Lonny, Zander, and I can handle it." I give him a tight smile.

"Sitting around doing nothing isn't going to bring him back. Keeping busy will help me . . . move on, I guess." He nods in understanding. I walk in to see Williams once again bombarding his guard with countless inquiries about Sentri.

"Thanks, Zed, we've got it from here." Zed nods and gives us a grateful smile before exiting the hut.

"I hear congratulations are in order!" He's met with silence. He looks anxiously between the two of us before a look of horror crosses his face.

"Oh! Oh my gosh . . . and of course, my deepest sympathies for your friend . . . Adira, I know that you two were very close, and I—"

"I'd shut the hell up if I were you." He does so promptly. "I don't need another reminder of the invasion of privacy that has been my entire life." He starts nervously picking at his nails again.

"We need to figure out a plan," I continue. "We don't know where to start. We thought you might." He's about to say something before Zander, Lonny, and Leia walk into the room. He looks like he's about to say something to her, but I quickly silence him with a look promising violence if he dares to speak Vince's name again.

"So, any thoughts?" He continues to fidget with his hands.

"Wh-why should I help you?"

"Well, it's that, or we kill you," Lonny says nonchalantly. "I'm fine with either." Williams pales and clears his throat.

"What exactly is the goal?"

"To shut it down," Lane answers immediately. Williams lets out a humorless laugh.

"I'm sorry, but that's impossible. You can't expect to shut down an operation that is more than a millennium in the making. It-it's impossible."

"Well, then suggest something useful, asshat," Lonny spits. Williams seems to contemplate for a moment.

"I mean, Sentri is all but forgotten in the program without any ability to observe. The only way in is through where we came through the lab and through the underwater tunnel from Maurea. If you can get everyone from Maurea here, then you won't be under surveillance any longer." He looks to each of us with a hopeful gaze.

"That leaves the issue of your father." I turn to Lane. "And getting everyone here. It's a difficult swim, and it seems as though everyone

is convinced that Paul is the one looking out for their best interest."
He nods.

"We need to make another trip back. See how things have progressed," he says.

"Won't they be able to track you again though?" Zander asks.

"Actually, that shouldn't be as big of an issue due to the tsunami. Paul has only been able to set up one camera since then. It's placed on the front of his tent. If you can get rid of it, you could plan accordingly," Williams says with a little more confidence. I nod.

"What do we do once they all get here?" Zander asks.

"It's a first step. We can figure out the rest as we go," I answer. He looks unconvinced.

"Adira, you have a very temporary solution to a permanent problem. They're going to see that you're all gone, and they'll come running here!"

"I don't see anyone else suggesting a more permanent solution!" Zander and I stare each other down.

"How do we get out?" Lane asks Williams.

"I'm not sure what you mean."

"Out of the ecospheres." The hut goes silent.

"Y-you want to leave?"

"I'm not seeing a lot of other options." Zander and Lonny curse under their breath. Their world has essentially imploded because of us. They were fine, living in blissful oblivion as to what is going on outside of Sentri. If we hadn't come here, they wouldn't be forced to leave their home.

"I'm so sorry . . . I know that us coming here has had terrible consequences for you and your people. I can't—"

"Save it, princess," Lonny interrupts me. "I'm sure these asswipes would have figured out sooner or later how to mess everything up here as much as they have in Maurea." I give him a grateful smile. Leave it to Lonny to find the bright side of things.

"The outside world isn't one that any of you will be acclimated to . . . The technology alone will be jarring. They could very easily find you!" Williams babbles on.

"You said they had set up nature reserves," Lane says.

"Yes, they have."

"We're plenty accustomed to nature. You'll take us to one of those. We'll find a way to settle there."

"The only one that's close enough isn't anything like Maurea and quite different from Sentri. You're looking at an environment that's far more similar to Tragdome."

"We weren't accustomed to Sentri before we were. We adapted once. We'll do it again," I say. Williams looks like he wants to argue but decides against it.

"So just so everyone is on the same page . . . We somehow try to get all of the Dorian to Sentri, and then bring the whole of the Amoran *and* the Dorian out of the ecospheres all together through Avil?" Lane says.

"Through Avil?" Williams asks.

"We were told that the only way out is through Avil."

"Ah. Another miscommunication. There *is* a way out. But not through Avil. I seriously doubt that such a journey through the desert wouldn't result in countless deaths . . ."

"Are you going to tell us the way out, old man, or do I get to beat it out of you?" Lonny asks taking a step closer.

"Through the lab! It-it's through the lab." Shit.

"How are we supposed to get past everyone who *works* in the lab?" I ask. He considers for a moment.

"How much time has passed since I've been here? How many weeks?"

"Roughly sixteen," Lane answers.

"I can't deal with roughly. I need exact numbers. Dates. There is one day that you might, *might* be able to pull this off."

"Keep talking," Lonny says.

"On June 25th, everyone who works for the project is going to be at a gala of sorts to celebrate the partnership of USDF. Only security will be in the building. If you have . . . weaponry of some sort, you should be able to make it through and out." That brings a smile to Zander's face.

"I'm sure we can manage," he says with a smirk.

"So, step one. We get the Dorian here. How do we manage that?" A devious smile graces my mate's lips.

"You know, my dad wanted me to be exactly like him. Just as conniving, just as manipulative. That's all he did in Maurea. He manipulated. Lucky for us he was a very good teacher."

"I'm not following," Leia speaks up for the first time. I give him a smile.

"We're going to beat Paul at his own game."

We figure out that we have exactly seventeen days before we need to make our move to get out of here once and for all. No time can be wasted. We make plans to leave in the morning to travel back to the pool so we can return to Maurea. Leia decides to come with. We should both be there when we give Simon the news about Vince.

Leia seems to be doing okay. As well as can be expected, I suppose. She's been going to see Lexa for the last three days, and oddly enough, helping Lexa is helping her come to terms with her own trauma. Leia tells me that she's seeing improvement in her already. I hope that having to pick everything up and move isn't going to make her recovery backslide, but at least Leia will be there to help her with the transition.

Having a plan of action is helping me put one foot in front of the other. It feels like there are times where I forget that he's really gone. Like my mind is still in a state of denial and that he's going to come waltzing out of the trees with a smug grin saying "Gotcha!" Lane seems to have an instinct for when I need comforting and when I need space. I couldn't bring myself to spend another night away from him after that initial night.

Today is our last day here. Not our last in Sentri, but our last here at camp where the Amoran have made themselves a home. We've only been here a few months, so I'm surprised at how sad I find myself as I walk from home to home, doing my rounds. Lane joins me today. He mostly just carries supplies and hands me tools and herbs when I ask for them, but I like the company. The last person I check on is Lexa and Arthur. Arthur is thriving, and Lexa really does look like she's improved. There's a little more color to her cheeks, and a smile teases at her mouth.

Afterward, we make our way back to the main fire for dinner. Lonny and Zander are sitting with Abe. When Abe sees us, he excuses himself and makes his way over to us.

"I hear a migration is in our near future."

"I'm sorry, Abe. If I could go back and change things . . ."

"It wouldn't have made a difference, dear. As our ancestors did, we will adapt." He gives my arm a reassuring squeeze, and I smile.

"Nothing left to do but move forward." He nods.

"Will you need any of our hunters to go with you tomorrow?"

"No. We've made the trip enough times, and I think between Lane and I, we can manage the journey on our own." He gives an approving smile.

"In that case, I will see you two at the start of the next journey." I step forward and wrap him in a hug. He returns it without hesitation and chuckles softly.

"Thank you for everything, Abe."

"We'd do it all again if given the chance." He shakes Lane's hand and retreats to his hut for the night. Lane and I grab our portion of dinner and settle in by Lonny and Zander. Lonny strings an arm around my shoulder.

"Are you sure that you don't want us comin' with you tomorrow?" I shake my head.

"We need you to help everyone here get ready to move. A little comic relief will probably be more than welcome," Lane says with a chuckle. I stifle a yawn the best I can. We should probably call it a night, but I want to stay awake. To soak in every bit of this place before I leave it and never have the opportunity to come back. Tears prick at the back of my eyes, and I bite my bottom lip to keep it from trembling. Lonny rubs at my arm, and Zander gives an understanding smile.

"It's just a place. Home is all about where your family is," Zander says.

"And you are *never* getting rid of us," Lonny yells. We burst into laughter.

"What's so funny?" Leia asks from behind us. She takes a seat on the other side of Lonny.

"Just the fact that we're stuck with Lonny. Forever." Her singsong laugh rings out, and I catch a moment of infatuation in Lonny's gaze as he looks at her. When he turns back toward me, I raise an eyebrow at him, and he shakes his head quickly. I give him a knowing smirk, and he *blushes*. It's way too soon for her after Vince, but maybe sometime in the future. Someone like Lonny would be good for her.

"We've got a long day tomorrow," Lane says standing up and offering his hand to me. I stand and take it. I turn back to Zander and Lonny, about to say goodbye before Zander puts up a hand to cut me off.

"We'll see you off tomorrow. Go get some rest. Or whatever else you do to reenergize," he says with a wink. Lonny chortles, and I roll my eyes as we make our way toward our teardrop for one last night. I try to keep a hold on my anxiety about tomorrow and going back to Maurea. Part of me feels like I need to sleep for hours on end, and another part of me feels like I need to run off the nervous energy. I quickly climb up into the dwelling and make quick work of setting up our firs for the night. Lane must pick up on my restless energy. He stops me and puts his hands on my arms and gently strokes them up and down.

"What's wrong?"

"Just nervous about . . . everything, I guess." He hums and moves his hands to my waist.

"You seem tense." His voice drops, and his eyes darken. I swallow the lump in my throat.

"Yeah, I guess a little." A sultry smile tugs at his lips.

"Let me help you relax," he whispers as he drops to his knees in front of me.

Well, that's one way to do it.

39

THE HIKE BACK to the pool takes longer than usual. Leia has come a long way in her recovery, but long treks are still uncomfortable. Around halfway there, she finally accepts Lane's offer to carry her the rest of the way. It's been dark for a few hours by the time we finally arrive. I get to work at starting a fire while Lane goes out to find something for us to eat.

"So, how bad is it? Back home, I mean," Leia asks. I finally get a good enough strike to spark a flame.

"Don't expect it to look anything like how it was before the storm. They've been able to set up tents for temporary living spaces, but that's about it. People also will stare at you and likely avoid talking to you. It's not going to be easy," I say looking into the flames. "It's not easy feeling all of that mistrust from the people you almost died for. I'm still a little bitter about it if you hadn't noticed." She chuckles softly.

"You have every right to be." I smile at her.

"Did you get a chance to see my parents? How are they doing?"

I throw some more kindling on the fire and lay out some wet twigs by the flames to try and dry them out.

"We didn't see them while we were there. I'm not going to lie, I was grateful for it. I had no idea how to tell them that their daughter was . . . gone. Or whatever it was you were for a while." Lane comes back with a small kill and starts skinning it. "I suppose we're going to have to figure out how to have that conversation anyway," I mutter. Leia doesn't say anything. Just stares into the flames.

"How exactly did you want to go about that?" I ask softly.

"I don't know. How do you tell someone that their son is dead?" She looks up at me with tearful eyes.

"Do we tell him how it happened?" Lane asks.

"You know he's going to ask," I respond.

"We could lie . . .," Leia says softly. I consider it for a moment. Sometimes I wonder how different Vince's death would feel if it had happened in a different way. What it would be like to think of the death of a friend and not feel an overwhelming amount of guilt associated with it. To hear that someone you loved decided their own life wasn't worth living . . . it's basically unheard-of.

"He is dead either way," I say in a toneless voice. "Lying about the way it happened isn't going to help him."

"But it might, Adira," Leia disagrees. "I can't imagine—"

"Everyone in Sentri saw him," I cut her off. "Sooner or later, Simon is going to be living with them. The truth is going to come out one way or another. It's best that it comes from us." After a moment, she nods.

"I'm sorry," I say with a sigh. "It's all just . . . a lot." She gives me a smile that doesn't reach her eyes.

"We're all coping the best we can." I lean forward and give her hand a squeeze. Lane hands us each our portion of food, and we eat in silence. I go to the pool to wash up after I'm done and find myself staring at my dark reflection. I look different. That much I can tell. I used to be slim with mostly just broader shoulders due to the constant swimming. But I've filled out now. I've got muscles where it used to just be skin and bone. I'm grateful for the changes, even if they are

slight. It wouldn't make sense if I looked the same as I did before the storm blew away any and all normalcy. At least some of the change I've experienced on the inside is reflected in my outward appearance. Lane's reflection shows up behind mine.

"Admiring something?" he asks with a grin. I let out a dark chuckle.

"Something like that," I say as I dry off my hands. He cups my face and brings my mouth to his.

"You ready for this?" he asks. I shrug.

"Do I have a choice?" He laughs softly.

"Good point." He takes my hand and leads me back toward the fire.

"So, how exactly are we planning on changing everyone's minds about this whole thing? We only have fourteen days before everyone needs to be back here to leave," Leia says.

"I think you and Adira are the main people who need to do the convincing. People inherently *want* to trust you. Dad thought that by telling them about the ecospheres that he could control the rhetoric, but it might work in our favor. They know just enough to have more questions. If you guys show up with answers, it could be enough to start slowly convincing them to trust us."

"What're you going to do then?" A devious smile tugs at Lane's lips.

"If there's one thing I'm good at, it's making him angry. We'll use his own faults against him. If they see his real nature, I have a feeling they won't be anxious to follow his lead." Leia chuckles.

"Well then, we've got a lot of work to do."

~~~~~~

The swim back to Maurea went far smoother than our initial swim away from it. After giving ourselves a chance to catch our breath, we make our way toward the horde of people. I was hoping to run into Geode first again, but it looks like he's moved camp. When the first person notices us, it's like a tidal wave of shocked glances.

"Addi!" I hear Avery's scream. A second later, he's barreling through the crowd and jumps into my arms. I pick him up and spin him around. The sight softens some people's gazes while others remain suspicious.

"You're back!"

"I promised I would be!" I set him down, and he bounds over to Lane. He goes to hug him, and Lane launches him up and sets him on top of his shoulders. Avery squeals with delight, and more people around us can't help but laugh at the sight. I see Mom peer at us over the crowd that's formed, and a smile lights up her face.

"Hey, Mom!" I shout. She turns behind her and motions to someone I can't see. A moment later, Leia's parents, Harold and Lucy, come into view. Lucy's eyes immediately fill with tears, and the three of them run toward us. Leia meets them halfway, and they collapse to the sand upon their reunion.

"My baby girl . . . we were so worried about you," I hear Harold mutter. Lucy looks her daughter up and down, assessing for injuries.

"I missed you guys," Leia says through her own tears. Lucy kisses her hair and smiles at me and Lane. Mom finally gets to us and pulls me into a hug.

"I'm happy to see you're safe," she whispers. I look over her shoulder and see Paul and Camille. I look to Lane, and a smirk lights up his face.

"We're more than safe," he says loud enough for everyone to hear. "We actually have wonderful news! Adira and I underwent the ceremony to be mates!" he announces, taking my hand in his. Avery shoots his fist to the air in victory, and my mom wraps me in a hug again.

It starts off with just a few people clapping their hands until I hear Geode's voice from the back of the crowd scream, "News worthy of celebration!" This causes everyone else to join in on the applause and cheers. Lane pulls me in for a kiss, and Avery gags, causing little teeters to spread throughout the crowd.

"Smart," I whisper against his lips. He hums and give me another small peck. He turns his head toward Paul and *winks*. His face turns red, and it takes him a moment for him to scold his features. It's a second too late. Some noticed and are now giving *him* the apprehensive glances. He notices and tries to mold his features into pleasant surprise.

"What wonderful news!" he crows out. "Although I can't imagine why you would do such a thing in a foreign place when you could have done it here?" Some mutters of agreements come from the crowd. Lane doesn't skip a beat.

"We figured, why wait! After all, we had the blessing of the Legions. We thought what better way to honor Maurea and the Dorian than revere the approbation given to us!" Lane's smile is one of glorious indifference. "After all, our first priority always has been and always will be for the good of the Dorian." His voice starts to drip with severity. The crowd picks up on it, and you can see that they realize we know. We know what's been said about us, and we're here to prove them wrong.

"I couldn't agree more!" I try not to let my face drop at the sound of Simon's voice. I look to Leia and see her bury her face into her mom's shoulder. Simon reaches us and wraps me in a hug.

"It's so good to see you! Is Vince here?" he asks a little softer.

"Let's talk in private," I say with forced cheerfulness. Concern crosses over Simon's features, and he nods. Mom leads us back toward where they have set up camp. Paul tries to stop us as we pass, but Lane cuts him off before he gets a word out.

"We're celebrating with family privately first. We will come see you later," he says without a second glance. I see the hurt flash in Camille's gaze at the implication that his words set. I hear Leia tell her parents that she will come find them soon, and she rushes to catch up with us. I take her hand in mine as we enter the cramped space of my family's tent. Between the six of us, there isn't really room for us to sit.

"Mom, why don't you and Avery go find something for us to eat?" She takes the hint and shoos Avery outside.

"I'll go help," Lane says. He gives me a kiss on the forehead and follows after them. When it's just Leia and I with Simon, he crosses his arms and faces us square on.

"What's going on?" Suspicion and worry are laced in his tone.

"Maybe you should sit, Simon," Leia suggests in a gentle voice. His concern deepens, and he sits on the ground. We sit across from him, and I debate grabbing on to his hand. I decide against it.

"Just say it," he says, voice trembling. I swallow the lump in my throat and fight the tears that prick at the back of my eyes.

"He's gone, Simon," I whisper. He stops breathing for a second, and I see his whole body tense up. Leia reaches for my hand again, and I grab on to it.

"How-why-when," he tries to start multiple questions without having the ability to finish them.

"It was a little over a week ago," Leia says softly, tears flowing down her face.

"How?" His voice breaks. Leia looks to me with pleading eyes.

"He . . . he couldn't . . . cope. With everything. We all found different ways to handle everything. Survive. I knew he was struggling, but he was so angry at me. Angry at *everything*. I didn't think he wanted my help—"

"Wait," Simon cuts me off. "He did—he did it to himself?" His expression is one of horror. I nod.

"Oh god," he sobs. "My boy," he starts weeping. I reach forward and grab his hand.

"I am so, so sorry, Simon," I choke out.

"He had told me," he says between sobs. "He told me how much he was struggling when he came here. He-he said that he just wanted a way out. Any way out. I had no idea . . . I couldn't even begin to think he would . . ."

"None of us did, Simon," Leia says. "It was a shock to everyone. We thought things were starting to turn around."

"Where is his body?" He looks up at us.

"His ashes are being kept safe for you." He nods, contemplating.

"Thank you. For telling me." What a terrible, awful thing to be thanked for.

"Is there anything that we can do for you?" Leia asks.

"I would like some time alone, if you don't mind." His voice goes devoid of emotion. I remember how numb I felt at first. I give his hand another squeeze.

"Take as much time as you need. We'll bring you food and water." He nods without expression. Leia and I leave the tent and see Mom and Avery crying beside the fire. Avery is sitting in Lane's lap and holding on to Mom's hand in a death grip. When he sees me, he jumps out of Lane's lap and wraps his arms around my waist in a hug. I give him a kiss on top of his head and look over to Lane.

"I told them," he says.

"Everything?" I don't know how I feel about Avery knowing the intricacies of suicide.

"Yes," he answers. I grind my teeth together. Arguing with Lane about this now isn't going to help the matter, and it's not like we can untell Avery.

"Avery, I need you to do me a favor." I kneel down, bringing my face level to his. He nods and wipes at his nose.

"I need you to not talk to anyone about Vince, okay? I know it'll be hard. But it won't be forever. There are people that could use what happened and twist it to mean something else. And we have to respect Simon enough to let him decide when people should know and how they'll find out. Can you do that for me?" His lip trembles as he nods again. I wrap him in another tight hug.

"You're so brave," I whisper.

"Not as brave as you," he mutters. Lane comes up and ruffles his hair.

"Not a person alive is as brave as your sister." That brings a smile back to Avery's lips. I sit down next to Mom, and Leia gets a portion of the food and water and brings it to Simon before coming back out and sitting with the rest of us.

"What's changed around here?" I ask my mom.

"Nothing of too much note. I've actually used up all of the supplies you brought. It took a while for people to trust me enough to let me use it. But one night, little Ellory got terribly ill, and nothing was working to help her. Her parents were worried she wouldn't last the night with the fever. Her mother finally broke down and let me help. She improved drastically. After that, the majority of the supplies was gone within a few days."

"Did Paul retaliate in any way?" Leia asks.

"He tried. It didn't have his intended result though. People saw something from Sentri have immense use and save someone's life. When they see their leader get upset over such a thing, they begin to question the morality of his character. *As they should.* Ellory's parents are firmly on your side now. A few others have come up to us parents and let us know that they, too, support you. If you ask me, Paul has started to write up his own demise." A smile graces my lips. Of course, he is. Evil will always show even if you try to cover it with the façade of good deeds.

"We didn't bring as much supplies as last time, but we brought the important roots and herbs for healing." I drop my voice lower. "We have thirteen days to get everyone on board with going to Sentri. I can't explain everything here, but unfortunately, we can't even stay in Sentri. We're leaving. We're leaving for good." My mom's eyes widen.

"You mean we're leaving the ecospheres?" I nod. She shakes her head.

"Adira, we have no idea what is out there. What we could run into," she shout-whispers at me. I look around to make sure no one else is listening.

"No, but we have someone who does. Trust me, Mom. If we want to live our lives without profound interference, we have to leave. The ecospheres aren't safe anymore." Her eyes go to Avery before settling back on me. I know that all she wants is what's best for her children. After a moment, she sighs and takes my hand.

"Of course, I trust you, Adira. Just tell me what you need me to do."

"Exactly what you've been doing," Lane says. "Continue to steer people away from my father and toward us. We can't do anything without their trust, and we don't have a lot of time to gain it." My mom nods, and Avery stands up quickly.

"I can help, too!" he shouts. I shush him and pull him back onto my lap.

"Okay, bud. You talk to the kids. If the kids trust us, their parents might just follow. I also have a *supersecret* job I need for you to do." His face lights up with the prospect of responsibility. "There's this thing called a *camera* that is somewhere on the entrance of Paul's tent. It looks like a perfectly round, tiny rock. I need you to get rid of it for me."

"Okay!" He turns to Lane. "I won't let you down." Lane gives him a smile and bumps his fist against Avery's.

"Never thought you would, kid." Avery's face splits into a smile and runs off—I'm assuming, to start his new job. Luckily, the day is still young. We have plenty of opportunities to get started on our parts as well. Leia leaves to go spend some time with her parents, and Lane helps me put together a small healer's kit to do my own version of rounds here. Before we set out, I brew Simon a cup of tea that should help him rest and calm his nerves.

Our first stop is at Ellory's. If we can make a public scene of helping someone that will *let* us help them, it should help people accept our assistance moving forward. Mom points us toward their camp, and we're met with friendly smiles as we greet them.

"Hi! I heard miss Ellory got pretty sick while we were away," I say loud enough for people around us to hear. A couple heads turn our way. Ellory's mom, Hazel, gives me a hug.

"She was. We really can't thank you enough for bringing what you did that first time you came back. She's doing so much better."

"Do you mind if I take a look just to double-check?"

"Please do! She still isn't feeling completely well. Ellory, baby! Come out. Adira wants to check up on you," she shouts into the tent. The little eight-year girl comes out and gives me a wide, toothless smile. I bend down level to her.

"Hi, Ellory. I'm Adira. How're you feeling?" She looks up at her mom, and Hazel nods. She looks timidly back at me and Lane.

"Sometimes my tummy still hurts, and I throw up after I eat . . .," she says softly. I nod and rummage through my bag. I find what I'm looking for and hold it out to Hazel.

"Have her chew on this if she's ever feeling nauseous or after she throws up. It'll help soothe her tummy and will also help with the taste in her mouth after vomiting." I hand her bundle of roots. "And have her eat one of these with each meal. Hopefully it'll make it easier for her to keep food down. I'll be around for a while, so come to me if anything all of a sudden gets worse." I turn back to Ellory. "I'll come check on you in a couple days and see if you're feeling better, okay?" She gives me another toothless grin.

"Okay!" she shouts. Lane and I laugh with Hazel.

"Thank you so much. And congratulations!" she croons. Lane puts his arm around me.

"Thank you. We couldn't be happier." He plants a kiss on my head. We turn to leave and see that we've attracted quite the crowd. I have to fight the urge to do a happy dance. Geode is at the front of the crowd.

"I've got this sore on my leg, Adira. Help a lad out?" I give him a smile and get to work. Slowly, sick and injured people start lining up behind him. As soon as I finish wrapping up Geode's leg, I stand and see Paul staring at us from a distance. I can't see much from here, but from the look on Lane's face as he gazes at his father, I know that the war is far from over, but we just won a battle.

40

DARKNESS FALLS BY the time we get through all the people needing medical aid. I'm hoping that we don't have many more days with this amount of people needing supplies, or we'll quickly run out. Today was good though. We gained a lot of trust. As people were treated, they asked questions. Some just asked how the ceremony was and how we were doing. Others were braver and asked questions about Sentri and the Amoran.

I think that Paul underestimated the Dorian. They may have been quick to cling on to some sort of security right after the disaster, but now that time has passed and it seems they're settling into a new routine, people are seeing the faults in his logic. The improbability of it all. They also don't seem to be a fan of the way things are running. I don't think that if I stood up and announced to everyone that they all need to trust me to swim into a super-deep, secret tunnel to enter a jungle so we can escape the ecospheres through a lab, that anyone would be on board. But it's a start. Today we took a huge step toward gaining their trust. As we start to walk back toward Mom and Avery's tent, we're met with smiles and waves rather than hesitant gazes and glares. Simon is sitting with Mom and Leia by the fire when we arrive. He's pale and has a devoid look about him, but at least he's eating. I sit next to him, and Mom hands me and Lane a portion of dinner. We eat in amicable silence. If I close my eyes, I can almost pretend that everything is as it used to be. The smell of the combination of fire and cooked fish mixed with the salty scent and sound of the sea reminds me of the countless nights that Vince and I spent under the stars. We talked about the dumbest, most juvenile things. We also talked about the most serious details of our lives. Well, *almost* all of them. I open my eyes and turn to Leia.

"When did you and Vince become more than friends?" I ask. She considers for a moment.

"Um, probably close to a year now. Walter was getting on me about not bringing in the same numbers as everyone else. Vince overheard, and the next day, he had caught enough to make up for what I missed that day and the one before," she says with a smile tugging at her lips. "The rest was history, I guess." Her bottom lip starts to quiver.

"Have you talked to your parents about it?" my mom asks. Leia nods, and Mom gives her a tight smile. Simon looks up from his meal and gazes at Leia. He opens his mouth to say something before a shrill voice cuts him off.

"Lane dear, you never stopped by to see us," Camille tuts.

"Yes, well, we've been busy today, Mother," Lane says apathetically. Camille glares at her son for a moment before turning to me.

"Adira, could I have a word?" All apathy leaves Lane's face, and he looks like he's about to jump between me and his mother.

"Of course," I say standing up. I look to Lane. *Trust me.* He hesitates for a moment, then nods. She takes me away from the horde of people, smiling and waving and offering polite greetings to everyone we pass. Once we're out of earshot, I see the mask fall and the real Camille stand before me. All kindness, all impassive pleasantness vanished.

"What the *hell* do you think you're doing?" she asks between clenched teeth. I look at her in feigned bewilderment.

"What do you mean, Camille?" I can see the anger boiling in her.

"I saw the way you looked at my son at the choosing ceremony. You don't love him. You're using him. Everything has been going as planned. *Everything.* Then all of a sudden, you show up, and you're what? In love?" She scoffs. I hold up my hand to stop her.

"First off, you're not wrong about the ceremony. I was far less than thrilled to be matched to your son. However, a lot has changed since then. I have changed. Your son has changed. And I do love him. Far more than I think you ever did or ever could." Her fists ball at her sides.

"How *dare* you—"

"How dare I what?" I raise my voice. "I'm sorry, in what ways have you shown him that you love him?" Her face starts to redden. "Was it in the lack of support for him to be the person he wanted to be his entire life? Was it in the way that you painted him as a person the entirety of our people couldn't trust when he risked his life for them?" She starts visibly shaking. I see a person in my peripherals looking our direction. I lower my voice so only she can hear my final blow. I let every ounce of anger I feel toward this woman and her husband drip in my tone.

"Or was it in the way that you stood by and watched him get beat for not being up to your bullshit expectations?" Just as I thought she would, she slaps me across the face, and I see stars for a moment. The coppery taste of blood fills my mouth. I touch my lip, and my finger comes back red. She's stronger than I thought. A startled gasp comes from our singular audience. Camille realizes her mistake a second too late, and the individual scampers off before she can recognize the person who saw. She looks back at me absolutely *livid.*

"You bitch," she seethes. "I don't know how you figured it out or how you plan to screw this up for us, but Paul *will* find a way to stop you." I wipe at my mouth again, still bleeding freely.

"We won't need to, Camille. You and Paul will bring your own ruin." Panic flashes in her eyes. For a moment, one singular moment, I feel pity for the woman before me. I wonder if she was always like this or if Paul just manipulated her into a bitter shell of the woman she was before. I turn without another word and walk away. When I get back into the main area where the cluster of camps are, eyes filled with pity and curiosity follow me. The second Lane sees me, he shoots up and runs to me.

"Lane, I'm f—"

"Don't say it, Adira," he says as he tilts my face up to get a better look. I grab at his hand and pull it away from my face.

"Relax. I've got what I need to fix it. I don't think I even need to stitch it." He just stares at me with a mixture of anger and worry.

"I provoked it," I mutter.

"Doesn't matter. She shouldn't have hit you. I'm going to go talk to her." I grab on to his arm before he can walk away.

"No, you're not. She got caught. People saw. Just stick to the plan, okay?" His jaw ticks as he looks back and forth between me and his parents' tent.

"The plan was never for you to get hurt," he says between clenched teeth.

"I've been mauled by a jaguar. You think this is anything?" I try to smirk but wince at tugging pain. He cups my face and tilts it up again.

"Let's get you cleaned up." He takes my hand and brings me to the fire. Shocked gasps from everyone come at me, and I wave them off.

"Relax, I'm fine." Lane grabs a rag and some fresh water and starts dabbing at the wound. Once it's cleaned out, I find what I need in my bag to help the healing go along faster. As I smear it over the cut, I look up and see Simon staring at me.

"Did you want some more tea, Simon?" I ask. He flinches as if he didn't realize he'd been staring.

"I'm sorry. You just look so much like your father right now. You'd be surprised how many busted lips I had to fix in our youth." A shadow of a smile crosses his face. "Some tea would be nice," he says barely above a whisper. I make quick work of boiling the water and crushing the herbs. I add an additional one to help him sleep.

"I suggest drinking this back in your tent. It'll make you very sleepy." He nods and stands and gingerly takes the cup I offer to him. He looks down at it for a moment before meeting my eyes again.

"I've said it before, but your father would be profoundly proud to see you where you are today. And—" His voice breaks, and tears start to well up in his eyes again. "I can't begin to tell you how grateful I am that you were such a good friend to Vince." Emotions boil to the surface, and I choke out a sob.

"I wasn't, Simon. I'm so, so sorry. I should have been better to him when we got there. It's my—"

"It's no one's fault, Adira. No one's. Don't torture yourself with the inclination that you are of culpability. It helps no one, and it won't bring him back." Fresh tears flow down his cheeks. I pull him into a hug, careful to avoid the tea. He gives me a tight squeeze for a moment before letting go, bidding everyone good night and heading to his own tent. I plop down next to Lane, and he picks me up and puts me into his lap. He starts playing with my hair as Leia excuses herself to go be with her parents for the rest of the night. My mom is openly staring at my lip and looks like she's going to go punch someone out.

"Don't do anything dumb, Mom."

"What, like provoke a crazy woman—no offense, Lane."

"None taken."

"To slap me across the face? Something dumb like that?" she seethes. I give her the best smile I can manage.

"Exactly." She scoffs, and Avery giggles. Lane chuckles into my hair.

"We made a lot of progress today. More than I thought we would on our first day back," he says softly. I nod.

"We still have a long way to go," I mutter. He hums and resumes running his hand through my hair.

"Avery, any luck today with your *secret* assignment?" He perks up and nods quickly.

"Yep!"

"Awesome! Where is it?" He giggles and pats his stomach. My eyebrows furrow together. He laughs again.

"Did you—did you *eat* it?" He laughs harder.

"Uh-huh!" I'm dumbstruck silent. Lane bursts out laughing, which in turn makes Mom laugh, and before long, I'm joining in.

"You're a genius, kid," Lane says as he wipes tears away from his eyes. Avery looks like this is possibly the best moment of his life. Before long, he settles back down and falls asleep. Mom carries him into the tent and bids us good night. Lane and I stay by the fire and watch the flames for a while. I don't even realize that I had started to drift off until Lane nudges me awake.

"Let's get you in a proper bed." We make quick work of setting up our own tent for the night. I give Avery a hug and make myself comfortable on the thin blanket. Lane comes in a moment later and lies next to me. I rest my head on his chest, and he pulls me closer. I close my eyes, about to fall asleep when speaks.

"Please don't put yourself in that position again," he says barely above a whisper. I'm too tired to keep my eyes open as I respond.

"Don't act like you weren't planning to do the same thing with your dad."

"It's different. I'm used to it." I flinch, and my eyes fly open. I prop myself up on my elbow so I can look him in the face.

"You think that makes it any better?" He starts running soothing lines up and down my back.

"I just—Adira, I promised myself that it would never be you. That they would never hurt you. And this is *twice* now that they have." His voice breaks. I cup his face in my hand.

"Hey, I'm okay. I won't do something like I did today again. At least not without talking to you first." He hesitates for a moment and nods. "Just promise me you'll be careful. I know you could take Paul if it came to a real fight, but I also know he's willing to fight dirty."

"I promise," he whispers. I give him a small smirk.

"I'd kiss you if it wouldn't get green goo all over your face." He chuckles and plants a kiss on my cheek.

"Get some sleep, little fish." My heart leaps at the nickname. "We've got work to do."

Lane wasn't kidding when he said that his parents would spell out their own downfall. The day after Camille hit me, I had multiple people coming to check in on me and even offer some of the healing herbs I gave out if I needed any for myself. With the help of my own stash, my face is looking remarkably better already. Throughout the rest of the week, more and more people became comfortable with us again. We started telling them stories about what we saw in Sentri. We also talk a lot about the Amoran people. I have enough hilarious stories involving Lonny to keep everyone thoroughly entertained. I had originally thought that Lane was planning on confronting his father and doing something similar to what I did with Camille. So far, it hasn't even been necessary. Us avoiding Paul and Camille has made him angry enough that he hardly comes out of his tent anymore. There's been a few nights where we've seen him try to sneak out to go back to the lab, but we've been able to set it up so that *someone* always conveniently runs into him and asks him where he's headed. He's stuck as long as we're here, and he knows it.

We knew that we were really on our way to dismantling whatever hold Paul had when people started bringing their issues to Simon. He's starting to take over the unofficial job as the man in charge. Simon has had a similar way of dealing with Vince's death as I did— throwing himself into work. So far it's just Leia's parents, Simon, Mom, and Avery who know the full extent of what is going on. Now that we only have six days until we need to be back in Sentri, we have to start being more proactive about including more people on what's going to happen by the end of the week. I have an idea on where to start.

"Hey, Avery, how come I haven't seen Eliot around?" I ask my little brother as we prepare breakfast together.

"He's doing what Walter used to do. He takes care of the fish and stuff. He doesn't really talk to anyone," he says. I hum and turn to see Leia's parents heading our way. I dust off my hands and hold one out to Harold.

"Good morning," I greet them with a smile. Lucy gives me a warm smile back.

"We're sorry that we haven't been by sooner. I suppose we're just coming to terms with everything," she says. "We wanted to offer you our assistance. Whatever it is you need, we're here to help." I nod and contemplate for a moment.

"Harold, the swim back to Sentri isn't an easy one. Maybe you can work with some of the kids on different exercises to help build up some endurance. What is our youngest?"

"There's a set of twin five-year girls," Harold answers. No way that they can make that swim fast enough and not run out of air.

"We'll need to have some people that are willing to have the youngest clinging to them. They won't make it on their own. I'm going to take a chance and go find Eliot. Maybe he'll have an idea on how to handle the swim that I'm not thinking of." They both nod at me and head off to talk to different parents about extra swim lessons.

"Hey, kiddo." I turn back to Avery. "Can you lead me to where I can find Eliot?" He drops what he's holding and rushes to grab my hand.

"Yep!" he shouts, pulling me with him. We make our way toward the outskirts of camp. I see him surrounded by different makeshift barrels counting out the different fish.

"Hey, stranger," I say in greeting. "Avery, why don't you go help out Lane with whatever he needs." He nods and runs back in the opposite direction. Eliot appraises me for a moment before lifting his hand in greeting.

"Welcome back to hell," he says in a gruff voice.

"That bad?"

"You've been here about a week now. What do you think?" There's a bitterness to him that's new. He was always quiet, reserved. But never bitter. Loss can do that to you.

"What do you need, Adira?" He gets right to the point.

"I need you to hear me out on something." He considers for a moment and looks back down at the barrels of fish.

"Fine. On one condition." I raise my eyebrows, and he takes it as a gesture to continue. "I'm low on stock. Help me catch up, and I'll listen to whatever it is you've got to say."

"Are you the only one that's been fishing?" He lets out a humorless laugh.

"Yeah. Part of Paul's new 'plan.' Minimizing risks and all." I can see the strategy behind it. He knows that Eliot was going to be the head Legion of our group. It makes sense that he would try to keep him as preoccupied as possible in order to keep him from being a threat.

"All right, deal." He throws me a spear, and I revel in the familiarity of it. I haven't had a lot of chances to swim since being back. Our days have been full. I dive under the water, and a smile breaks out on my face. I let instinct take over as I hunt. I didn't think I'd be able to use the skills I had learned in Sentri underwater, but I was wrong. I'm faster, even more efficient now. It isn't long before my spear is full and I ascend to the surface. I go to one of the empty barrels and drop each one in and head back to the ocean. By the third time I dive under, Luna joins me. I stroke her belly the way she always liked as I head for a coral reef. When I get close, I see that Eliot is already down there. I stick to one side of it in hopes that I won't interfere with whatever strategy he's in the middle of. When I fill my spear again, I give Luna another belly rub and head to the surface. Eliot follows close behind. I unload my fish into the barrel and watch Eliot as he does the same. He mutters to himself as he counts what we've got for the day. A satisfied look comes to his face as he shifts his gaze to me.

"I forgot how good of a fisherman you are."

"I'm a halfway decent hunter now, too." His eyebrows crunch together, and he wipes off his hands before placing them on his hips.

"All right. I'll hear you out."

41

I DON'T KNOW WHAT I expected Eliot's reaction to be. Nonchalance was not it, though. The only time that he ever seemed to have anything other than indifference was when I told him about the experiments they had started on Leia. When I finish, silence drags out between us as he seems to contemplate everything I just laid out in front of him.

"How much time until we need to be in Sentri?"

"Six days. We'd leave the following day through the lab."

"Led by some imbecile named Williams."

"Precisely."

"Ah." He goes silent for another minute. "And if he leads you right into a trap?"

"Lonny will kill him."

"It'll be too late by then, though."

"Williams is a coward above anything else. The important thing is that he *knows* Lonny will kill him. Probably creatively too. He won't double-cross us." He contemplates for a moment before shrugging.

"Okay, what do you need?" I gawk at him.

"That's it?" His eyebrows shoot up. "I mean . . . you don't have any other questions?"

"You talked a lot, Adira. You answered any questions I had before I had the chance to ask."

"Um, okay. I guess the main thing right now is we need to get everyone on board with going to Sentri, and we need to figure out how to get everyone there without someone drowning."

"How long is the swim?"

"The first time was pretty terrible, but we were also searching for the entrance, and so we lost minutes. Fastest we've done it is around fifteen minutes. But we're good swimmers. I'm worried about the elderly and our youngest ones. I mean, I don't think Geode has swum in years." He nods, deliberating to himself.

"If we can pair off some of the strongest swimmers with the weakest ones, we might be able to pull it off," he says.

"Only thing is that it's going to take more time, then. We did it in fifteen minutes without carrying a whole person on our backs."

"But between you and Lane, you can hold your breath for close to twenty minutes. Maybe longer now that you both are in better shape. Leia can stay on the other side while you two help the weakest members get there." My muscles ache just thinking about it.

"Only other issue is that most Dorian range around twelve to fifteen minutes for their best time underwater. With us carrying people, we can *maybe* make it in seventeen minutes."

"But that's twelve to fifteen minutes of them doing the work and exerting themselves. If all they're doing is riding and hanging on to someone, it could make up for the time lost."

"*Could* doesn't mean it will."

"You don't have any better options." I grind my jaw and look toward the shoreline.

"Fine," I mutter.

"I'm not sure what I can do for you in regard to convincing people to go," he says as he picks up one of the barrels and carries it under a tent.

"People listen to you. They respect you." He scoffs.

"Yeah, maybe they did before Paul came in and screwed everything up. I'm no one but the fisher boy now."

"You made yourself into that," I counter. He drops the barrel and faces me.

"You don't know a damn thing about me."

"Right. Because we didn't grow up together, have countless lessons together, and both lose a parent. I have no idea who you are or what you might be going through." His jaw ticks. "Eliot, I just need you to help people trust us again. We've already made a lot of leeway. If you would bother joining society rather than sitting out here like a hermit, you might have noticed that Simon is controlling more things than Paul nowadays." His eyes lighten at that.

"Okay. I'll do what I can." I launch forward and wrap him in a hug before he can back away. He stays frozen for a moment before putting tentative arms around me and hugging back.

I head back toward our tent with a little extra pep in my step. Things are slowly happening in our favor. It feels good to have a win. I'm halfway back when I realize that it's far too silent. A crowd has formed around our tent, and panic seizes me. I start sprinting, thinking of the last time I saw a crowd gathered like this. Please no. Please, please no. When I break through, Simon and Paul are standing in the center in what appears to be a silent stare off. Simon looks like he's on the verge of either punching Paul out or on the cusp of tears. Paul has a smug look of feigned pity.

"I mean really, Simon," Paul exclaims. "You have my deepest sympathies." Anger boils in my blood. How the hell did he find out? "But if you couldn't keep your own son safe, how do you expect to keep the rest of us safe?" he asks gesturing around. "And let's consider," he says facing the crowd, "what kind of a place Sentri must be if it drove poor Vince to such measures." Absolute fury rages in my very bones, and my feet step forward on their own volition.

"How *dare* you," I seethe. All eyes turn to me. "How dare you use the death of one of our own for your own venal agenda!" He gives me a pitiful, sympathetic look.

"Adira, dear. I'm simply looking out for the best interest of the

Dorian. Something that you don't seem to know how to do. You spread lies about peaceful people and plentiful land, and yet four of you left, and only three came back. Why should anyone believe what you have to say about the possibilities of a happy life if Vince was *so* unhappy that he—"

"Be mindful of the what you say next, Father," Lane cuts him off. "You're looking out for the best interest of our people?" Lane scoffs.

"Of course!" Paul exclaims.

"Yeah, I'm going to call bullshit on that." The crowd gasps. Paul's jaw ticks.

"Call it whatever you want, son. But let's not forget *who it is* you're speaking to." I'm sure that line at one point would have had Lane quivering to the bone, but not anymore.

"Or what?" he challenges. Paul's face starts to turn red. "Go on, Dad," Lane says in a lower tone. "Show them how you kept me in line at home." His voice drips implication, and several looks of horror shoot toward Paul.

"You *lie*," he says in a gravely tone.

"No, I don't. But you do. Shall we divulge just how 'selfless' your intentions are?"

"Spew whatever you want, boy. That doesn't make it the truth."

"I'd like to hear what he has to say," I hear Eliot shout from the back. Several people mutter their agreement. Okay, we're doing this now, I guess.

"You all know about the ecospheres," Leia says from the other side of the circle that's formed. She steps into the center and eyes Paul as she goes to stand next to Simon. "What you don't know is that the people who created the ecospheres are still there. Watching us. Observing. At least they *were* just observing. Until the storm hit."

"Oh, this is ridicu—"

"Shut up, Paul!" Geode shouts. I fight the smile that comes to my lips.

"The initial experiment is done," Lane picks up the explanation. "They needed a new one in order to keep the funding for the program going. They decided that Maurea was the best world of the four to conduct it in."

"It's a social experiment," I cut in. "One where they're trying to determine if a society is better run if it is run by a dictator. Where one person and one person only has any and all say over every single aspect of your lives."

"I present to you," Lane announces, "the man who graciously volunteered for the position." He gestures toward Paul, who is now bright red in the face. "He has no agenda here other than attaining power over you. Give it to him if you must, but as for my mate and I, we refuse to live in a world where we're not only being watched, but one where we also would have no say in the way we live our lives."

"This isn't your only option," Leia says. "We've found a way out. Not just out of Maurea, but out of the ecospheres altogether."

"We'll lead you all to Sentri. There's an exit there that will lead us out. We'll start a new life on the outside. One out from under the thumb of my father and the people who would sooner see us dead than free," Lane concludes.

"This. This is what I've been trying to tell you all!" Paul squeals. "They've gone mad. My poor son . . ."

"How do you know the way out?" someone in the crowd asks, cutting Paul off.

"The last time we were here, we followed Paul when he left in the middle of the night to go to the lab where the scientists reside that run the experiments. It was there that we found Leia hooked up to machines. They were running tests on her blood and marrow." Leia lifts her shirt and trousers to show the scars in her hips and knees. Several gasps sound out from the crowd. "While we were there, we . . . acquired one of the scientists that worked for them. He'll lead us out."

"How can we trust him?" another voice calls out.

"I'm not asking you to trust him. I'm asking you to trust me," I answer. Silence follows.

"This is madness," Paul mutters.

"Why have there been multiple of us that has ran into you trying to leave in the middle of the night then, Paul?" a voice calls out.

"And why have you shut down anyone else's ideas when they're brought to you?" another voice asks. I can see that he's about to break. The spear is waiting over his head, just aching to fall and finish him.

"Why did you leave me in that lab when you saw what they were doing to me?" Leia asks, and the spear falls. I don't know if he ever actually saw her, but either way, the way that everyone in the crowd is looking at him now, I know. We've just won the war.

~~~~~~

The debate over what to do with Camille and Paul drags on for five days. They ended up staying under guard in their tent while decisions were being made. In the end, it just came down to a vote. They will stay here when we leave. Lane and I will be the ones to tell them tonight.

Tomorrow is the day we leave Maurea. I thought it would be more difficult leaving this place, but I've found myself more anxious to just get to the next part of what life holds. I've gone out with Harold and the kids to help with the swimming lessons every day. I don't know if Luna knows that our times to swim together are coming to an end, but I'm grateful that she's been at my side every day. The kids love her too.

Eliot has been the mastermind behind us getting to Sentri. He's set up an intricately scheduled plan for pairing up the weaker swimmers with the stronger swimmer like himself, Lane, and me. We'll be bringing people throughout the day over a long period of time so that we have plenty of time to rest between trips. It's going to be an extraordinarily long day. Lane is waiting for me at our tent when I come back from the last set of lessons.

"Ready?" he asks.

"Are you?" He hasn't had much to say about his parents being left behind. He shrugs and takes my hand. We take our time walking toward what has become a prison for Paul and Camille. Weston is the one standing guard when we arrive. He gives Lane a sympathetic glance and steps aside for us to go in.

"Mom, Dad," he greets them. They flinch at the sound of his voice. They look at us with equal disdain and ire.

"You'll be staying here," Lane states. Paul laughs.

"You're a damn fool. You do realize I can just go directly to USDF once you all leave and tell them exactly how you just left the ecospheres? This solves nothing, you fools!" he spits at us.

"I really couldn't care less what you do after we leave here, Dad. Although I'd be careful if you decide to go to them once we're all gone. There's no way in hell you'll be able to find us, and you two will be the last Dorian standing."

"Get to the point, Lane," Camille seethes.

"Ask Dad what they did to the last Dorian that was stuck in their labs." Paul's face blanches.

"You're they're last hope," Lane whispers. All indifference leaves Paul's face and is replaced with bone-chilling panic.

"You're leaving us to die. To die, son! Is that what you want? To kill your own parents?"

"I told you," Lane says in the same calm voice. "I don't care what happens to you when we leave this place." He gets within an inch of his father's face. "You. Mean. Nothing." Camille looks like she's on the brink of tears. Unlike her husband, she isn't above begging.

"Lane baby, everything we did to you was for your own good. Because we love you! I mean look at who you are today! Strong, skilled, smart, a leader!"

"Everything that I am is in *spite* of you. Not because of you. You don't get to take credit for me," he shouts at her with tears welling in his eyes. "I was a kid," his voice breaks. "I was *your* kid. You don't do what he did or watch it happen and cover it up and get to call that love." We all stand there a moment in time suspended. Lane abruptly turns and leaves the tent, leaving me alone with them for a moment. They give me twin looks of revulsion. I find that I have nothing to say. I spit at the ground and follow Lane. He storms away, and I have to jog to keep up. The second that we're out of sight of the tent, he pulls me aside and picks me up and kisses me. His tongue immediately finds mine, and he barges into whatever tent is nearest to us.

"Lane baby," I say as he moves down to my neck. "This isn't our tent."

"I don't care," he mutters against my skin. His hands start moving up my torso, and a small whimper escapes me.

"Maybe this isn't—" He shuts me up with a kiss that brands. Scorches.

"Just . . . help me forget . . .," he begs. I look into his eyes and see pain. Profound pain. I nod and bring his lips back to mine. And I help him forget.

42

THE FOLLOWING MORNING comes too soon. Eliot has everyone up and ready to go before the sun is even up so that we all have time to get everything we need together before we set off. Tears are everywhere. People have come to terms with why we need to leave, but they're still leaving the only home they've ever known.

Eliot breaks everyone off into the groups that they will be leaving with. The first group is mainly the best swimmers that can make it on their own and possibly help with making camp back in Sentri. Eliot, Lane, and I will be a part of every group. This way, we're taking three people who can't make the swim in each round. Leia is going with the first group and will stay in Sentri to aid in the introductions if the Amoran arrive before the last group makes the swim in. If everything went as planned back in Sentri, Kira, Lonny, and Zander should have arrived at the pool last night. Kira is there in case we have any less-than-ideal results from the weak swimmers.

"All right! First group, get ready to move out!" Eliot shouts as the first rays of light drip over the water. It's a beautiful morning. The water is so still. Little Ellory comes bouncing up to me and gives me her toothless grin.

"Ready!" she squeals. I laugh and take her hand. Lane gets Geode for the first trip today, and Eliot gets Anthony, another elderly gentleman. Lane and I will lead this group while Leia takes up the rear. I help Ellory hop onto my back, and without looking back, I plunge underneath. The worst part about the swim is that with every stroke, her hands close in on my throat and choke me. I look back to make sure that Lane and Eliot are keeping up all right with the heavier partners. Even in the darkness of the deep water I can see a smile on Geode's face. I turn my gaze forward and quicken my pace. Before long, I see the tunnel appear. Ellory's grip tightens, a sign she's starting to run out of air. I kick harder, willing myself to swim faster. I finally break the surface in Sentri, and Ellory starts coughing up water. I see Kira run to the side of the pool and help her climb out. She gets Ellory on her side and helps her cough up the water. I jump out of the pool as quickly as I can to make room for everyone else to get through. I sit on the side and rub out my neck as I catch my breath.

"Good to see you, princess." I smile at the familiar voice. I turn around to see the two biggest idiots smiling down at me.

"I missed you two." They laugh and plop down next to me. Lane and Eliot emerge, and Zander and Lonny help the two elderly gentlemen out of the pool.

"Geode, Anthony, meet Lonny and Zander." Geode is still catching his breath but manages to point at Lonny.

"I've heard many things about you," he says with a low chortle.

"Did she tell you she's secretly in love with me?" He tuts. "I knew it!" Lane laughs and swims his way over to me.

"Something you'd like to tell me, darling?" he asks with a smirk.

"Mmm, so many things," I say as I kiss him. Zander and Lonny gag.

"Didn't miss that," Zander mutters. Everyone laughs. By the time I'm thoroughly embarrassed, the whole group has made its way through. I don't miss the look of relief and excitement that flashes in Lonny's eyes when Leia swims up.

"Once you two are ready to go back, we'll move back for group two," Eliot says. I nod and wade myself back into the water. Lane follows after me, and Eliot hops in.

"See you soon, sweetie!" Lonny calls out. I roll my eyes and make my way back to Maurea.

The rest of the day goes by smoothly. I made sure to tell everyone that came after Ellory to put one hand on each of my shoulders instead of around my neck to avoid the choking. We have to take longer breaks after each group, but before we know it, the sun is starting to set, and there's just one group left. This one is with Simon, Mom, and Avery. Avery will swim with me. But before we leave, there's something Lane has to do. We make our way back toward Paul and Camille's tent. When we arrive, they're already tied at the hands and feet. Lane holds up one dagger and throws it out of the tent. It lands about fifty feet from them. He walks over to them and kneels so he's level with his father.

"By the time you two are able to make it to that knife, we'll be long gone." Paul just stares back at him. Camille starts crying again.

"So, this is it," Paul glares. Lane nods.

"This is it." There's a brief moment where I think I see sadness in Paul. Maybe an ounce of regret. Lane stands up and retreats back to leave the tent and his parents behind.

"Good luck," he says over his shoulder. And then he's gone. I follow him without a second glance. Camille's sobs follow us back to the beach.

"Ready?" Eliot asks.

"Yeah," Lane replies. I reach for his hand and give it a squeeze. He gives me a half smile and pulls me into his arms. I look out at the setting sun kissing the ocean, and I let myself have this moment. This moment to be sad to go. This moment to mourn the place that's been my home. I don't fight the tears that come. No one does. I don't know where we will end up settling once we leave these forged worlds, but I make a promise to myself in that moment to someday make it back to the ocean.

"Let's head out," Eliot says as he helps the little boy onto his back. Avery comes up to me, and Lane picks him up and sets him on my back. The last of the elderly population makes her way to Lane. He gives her a polite smile and helps her up. Mom gives my hand a tight squeeze, and we make our way to the water. I dive under and make myself take one last good look around. Luna finds me again, as she has been for most of the day. Avery lets go of one of my shoulders to glide his hand over her. Luna follows us all the way to the tunnel. Avery seems to be doing okay, so I point the direction for him to go for the last hundred yards, and he nods, following Lane. I float there with Luna for a minute more. I rub her belly and stroke her head and bestow every thought in my head to her. *Thank you, friend. I don't know how I could, but I hope I'll see you again someday.* I turn to go down the tunnel when a low moan emanates from behind us. I turn back to see another old friend. The blue whale lets out another moan, and Luna turns to swim toward him.

What a funny thought. A whale and a manta ray being friends. Then again, a manta ray being one of the best friends of a human is also probably strange.

By the time I emerge from the pool, I find myself profoundly grateful that I'll never have to do that swim again. It's started to rain in Sentri, and it looks like the rest of the Amoran have started to arrive. Abe and Simon are engaged in deep conversation, and Avery is off playing with some of the other Amoran children. Kira and Mom are going around together, helping wherever is needed. So far, it looks like everyone is getting along. Although it is crowded. In total, there are about 225 of us. My eyes catch on the one man this is all riding on. I make my way over to Williams. He sees me and waves enthusiastically.

"Adira! Looks like everyone is getting along. Good news!" Man, this guy really doesn't ever turn off.

"Yeah. A lot of people here. Children too," I say looking him dead in the eye. It takes him a moment to catch my point. He stutters for a moment, trying to find the right words to say.

"I've spent a good deal of time with you all at this point." I nod for him to continue. "I've come to realize the error in the ethics of our projects . . . When all you see are videos and surveillance of people without ever really *seeing* them, it's easy to . . . forget. Forget that you're real. And for that, I apologize." My eyebrows shoot up, and I cross my arms. I was not expecting that.

"I know that I can't take back whatever part that I had in it, but I can hope to at least try to make it up to you all by helping you get out." I search his eyes for a lie. Any tell that he's being dishonest, I find none. I still have a lot of grudges to work out with this man, but this is at least a start. I hold my hand out to him, and he looks at it for a moment in utter shock before grasping it with both hands and shaking it vigorously.

"There's a lot riding on you, Williams," I say.

"Scott. Please call me Scott. Williams is my surname."

"I don't know what a surname is, but sure, Scott." I pat him on the back and turn to find my mate. I find him sitting underneath some overhead rock with Avery in his lap and Mom at his side. I plop down next to him, and he gestures toward where Leia and Lonny are currently talking.

"What do you think about that?" he asks with a smirk.

"I think *we* shouldn't get involved and that Leia will move on when she's ready."

"But when she moves on . . ."

"Oh, it'll be with Lonny for sure." We chuckle, and Avery wiggles until he gets comfortable.

"It smells heavy here." I can't help but chortle at my brother's description of humidity.

"Well, I'd say you'll get used to it, but we're going to be here less than a day. So instead, I'll say get over it," I tickle him, and he squirms and giggles until he's out of Lane's lap. I lay my head down on it, and he starts playing with strands of my hair. Now that I have a moment to rest, the exhaustion of the day sets in. My bones feel like they're turning to liquid. Every muscle is sore. Almost as if he can hear my thoughts, Lane starts absentmindedly massaging my back.

"You're a good man," I mutter. He laughs.

"Go to bed, little fish." I hum and cuddle into the warmth and comfort of my mate. It's funny to think that I used to be a light sleeper. Now I'm at the point where I can fall asleep to the sounds of countless conversations amongst strangers who, by morning, will be nothing of the sort.

43

I WAKE UP SORE and restless. I feel like I could very well throw up. I'd make myself some tea to help with the anxiety, but it usually makes me feel a little foggy, and I need to be alert today. I nudge Lane to wake him and get up to wash away some of the fatigue. I set my arms in the pool and pull my hair back into a top knot. Lane does the same beside me, and I give him a grin. I love it when he wears his hair like that.

"Morning, lovebirds," Lonny says far too loudly. Multiple people around us wake up. I give him a scolding look, and he shrugs.

"About time to get moving, anyway!" he shouts loud enough to wake up the whole camp. Lane chuckles beside me, and I elbow him.

"Don't encourage him," I chide.

"What? It's funny!" I splash him with water, and he laughs harder. It feels good to laugh on a day like today. I still can't believe that we were able to convince all of the Dorian to come here. We had so much bad fortune for a while that I guess the luck is finally turning in our favor.

The Amoran brought most of their salted meats with them since they weren't going to do any good sitting in their huts anymore. So luckily, we don't have to worry about trying to hunt down breakfast for everyone this morning. I do my best to stomach my portion, but my stomach is in so many knots that I find myself nibbling on it.

"How very . . . Old Testament of us," I hear Williams—I mean Scott—mutter to himself.

"What now?" Lonny asks. Scott turns to him.

"There is a very famous story about a lad named Moses. A story that is integral for not one, but *two* different religions back in the outside world. He-he delivered people out of a hostile area and into one that was promised to be better," he explains.

"Does Moses win?" Zander asks. Scott chuckles softly.

"Not without some difficulties. It did take plagues and a few decades of wandering in a desert, but I suppose you could say yes! He won."

"Goody-goody," Lane mutters, taking another bite of his meat.

"Do you have a family, Scott?" I can't believe I hadn't asked sooner. He might have someone who's missing him.

"Ah. Unfortunately, not. Only child and parents died almost a decade ago. I did have a girlfriend once, but there was this, um, biker fellow, and well, it simply . . . never mind. No, no family. I always say that science was my one true love."

"Well, that's the most depressing shit I've ever heard in my life," Lonny says with a full mouth. I bite back the laugh building in my throat, and Zander elbows him.

"Adira," Eliot comes up behind me.

"Hey, Eliot, what's up?" He sits down and nods at everyone in greeting.

"I was hoping to get filled in on what the plan is for when we're getting out of here." I give the rest of my portion to Lane, giving up on finishing it.

"Scott here is going to lead since he's the one that knows the way. Me, Lane, Lonny, and Zander are going to be up front with him along with the other best fighters that Sentri's got. We'll take out whoever is left in the lab. You and the rest of the fighters will be interspersed throughout the mass and come up the rear." He nods.

"And Leia?" Lonny looks up at the mention of her name.

"She's not a fighter. She'll be with the mass of people," I answer. He nods again and walks away without another word. As people finish eating, it gets closer to the time for us to make the hike toward the entrance. Avery insists on staying with me and Lane. We let him stay if he promises to stay in the middle when we go through the lab. He eagerly agrees. It takes an hour or so before everyone is up and ready to move. Lane, Leia, and I move to the front with Lonny and Zander, and we start the hike toward the entrance.

There was a part of me that hoped it would rain. It doesn't seem right to leave Sentri without one last shower from her. But I'm sure the second we get into the cold lab, I'll be grateful. I find myself double- and triple-checking all of my weapons. The spear isn't exactly the smartest weapon being that whatever fighting we'll be doing will hopefully be from a distance, so most of us are armed with a bow and arrow and knives. I've got all of my arrows attached to my back and a dagger strapped to each thigh and each forearm. By the fourth time I start checking them, Lane grabs my hand and kisses it.

"Relax, baby. You're going to get throw-happy and end up landing a dagger in Lonny's ass."

"He could use a dagger in the ass," I mutter.

"Heard that!" Lonny shouts from ahead of us. Avery laughs next to me, and I pull him into my side.

"Hold up," Lane says. He walks ahead of the group and bends down to check something. After a few minutes of him stomping around, he bends down and pulls up the ground. He found the door. My heart starts beating out of my chest. Lane shouts for Scott, and he comes scampering forward. I stop him as he passes me.

"Please, Scott," I beg with tears building up in my eyes. He looks at me with bewilderment and regret.

"I promise, Adira," he says. I tentatively let go of his arm, and he makes his way down into the tunnel. I turn to Avery.

"Go find Mom and *don't leave her side*." He sees the fear in me, and I can tell that I've scared him. I drop down to his level.

"I'm sorry, Avery. I-It's going to be fine. I'm just a little nervous."

"It's okay to be scared, Addi. As long as you do the thing anyway," he says with a tentative smile. I bite my bottom lip to keep myself from crying and pull him into a bone-crushing hug. I can't lose him. I won't. I refuse to.

"Okay, go find Mom," I shoo him away. Lane is waiting for me next to the entrance. I take his hand and let him help me down. I cannot believe that we're back in this terrible place. We're in the room between Sentri and the lab. Scott goes on his toes to look through the little see-through wall to make sure no one is coming and cautiously opens the door. He pushes it all the way to the wall until I hear a *click*, and the door stays open.

"Okay, let's be quick," he whispers behind us and sets off at a trot. Zander is the first to follow after him, followed by Lonny, then Lane, then me and the rest of our crowd. We make the first turn, and before the first guard can say anything, Zander's arrow is in his throat. We move on without breaking stride. When we pass a four-way path, I take out one guard with an arrow from the hallway to the left, and Lane takes one out with one of his daggers on the right. We keep moving forward, making turn after turn in this endless maze. I hope Leia is doing all right with seeing all of this again. I wasn't the one abused here, and being back is giving *me* the creeps.

"Hey! Stop!" a voice calls from behind us at. One of the fighters in the center reaches back for an arrow. A loud *bang* sounds, and all of a sudden, he's bleeding from his chest. I leave my spot at the front of the group and sprint back toward him.

"Adira!" Lane calls after me. I reach back and nock the arrow into my bow and shoot it at the guard before I crouch down next to the hunter and feel for a pulse. Nothing.

"*Dammit.*" I look toward the guard and see he's down, but alive. He's talking into something at his shoulder. I run at him, and he reaches for his weapon. I kick it away at the last second.

"Copy. On our way to you," a voice says from his shoulder. I pick him up by the collar.

"Who's coming?" I demand. He gives me a bloody smile.

"Everyone," he gasps out between bloody coughs. I must have nicked a lung. He'll slowly drown in his blood. I unsheathe the dagger at my side.

"Consider this a favor," I say as I drive it into his heart. He lurches for a moment before sagging to the ground. I make my way back toward the horde of people

"We're about to have company!" I shout.

"How many?" Zander asks.

"He said everyone." I turn to Scott. "Give me a rough number."

"I-I-I," he starts stuttering. Lonny slaps him across the face, and that shakes him out of it.

"If I had to guess, around thirty. Maybe less with the ones you've already killed. I know that there are around thirty guards here at all times, and it should just be the core guard staff here right now." Zander nods and shoots into action, giving out instructions for all hunters present.

"All right, everyone willing to fight, make a perimeter around the crowd. We keep moving. Shoot and throw to kill. Lonny, I want you to stay with Scott and make sure he stays alive. He's our way out of here. Scott, keep your head down and keep us moving forward."

"Zander, I don't know what weapon did this," I say gesturing to the hunter who died. "But it was so fast I didn't even see it go in."

"Guns," Scott answers. "They have guns."

"Well, then," Zander says, nocking an arrow into his bow. "Shoot them first." The sound of running footsteps closes in, and we take our positions. A flash of black moves in my peripheral vision, and I aim and shoot. I have another arrow nocked by the time the woman hits the ground. It takes me a minute to adjust to the awkward shuffle as we keep moving while trying to fight. Luckily, we have more fighters than them. Lucky for them, they have better weapons than us. Guns go off one after the other. For every fighter that gets hit, we lose another that stops shooting to carry their friend to safety. We're losing, and I'm down to my last few arrows. I chance a look toward Lane and see that he's down to his last one, and it's already in his bow, ready to be shot. We need to start taking them on with the daggers.

"Lane, stay with me."

"Always." And then we're off. Us running straight toward them throws them off enough that they fiddle with their weapons for a second too long. Before they can shoot, I shoot off of the ground at a leap. Lane grabs the back of my shirt and directs the flow of my kick. My boots slam into both of the guards standing side by side before he follows through, and I land on his shoulders before shooting off again, attacking the two guards behind them with the daggers in my hands. Three come at us from behind, and Lane slits the throat of two with one stroke. The other shoots and misses. He's reaching for another weapon.

"Duck!" I yell, and he does immediately. My dagger flies its way home into his eye socket. Lane yanks it out and hands it back to me as we make our way down the hall.

"We're getting farther from the group," he says as he shoots off his last arrow.

"Remember each turn we make. I'm incredibly directionally challenged." He laughs right before he launches his second-to-last dagger at the woman who just turned the corner.

"I know you are," he says with a chuckle. I turn to give him a smile, and a second later, a gun goes off, and my arm is in excruciating pain. Lane curses and throws his last knife. From the grunt and thud I hear, I know it hit its target. Lane rushes to me and kneels at my side. As I inspect the wound, I notice two holes. Whatever the ammunition is, it went through and through. Lane tears off the bottom of his shirt and then bites the piece in half. I grit my teeth and hold back a scream as he shoves one of them into the hole to staunch the bleeding. Once the bleeding stops, he wraps the other piece around it, bandaging the wound.

"You okay?" He cups my face and searches my gaze.

"Yeah. Let's get the hell out of here," I say, taking his hand. He remembers every turn and hallway that we go down, and soon enough, we catch up with the tail end of the group. We run up to the front, back to our original positions. Lonny notices my arm first.

"Damn, princess. You sure like the scar look," he says with a grin. I give him one back.

"Are we good? Did we get them all?"

"You and Lane got half of them on your little tirade. That was dumb, by the way. Badass, but dumb," Zander says with an approving smile.

"How close are we, Williams?" Lane asks.

"We got a bit turned around with the attacks, but I believe there's an exit right up here on the other side of one of the observation rooms!"

We make our way down the long hall, and I feel like I can *smell* freedom knocking on our door. Scott abruptly stops and curses under his breath and hugs the wall.

"What?" I shout at him in a whisper, fingers itching toward my last dagger.

"They're here," he says with panic in his eyes.

"Who's here," Lane asks between clenched teeth.

"My boss and everyone from the gala. He's giving a tour. *Shit*, why didn't I think he'd give a tour?" Sweat is starting to flow down his face. I chance a look to see what we're dealing with. There's at least seventy-five people in a massive room. There are guards that surround the entire group, but they're in a different uniform than the ones we just took down.

"How did all of these guys not come out earlier when everything was going on?" I ask. It's a good thing they didn't because we'd be out-ammunitioned by a long shot.

"Those are USDF soldiers. They don't communicate with our guards. And the room is soundproof. It helps for when they wanted to pick up certain things during observations."

"Is there another way out?" Zander asks. Scott starts crying and shakes his head.

"It's *right there*. Less than thirty feet to our right. That emergency exit leads straight into the Tyresta forest." Dammit. It's *so close*. But there's no way for us to get everyone through without them noticing. Unless . . ."

"We need a distraction of some sort," I say.

"Any suggestions, princess?" Lonny asks. I curse under my breath.

"I might have an idea . . .," Scott says with bated breath. For the first time since I've known Scott, I see a surety to his demeanor. No insecurity, no fear. Without warning, he shoots off toward the group and screams, getting their attention. For a second, I think that he just sold us out. Until he turns and grabs a large gray pole and starts smashing everything. The group springs into action and runs for him. Scott screams like a crazy man in the opposite direction of our line of sight.

"Go, go, go!" Zander shoots toward the door and launches it open. The door isn't wide enough for more than two people to get through at a time. Lane and I stay on the inside, making sure that everyone gets out while Lonny and Zander lead everyone into the forest. I suddenly hear shouts in our direction.

"Hey! Hey! People are, people are leaving! They're leaving!" Suddenly there are countless high-pitch sounds emanating from the walls. I plant my last arrow in the man's chest. More of the new guards flood from the pathways. Lane grabs arrows from the back of a retreating hunter before the man runs out of the door. Lane and I take them down one by one before they reach our people. How close are we? How close are we to the end?

"Did you see Mom and Avery?" I shout at Lane.

"Yes, they got out right before these assholes showed up," he says, shooting another arrow. Suddenly, a heavy smoke erupts from one of the pathways. I can't see anything past it. Lane and I utter curses. We have to be close to the end . . . Suddenly Eliot emerges from the smoke coughing.

"Go!" he shouts.

"Is everyone out?"

"Yes, go!" I don't wait a second more. I exit, and Lane shuts the door behind us. He grabs my last dagger and jams it into the keypad on the outside. Hopefully that'll stall them long enough for us to get away. The sun is *glaring*. It's like I've always been seeing it in its muted form. I stumble as I try to scamper away. Lane grabs for my hand, and we run like hell. I can hear Eliot running right behind us. Once my eyes adjust, I'm able to move even faster. My arm is throbbing, but I do my best to ignore it and put all focus into putting one foot in front of the other. I don't know how far behind we got, but we run for what I assume is close to seven miles. Everyone must be running on adrenaline. On the instinct to survive. I'm shocked that I haven't even run into any of the elderly people yet. Or the kids, or the injured . . . I have no idea how they're keeping up. It seems . . .

"Wait!" I shout and stop in my tracks. Lane stops a second later, and Eliot looks like he's about to pick me up and throw me over his shoulder to keep me running.

"*You* said we had everyone," I say, short of breath. He doesn't respond. I get up in Eliot's face and say it louder.

"You said we had everyone!"

"You can't save everyone, Adira! The plan went sideways. The smoke came, and people started slowing down. Some even passed out. There was *nothing we* could do."

"You don't just leave them behind!" I scream at him with tears running down my face. "They trusted us. They trusted me! I told them they would be safe! There are kids in there, Eliot!" He doesn't answer. I throw my fists against his chest "Damn you!" Lane holds me back, and Eliot takes a step back.

"I did what I thought was right."

"They're just children, you son of a bitch! They're your people. Our people!"

"I'm sorry," he mutters before turning and continuing the run. I turn around and gawk at the massive domes that seem to go on for*ev*er. It looks so depressing. So void from the outside. I fall to the ground and scream. I don't care if they find me. I don't care. I let them down. I let them all down. Lane bends down and puts my face in his hands.

"Ad, we can't help them now."

"We should go back," my voice breaks.

"You and me go back now, we die, and that helps no one. Think of Avery. Think of your mom and Leia. We need you. Lonny, Zander, Kira, me—we all need you, baby. We can come back at a later time when we recuperate and find a way to do it that doesn't end with my mate getting killed." I stare into his cerulean eyes and breathe with him until I feel my heartbeat settle.

"Do you promise?" I ask between tears.

"I promise, baby. I promise." He's right. Going back now is going to do nothing but get me tied up to one of those beds or killed. But I make myself a promise then and there as I stare up at the prisons that I used to think were a home. I promise that even if I do it alone, I'll be back. If I'm going to be a leader for my people, they deserve someone that will fight for them. I'm leaving now so I can fight another day. I will be back. I promise I'll be back.

I nod and get to my feet and force them back into a run. I run away from the only worlds that I've ever known as home. I run away from the eyes of strangers and the oppression of my circumstance. I run away from lies and agendas. I run away from the worlds that broke me and sewed me back together. I run away from the old. Only thing is . . .

I have no idea where I'm running to.

ACKNOWLEDGMENTS

THE COMPLETION OF this novel is something that never would have made it to your eyes without the help and support of some very important people.

Rachael, thank you for the encouragement to keep going when other circumstances made me want to give up. I'm extraordinarily grateful that we've come into the stage of life where your sister is no longer your nemesis.

Gammon, thank you for keeping my head afloat. You exemplify what it means to be a leader, and your support of my goals outside of the military is one of the reasons I was able to finish this book. Hooah, Sergeant.

Joy. Dear, dear Joy. You're an actual angel. You helped bring a new dimension of life into this story through your suggestions, and I'm forever grateful not only for your expertise, but also your friendship.

Jameson, this book quite literally would not exist without you. You were one of the first people I told about my wild idea for a story, and you ran with it from the beginning offering suggestions and encouragement. You're truly one of the best friends a writer gal could have, and I hope to return the favor for you someday.

My dear son, Finnick. Do not read this until you are at least fifteen years old. Know that everything I do, I do for you.

I saved the best for last. To my amazing husband, Hunter. Your support has been unwavering from the start. I remember the day I woke you up super early one morning, babbling about a book idea that would finally make it all the way from start to finish. You wiped at your eyes and gave me a sleepy smile and said, "Go for it, babe." You were the first to read every chapter and always insisted that each new chapter was the best one yet. Thank you for your steadfast support and love throughout this journey. From being my cheerleader to watching the baby for hours so I could finish that chapter. I'm so grateful that I have a soul mate like you to take on every challenge with. I love you.

9781664110885